LET THE WIND RISE

Books by Shannon Messenger

The SKY FALL Series
Let the Sky Fall
Let the Storm Break
Let the Wind Rise

The KEEPER OF THE LOST CITIES Series
Keeper of the Lost Cities
Exile
Everblaze
Neverseen
Lodestar

Coming Soon . . .
Nightfall

LET THE WIND RISE

BOOK THREE IN THE SKY FALL SERIES

Shannon Messenger

Simon Pulse

New York   London   Toronto   Sydney   New Delhi

SIMON PULSE

An imprint of Simon & Schuster Children's Publishing Division

1230 Avenue of the Americas, New York, New York 10020

First Simon Pulse paperback edition April 2017

Text copyright © 2016 by Shannon Messenger

Cover illustration copyright © 2016 by Shane Rebenschied

Also available in a Simon Pulse hardcover edition.

All rights reserved, including the right of reproduction in whole or in part in any form.

SIMON PULSE and colophon are registered trademarks of Simon & Schuster, Inc.

For information about special discounts for bulk purchases, please contact Simon & Schuster Special Sales at 1-866-506-1949 or business@simonandschuster.com.

The Simon & Schuster Speakers Bureau can bring authors to your live event. For more information or to book an event, contact the Simon & Schuster Speakers Bureau at 1-866-248-3049 or visit our website at www.simonspeakers.com.

Cover designed by Regina Flath

Interior designed by Mike Rosamilia

The text of this book was set in Adobe Caslon Pro.

Manufactured in the United States of America

2 4 6 8 10 9 7 5 3 1

The Library of Congress has cataloged the hardcover edition as follows:

Names: Messenger, Shannon, author.

Title: Let the wind rise / by Shannon Messenger.

Description: First Simon Pulse hardcover edition. | New York :
Simon Pulse, 2016. | Series: Sky fall ; 3 | Sequel to: Let the storm break. |
Summary: When Audra is imprisoned by Raiden and the Stormers she is forced to sever the bond between her and Vane, while Vane, frantic that he is losing her, can only turn to former enemies to rescue Audra.

Identifiers: LCCN 2015042470 | ISBN 9781481446549 (hc) |
ISBN 9781481446563 (eBook) | ISBN 9781481446556 (pbk)

Subjects: | CYAC: Supernatural—Fiction. | Winds—Fiction. |
Love—Fiction. | Fantasy. | BISAC: JUVENILE FICTION / Fantasy & Magic. |
JUVENILE FICTION / Legends, Myths, Fables / General. |
JUVENILE FICTION / Love & Romance.

Classification: LCC PZ7.M5494 Lft 2016 | DDC [Fic]—dc23

LC record available at https://lccn.loc.gov/2015042470

For anyone who has ever fought and doubted and struggled, because hope is always on the horizon

CHAPTER 1

VANE

They're calling it "California's Worst Natural Disaster in Decades."

But there was nothing "natural" about it.

It's easier if people blame global warming, though. Or Mother Nature. Or any of the other theories scientists have been tossing out, trying to explain the freaky tornadoes that stomped the mansions and country clubs in my stuffy valley into million-dollar heaps of rubble.

Nobody would know how to deal with a reality filled with "sylphs" and "wind wars" and "storms that fight like monsters."

Plus, then I'd have to tell them the worst part—the part that makes me want to curl up into a ball and never move again.

It was my fault.

If I'd moved to one of the Gales' bases in the middle of nowhere, or taken my training more seriously, or insert-any-of-the-mountain-of-Vane-fails here, none of this would've happened.

My hometown wouldn't be a federal disaster zone.

Innocent people wouldn't have died.

And Audra . . .

I'm trying not to think about where she is or what she might be going through. Or how I was the one who insisted she trust her mother and made her fly off with Gus, straight into Raiden's trap.

Or how she broke our bond.

I want to believe she did it to protect my heritage—stripping away any knowledge she had of the Westerly language so she couldn't give Raiden what he wants. But I wouldn't blame her if she hates me.

I definitely hate myself.

But I'm going to fix this—all of it.

I have a plan.

I have the power of four on my side.

It's time to be the hero everyone's expecting me to be.

CHAPTER 2

AUDRA

'm stronger than this.

The words have become my lifeline, warming me with their promise as I whisper them in my frozen cell.

Ruined Northerlies tear at my hair, my skin, the flimsy fabric of my dress. The rough stone floor cuts into my bare legs. Still, I don't move—don't blink—as I count my shallow breaths. Waiting for Raiden to return.

Whatever he has planned, whatever horrors lie ahead . . .

I'm stronger.

I have to be.

For Gus.

For the Gales.

For *Vane.*

Thinking his name should claw at my heart with longing and regret.

Instead, I feel nothing.

No pull.

No pain.

Just an empty void where something precious used to be.

But it's gone now.

All that remains is a ghost of a memory that would almost feel more like a dream—if it weren't for the calm breeze wrapped around me.

I can no longer understand its words, but I know the gentle Westerly is loyal.

And that gives me the courage I need.

Raiden has power and pain on his side.

But I have the wind.

Change is in the air—I can feel it as clearly as I can hear the brave melodies of the untainted drafts slipping through the cracks of Raiden's supposedly impenetrable fortress.

A hum building to a crescendo.

The wind starting to rise.

CHAPTER 3

VANE

I'm pretty sure I've made a deal with the devil.

But I'll do whatever it takes to get Audra back—even if it means trusting her psychotic mother.

I can see Arella from my bedroom window, her long dark hair tinted blue in the moonlight as she stands in the middle of my front yard with her face tilted toward the stars. The pose should be peaceful, but her brows are pinched, and she keeps scratching at her pale, skinny arms, leaving finger trails along her skin.

"You're wearing the Gale Force uniform," Solana says behind me.

Her voice is barely louder than a whisper, but the sound still makes me jump. Probably because I've been avoiding her.

I don't turn around, even though I know I'm being stupid.

Solana's coming with me on this mission—quest—whatever-you-want-to-call-it—thing. So I'm going to be spending *lots* of time with her.

But . . . every time I look at her I can't help thinking, *I saved the wrong girl.*

It's not that I regret rescuing her—there's no way I could've left her trapped in the crushing grip of a Living Storm. But I was still helping Solana while Raiden was dragging Audra and Gus away.

"Yeah," I mumble, realizing she's expecting me to say something. "Figured I should start dressing the part."

She's quiet for a second, and I hope that means she's going to leave me alone. Instead she says, "It suits you."

I snort, but manage to stop myself from pointing out how the heavy black fabric is stiff and scratchy and pretty much the most uncomfortable thing I've ever worn. I'm done whining about the role I'm expected to play. Plus, it's cold where we're going, and this is the warmest thing I own.

"You didn't hurt your elbow getting the jacket on, did you?" Solana asks.

I did, but I don't feel like telling her that. So I shrug—which turns out to be a really bad idea.

Pain shoots from my shoulder to my fingertips, hot and sharp and so intense that a tiny yelp slips out before I can stop it.

Painkillers would come in really handy right now—or so I hear.

Sylphs are allergic to human medicine.

Solana rushes to my side, and I can't help noticing that she's changed into a pale blue dress, so short and tight it looks painted on.

I'm used to the skimpy clothes she wears to keep her skin exposed to the wind, but I still have to turn away before my eyes can focus on the parts of her it *doesn't* cover.

"Aren't you going to freeze in that thing?" I mumble.

"I'm a Southerly," she says. "My winds keep me warm."

That doesn't make a whole lot of sense, but very few things do when it comes to my life these days. If it's weird and windy, I'm learning to say "Okay then."

Solana pulls up my left sleeve, and I cringe when I see how the bandage is bunched and twisted, with the skin swollen all around it.

"I'm sure that has more to do with the fact that my elbow was torn out of joint—twice—than it does with me tweaking it as I got dressed," I argue.

She sighs and starts rewrapping the wound. "You still could've asked me for help."

"Right, because that wouldn't have been awkward at all."

Nothing says "no big deal" like having my sorta ex-fiancée help me put my pants on.

Solana rolls her eyes. "I know this might be hard for you to believe, but things don't have to be uncomfortable between us. I'm not the kind of girl who chases after a guy who doesn't want me. I know a lost cause when I see one."

I feel my jaw drop, and realize I must look like an idiot. But seriously, what am I supposed to say to that?

She laughs. "What? You thought I was still pining for you?"

"I . . ."

Nope, I've still got nothing.

But I'm looking pretty lame here, so I go for a subject change. "What exactly *is* pining?"

"Um, it's like yearning, I guess?"

"And how does someone *yearn*?"

"I don't know. But I'm not doing it for you."

"Okay, I'm starting to feel insulted."

"And here I thought you'd be relieved."

I am, I guess.

Though I'd feel better if her left wrist didn't still have the wide gold cuff with the letters *S* and *V* etched into the design.

Her *link*.

Basically the Windwalker equivalent of an engagement ring—and this one was given to her by the Gales to symbolize our betrothal. I'm tempted to ask her why she hasn't pitched that thing in the nearest trash can but decide it's easier to pretend it's not there.

"So, we're good then?" she asks, tying a careful knot at the end of the bandage. "No more weirdness?"

"Sure. No more weirdness."

I want the words to be true, but she's resting her hand on my skin and . . .

Her touch is too warm.

Not hot and electric, like Audra's touch always feels. But it's a far cry from the cold emptiness I usually get from other girls—and I swear when our eyes meet, I can tell Solana knows it.

My bond is not fading, I repeat over and over in my head, ordering the words to be true.

Audra may have broken our connection on her end, but I'm still holding on with everything I have.

"You okay?" Solana asks, pointing to my shaking hands.

I pull my sleeve down and scoot away from her. "We should probably get going. Arella's waiting outside."

Solana doesn't follow me as I move toward the door, and when I glance back, she's biting her lip.

"If you've changed your mind—"

"I'm coming with you," she interrupts, tucking her long, wavy blond hair behind her ear. "It's just . . . do you really think we can trust her?"

She tilts her head toward the window, where Arella's watching us with narrowed eyes.

If I had my choice, I'd drag Arella back to her suffocating prison and let the Maelstrom finish draining the life out of her. She deserves that and more after betraying Audra *again*—not to mention the zillion other creeptastic things she's done.

But her gift allows her to feel things on the wind that no one else can—things that will hopefully give us a better chance of sneaking into Raiden's fortress and getting Audra and Gus out of there alive.

"We need her," I tell Solana, reminding myself as much as her.

Solana opens her mouth, then closes it again. "I'll get my stuff," she says, and disappears down the hallway.

I use the time alone to take one last look around my room, making sure I'm not forgetting anything—not that there's anything worth taking. I shove a bottle of pain pills into my pocket, since those helped me poison a Stormer in one of my previous battles. Everything else is just a bunch of video games and dirty clothes and random-crap-that-won't-matter-in-a-wind-battle, and proves how supremely unprepared I am for this.

Even my cell phone is useless. The battery died while I was trying to text my mom answers to all her questions. So it looks like the last thing I'll be saying to my parents—maybe ever—is:

I didn't destroy the house, but it's safer if you don't come home yet. I'll call you if I make it back. ☺

I'm sure the smiley face really set my mom's mind at ease.

I hate telling my parents to keep running, but I didn't know what else to say. They'll never be safe here. Not unless . . .

I kill Raiden.

The thought makes my legs wobble and my vision dim as my peaceful Westerly instincts rebel against the idea of violence. But I grit my teeth and remember that everyone's counting on me.

Audra's counting on me.

So is Gus.

I repeat their names until the fear fades into something I can swallow.

But it's still there, so deep and solid it feels like a stone sloshing around in my stomach.

I need air.

I jam my phone onto the charger—it's better to plan on making it back, right?—and run outside, hoping to find a few breezes to clear my head.

But nights are stuffy in the desert. The only winds I can sense are miles away, skirting the base of the mountains. So, by the time

I reach Arella, my jacket is soaked with sweat. I've also had to swat away about fifteen bugs.

"The sky is restless," Arella whispers, rubbing at the goose bumps covering her arms. "A storm is coming, but I can't find the source of the turbulence."

"Then perhaps you shouldn't be leaving," a deep voice says behind us.

I fight off a sigh as I turn to face the captain of the Gales. "We already discussed this, Os, and—"

"I know," he interrupts, reaching up to smooth the narrow braid that hangs down the left side of his face. The hairdo is supposed to represent his authority over the guardians. Mostly I think it looks super dorky.

"But I've taken some time to think," he tells me, "and the fact of the matter is, we need you here."

He points to my back patio, where the faded lawn chairs have been dragged into the dim glow of our porch lights to create some sort of makeshift triage center. Only seven guardians survived our last fight—and most of them barely. The few who can actually move are working to bandage up the others with the meager supplies I tracked down in my bathroom.

Guilt makes the stone in my stomach burn hotter than asphalt in the sun, but I let my bigger worries snuff out the pain.

Os put out a call for the remaining guardians at our other bases to gather here and provide additional support and supplies.

I'm the only chance Audra has. I know Os. He may be worried about Gus, but he'd celebrate if Audra didn't make it back. Shoot—a few days ago he threatened to break our bond himself.

He's the president of Team Solana, still rooting for her to be queen. Which I'm not opposed to, as long as *I* don't have to be king—but that's a whole other complicated nightmare I'll worry about later.

"You ready?" I ask Arella.

Os blocks us as we try to walk away. "Being king is about what's best for your people, Vane. And your people need you alive. We *will* battle Raiden's forces again. We *will* finish this. But first we need to ensure we're properly prepared."

"Gus and Audra don't have that kind of time," I remind him. "Besides, this is a rescue, not an invasion."

I'm probably being naive, but I keep hoping we can run this like a heist movie, sneaking in and out like clockwork. All I have to do is come up with an actual plan for how to pull that off.

I try to look confident as I call the drafts I can feel in the distance, choosing one of each of the four winds. They whisk smoothly to my side, and I weave them into a deep blue wind spike infused with the power of four. Os watches me work, rubbing the fresh scabs along the scar under his eye.

It used to be a *T* for "traitor"—a present from Raiden—but the last battle added a new cut that crossed the whole thing out.

"You harness a tremendous power," he says. "But you're still not strong enough to challenge Raiden alone."

"He won't be alone," Arella reminds him.

She straightens up, looking a bit more like the scary Arella I'm used to—until the air shifts and the ache of her gift makes her double over.

Arella's always been affected by the wind, but being separated from the sky for so many weeks must have weakened her further.

"I'm going too," Solana says, marching up beside me.

She pats the windslicer she's strapped around her waist, and I'm sure she means to look tough and soldierly. But something about her tiny dress and fluffy hair makes it a little hard to see her as *scary*.

Os sighs. "Oh good, a princess, a deranged murderer, and an inexperienced, untrained teenager incapable of violence will be flying across the continent and trying to sneak past the greatest warrior our world has ever seen—and his entire army. How could that possibly go wrong?"

"You're underestimating my power," I tell him, holding up my wind spike.

"No, you're *over*estimating it, Vane."

He hisses a word I can't understand, and the Northerly in the spike screams, twisting and writhing and turning a sallow yellow as the spike hums with a different energy.

The power of pain.

Solana cringes, and Arella covers her ears and collapses to her knees.

I can't blame them. The sound of a draft shattering makes me want to cry and vomit and punch something really hard all at the same time.

Instead I drop the spike and kick it away from me. Then I grab Os's shoulders.

"What gives you the right—"

"What gives *you* the right?" he asks, shoving me away. "We've sacrificed everything to protect you and train you and make you a king worth serving—a king who will lead our people out of these treacherous times. And what has it gotten us?"

He turns to the wounded Gales again, and the reminder stings worse than if he'd smacked me.

"That doesn't change the fact that you're destroying the wind," I say when my voice is working again.

"Raiden's left us no choice! We wouldn't be here right now if I hadn't broken the drafts in your worthless weapons."

I want to argue, but I remember the battle all too well.

My spikes bounced off Raiden's Living Storms like we were pelting them with giant Q-tips.

"In war," Os whispers, "sacrifices have to be made."

He retrieves his yellowed spike, running a trembling hand over the edge and examining his creation with a look that's part horror, part fear, but mostly a whole lot of something else. It takes me a second to figure out that it's awe.

Audra warned him that the power of pain is like a drug—a craving that feeds on itself, getting worse every time anyone harnesses it.

"You have to stop, Os," I say. "You're deluding yourself if you think the power isn't corrupting you."

Os's laugh sounds like thunder. "The only one deluding himself here is you, if you really think I'm going to let our future king run off on a suicide mission."

"Is that a threat?" I ask, not missing the way he's lowered the ruined wind spike so it's aimed right for my chest.

"Think of it as an order."

I glance at Solana, who looks about as dangerous as a hissing kitten. And Arella's still on the ground, clawing at her skin, crippled by the wind's pain. So . . . Os may have a point about my backup.

But I'm still going.

"I'm not afraid of you," I tell him, calling the nearest Westerly to my side.

"You're also not nearly as strong as you think," he warns.

"Funny, I was just thinking the same thing about you."

His fist tightens around his spike, and I brace for him to throw it. So I'm completely caught off guard when he ruins another draft and sends it crashing into me like a semi.

I skid across the grass, careful to shield my injured arm as I beg my instincts for a command I can use to retaliate.

Another shattered draft slams into me first, pinning me to the ground and pressing on my chest and throat, closing off my windpipe.

Voices scream around me—Solana? Arella? I can't tell. The roaring winds sweep them away as the world turns to a mushy haze.

Just before the darkness swallows me, the pressure eases enough for me to roll to my side and cough and hack until I'm pretty sure I'm bruised both inside and out.

Os leans over me as I lie in the dirt like a Vane-crumble.

"It's time to admit that your powers are useless, Vane. Dust yourself off and rest up for a long day of training. Every Gale—including you—is going to learn to harness the power of pain."

CHAPTER 4

AUDRA

The Easterly winds surrounding me have carried a steady stream of whispered assurances.

Stay calm.

Have hope.

Believe.

But as the final strands of darkness fade to morning gray, their songs change to a verse that chills me far worse than the frigid air.

He's coming.

I barely have time to process the words before the drafts whisk away, vanishing through the invisible cracks they came from and leaving me with nothing but the echoey thud of footfalls climbing the tower stairs.

I pull myself to my feet, determined to face Raiden from a

position of strength and confidence. But I can't help falling back a step when his tall form appears through the darkness.

The majority of the tower is taken up by my cell, but there's enough space beyond the bars for Raiden to stand in his fur-lined white cloak, his long blond hair whipping in the ruined winds, his figure silhouetted by the dawn light as he studies me with an expression that's more curious than menacing.

He's brought no guard and carries no weapon—but he doesn't need them. One carefully chosen word can make his winds beat me, break me, ruin me a million unimaginable ways.

I've seen the effects of his methods firsthand, and the memory alone of the thousands of holes bored through Aston's body is enough to make my knees shake so hard I have to steady myself against the icy wall.

And Aston was simply a captured Gale, not someone Raiden suspected of speaking Westerly.

I'm stronger than this.

I am.

"You look cold," Raiden says, a hint of a smile playing across his lips. "I can't say I blame you. You've spent how long sweating away in that dusty desert?"

"Almost ten years."

I feel a hint of pride when his smile fades. He must've thought we kept Vane on the move, constantly running to stay undetected. But placing Vane with groundlings hid him so well that we never had to take such extreme measures. And Raiden fell for my mother's trick and believed Vane died in the attack. He only learned the truth four years ago when he broke Aston and Normand during his interrogations.

He won't break me.

"Where's Gus?" I ask, bracing for the worst possible answer.

Raiden's smile returns. "My questions first."

He hisses a word, sending a draft rushing toward me.

I square my shoulders, expecting pain—but the breeze is feather soft and warm as sunlight. It drapes around my body like silk and sinks under my skin, calming my nerves, easing my aches. Even the windslicer gash on my side—a wound left over from my confrontation with Raiden in Death Valley—seems to dull under its bandage.

A sigh escapes my lips and Raiden's smile widens. "Better?"

I give him a nod, even though he doesn't deserve it.

The draft is a ruined Southerly, robbed of its will and its voice, and no more than Raiden's slave.

I hate myself for drawing comfort from it.

But it's so nice to be warm.

"I'm glad," Raiden says, and I'm surprised by the sincerity in his tone. "Regardless of what you may think, Audra, I want you to be comfortable here."

I want to tell him that he shouldn't have left me trapped like a flightless bird in a frozen cage. But the words stick in my throat when I meet his eyes.

He's looking straight at me, studying me with an intensity that makes my cheeks flame.

"A short red dress seems like a strange choice for such a fierce warrior." His gaze travels over my body, making my face burn even hotter. "Dressing to impress?"

"*Are* you impressed?"

I don't know where the question came from, but I want to suck the words back as soon as they leave my mouth—and kick myself for saying them.

Especially when Raiden says, "Incredibly. I see so much of your mother in you."

He stalks closer, running his hands down the bars. "I don't use this tower cell often. But I couldn't lock you away in a dim, filthy dungeon. You're too . . ."

"Too what?" I whisper, not realizing I've moved forward until I feel my knees graze the frost-coated bars.

I'm so close now that I can see the blond stubble that lines his jaw, and the blond lashes rimming his ice-blue eyes.

His features aren't handsome, but there's something striking about him.

Something *powerful*.

My hands curl into fists when I realize what I'm thinking, and I shake my head to clear it. But the sweet, soothing wind is making everything spin too fast.

Or maybe it's Raiden's piercing stare.

"You're different," he whispers. "Most prisoners I can read in an instant. But you . . ."

He licks his lips, and my stomach turns sour even as my heart starts racing.

I want to look away but I can't. His gaze is the only thing keeping me from melting with the rushing warmth.

He reaches through the bars and tucks a strand of hair behind

my ear. I should flinch away, but I'm rooted to the floor. A tree clinging to the earth as a storm rages around it.

"If I told you that you belong as a queen, what would you say?"
he asks.

My breath catches.

I can see myself sitting on a gleaming throne. And beside me
stands . . .

I rub my head, trying to concentrate on the man beside me, but
he's blurry and shifting.

Old one second.

A boy the next.

Blond, then dark haired. Stolid, then smiling.

A jumble of contrasts I can't make any sense of—but one feels
warm and safe, like the wind whipping around me.

The other feels empty.

I don't want to be empty anymore.

I try to focus on the man, try to wrap myself in the steadiness
of his safety.

But I can't forget the boy.

He materializes in my mind.

Beautiful.

Heartbreaking.

Why can't he be mine?

"Perhaps that's the wrong question," Raiden says as I back
against the wall and let the cold stones press against my skin.

I try to shove the fog from my thoughts, but it's too heavy to lift,
and my mind keeps drifting with the sweet, soft breeze.

"You love the wind, don't you?" Raiden asks.

"The wind is all I need."

I laugh when I hear the words out loud.

I've said them in my head hundreds of times, and at some point I must've believed them.

But can the wind ever really be enough?

Can the wind fill the space between the things I've lost?

"You miss someone," Raiden says.

It's not a question, but I still answer.

"Yes."

The confession is sharp as knives, and I realize that I've crossed my cell again. This time I must've crawled, because I'm on my knees, clinging to the bars like a child.

Raiden covers my hands with his. His skin is warmer than I expected. His grip comforting.

Protective.

"Who do you miss?" he asks, his voice as soft as his skin. "Who have you lost?"

"My father."

Tears drip off my cheeks, and my hold tightens on the bars.

I don't want to cry for my father—not here. Not with the man responsible for his death.

But *is* Raiden responsible?

I thought it was him—but with my head floating and the world spinning, I realize these warm hands wrapped around mine couldn't belong to a killer.

A killer couldn't be so soft.

21

"You've had to grow up too fast, and you've had to do it alone," he whispers. "But it doesn't have to be that way anymore, Audra. I can keep you safe."

"Safe?" Repeating the word doesn't help me understand it. "But . . . I'm in a cage."

"To shield you from the others. The ones who took away your father."

My mother's face fills my mind. "You can protect me from her?"

"That's why I brought you here. Now she can never hurt you again."

I close my eyes and lean against the bars, grateful to feel them.

"You'll keep her away?" I whisper.

"As long as you stay here. But I might have to send you off alone."

I try to open my eyes but my eyelids feel too heavy. "Why?"

"Because you're hiding something from me. The secret I need in order to protect you."

"I don't have any secrets."

"That's not true, now is it?"

"It is."

At least, I think it is.

It used to be true. But everything feels so faded and blurry I can't be sure anymore.

He sighs, slow and sweet. "Don't you trust me, Princess?"

"Of course I . . . what did you call me?"

He leans closer, stroking my cheek. "Tell me what you're hiding, *Princess*."

I jerk away and crawl backward across the floor.

My father had a dozen nicknames for me. But he never called me Princess.

Raiden is not my father.

The statement feels so glaringly obvious—but it's earth shattering too.

Raiden. Is. Not. My. Father.

Did I really think that he was?

How could I . . .

The wind.

This ruined, Southerly wind.

It's clouding my mind somehow and shifting my emotions.

I pull myself to my feet and press my cheek against the wall, letting the shiver clear my head. "Does that usually work?"

Raiden sends the wicked Southerly away, stealing the last of the warmth—but I'm grateful for the cold.

Each shiver makes me *me* again.

Even the pain that floods back to the wound on my side is a welcome reality check.

"Actually you're the first person I've tried it on," Raiden says. "Your mother taught me the trick while we waited for you and your friend to arrive at the Maelstrom. She claimed it would be the *only* way to get answers from you."

"Leave it to my mother to help you capture me *and* torture me."

Raiden laughs—as bitter and cold as the air. "Actually her method was far gentler than what you'll face now."

I can't stop myself from shaking. But I force myself to meet his eyes, noting that they're rimmed with dark smudges. Further shadows line his brow and deepen the creases around his frown.

He looks tired.

The realization boosts my confidence as I tell him, "I'll never give you what you want."

"They all say that in the beginning."

He snarls a word, and a ruined Northerly coils into a whip and cracks my face so hard it knocks me to my knees.

Pain stings my cheek. But when I reach up to check for blood, my hand comes away clean.

Raiden seems as surprised as I am and lashes me again, this time across my chest.

The force of the blow makes me wheeze, but a second later the pain fades and no marks line my skin.

My loyal Westerly shield must be strong enough to protect me.

"I *knew* you had more to hide!" Raiden shouts, his voice a strange mix of fury and triumph.

"No—everything's gone."

Everything Vane shared with me.

Everything that mattered.

I stripped it and shredded it and scattered it on the wind—whatever I had to do to make sure it was safe.

"Then why did your friend's shield abandon him at the first blow?" Raiden asks. "The draft you wrapped around him before we took you both away rushed back to the sky at the first crack of my whip."

"You're lying."

"Am I?"

He holds his sleeve up to the moonlight so I can see the splashes of red staining the fabric.

I turn away, trying not to imagine Gus—smiling, handsome Gus—bloody and alone in some dark dungeon.

"Let him go," I beg, knowing it's pointless but needing to try. "He has nothing to give you."

"Ah, but that's where you're wrong. Your Westerly won't let me hurt you. But I can hurt *him*. And I'll make you watch, until you tell me what I need."

CHAPTER 5

VANE

I'm starting to worry that Os is right.

Not for attacking us. Or taking our weapons. And definitely not for tying Solana, Arella, and me to the sturdiest palms in the grove and telling us we can sweat here until we're "ready to cooperate."

But the fact that he was able to do all of that—and create some sort of weird vortex around us that's spooking all the winds away—makes it pretty hard to argue that the power of pain isn't more effective.

Come on Westerlies—time to prove you're the big, legendary things you're supposed to be. . . .

I close my eyes, waiting for my instincts to whisper something that will get us out of this mess. But all I hear is the creaking palms and the chirping bugs and the wails of the ruined drafts whipping past, trapping us with the heat and the swirling sand.

The sun rose a little while ago, so we've lost at least seven or eight hours.

Looks like I'm failing pretty epically at this "hero" thing.

"You're going to tear your elbow out of joint again," Solana warns as I try to squirm free of my ropes.

"If that's what it takes to get out of here, I'll deal with it."

But all I'm really accomplishing is scraping the hell out of my skin.

I curse my dad for having a stockpile of industrial strength, rampaging-elephants-couldn't-break-this-stupid-rope in our garage—though I guess I should be grateful Os didn't use draining winds to bind us instead.

"Save your energy," Arella tells me. "This vortex isn't all that different from a Maelstrom. It won't kill us—but it is slowly sapping our strength. Os is making sure I have no means of escape."

The bitter edge to her voice reminds me that this isn't the first time Os has held her prisoner—just the first time she didn't deserve it.

"Why did you refuse to train with them?" I have to ask.

She's sacrificed everything in her quest for control.

Her daughter.

Her husband.

Even her own life.

And yet, here was a chance to learn this incredible new power, and instead she chose to be tied to a tree.

Arella stares at the sky for so long I assume she's not going to answer. But then she whispers, "I could never destroy the wind."

Her whole body quivers with the words and I'm . . .

. . . not sure how I feel about that.

She murdered both of my parents with a couple of flicks of her wrist. Does she really think the wind is more important than *them*?

Then again, if even *she* wouldn't cross that line . . .

I honestly have no idea how I feel about Os teaching the Gales the power of pain. I know I could never do it. And part of me wants to drag him underground and never let him near another gust of wind again.

But another part of me—a part I'm not necessarily proud of— can't help wondering if it's the only way we stand a chance against Raiden.

How else do you win when someone doesn't fight fair?

"So what's our plan?" Solana asks when I finally admit that wriggling out of these ropes isn't going to happen.

Arella shakes her head to shoo the gnats away from her eyes. "We wait for Os to come back and convince him to let us go."

I snort. "You really think he's going to do that?"

"I can be very persuasive."

She definitely can.

She's fooled me a pathetic number of times—but she's never managed to convince *Os*. He was ready to let her die in the Maelstrom. The only reason she's still breathing is because I dragged her out, needing her alive so she could tell me what happened to Audra.

What she did to Audra, I correct.

And now she's just standing there, waiting for a chance to try to talk her way out of this—after we've already lost so much time.

"That's not good enough!" I shout, wishing I had a way to fling something at her head. "Don't you care that Audra's a hostage right now? That Raiden might be . . ."

I can't say it.

Can't even think it.

"Of course I do," Arella says. "But caring doesn't change anything. All it does is waste energy."

I know she's right.

But I hate how calm she is.

I hate *her*.

"This is *your* fault!"

"I know." Her voice hitches, and for a second she sounds like a mother who's actually worried about her daughter. But her tone hardens again as she tells me, "Raiden left me no choice."

She keeps using that as her excuse, but she still hasn't explained what Raiden threatened her with. Not that it matters—nothing matters except getting to Gus and Audra.

"We *will* find them," Arella promises. "We just have to bide our time. Without the wind I have nothing except—"

She sucks in a breath.

"Except what?" I ask, but she's too busy bending into a position that would make even a yoga master yelp.

Somehow she stretches around her ropes and gets her head close enough to her hands to slip her fingers between her lips.

The high-pitched, shrieky whistle makes my ears ring, and

Arella's practically beaming as she pulls herself back up. "Os always forgets about the birds."

I glance at Solana, glad to see she looks as confused as I am. I know Arella has a special connection with birds—it's one of the few things she and Audra share. But I don't see how that's going to help us. All a bird is going to do is flap and screech and peck and . . .

"Oh God," I groan, realizing what her plan is. "You've got to be kidding me."

A minute later I see dark shapes moving toward us on the horizon, and the blood drains from my face.

Solana laughs. "Are you seriously afraid of birds?"

"Hey, they've made horror movies about them for a reason!"

The cloud of birds streaks closer, and I abandon all hope of playing it cool. There are dozens of them—huge black crows and vultures. It's officially my nightmare come to life. All that's missing is the screeching violins playing in the background as they dive.

I try to hold still, but there's so much flapping and cawing, and I can feel their talons digging into my skin as they peck and peck and—yeah, I'm definitely going to be sick.

"Close your eyes," Solana tells me, so I'm guessing I look as awful as I feel.

I take her advice, but I still hear all the flapping and pecking—and now it makes me imagine they're stripping away flesh.

"Okay, that's *so much worse!*" I yell, ripping my eyes open again.

I'm relieved to see there's still skin on my hands. But I also have five evil crows perched all over me, and I flail harder than I've ever flailed before—which is especially impressive considering how tight my bonds are.

"Stay calm," Arella orders. "Remember why you're doing this."

I try to focus on Gus and Audra as the crows land on me again. But I still flail—it's a reflex. *Creepy birds wanting to peck my eyes out—run away!*

I'm trying to come up with a plan C when I hear a familiar screech, and as I turn toward the sound, I see a gray hawk heading straight for me. This time I'm not afraid.

Gavin and I have come a long way since the days when he used to terrorize me if I accidentally wandered too close to where Audra was hiding. I still don't *like* him—and I like him even less when he lands on my bad arm and glares at me with his beady, red-orange eyes. But then he goes to work on my ropes with his razor-sharp beak, snapping through the strands like they're made of paper.

"We have to hurry," Arella says, slipping her hands from her shredded bonds. "Os could've spotted the birds as they swooped in."

She unties her ankles and rushes over to me, shooing Gavin away as she unravels the last of my frayed ropes.

Gavin screeches and I tell him, "Don't try to follow us—and don't go near Os."

I watch him land among the palms, and our eyes meet for a second.

"I'll bring her home," I whisper.

I swear when he blinks, it feels like a nod.

"Come on," Arella says, ruining the moment.

"Wait for me," Solana calls, still struggling to break free.

Arella shouts that we don't have time, but I turn back and tear at Solana's ropes—not that I'm much help with only one strong hand.

"We don't need her," Arella insists.

"Excuse me?" Solana asks. "I'm the one who's guiding us to Raiden's fortress."

"I can do that," Arella says. "In fact, I'm fairly certain Vane's the only Windwalker in our world who doesn't know how to get there."

"Uh, maybe I would if you hadn't scrambled all my memories with your little wind tricks," I grumble. "Especially since you only did it so I wouldn't remember that you *murdered my parents*."

I want to argue more, but now's not the time to think about the list of Shady Things Arella's Done. Instead I help Solana pull herself free, and we follow Arella through the vortex of ruined winds. The drafts scrape like sandpaper, and as soon as we cross to the other side, I hear sounds of the Gales crunching through the trees to find us.

Arella sends her creepy birds after them, and I call as many winds as I can find until I have enough to tangle us in the power of four. Then we're streaking through the blue-white sky, blurring over sand dunes and flattened houses and what's left of the San Gorgonio Pass Wind Farm. I don't dare slow down or look back or even let myself think about what Os is going to do while we're gone.

I picture Audra and Gus and beg the winds to get us to them as fast as they can.

"I need you to steer us north," Arella tells me, pointing toward the mountains in the distance.

"Raiden's fortress is to the east," Solana corrects.

"I know. But Os took all of our weapons. I keep a stash of replacements at my house."

I'm not convinced that windslicers will do us any good against the power of pain, but I guess it would be pretty stupid to storm a fortress unarmed. And we already know my wind spikes aren't very useful.

Arella's directions take us over a forest of Joshua trees and end at a small, square house in the middle of an endless stretch of barren desert. It looks like the kind of place where a serial killer would hide, which . . . is pretty accurate.

I set us down in the shade of the only tree—a giant oak that should be dead, considering the dry ground all around it. The soft ringing of wind chimes fills the scorching air.

Arella gasps and races toward her house, staring up at the eaves where silver chimes dangle from an intricately carved blackbird. The melody feels haunting and sad as they ping against each other in the late morning breezes.

"Audra must've come here," she whispers, reaching up and removing a black necklace that's been tied around the bird's neck. A silver feather pendant dangles from the cord, and I vaguely remember Audra tearing it off her mother's neck after she realized her father's death had been Arella's fault all along.

"That belonged to Audra's father." I don't say it like a question, but Arella nods anyway.

"I found it in the rubble after the storm." She traces her fingers along the cord. "I'd been holding out hope, refusing to believe Liam was really gone. But then I saw the black, and—"

She chokes back a sob as she clasps the necklace around her neck.

"A guardian exhales a bit of their life force into their pendant," Solana explains. "As long they're still breathing, the cord is vivid blue. But once they return to the sky . . ."

Tears stream down Arella's cheeks, but I stop myself from feeling sorry for her.

It was *her* fault.

Everything is.

My fingers find their way to the copper compass bracelet Audra gave me, the only thing I have left from my parents after Arella slaughtered them. The needle usually points west, but for the moment it's just spinning and spinning.

"We need to keep moving," I say, and Arella nods.

Before she goes inside, she takes down the wind chimes, bringing them with us as we follow her up the weathered porch steps.

I don't really know what I was expecting Arella's house to look like—but I definitely would've been less surprised by cobwebs and creepy chandeliers than I am by the sparse emptiness. Each room has a couple of pieces of worn, dusty furniture—and that's it. The rest is bare walls and creaky floors and still, stuffy air. It's barely better than the burned-down shack Audra squatted in on my parents' property.

Arella hangs the wind chimes over a plain wooden table in the kitchen and disappears down the hall, promising to be right back.

"Is this where Audra lived?" Solana asks.

I'm honestly not sure, but I nod anyway. I don't feel like admitting how little I know about the-girl-I-was-bonded-to-and-am-planning-to-bond-to-again.

But Audra didn't like to talk about . . . well . . . almost everything. Especially when it came to her past.

Mental note: Ask more questions next time.

I'm studying the depressing rooms, trying to memorize every detail when Arella returns, carrying a silver scabbard and two wind-slicers.

She's changed into clean black pants and a tank that probably used to fit better—but thanks to her days in the Maelstrom the fabric hangs off her scrawny shoulders and bunches in weird places.

She hands Solana one of the windslicers and straps the other to her belt.

She gives me the scabbard.

My hand shakes as I slide out the knife and stare at the blade molded from thousands of needles. It's feather shaped, like a mini-windslicer, designed to shred drafts and skin alike—and there's a tiny speck of dried red near the hilt.

I hand it back to her as the room starts to spin. "I can't."

"You have to," Arella tells me. "There's no point getting anywhere close to Raiden's fortress if you're not ready to kill."

There's that word again.

Kill.

I know I can't avoid it forever. But I'm not sure how I'm going to get through it without shattering to a million pieces.

She's right though.

If a Stormer spots us during our mission, there's only one option.

I try to slip the scabbard into my boot, but it doesn't fit—clearly I shouldn't take weapon ideas from movies.

Solana shows me how to strap it to my belt.

"I also found this," Arella says, holding up a silver instrument the size of her palm with cuplike ends dangling off some sort of pinwheel. She nudges it with her finger, making it spin with a soft creak.

"Is that one of the Stormers' anemometers?" Solana asks, leaning closer.

"I stole it off one of them a while back," Arella agrees. "Thought it might come in handy someday."

"What does it do?" I ask.

"I'm not sure. It never seems to respond to the wind. But if Raiden has his Stormers carry them, they must be important." Arella slips the longer end through her belt, leaving it dangling next to her windslicer as she walks to the window, pulls it open, and traces her fingers across the filthy screen. "We need to figure out our flight path."

She and Solana start discussing jet streams, but I'm not listening—partially because I don't know crap about that stuff. But mostly because I keep staring at the fresh welts on my wrists from the ropes I just escaped.

If Os—with his limited experience in the power of pain—could capture all three of us in one fell swoop, it won't matter how we fly, or what weapons or gadgets we bring with us.

If we have to face off against the Stormers—and let's be honest, there's a pretty good chance we will—we'll need to fight like them if we want to win.

And since none of us want to sink to that level, we need to get someone else on our side who can.

I know a guy for the job—assuming I can find him.

And assuming I can convince him not to kill us.

CHAPTER 6

AUDRA

I try to count my steps and memorize the turns as Raiden leads me to his dungeon, but his fortress is a labyrinth of narrow paths and twisting stairways that take us up and down and every possible direction. By the time we reach the dim, windowless room lined with dark-barred cells, I'm so turned around, I can't tell if I'm deep underground or high in a different tower.

Raiden shoves me into a cell in the center of the row and locks the barred door behind me. I crawl to a corner, curling my legs into my chest and wrapping my arms around them, trying to preserve what little heat I can.

The cold is different here.

Damp and heavy.

It presses against my skin with a million icy fingers as my breath puffs into clouds that seem to hang permanently in the air.

The gray floor and walls of my tiny cell are bare, save for deep scratches where a former prisoner must've clawed at the stones.

"It's definitely not as nice as your last cell," Raiden tells me. "But the view is *infinitely* better."

He steps to the side, and everything inside me unravels.

"Gus?" I whisper, squinting through the dim light, hoping the crumpled figure on the floor of the opposite cell won't respond.

For a second he doesn't move. Then he slowly lifts his head, scanning the room until his pained eyes find mine.

I choke down a sob.

His face is so bruised and swollen I barely recognize him. But somehow he still tries to smile.

"Clearly you two have some catching up to do," Raiden tells us, and the smugness in his voice makes me wish I could claw off his skin.

I wait until his footsteps fade before I scoot closer to the bars. The damp chill makes my muscles ache, but I refuse to think about the pain. Not when Gus looks like . . .

"So it's that bad, huh?" Gus asks, studying my face. "I guess this is the end of my Best-Looking Guardian days."

I force a smile, trying to be brave for him. But as he pulls himself into a sitting position, my eyes brim with tears.

Thick gashes as wide as my fist have turned his broad chest into more wound than skin. Some of the cuts are covered with scabs, and others are still seeping red—but it's the dark spot on his left shoulder that makes me feel like I'm going to be sick on the floor.

A hole.

Perfectly symmetrical and about as wide as my finger.

Bored through flesh *and* bone.

Aston had twenty-nine just like it. One for every day he resisted the power of pain, until Raiden found a different way to break him.

"Gus, I'm so—"

"Don't!" he interrupts, shaking the crusty strands of his long blond hair out of his eyes. "Please don't apologize—this has nothing to do with you."

"How can you say that?"

"Because we're at war. Soldiers get captured and interrogated. It's as simple as that."

But it isn't.

My mother handed us over to Raiden like animals to the slaughter.

And the only reason Gus was with me was because he was trying to guard me, to keep the Westerly language safe—a language I only knew because I broke my oath as a guardian and bonded myself to Vane.

Everything goes back to me.

My mistakes.

My fault.

Gus winces as he reaches to tear a strip of fabric from the end of his pants. I try not to notice that his back looks just as shredded as his chest.

"If you need more bandages I can tear off part of my dress," I offer.

Gus laughs. "You barely have enough fabric to cover you as it is. Pretty sure Vane would kill me."

"I don't care about Vane."

I didn't mean the words the way they sounded—or I don't think I did. But they seem to echo off the walls.

"Is that true?" Gus whispers. "I heard Raiden say something about you breaking your bond. . . ."

I focus on rubbing my hands together, letting the friction warm my fingers.

"Do you really not care about him anymore?" Gus presses.

"I . . . don't know. My head and my heart don't match. I still remember everything. But I can't *feel* it. I'm just sort of . . . empty."

Gus nods as he ties the strip of fabric across the widest gash on his arm. "I guess that's better. Maybe the broken connection will keep Vane from trying to rescue you."

"Do you really think he'd come after us?" I'm surprised the thought hadn't crossed my mind.

"It's *Vane*. He's the master of taking stupid risks. Besides—he'd do anything for you. Or he would have, before . . ."

"Well," I say, my voice cracklier than I'd expected. "Hopefully he's over it."

"Do you really mean that?"

"I have to." It'll be safer for Vane if he lets me go.

"Wow," Gus breathes. "And I thought *I* had it rough."

"How can you even compare the two?" I wave my arm toward his seeping wounds.

"Uh, I got smacked around a bit. You ripped away half of your essence and gave up the guy you loved. Don't even try to pretend that wasn't agony."

It was.

And the cold hollowness that followed was worse.

"You got more than smacked around, Gus," I remind him. "You have a hole in your shoulder."

"Yeah, well . . . it's only a little hole." He tries to smile as he traces his fingers along the edges. But I can hear the pain in his voice.

"I have a bandage on my side," I say, wishing it weren't such a pathetic offer. "Part of it's soiled, but Vane's mom used way more gauze than I needed. It might even have some ointment on it."

"Not worth it. This is the kind of wound that's never going to heal."

He presses his palm over the hole and a hint of fear creeps into his eyes.

"How did Raiden do it?" I whisper.

"You don't want to know."

I don't.

But I'm going to have to *see* it.

The realization sends me spiraling, and I can't tell if I fall backward or crawl. All I know is that I'm somehow pressed against the wall of my miniscule cell, gasping for air.

"What's wrong?" Gus calls.

I try to relax—to focus on slow, deep breaths. But even when my heartbeat steadies, it doesn't calm the panic.

I close my eyes, swallowing the bile on my tongue as I tell him, "I can't watch him hurt you."

"It won't be as bad as you think."

"No—it'll be worse. I saw Aston. One hole is only the beginning."

All the color drains from his face. But he straightens up, promising, "I'll be okay."

"How?"

I trail my fingers along the scratches in the floor, wondering if a prisoner made them while they were being tortured—or a friend who had to sit there and let it happen. . . .

My hands shake with rage, and I'm not sure if I'm angry with Raiden or myself. All I know is: "I can't do this."

The words hang in the silence between us until Gus sighs, sounding so weary and broken a few tears creep down my cheeks.

"So what's going to happen, then?" he asks. "Are you going to teach Raiden Westerly?"

"I don't even know Westerly anymore—I tried to tell Raiden that, but he wouldn't believe me. Because of this stupid wind!"

I claw at the draft still whipping around me, wishing I could pry it off and fling it away.

I don't care that it's loyal or protecting me. "I don't deserve to be shielded!"

"Stop it!" Gus shouts, and the anger in his voice makes me freeze.

He takes a deep, labored breath before he speaks again.

"I know you're worried about me. But my dad used to say, 'No matter what happens—trust the wind.' It's part of us. It's our kin. And that draft—for whatever reason—has decided it needs to protect you. So trust it. Let me deal with Raiden."

"You don't know what he'll do to you."

"I have a pretty good idea." He uncovers the hole in his shoulder again. "But I can take it, Audra. Raiden's already attacked my mother.

Murdered my unborn sister. Turned my father into a Living Storm and forced me to kill him. And I'm still here. Still fighting. I'm stronger than Raiden. He did all of this to me, and still has no idea you taught me that command—and he never will."

The words bury me in shame.

I'd forgotten I taught him Westerly.

Only one word—and I didn't even tell him what it means. I didn't want to trigger the breakthrough and put him in more danger.

And now he's bruised and bloody, facing who knows how many more rounds of torture. Yet he has no doubt that he can bear through it, while I'm wallowing in self-pity.

"I can't believe you know more Westerly than I do," I whisper.

"Gotta love the irony, right? But it's good. It gives us an advantage. We know that Raiden has his suspicions backward."

I don't understand how he can stay so positive, but I try to draw from his confidence.

There has to be something we can do—a way to change Raiden's mind, or get us out of this somehow, or . . .

I jump to my feet when I realize what I'm forgetting.

Aston gave me some advice before I left his cave—something that could be the answer to everything. I scour my cell, but all I find are the scratches in the floor, and no matter which way I study them, their pattern remains random.

"Do I want to know what you're doing?" Gus asks as I squint through the bars of one of the cells next to mine.

I scan the dungeon for hidden guards before I lower my voice to the softest hint of a whisper. "When I left Aston's cave, he told me that if I ever got captured by Raiden, I should look for the guide he carved into his cell. He said it would help me escape."

"Did he say how?"

"He was obnoxiously vague. But if we can find it . . ."

"I think I already have. There are some marks in here that are clearly supposed to mean something. I don't know how they could be a guide, though."

He points to the back corner of his cell, but all I can see is shadow.

"Can you describe it to me?" I ask.

"It just looks like a bunch of dashes and scribbles. Do you really think it matters? I'm sure Raiden's figured out how Aston escaped and made changes to prevent it from ever happening again."

That sounds like Raiden.

But it's the best chance we have.

"Aston is smart—and he was convinced the guide would get me out of here," I tell Gus, hoping I sound more confident than I feel. "I wish I could see it."

Gus nods and crawls toward the shadowy corner. "I guess it's a good thing I have all these handy wounds, then."

He rubs his finger against his chest. Then draws a red line on the floor, painting a copy of the guide in his blood.

CHAPTER 7

VANE

'd really been hoping to face psycho cave-boy with at least a little bit of daylight. But the sun is long gone by the time Arella picks up hints of Aston's trace.

I have no idea what she's sensing. All I see is an empty beach—which looks exactly like the zillion other empty beaches we've been flying over for the last few hours.

She points to a dark patch among the rocks and whispers, "I feel him testing the air, getting a sense of who we are."

"Oh, I *know* who you are," a deep, accented voice calls from the darkness. "And the only reason you're still breathing is because I've decided to let you. But that can change."

A cluster of cold, scratchy drafts yanks us out of the sky and slams us against the beach in an explosion of sand. I can't see—can't breathe—can't tell if I'm sinking or rising. And as the winds crush tighter, everything goes dark.

The last threads of my consciousness are about to unravel when the winds vanish, and I cough and wheeze through the lingering silt.

I force my eyes open, squinting through the falling sand to spot . . . a blond head.

Just a head.

A *lot* of shouting and panicking follows, along with a ton of failed attempts to thrash before I realize I'm pinned and—most important—that I didn't see any blood.

The head is also talking to me, which I probably should've noticed right away. But my brain was too busy screaming, *AHHHHHH—DISEMBODIED HEAD!!!*

I take another look and realize the rest of Solana is buried in the sand.

The fact that I can't move seems like a pretty good sign that I'm in the same boat.

I'm trying to be glad that at least I don't feel any new injuries—or any extra pain shooting through my bad elbow—when I realize we're stuck in the wet, squishy sand. The kind of sand you only get when you're on the part of the beach where the waves come crashing down.

Almost on cue, a freezing, foamy wave slams into us, stinging my eyes and nose and filling my mouth with salt water. The sand loosens around my shoulders as the ocean retreats, but not enough to pull myself free before the next wave hits.

Then another.

And another.

Laughter rings between splashes, and I decide that as soon as I get my arms free I will blast every square inch of this beach with wind spikes until I find his smug face and—

"I think that's enough to make it clear who's in charge here, don't you?" Aston's voice asks as the waves stop and we shiver through the eerie silence. "Not that any of you seem capable of putting up much of a fight. Still, now your silly notions of superiority can flutter away with your pride."

His voice is everywhere and nowhere, and I want to turn my head to follow it, or at least figure out how he managed to stop the ocean. But my muscles will only let me twist so far. All I catch is a glimpse of Arella's head sticking out of the sand on my other side, rocking the drowned-rat look.

"Well, if it isn't the jilted princess, the questionable mother—who reeks of Maelstrom, by the way—and the heartbroken lover-boy," Aston's voice calls from his cave. "I figured I'd be hearing from at least some of you after all the turbulence I've picked up—though I can't say I expected this particular combination."

He hisses a word I can't understand and a sickly Easterly crawls under my skin, its icy needles prickling all the way to my core.

"Still clinging to your side of the bond, I see," he says. "Too bad it won't matter. Shattered bonds rarely linger. Especially when faced with so much *temptation*."

He hisses another word and the sand explodes again, sending me tumbling across the beach. When the world stops spinning, I notice I'm tangled up in something warm.

"Sorry," Solana mumbles, sliding out from underneath me.

I try really really really hard not to notice whether the water turned her dress see-through.

Aston laughs from the shadows, and I call a Westerly to my side, ready to get started on my attack-the-crap-out-of-this-beach plan.

But then I remember the reason I dragged us here in the first place.

"We need your help," I call toward his cave.

"Yes, I can see that. This is the rescue party, right? Funny, I thought it would be bigger. Having a little trouble controlling your army, are we, Your Highness?"

"Yeah. The Gales are too busy learning to destroy the wind," I snap back, finally getting his attention.

A cloaked figure steps out of the shadows, like he's following the Shady-Dude-Dress-Code. "You're teaching them the power of pain?"

"*I'm* not teaching them anything." I wrap my Westerly around me as a shield and struggle to stand. "Os is the one behind it, and when I tried to stop him, he tied me to a tree. He thinks the only way to beat Raiden is to fight like him."

Aston's laugh is slow and bitter. "Os is right. But he's going to ruin himself."

"He knows," I agree. "He doesn't seem to care."

"And what about you?" Aston asks as he crosses the beach to join us. His feet barely leave marks in the sand. "If you see so little value in the power, why beg me for assistance?"

"It's not that I don't see value," I say. "It's that I don't think it's worth destroying myself for it. But if you're already under its influence . . ."

"Ahhhh, I see. So I'm a lost cause and get to do your dirty work for you. Is that why you brought the murdering mother as well?"

"Actually, he brought me to see through the tricks of silly fools," Arella says, slithering out of her sandy prison.

"Don't get too cozy," Aston warns. "Just because I haven't killed you yet, doesn't mean I won't."

"I don't believe you," Solana says, taking a small step toward him. "You were one of the Gales who came to help after I lost my first guardian. I'll never forget how kind you were. How safe you made me feel."

"Yes, well, things have changed a bit." Aston raises his arm, and I reach for another Westerly. But instead of attacking, he peels back the sleeve of his cloak and waves his hand back and forth.

A strange whistling prickles the air, and glints of moonlight leak through his skin.

It takes my brain a second to realize it's because his arm is covered in pin-size *holes.*

I squeeze my eyes tight, but I can't wring out the horrifying image. And I can't stop myself from imagining Audra looking just as Swiss-cheesy.

"How long after you were captured did Raiden start to . . ." I don't finish the question.

Aston turns away, wrapping his arms around his chest. "The torture began immediately."

I sink to my knees and punch the sand so hard it sends the grit flying into my eyes—but I'm already tearing up.

"I'm sorry," Aston tells me. It almost sounds like he means it. "If it's any consolation, she's definitely still alive—for the moment, at least." He tosses something on the beach. "She left this here during her last visit."

My blurry eyes only see a smudge of blue, but Arella whispers something about guardian pendants, and I scramble to grab it before she can.

The cord is blue.

The sobs hit me then—huge heaving wails that could rival any toddler.

But I don't care.

She's alive.

I squeeze the proof as tight as I can as the sobs keep coming.

Pretty soon I'm choking on my own snot, winning the prize for the Most Pathetic Dude in the History of Pathetic Dudes. Until gentle arms wrap around me, followed by a soft breeze.

I lean into the warmth, my mind drifting with a rush of sunny memories.

Chasing magpies in a field, stretching out my arms and wishing I could fly away with them.

"Someday," my mom tells me. "Someday you'll rule the whole sky."

Then somehow I'm sneaking through an orchard with my dad, grabbing peaches off the branches.

Juice dribbles down our chins, and he tells me, "We'll have to jump in the lake before your mother finds out."

Their voices feel so familiar, and so foreign at the same time.

I try to remember more, but cold fingers squeeze my arms, dragging me away from the warmth.

"He doesn't need your comfort," Arella snaps.

"Shouldn't that be his decision?" Solana snaps back.

"He made his choice. And it had nothing to do with you."

It's obvious what Arella's implying—and she's technically right.

But *she* doesn't get to be the one to say it.

"You certainly are an interesting group," Aston says, as I pull away from both of them, nearly wrenching my elbow in the process. "I'd almost love to keep you here to watch how this all plays out. But I don't think I could stomach Loverboy's sniveling."

"I'm not *sniveling*," I say in . . . a pretty snivel-y voice.

I dry my nose on my sleeve and clasp Audra's pendant around my neck, trying to keep focused on what's really at stake here.

"Ah, there's the look," Aston says. "The *I'm going to throw my life away* look. Your little girlfriend had it too, when she decided to leave my protection. And it's worked out so well for her, hasn't it?"

I *really* want to punch him.

But since we still need him, I mumble, "If you help us, we can get her out of there. I'm betting you know that fortress better than anyone."

"I do. And I hate to crush the dream, but no one can break into Brezengarde."

"My father escaped," Solana argues.

"As did I," Aston reminds her. "But breaking in and breaking out are two very different things. There's a chance she might make it out on her own—if she uses that brain of hers. But even then . . ."

"I can find a way in," Solana insists.

I wish I could feel her confidence. But it doesn't matter. "I have to try something."

"Yes, I'm sure that's what Raiden's counting on," Aston says. "Not that he *needs* your power. But he does so love to collect things. And what are you going to do when he catches you?"

"*If* he catches me," I correct. "And . . . I'll find a way to kill him."

The words would be a whole lot more convincing if my voice wasn't shaking.

Aston sighs. "Sadly, that's not what I meant—though we'll need to circle back to the Worthless Westerly Conundrum later. You have a much more fundamental problem than that. There's a reason Raiden rarely bothers with bodyguards. Anything you throw at him. Any deathblow you try to deliver. It all ricochets right back onto you. He calls it his *backlash*. I never could find a way around it."

My mind flashes to our escape from Death Valley, when Audra, Gus, and I were hiding under our Westerly shield and Raiden practically dared me to attack him.

I'd been *very* tempted. But . . . it felt like a trap.

"So you're saying Raiden can't die?" I ask.

"I'm saying you can't kill him. At least not by any *conventional* means."

Well . . . that definitely falls into the category of Crappy News I Didn't Need to Hear. But killing Raiden isn't my goal right now.

My plan is much more simple.

"Look," I tell Aston. "I'm the first to admit I have no idea what I'm doing. That's why I'm here. You think I wanted to waste all this time finding you? I need help—and I thought maybe you had a little decency left. If not, I thought you'd at least jump at the chance to piss off Raiden. I mean, what better way is there to drive him insane than stealing two of his prisoners while working with the one Westerly he's never been able to capture?"

Aston circles me, and the wind whips back his hood, revealing his pale, scarred face and blue-tinged lips.

He's honestly not as scary as I'd imagined. Just a few scars—nothing like his arm.

Then again, we haven't seen the rest of what's under that cloak. . . .

"Please," I beg. "I have to get her back. It's my fault she was captured."

"Is it? I thought it was mostly hers." He points to Arella and she looks away, mumbling her same excuse about having no choice.

Aston doesn't buy it either.

He widens his circle to make a slow path around all three of us. "What would you give me if I agreed to help?"

I open my mouth to tell him "anything"—but "I won't teach you Westerly, if that's what you're asking," comes out instead.

"Not even to save your precious love?" he asks.

"My instincts won't let me."

"The infamous Westerly instincts strike again. Surely they'll be the death of us all. And yet . . . your winds can be very comforting. They used to visit me during my years in Brezengarde. Somehow they'd slip through the cracks in the fortress walls. I couldn't under-stand them of course. But their songs were so beautiful." His eyes look glassy as he stares at the stars. "Your girl sang one for me when she stayed here. I'll never forget it."

"She has her father's talent for song," Arella whispers.

"Careful," Aston tells her. "You *almost* sound like a loving mother."

"I *am* a loving mother," Arella snaps.

"Well then, here's your chance to prove it—and this will be a one time only offer, so think it through. I'll give you my help. I'll even figure out a way to sneak into Brezengarde. But only if you agree to give me your pain."

I have absolutely zero idea what that means, and judging by Arella's expression, she's just as clueless—until Aston raises his arms and tangles a draft around her.

Arella screams and drops to her knees.

I try to help, but the wind knocks me back. Same thing happens to Solana.

Several terrible seconds pass. Then the wind calms and Arella falls still.

Aston, meanwhile, is smiling so wide, his whole face looks stretched. "I'd heard stories of the ache her gift caused her, but I never realized it was so deliciously intense."

"What did you do to her?" Solana asks.

"I absorbed her agony. Usually I'm forced to draw on the wind's pain to hold myself together. But hers is so much stronger—so much more liberating." He stands over Arella, the moonlight casting his strange speckled shadow over her. "That's my offer. My help, in exchange for your pain three times a day."

"So . . . basically, you want to torture her," I clarify.

"Only for a few minutes. Don't tell me she doesn't deserve it."

She does—but something doesn't add up. "Why would you offer that when you could just capture her right now?"

"Because he would never be able to keep me here," Arella whispers.

"Your gift does give you a very specific skill set," he agrees. "Os was right to contain you in the Maelstrom. Separating you from the sky is the only way to truly contain you—unless you cooperate. But don't think that means I don't have ways to *control* you. I know what you crave." He squats to make sure Arella's looking at him. "I want your word that when this is over, you'll return here with me to keep our arrangement going. Break it, and I'll destroy everything you care about."

"Keep Audra out of this," I warn.

"I meant what she *really* cares about. Oh yes—" he adds when Arella sucks in a breath. "I know how to find him. But I won't if you're a good girl. And as a bonus, I'll help you save your daughter."

I can't imagine Arella agreeing to any of this—but maybe I don't know her as well as I think I do.

Or maybe she thinks she can outsmart Aston.

Or maybe she's afraid.

Either way, she whispers, "You have my word."

CHAPTER 8

AUDRA

The swirling patterns of lines make me dizzy—or maybe it's the blood.

Or the fact that I have no idea what Aston's guide means.

"You're sure you re-created it exactly?" I ask.

"I'm not an artist," Gus says. "But the original is just as confusing."

Weariness weighs down his words, and a pained stiffness has settled into his motions.

"You should rest," I tell him.

Gus nods.

"I hope you've memorized this," he says as he pulls off one of his bandages and smudges the guide with the soaked fabric.

When the marks are reduced to a smear, he lies down on top

of it to make the bloody puddle seem as if it seeped from his many wounds.

"'Raiden's greatest weakness is that he *has* no weakness,'" I mumble.

"What does that mean?" Gus asks.

"I wish I knew. It was something Aston told me while I was his hostage. He also said, 'His fortress has more security than anyone could ever need and none all at the same time. Once I figured that out, getting away was easy.'"

Gus sighs. "I've never been good at riddles."

Neither have I.

But I close my eyes and picture the bloody lines of the guide, trying to imagine anything that could make a similar pattern. Some of the lines intersect, separating the design into clusters of three, four, and five.

Seventeen clusters in all.

Seventeen is a prime number—but I doubt Raiden pays attention to basic mathematics. It's also my age—though I'm certain my lifeline holds no importance.

Still, the reminder startles me.

I'm only seventeen.

Most days I feel much older, but it suddenly feels too young—too inexperienced to face a foe with triple my lifetime's worth of wisdom.

Panic tightens my chest and I lean against the wall, closing my eyes and counting my breaths until they slow into a pattern I can manage.

Behind me, I hear Gus shift positions.

Then shift again.

And again.

Each time he moves, he grunts in pain.

I watch the red trickle across the ground, wishing I had a way to comfort him. But I have no wind. No warmth. Nothing except . . .

My voice.

For years my songs were silenced—the loss of my father too thick in my throat. But now that I know the truth of his loss, I've been slowly reclaiming the melodies.

I choose the song my father sang to calm my mother during her worst bouts with pain:

> *Another day, another night*
> *Hollow darkness, blinding light*
> *Both have to share.*

> *Another calm, another storm*
> *Calls of peace, violent swarms*
> *It's never fair.*

> *Might be grounded now, but the sky still calls for you*
> *Hush now*
> *Rest your wings*
> *Sleep now*
> *Close your eyes and let the wind sing*
> *And be miles away*
> *Until yesterday*
> *Is just a long forgotten dream.*

The last lyric fades into a hum, and I notice that Gus's breathing has softened. His brow is still pinched with pain, but for the moment he sleeps.

I should do the same.

I tuck my legs underneath me and pull my hair tight against my shoulders. I've barely closed my eyes when pounding footsteps jolt me back to the present.

"On your feet!" a Stormer orders as he marches into the dungeon.

Everything about him is pristine—his gray uniform perfectly pressed, his weapon polished to a gleam—save for the pale scars marring his black skin along his neck and wrists.

He uses rough yellow winds to bind our hands before unlatching our cells.

Our path through the halls is straighter than my previous route, and I'm trying to figure out if that means there are multiple routes to the same place or if we're going somewhere new when the Stormer shoves his way past us and snarls another word.

A door appears in the wall, and we stumble outside to the gray, frosty day—far colder than I'd expected given the time of year.

Scratchy, ruined drafts thicken the air, and I sense no trace of the brave winds that snuck into my tower cell and kept me company.

My thoughts blur as my bare feet sink into the knee-high snow. I wait for numbness to take over, but the ice is too sharp. By the time we've crossed the courtyard, my head is spinning faster than the enormous silver windmills lining the walls.

"Up there," our escort says, shoving us toward a staircase barely wide enough to fit my narrow frame.

Gus is forced to turn sideways, pressing his wounded back against the stones and leaving a trail of speckled red across the icy wall.

The Stormer doesn't follow, stationing himself at the base with a second Stormer and blocking any possible escape.

The air grows thinner as we climb, and by the time we reach the top, I can't remember who the tall blond figure dressed all in white is. He eyes the boy I climbed with—I can't recall his name either—then frowns at me.

"We're going to need you to be a bit more lucid than this," he says, waving his arm.

Something gray and heavy is draped over my shoulders, smothering me in a sticky kind of heat. It melts the fog in my head and thaws the ice in my veins.

My shoulders relax—until I realize I'm wearing the coat of a Stormer. I want to fling it away, but the warmth is the only thing providing clarity.

"Not used to the cold, I see," Raiden shouts over the raging winds. I can't believe I didn't recognize him. "And here I gathered the squalls just for you. Can you feel their energy?"

He grabs my wrist and presses my palm against the wall, which hums with a steady vibration.

"The power of the earth meeting the sky," he breathes in my ear. "And it's only the beginning. I've learned so many incredible things in my years living here. There's so much I could teach you."

I jerk my hand away.

"Clearly you have other lessons to learn first." He points behind us, to where Gus—*how could I forget about Gus?*—has been dragged to the side of a tower and bound to the stones.

"What are you doing to him?" I ask.

Raiden smiles. "Patience, my dear."

"I'm not your dear."

"No. I suppose not." He raises his fingers to his lips and blows a screechy whistle.

Metal scrapes across the courtyard, and I turn to find five Stormers dragging open a heavy door. Behind it is an enormous round grate, and just beyond the bars I catch a glimpse of fans spinning at top speed, filling the air with an unsettling howl.

"This might be my favorite creation," Raiden says. "I call it the Shredder. It's Brezengarde's air purification system. No wind can pass near my fortress without learning to be *submissive*."

Goose bumps prickle my arms as I realize the strange howl is the cry of innocent drafts being torn into Raiden's ruined slaves.

"The true brilliance of the Shredder, though," Raiden adds, "is that I can concentrate its force. For instance . . ."

He whistles again, and the Stormers crank a wheel next to the grate.

Metal panels curl inward, creating a beam of wind that blasts into Gus.

He stands silent and still, but his agony is carved across his face.

"Are you getting the idea of how this is going to work?" Raiden asks, steadying me as my body shakes with rage. "If I have them narrow it one click further, it gets rather dangerous for your friend—especially fueled by these violent Northerlies. So, is there anything you'd like to tell me?"

My eyes stay focused on Gus. He's watching me, mouthing the same three words again and again.

Trust the wind.

Still, I can't help feeling like a coward as I tell Raiden, "I have nothing to say."

"I was hoping you would say that. Now we get to have a little fun." He smiles as he whistles the command.

The Stormers narrow the grate to a jet stream that slams Gus in the stomach, and this time Gus can't fight back his screams.

I try to look away, but Raiden grabs my neck. "You will watch every second, or I will gouge out your eyes, understood?"

I turn back to Gus, feeling my heart break when I see his beautiful eyes pleading with me to be strong.

I owe him that much.

So I watch every minute, trying to pretend it's not really happening. But my stomach heaves and I cough up bile onto the snow.

Raiden whistles to end Gus's agony and offers me a white handkerchief to dry my mouth.

I refuse, using the sleeve of the Stormer's coat instead.

"Ready to talk—or do we need to continue?" Raiden asks.

I shake my head, spitting out the same worthless response I gave him before.

The wheel cranks again, and Gus's screams turn into deep, guttural groans that will echo in my mind from this day forward. When it's over, his breaths are so ragged they sound more like gurgles, and blood is streaming from his nose.

"Very few have survived a third blast," Raiden tells me. "And none when the Shredder was fueled by the squalls."

My mouth tastes of iron as I bite my tongue.

But Gus is still staring at me. Still pleading with me to keep going.

Raiden gives the command, and I curse the wind for obeying— for blasting Gus so hard he goes silent.

I don't realize I'm sobbing—or that I'm digging my nails into my hands—until the Stormers at Gus's side declare him alive.

"You're both stronger than I thought," Raiden says, ordering his Stormers to haul Gus away. "But don't worry, the strongest things are the most fun to break."

"Then take a turn on me!" I shout.

"I intend to. But for you it needs to be *special*."

He stalks away then, leaving me to imagine the horrors he'll dream up as the Stormer with the scars hauls me down the stairs.

Another Stormer is waiting for us in the courtyard, and he strips off my coat, sending sharp pain shooting through the wound on my side. I suck air through my teeth, trying to keep it together. But when he shoves me again, I heave more bile, not sorry at all when most of it ends up on his shoes.

He pins me against the wall, proving he's less disciplined than the others.

I can use that.

I spit accidentally-on-purpose onto his coat, and he grabs my hair, yanking my face closer to his.

"You'll have to do something to make that up to me," he growls.

"We need to keep moving," the Stormer with the scars warns him. "Raiden ordered us to take her straight to the hold."

"Raiden's not here right now," he argues, sliding his hands to my waist.

I knee him as hard as I can.

I only manage to hit his thigh, and he grunts and grabs my throat.

The scarred Stormer pries him away and shoves him into the snow. "Get down there and cool off! I'm not facing the Shredder over you."

The other Stormer snarls threats, but doesn't follow as I'm dragged away.

"Thank you," I mumble, tripping over my shaky feet.

"I didn't do it for you," the scarred Stormer says.

I follow his eyes to his marked hands, where the pale lines almost glow in the dim light.

"You've faced the Shredder before?" I guess.

He doesn't answer. But the set of his jaw tells me all I need to know.

I probably shouldn't ask my next question, but . . . I have to.

"What did it feel like?" I whisper.

"How do you think? The Shredder has seventeen fans, and each one carves different edges into the drafts. So when the wind hits, it's like having seventeen spinning blades liquefying your insides."

If my stomach weren't so empty, I'd vomit again.

Instead, I let out a sob for Gus—but only one.

I spend the rest of the walk trying to compose myself. Which is why I don't realize the crucial information I've been given until I'm locked away in my cell.

Seventeen fans.

Now I know what Aston meant about the fortress having more security than anyone could ever need and none all at the same time.

Aston escaped through the Shredder.

CHAPTER 9

VANE

Flying with Aston sucks.

Actually, "sucks" isn't a strong enough word—but breaking my parents' Language Rules feels like admitting that I'm really not planning on seeing them ever again.

It's not just the scratchy broken winds Aston uses, or the way they turn the world into a blurry mess.

It's that Aston's, well . . . *holey*.

He's still wearing his cloak, but he has the hood down and his sleeves keep blowing back. And when you surround any of his skin with a ton of rushing wind, it makes this constant *screeeeeeeeeeeeeeeaaaaaaaaaaaaaaaaaach*.

I lose track of how many hours I spend gritting my teeth through the nails-on-a-chalkboard whistle, but my jaw is aching when we set down in the middle of a field with long, swooshing grass and one of those round, silver windmills with the fin sticking out of the back.

"Why are we stopping?" I ask.

"I know I may ooze power and prestige," Aston says. "But I do occasionally need to rest."

The confession reminds me how long it's been since the last time I slept. Raiden spent weeks using his shattered winds to torment me with nightmares—and now I can't sleep. Not when Gus and Audra are . . .

"What time is it?" I ask.

Arella glances at the sun. "Looks like it's getting close to noon."

"NOON?"

"Oh, spare us the freak-out," Aston tells me. "We're losing time as we head east."

"How does that make it better?" I ask.

Aston shrugs. "If you want to move faster, we'll have to ditch some dead weight."

His eyes dart to Solana, and she gives him a glare that practically shoots ice beams.

"You call *this* 'dead weight'?" She stretches out her arms, and all the nearby breezes sink under her skin.

"You do realize that windcatching is essentially the worst thing you can do when you're facing the power of pain, right?" Aston asks. "What do you think will happen to all of this"—he waves his hands in front of her, outlining her curves—"if I shatter those drafts you've tucked away?"

The color drains from Solana's face. "Can you really do that?"

Aston pulls aside his cloak to reveal a long row of perfectly round holes, piercing through skin and bone. "Anything can be broken."

"Well, he won't break me," Solana says, calling more breezes and soaking them up.

Aston shakes his head and growls a scratchy word.

A grayish draft tangles around her, but Solana absorbs it like the others. "You were saying?"

"That is . . . unexpected," Aston says.

He studies her so closely that Solana starts to fidget.

I save her by getting back to the much more important subject. "I think we should use pipelines for the rest of the journey."

I hadn't suggested the rapid wind tunnels before, because they can be unstable and deadly. They also suck worse than traveling with Captain *Screeeeeeeeeaaaaaaaaaaaaaaaaaaaach.*

But we're wasting too much time.

"We're moving faster than you think," Aston promises. "We've already made it to that middle part of the country where there's far too many cows for my liking. Kansas, is it? Or Dakota something?"

"Nebraska," Arella murmurs.

The name feels fuzzy in my ears, matching the memory that resurfaces with it.

A hazy afternoon—the sun so bright it whites out the blue. I follow a dark-haired girl as she finds the tallest tree and climbs. I can't see what's in the nest, but I'm mostly there for the songs. Her voice makes me forget that I'm supposed to be afraid.

I close my eyes, trying to remember more, but my past is still too jumbled up.

Audra's a part of it, though.

And she's still a part of me—even if the ache I'm clinging to is growing fainter every hour.

"Are you okay?" Solana whispers, resting her too-warm hand on my shoulder. "Isn't this where your family . . ."

I nod.

Arella clears her throat. "Actually, we're a little to the north. But it does look the same."

I study the field we're standing in—rolling waves of grass and wildflowers as far as the eye can see.

It's pretty, I guess.

But it makes me uneasy.

There's too much sky. Too much wind. Too few places to hide.

It feels like the last place on earth for a family of sylphs to be when they're trying to hide from Raiden—which was probably why Arella chose it.

"I know what you're thinking," she tells me, scratching at her arms. "If I could undo it, I would."

"Oh please." I kick a clump of wildflowers, sending their yellow petals scattering. "All you regret is that your husband sacrificed himself to save me."

She doesn't deny it.

"Well then," Aston says, "this seems like a fitting time for my afternoon fix."

He tangles Arella in ruined drafts, soaking up her pain as she sinks to her knees. Solana covers her ears—but I memorize each one of Arella's screams.

"Look at you," Aston says. "I must say, this is the darkest side I've ever seen in a Westerly. You're almost smiling."

"She deserves it."

"Ah, yes. Pain for pain. Does that make it all better?"

It doesn't. Just like whatever he's doing to Arella doesn't make his holes disappear.

But it *helps*.

Aston smiles. "You definitely got some of your girl's fire when you bonded, didn't you? Might keep you alive—if we learn to use it. So why don't you make one of those fancy wind spike things and we'll see what you've got?"

"We don't have time to play around," I argue.

Aston points to where Arella lies curled up in the long grass. "She won't be up to traveling for a bit. And I'm not getting you anywhere near Brezengarde until I know you can defend yourself. So be a good boy and make a wind spike."

He claps his hands like I'm some puppy he's teaching a new trick.

I hate myself for obeying.

As soon as I form the spike, Aston snatches it away—but I shout, *"Come,"* in Westerly and the spike snaps back to my hand.

"I bet you think that gives you an advantage, don't you?" Aston asks.

Before I can respond, he grabs my spike and gags me with one of his ruined winds.

"Now try to call your weapon back." He points the wind spike at my heart. "Oh wait, you're dead. Pity."

For a second I wonder if he's really going to impale me. Solana must be worried too, because she drags Aston back.

"Oh, relax, Princess. If I wanted him dead, he would be. I'm merely trying to show him how pointless his little tricks are against Raiden's methods."

He hisses another command and my gag unravels.

"Let's assume for a moment that you manage to hold on to your weapon and get close enough to actually have a clear shot at one of the Stormers." He hands me back my wind spike. "Could you kill them?"

"Is it necessary?" I ask.

"It's always necessary. *They're the enemy.*"

"Right, but are they actually, like, threatening me?"

"Fine, let's make this easier and say they have their weapon pointed at your true love—and they've been murdering kittens all day. *Now* could you destroy them?"

"Of course."

The squeak in my voice says otherwise.

"Stop thinking like a Westerly! You need to channel some of that inherited darkness." He grabs my wrist and drags me closer to Arella. "There she is—the woman who murdered your parents and betrayed your beloved. Stab her."

"What?" Solana and I ask as he pins Arella with sickly winds and silences her screams.

"I don't mean anywhere fatal," he says. "I need her around for my pain doses, after all. But why not take a bit of revenge? Slice off a finger or something. She doesn't need all ten."

Arella twists in her bonds, but Aston has her held fast. "I'd stay still if I were you. He might chop off something *important*."

"Vane?" Solana asks from somewhere behind me. "You're not going to do it, right?"

"Quiet, Princess," Aston tells her. "We'll get to your problems next."

"I don't have any problems."

"Oh, trust me, you do. But first we need Loverboy to prove he can actually hurt his enemies."

"I've already proven that," I argue. "I killed two Stormers."

The guilt and grief of it almost shattered me—and probably would have if Audra hadn't bonded with me afterward—but Aston doesn't need to know that.

"That could've been a fluke," Aston says, leaning close to whisper in my ear. "This isn't hard, Vane. Think about your parents' faces—their screams. The splash of their blood as she murdered them. Or if that doesn't get your anger flag flying, think about your girl locked away in Raiden's dungeon. Shall I describe what it's like down there? The kinds of things Raiden likes to do?"

He drops his cloak, revealing the full horror of his wounds.

"And let's not forget that I'm not a gorgeous young girl with deliciously pouty lips. How long do you think it'll be before he—"

"STOP IT!" I scream, covering my ears.

Don't picture it.

Do. Not. Picture. It.

"Leave him alone," Solana says, trying to take my hand.

Aston blocks her. "Not until he proves that his life is worth all the guardians who've died to save him. Come on, Vane—what's the big deal? A few minutes ago you were reveling in her pain. All I'm asking you to do is take the next step."

My grip tightens on the wind spike, and I raise it over Arella's hand.

She won't die if I stab her pinky . . . and she's done a million worse things.

"And still, you hesitate," Aston says. "Behold, the worthlessness of the Westerlies."

I reel around, pointing the spike at his head.

"Go on, then," he says. "I'll even make it easy for you." He holds his palm in front of the wind spike, wiggling his pinky. "Slice away."

I'm tempted.

I really am.

But I can't do it.

Aston shakes his head, disgusted. "Here you are, racing across the country, pretending you're willing to do whatever it takes. But your instincts will always slow your hand, won't they? And when they do, your little girlfriend will die."

"Shut up!"

"You can't stop me," Aston says. "And you can't stop Raiden. He'll break your girl down piece by piece. And when she finally takes her last ragged breath, she'll do it knowing the boy she sacrificed everything for—the Westerly she spent her life protecting—couldn't find the will to save her."

"THAT WILL NEVER HAPPEN!"

"Prove it, then. Hurt me. Or hurt her." He points to Arella. "Show me you can inflict some pain."

"You want pain?" I ask, squeezing my wind spike so hard the winds feel ready to unravel.

"I want you to prove you have the stones to do what needs to be done."

"Fine."

I take a deep breath.

Then I kick him in the nuts.

Aston collapses to his knees, letting out the same wheezy groan I remember making after my friend Isaac accidentally nailed me in the balls during PE.

It's a pain only guys understand—one I honestly wasn't sure if Aston could feel, since I had no idea if Raiden had left his dudehood intact. But clearly Raiden did, because Aston's clutching his stomach and looking ready to hurl.

"This—doesn't—prove—anything," he mumbles.

"It does, actually. It proves that if I fight my own way, the violence won't get to me. I just inflicted a crap-ton of pain on you, and I'm not even queasy."

"You think Raiden will ever let you get close enough to kick him?"

He hisses a command through his teeth, and a draft coils around my neck, twisting so tight, spots flash across my eyes.

"LET HIM GO!" Solana screams, but her next words sound very far away.

I'm stuck in that weird haze between panic and blacking out, so I can't really tell what happens next. All I know is that the draft unravels and I get some much-needed air.

When my chest is done heaving, I find Solana and Aston in the middle of some sort of epic stare-down.

"Time to tell your fiancé what we've just discovered," Aston tells her. There's no teasing in his voice. "Five seconds . . . four . . . three . . ."

"I gave the command, okay?" Solana asks, not looking at me.

"Judging by the idiotic look on your face," Aston adds, "I'm guessing you have no idea what that means. Think it through. The draft I attacked you with was broken. So the only people who can command them . . ."

I stumble back when I figure out how to finish the sentence.

Solana used the power of pain.

CHAPTER 10

AUDRA

Gus is vomiting blood.

Between every retch he keeps begging me not to worry.

But I doubt he'll survive another round of Raiden's torture.

I don't even know if he'll survive this one.

I try to convince myself that Raiden won't let him die—that he needs Gus to pressure me.

But Aston was captured along with another Gale.

Only Aston made it out alive.

Even the Westerly shielding me seems worried. It keeps stretching thin, offering Gus gentle breezes of comfort. But whenever a noise warns that a guard might be approaching, it snaps back to protect me.

I wish it would shield the person braving the torture, not the one standing uselessly by.

But the wind is making its own decisions.

And it keeps choosing me.

So I sing until my throat turns raw and Gus finally falls silent. I can't tell if he blacked out or fell asleep, but his labored breaths promise he's still holding on.

I try to do the same.

I'd thought knowing what the guide meant would give me hope. But Aston's escape plan is far more dangerous than I'd realized. We don't just have to get out of our cells and through the mazelike fortress and past the myriad of guards—without any useable winds to assist us.

We have to survive the blades of *seventeen* fans.

There's also no way to know if Raiden has adjusted the blades since Aston's escape. And I don't understand how he found a path through the Shredder—or how he mapped it out ahead of time.

But we have no other options. So the first step will be finding a way into Gus's cell. I need to study Aston's exact markings. There's no room for guesses or errors.

Maybe I can convince the Stormer who helped me today that I need to ensure Gus doesn't choke on his vomit. He wasn't necessarily kind, but he seemed afraid of upsetting Raiden. I doubt he wants Gus to die on his watch.

I practice how I'll ask, choosing each word carefully. But the next Stormer who checks on us is the one who tried to choke me.

I can still feel his sticky breath on my face—his roving hands on my waist.

I pull the fabric of my dress as far as it will cover.

"Believe me, I intend to do all the things you're imagining right now," he says as he opens my cell. "But not while you belong to Raiden."

"I don't belong to anyone."

"Keep telling yourself that."

He sniffs my hair as he binds my arms behind my back, and keeps me pressed against him as he marches us up the stairs. He rests one hand on my shoulder, the other hand gripping my waist. When it slides toward my hip, I kick out his ankle.

He clings to me to regain his balance, but I shake him off, ignoring the tear of fabric as he topples back several stairs.

I run the other way, even though I can see the staircase dead-ends ahead.

A hand drags me through a hidden doorway before my assaulter catches up to me, and I scream until I realize it's the scarred Stormer from the day before.

He seals the door behind us, and his eyes dart to my chest—then away.

I realize my damaged dress isn't covering me as much as it was before.

Fury and shame burn my face as he ties the shreds of fabric back into place.

He clears his throat. "Did he . . . ?"

I can't look at him. "Not *yet*."

He mutters something I don't catch before he says, "I'll escort you to Raiden."

We walk in silence for several minutes, weaving through another tangle of corridors. Eventually I have to ask, "Why do you serve him?"

I don't understand how someone who appears to possess a few shreds of decency could choose Raiden's side over the Gales.

"The better question is: *Why do you resist?*" he asks. "Our people have been forced to the fringes of this world while the groundlings poison our sky. Raiden's only trying to reclaim what should be ours."

"Well, I guess that's the difference between us. I want no part of whatever world Raiden claims."

"Keep refusing to cooperate, and Raiden will grant that request."

He ends the conversation there. But when we reach a narrow staircase, he tells me, "You're not a fool, Audra. You're not like the others I've delivered. Give yourself a chance to see the value of Raiden's methods before you throw your life away."

He doesn't allow me to reply. Just pulls me to a rusty door at the top and gives the broken command to open the lock.

Please let Gus still be safe in his cell, I beg as I wade into the waist-high snow. The sky is the same dull gray, swirling with snowflakes that stick in my eyelashes while my teeth chatter as loud as my heartbeat.

The courtyard seems smaller.

Less wind—though I can hear soft chimes tinkling a quiet song.

Or maybe I'm imagining them.

I forget my name again and lose my grasp on anything I'm seeing. The dome of black metal we stop in front of seems familiar, but I can't figure out what it is.

"She's not good in the cold," a voice says beside me.

A figure in white seems to melt out of the snow. "Yes, I'm noticing that."

Someone drapes scratchy fabric across my shoulders, and as my head slowly clears, I realize I'm standing near a large birdcage housing two ravens. They eye me with a stern sort of wariness I'm not used to seeing from birds.

"If I'd known you were this weak," Raiden says, "I would've given you warmer clothes."

I should've guessed he'd be the figure in white at my side.

His cloak is feathered this time, plucked from soft, downy doves.

No wonder the ravens look wary.

"Of course, then I wouldn't get to watch your lips tinge with blue," Raiden says.

"You're not the only one watching her lips," the scarred Stormer mumbles.

He's no longer wearing his jacket, and yet his huge, muscled arms show no sign of shivers.

Raiden's eyes narrow. "You doubt my security?"

"Of course not, my liege." The Stormer dips a deep bow.

Raiden waves his hand to dismiss him, and the Stormer turns to leave. But he only makes it a few steps before he pivots back and drops to one knee.

"Forgive my boldness," he says, his words hasty and jumbled, "but I know you value whatever bond remains between her and the Westerly." He pulls back my coat and points to the torn sleeve. "I'd hate anything to damage that connection. Or *anyone*."

A bond can never form through force.

Still, the point gives Raiden pause.

"Tell Nalani she has a new charge," he tells the Stormer. "And to bring an extra uniform to the dungeon."

The Stormer stands and offers a salute, raising his arm straight in front of him and sweeping it toward his forehead in a wavy motion.

"I keep hoping you'll prove to be worth all of this hassle," Raiden says when we're alone. "And yet I fear I'm setting myself up for another disappointment. Still . . ."

He reaches for my cheek, his fingers grazing the breeze of the Westerly instead of my skin.

I jerk back.

Raiden laughs. "You have many reasons to fear me, Audra—but *that* is not one of them."

"Hard words to believe coming from the mouth of my torturer."

"Ah, but you haven't been tortured yet, have you?"

"Only because the wind protected me."

"Is that what you think?" He laughs and reaches for my torn sleeve. "The wind can only do *so* much. Surely you realize that."

Shame and rage burn my cheeks, and I refuse to meet his eyes, searching the courtyard for the source of the music I hear.

Small silver wind chimes dangle from the top of the birdcage, swaying in the gentle breeze.

"I see no reason to destroy you, Audra," Raiden whispers. "Why else would I try your mother's mind trick to interrogate you?"

"Do you think I only count what happens to me? Gus is—"

"Your friend is a separate matter," Raiden interrupts. "He challenged my authority."

I feel my lips smile as I remember that day in Death Valley. The look in Raiden's eyes—the shock and fury after Gus's wind spike hit its mark.

A teenager made him bleed in front of his army.

Proved he isn't the invincible force he claims to be.

And I realize.

Gus will never get out of here alive.

"My patience is wearing thin," Raiden tells me. "That's why I've had you brought here. One final attempt to make you see reason."

He steps closer to the cage, slipping his hand through the bars. The closest raven nips gently at his fingers.

"Your mother trained these birds. They were our messengers."

I meet the ravens' beady eyes, surprised to find my mother's connection in their gaze.

No one is ever the same once they trust my mother.

"I . . . don't understand."

The whole reason she came up with her bird-messenger system was so Raiden couldn't read the coded messages she sent to the Gales—unless that was another of her brilliant lies. . . .

A tempest swirls to life inside me as questions and theories crash together. I don't want to hear the answer, but I have to ask, "How long has she been helping you?"

"Helping me," Raiden repeats, his laugh as frosty as the wind. "Surely you know better than anyone that your mother is always the eye of her own storm."

It's a fitting description.

But it only adds to my confusion. "Why are you showing me this?"

"In the hopes that past mistakes might not be repeated. Your mother and I used these birds long ago—before you. Before your father. Years and years before our more recent interactions."

"You mean the times you tried to kill her?"

Not that I care.

My mother was trading lives—she should've expected to pay the same price.

But it dawns on me then that my mother might already be dead.

The last time I saw her, Raiden had sped up the winds of her Maelstrom, leaving her trapped in their draining pull.

No one was around to help—the Gales were all busy with the battle.

I'm . . . not sure what to do with that thought.

"I've spared you this far," Raiden says, snapping me back to attention, "because you're intriguing. An Easterly who speaks Westerly—"

"I don't speak Westerly," I interrupt.

"So you keep saying. But we both know there's more you're not telling me. End this ridiculous charade, or I will be forced to change my tactics—and trust me when I say you can't imagine the pain I will rain down upon you."

I believe him.

"Why do you want it so badly?" I ask. "Everyone claims the power of pain is greater than the power of four."

"What about the power of four pains?" Raiden counters. "Oh, don't look so disgusted. I seek power to rule our people. Our race has always been weak—no less pathetic than these caged birds. I'm trying to set them free. Trying to make them strong."

"No, you're trying make yourself strong."

"It's the same thing. No group can ever be strong without a strong leader. Look at the groundlings. Those powerless, talentless wastes have taken over this earth through the strength of a few great men. And yet you fault me for trying to do the same?"

"You and I have very different definitions of the word 'great.'"

"Indeed we do. You bonded yourself with that pitiful boy—do you honestly believe he'll become the leader the Gales desire?"

"No," I admit after several seconds of silence.

But Vane has other greatness to offer.

He saved me from myself.

Showed me the value in living—the value in who I am.

Even without our connection, I can still feel the strength of that gift.

"He will give our people peace," I whisper.

"Peace," Raiden scoffs. "Peace is taken—not given. All I'm asking for is the power to ensure that it happens. Let me rebuild our world the way it was meant to be. Let me give our people true security—a ruler who conquers everything. Even the wind."

"The wind will never be conquered. And our people don't want your power. Strong winds have their place, but we all crave the calm."

"That sounds like a final answer," Raiden says, turning back to his ravens. "Are you sure that's what you wish?"

I have to swallow, to make sure my voice is steady as I say, "Yes."

Raiden sighs as he reaches through the bars to stroke the birds. "I'd hoped you'd turned out smarter than your mother."

"I did."

"Perhaps," Raiden agrees. "I did make her a much better offer. She had a chance to blend her power with mine—and let mine blend with hers."

His meaning kicks in—but my brain refuses to accept it.

Even when Raiden adds, "She had a chance to be my queen."

CHAPTER 11

VANE

Solana knows the power of pain.

I guess that's what I get for trusting my ex.

She was supposed to be the *non*-psychotic, *non*-creepy person helping me with this rescue.

"How long have you been using it?" I ask. "Was it before or after Os told us about his new lessons?"

She doesn't answer, but her eyes tell me all I need to know.

"*Unbelievable!* So you stood there tied to a tree, pretending to resist the evil new power—and you were already using it?"

"It's not as simple as that," she says.

"Yeah it is. And you know what? You're going home—now. I'm sure Os will be thrilled to have you help with his training."

I turn and stalk toward the windmill, because we're in the

middle of freaking nowhere and it's the only place to stalk to.

She catches up with me and grabs my arm.

My *bad* arm.

"Sorry," she mumbles when I screech.

I jerk my arm away and succeed in wrenching it even worse.

My parents' Language Rules go out the window.

"Will you stop for five seconds?" she asks, getting a death grip on my wrist.

I want to keep fighting, but she's way stronger than she looks.

Plus my elbow has started shooting sonic blasts of pain that hit right in the pit of my stomach.

"Just let me check the bandage," she says. "And then can we at least talk about this? If you still want me to go afterward . . . I will."

"I'll still want you to go," I promise.

She drops her eyes, but I don't let myself feel guilty.

She uses the power of pain.

She tries to roll up my sleeve, but the salty ocean and the sand have made the fabric too stiff and crunchy. And since unbuttoning my jacket is a two-hand job, she has to help me.

Our fingers bump eleventy billion times. It gets extra weird when she has to peel off the whole thing—especially since the black tank underneath is so tight that even *I* want to make fun of it.

Aston whistles. "Well now, someone's been doing their sit-ups."

"Don't make me kick you again," I warn him.

"I'd love to see you try."

Solana ignores us, retying my bandage extra tight.

"Uh, are you trying to cut off the feeling in my fingers?" I ask.

"I need to limit your range of motion," she explains, helping me back into my coat. "If you tear the wound again, we're going to have to put your arm in a splint."

"Hey, this was your fault—not mine."

"I know." Her eyes move to her hands. "And I know what you must think of me—"

"That you're even creepier than her?" I interrupt, pointing to where Arella sits. She's free of Aston's bonds, but still lost in her own pain, and she keeps scratching at her arms and staring at nothing, like a monkey that's been in the zoo way too long.

"Even *she* won't touch that power, Solana. Think about that."

"I have," she says. "I try not to use it. I never wanted to in the first place. But I didn't have a choice."

"God—why is that everyone's excuse all the time?" I ask. "At least when I screw up, I can admit I was an idiot."

"You're always an idiot," Aston says, sidling up to join our conversation. "But this kind of thing doesn't happen by accident. Our girl here had to *choose*."

Solana's hand moves to her wrist, her fingers tracing the *V* in the design on her link, which definitely doesn't help my mood.

"Os was the one who taught me," she mumbles. "During the last battle, right before you found us in that cave."

I remember that moment. A Westerly had led me there, scream-ing about stopping a *traitor*. Guess there were two traitors I should've been worrying about.

"We were trapped," Solana says, like that makes it better. "The Living Storms were hunting us down—and there was no wind and no hope of reinforcements. The only things that worked were Os's altered wind spikes. So he made me memorize the command he was using to make them, in case anything happened to him. He taught me another word too, but I had no idea what it was for. I wasn't planning to use any of it—even when the Storm grabbed me, I held back. But then . . . you saved me. And we rushed to the Maelstrom. And when Gus and Audra weren't there, you started freaking out. You were pounding on Arella's cell—and I knew I was the reason you hadn't gotten there sooner, so . . . I tried using the command like a password. And it worked."

I vaguely remember her saying something I couldn't understand— but if I'd known it was the power of pain, I'd . . .

Actually, I don't know what I would've done.

Arella was my only chance of finding out what happened to Audra and Gus.

"So that's it?" I ask. "You only know those two words?"

"That's not how the power works," Aston jumps in. "You don't have a breakthrough. It's deeper than that. Once you use it, it becomes a *need*. That's why she was able to absorb that broken draft I coiled around her." He smiles at Solana. "Felt good, didn't it?"

"I never told it to do that," Solana argues.

"You don't have to. The need works on instinct."

He snarls a word, ruining a nearby Northerly before he swirls it around her.

The draft disappears under Solana's skin.

"There it is," Aston whispers. "The hunger in your eyes, craving that delicious rush as it takes over you."

"There's no rush," Solana insists.

Aston sounds almost dreamy as he whispers, "Yes there is. It's the sweet bliss of power mixed with the thrill of doing something so wrong it can't help but feel *right*. And it must be even better for you, getting to keep the wind swirling under your skin."

Solana tries to blink it away, but I can see what Aston means. She looks like a junkie who just took a hit of the *really* good stuff, and can't wait to get another.

"I have it totally under control," she promises me.

"Not possible." Aston tangles two more grayish drafts around her, and she soaks them up with a slight shiver.

"Like a true addict," he whispers.

"That's not fair! I can't send them off without using the power of pain. So either way I'm affected."

"Oh, there's another way," Aston says. "But the need blinds you. Believe me, darling. I know better than anyone. It'll be more gradual for you, because you aren't using it all the time—yet. But eventually you won't even think of the other languages. Pain will be the only words you speak—the only words you want."

"Which is why you need to go," I tell her. "There's already too many crazies on this mission. I don't have room for any more."

"But you need me," she says, still fiddling with her stupid link. "I'm the only one who can get us into Brezengarde—you heard Aston. He said it's impossible."

"It *is* impossible," Aston corrects. "But I'm sure I'll cook up something—"

"It won't be better than my way," Solana argues. "I know how to find the Royal Passage. It's the path my father escaped through—only those in my family know it exists."

"But how do you know about it?" I have to ask.

I'm not all that up on my Windwalker history, but I'm pretty sure I remember Gus telling me her parents died when she was still a baby.

"My parents sent me their memories as they were killed—kind of like passing on a gift. I didn't get everything. And some of them I still don't understand. But the details of my father's escape are incredibly clear. The fortress is mostly underground, in a web of tunnels. It's a defense mechanism—if anyone invades, they'd have to navigate the labyrinth. But the builder also had to ensure the royal family wouldn't get caught in the same trap. So he built the Royal Passage, a secret path in and out of Brezengarde. It's not on any of the maps or blueprints. The only people who can find it are those in the royal line who know the trick."

"Convenient how this is coming up *now*," Aston says.

"You think I wanted to share my family's oldest secret with *her*?" She points to Arella, then focuses back on Aston. "Or you? I figured I'd make sure you at least stayed loyal long enough to reach the base of Raiden's fortress. But Vane needs proof now, so . . ."

She finishes with a shrug.

Aston circles around her. "I can't tell if she's bluffing. I don't think she's that good. But I've been through every inch of that fortress and I never saw anything like what you're describing."

"That's the point," Solana says.

She turns to me, the craving for her new power gone from her eyes and replaced with something that feels a whole lot more inno-cent. "I can get us inside the fortress. We can save them, Vane. You just have to trust me."

"That's the problem," I mumble. "I don't."

"I do," Arella says from behind us.

She stands on shaky legs and stumbles to our side, looking pale and sweaty and haggard. "Can't you hear it?"

I'm pretty sure she's proving my point about too many psychos on this mission. But I strain to listen and . . .

Yep. Nothing.

"The Southerlies' songs have shifted," she says, drawing the winds closer.

The drafts drift around us, and even Aston closes his eyes to listen.

"Southerlies usually mourn change," Arella says. "And sing of things lost or slipping away. But now . . ."

The whispers are so soft I barely hear them. But all the drafts sing together, united in a single verse.

Rise beyond doubt and storm forward.

Solana blinks back tears. "They know I won't use the power of pain against them."

I'm pretty sure that's not the kind of promise she can actually keep. But if the wind is going to trust her, I guess that means I have to do the same.

"Fine," I say. "Let's go find that secret tunnel."

CHAPTER 12

AUDRA

Raiden proposed to my mother.

The words flit around my mind, refusing to settle.

I know my mother's beauty and power earned her attention from *many* men. And I know Raiden began his career as a high-ranking Gale.

But still.

The thought of them together makes me want to laugh—and throw up in my mouth.

"It was more about mutual advantage than desire," Raiden says, though I notice he's still stroking one of her ravens. "But when I see her fire in you, I can't help mourning what we could've created."

Now I really might throw up—and I silently thank my mother for marrying my father.

"You have too much of him in you," Raiden says, as though he knows what I'm thinking. "But you still have her drive and ambition. Don't squander it like your mother did. Give me one Westerly command, and you have my word that I will spare you through these final battles."

His tone is surprisingly sincere.

But I know better than to be tempted.

Raiden's a cyclone, snatching things up and hurling them back out when he's finished.

Nothing survives his path.

"You think you're so wise," I say, too disgusted to hold back my anger. "You think you're some brave leader destined to rule the world. But you're just a fool shouting at the wind, trying to pretend he's stronger."

Gusts crackle around me, turning the song of the wind chimes deep and ominous.

"Well," he says, turning slowly away from me. "Clearly I have my answer."

He strokes the raven one final time.

Then he snaps its feathered neck.

The other raven shrieks and flies to the top of her cage. I can feel her fury and heartache wafting through the air.

Ravens mate for life.

She will mourn this loss until her final breath.

"Sentiment," Raiden says as I bite back my tears. "Such a dangerous waste. Your mother proved that to me. And now I'll prove it to you."

He spins around, knocking me to the ground with his whip of

winds—but once again my Westerly spares me most of the pain.

"The wind won't shield you from blades. Did you think I'd forgotten?" His whip cracks against my side, right where his windslicer left its jagged gash. "You think it's fear you're feeling—but it's doubt. Your essence knows this isn't your fight. You're an Easterly. Your winds are survivors. But it's too late to change your mind."

He drags me to my feet and presses his knife against my right shoulder. The needled blade slices through my coat as though the thick fabric were made of air.

"One word," he tells me. "One word of Westerly."

I focus on the lonely raven, crying for the loss of her companion. "There's nothing you can do to me that will ever make me help you."

Pain stings me then.

And again.

And once more.

"No tears," he says, and I can't tell if he's livid or impressed. "Don't worry—they'll come." His breath is humid in my ear as he whispers, "My winds tell me your precious Westerly is on his way. He'll be here tonight. Then the real fun begins."

I feel another sting, on my left shoulder this time. Longer than the other, but I'm too dazed to react.

Vane came after me.

The thought cuts deeper than Raiden's blade as he slices me again, across the lower part of my back.

"That's enough for now," he says, sheathing the knife. "Can't have you losing too much blood. I want you awake when I tear your love apart piece by piece."

"I thought you wanted his power."

"That's how I'll get it. You share another thing with your mother. You both crumble to protect your *men*."

He drags me back to the dungeon, nearly dislocating my shoulder in the process.

A new Stormer is waiting for us there, a woman with black, angled hair. I assume she's Nalani.

"The prisoner needs new clothes," Raiden tells her, shoving me into her arms. "But do not treat her wounds. I want them to scar."

Nalani nods.

"What about that one?" She points to Gus's cell. "He doesn't have long left. And he's starting to smell."

Raiden's nose crinkles as he sniffs the air. "Put her in there with him. Let her watch his life drain away. And when he's gone, bring me his body."

He leaves us then, and my new guard shoves me into Gus's cell and tosses a gray uniform at me.

Gus seems to be unconscious, but I still move away from his eye line and slip out of my tattered dress. Warm wetness coats my hands as I pull the scratchy jacket off, but the wounds feel shallow. And my Westerly shield is doing all it can to soothe them.

When I've changed, I check on Gus. His skin feels sticky and feverish, his breaths a soggy wheeze.

I shred the remains of my dress and bind as many of his wounds as I can.

"He's bleeding on the inside," Nalani tells me. "Nothing can fix that."

Sobs burn in my throat and I choke them back, reminding myself that there's a reason our medics only know how to set bones and patch wounds.

The wind is our lifeline.

Fresh air will bring Gus's strength back.

And in his rage, Raiden just made a fatal error.

I roll Gus toward the wall, pretending to be moving him to cleaner ground. The new position gives me a chance to view the guide.

Gus's rendering was accurate. I try to do the same as I scratch the marks into my leg and let my new pants cover the evidence. The guide still doesn't make much sense—and I have no idea how to get us to the Shredder. But I have a plan to get Gus the wind he needs.

I prop Gus up, pretending I'm checking his breathing, and when his eyes slit open, I whisper in his ear, "If you can hear me, I need you to act like you're in as much pain as possible."

I can't tell if his grunt is a *yes*.

But the screams that follow are agonizing—horrible blood-curdling screeches as Gus thrashes and writhes, smearing more red across the floor.

"He needs air," I shout, letting my panic leak into my voice. "Please—you have to take him aboveground."

"You heard Raiden's orders," Nalani tells me.

Gus vomits. His legs and arms thrash, and I honestly have no idea if he's acting or finally admitting how much pain he's in.

"Please—he's dying!"

"I think that's the point."

"But you don't understand." I sweep the tears off my cheeks and new ones immediately replace them. "*He's* the important one."

"What's going on down here?" a familiar voice shouts, and the Stormer with the scars runs to the bars of my cell.

I reach for his arm. "My friend is dying. Please—you have to get us to the tower. Raiden would want you to."

"Then why did he order me to let you watch him die?" Nalani asks.

"Because he doesn't realize how important Gus is!" I hesitate then, warring over my next words, debating if the risk is too great.

Gus heaves again, making the decision for me.

"Gus is the one who can teach Raiden Westerly," I whisper. "I taught him a command before I broke my bond."

Nalani snorts. "How convenient."

"It's also true," I say, focusing on the scarred Stormer as he weighs my words. "I can't teach Raiden anything," I tell him. "All of my knowledge is gone. And Vane will die faithful like all the other Westerlies. So if Gus slips away now, he takes Raiden's last chance at learning the language."

"And you've just decided to tell us this now?" he asks. "Now that your friend's taking his final breaths?"

"That's *why* I'm telling you!" I turn to Gus, and a sob shakes my shoulders when I see the red oozing from his lips. "I thought I'd be strong enough. But I can't let him die. Not like this—not for a language that's not even mine. Or his. It's not our job to protect it. I'd teach Raiden right now if I could. But I can't. Only Gus can."

I can practically hear their minds chewing the words, deciding whether or not to swallow them.

I focus on the scarred Stormer and push where I know he's vulnerable.

"What do you think Raiden will do when he finds out that Gus knew Westerly? I'll tell him after Gus is gone—and I'll tell him I told you before it was too late. Do you think he'll reward you for blindly following his orders—or make you face the Shredder?"

Nalani grabs my throat. "You dare to threaten us?"

"I'll do whatever I have to do to save him," I rasp.

The scarred Stormer pulls her hand away, letting me breathe.

"Raiden needs to know," he mumbles. "If there's even the slightest chance . . ."

Nalani sighs. "We better get him to the tower cell, then. The boy doesn't have long without the wind."

The scarred Stormer nods, and his eyes focus on me.

For the first time I can see him as one of Raiden's trained killers. Especially when he says, "If this is a trick, I'll end you myself."

CHAPTER 13

VANE

The sky is dark by the time we reach the mountain that hides Raiden's fortress—and I mean *really* dark.

No stars.

No moon.

Just storm clouds blacking out the world and showering us with snow . . . in the middle of summer.

"I'm g-g-guessing this isn't n-n-normal," I stutter as Aston sets us down in an ice-crusted forest. It looks like Mr. Freeze came through and blasted everything with his freeze gun.

"It means Raiden knows we're coming," Aston tells me, pulling his hood up to block the snow. "I'd figured as much. But I'd been hoping he wouldn't be *this* prepared."

I know it shouldn't surprise me that Raiden can change the weather. But somehow the idea feels *huge*.

And the mountain *itself* is huge—way bigger than I'd imagined. We should've brought climbing gear—and about a million extra layers of clothes.

"Here," Solana says, blanketing me in a Southerly.

She does the same to herself before turning to Aston.

"I'll just absorb it," he tells her.

"And it would dull my senses too much," Arella adds.

I shiver just looking at them. The Southerly can't keep all the freezing air away, but at least I'll leave here with all ten of my toes.

Aston licks his finger and waves it back and forth, then curses under his breath. "Raiden's definitely gunning for you, Loverboy. He brought in the northern squalls. We'll have to limit flying to emergencies only, and Brezengarde will be at maximum power."

"The fortress draws strength from the wind," Solana explains when she sees my confusion. "There are windmills on every wall, and a system of tunnels to channel the wind to the heart of the fortress, where a central turbine powers all of Raiden's defenses."

"And his *offenses*," Aston adds. "Raiden isn't the type to sit back and wait for his fortress to be stormed. He likes to blast you to pieces long before you ever get there. And the squalls triple the range of his blasters—and quadruple the force of the Shredder."

"The ground isn't safe either," Arella warns, waving her hands to fan away the cloud of her breath. "I can feel patrols all over the mountain."

"Okay, so . . . how do we get around all of that?" I'm done hearing about problems. Let's get cracking on the answers.

Aston turns to Solana. "It might help if we knew where we're going. Care to tell us where we can find this mythical tunnel?"

"It's not mythical," Solana argues. "But . . ."

I feel a nightmare coming on.

Solana fiddles with her link. "I don't know exactly where it is—but I remember seeing train tracks near the exit my dad used in his memories. And some sort of structure."

"Train tracks?" I repeat. "On a mountain?"

"There's a train that takes people to the summit observatory."

She says it like that's good news, but uh . . . "There are *people* on this mountain?"

"Normally, yeah—especially at this time of year," Solana says. "But the squalls should be keeping them away."

I hope she's right.

There was enough collateral damage during my last battle with Raiden's army.

"Why would your family build their fortress so close to humans?" I ask. "And why hasn't someone noticed it and been like, dude—what's *that?*"

"It's tucked away quite brilliantly," Solana tells me. "And the winds help disguise it."

"You know, for a sylph raised by groundlings, you don't seem to know much about either race," Aston points out.

"Oh, please, like anyone normal knows about . . . um . . . what mountain is this?"

Okay, so maybe I'm an idiot. . . .

"Mount Washington," Solana tells me. "One of the windiest

places in the world. Also the highest peak in the northeast part of this continent."

"Well, look who's a walking geography book," I grumble.

"No—I just took the time to learn about my home," Solana snaps back. "Though I guess it'll be your home when all of this is over. You and your *wife*."

Oh good, so we're going *there*.

It gets even better when Arella says, "Audra will make a better queen."

"Okay, no one is getting crowned right now," I jump in. "Can we get through this alive and *then* worry about who gets to keep the castle?"

The sad truth is—assuming we find a way to defeat Raiden—if I don't marry Solana, I'll basically be usurping her family's throne. It doesn't matter who I love—or who loves me—or that I don't even want to be King Windwalker. It's all about the Gales' plans for rebuilding their world.

"Entertaining as it is to watch this little drama," Aston interrupts, "we're standing in the middle of enemy territory and clinging to the ever-unraveling hope of somehow eluding them. So perhaps we should stay a moving target?"

"Right," Solana mumbles. "Sorry."

"Me too," I tell her. "So . . . anyone know where the train tracks are?"

"I know how to find them." Aston pats the icy trunk of the nearest tree. "Get climbing, Loverboy."

"Great idea! Except, y'know, one of my arms isn't working right now," I remind him. "So how about you shimmy on up there?"

"I'll do it," Solana says, jumping to grab the lowest branch.

She misses by at least six inches.

"Honestly, if I'd realized I'd be working with idiots," Arella snaps, "I would've made this a solo rescue."

"Uh, we wouldn't need a rescue if—"

"Yes, I *know*," Arella says, cutting me off.

She cups her hands around her mouth and makes a warbling screech, and a small gray owl dives from a hole in one of the trees and lands on her wrist.

It's too cute to scare me—though it's super freaky the way it can spin its head around. Arella scratches its speckled feathers and makes a few more warbles until the owl blinks its huge yellow eyes and flaps toward the sky.

"The best way to get a bird's-eye view," Arella tells us, "is to ask a bird."

Sure enough, when the owl returns, it tells her we need to head northeast.

"Most of the tracks are under the snow," Arella says, "but it said there are several structures halfway to the summit."

"Oh good—time for some mountain climbing," Aston says, heavy on the sarcasm.

I'm right there with him.

I've always hated hiking. Hiking through ice and snow—without the right shoes or gear—is a million times worse. Hiking through ice and snow, when every creak or crackle could be an evil soldier coming to murder us?

Yeah . . . every minute pretty much feels like a thousand years.

I have no idea how long we've been trekking when Arella hisses for silence, waving her arms around, testing the air.

"I feel something," she whispers. "A deep shiver down my spine."

"I feel nothing," Aston tells her. "I think it's—"

A soft squeaking cuts him off, and we all focus on Arella's hip, where the silver anemometer has started spinning.

Aston grabs my arm. "Get us airborne—now! And use Westerlies!"

There aren't many around, but I manage to tangle a handful into a wind bubble. Solana, Aston, and Arella cling to me as I rocket us into the sky.

"What's going on?" I ask.

Aston pulls the anemometer from Arella's belt. "These only spin around other Stormers. Things are about to get very . . . explosive."

The word is still bouncing around our wind bubble when a thunderous crack erupts behind us, and one of the trees blasts into a million jagged pieces.

"Care to fly a little faster?" Aston asks. "And maybe make us a bit of a harder target?"

"On it!" I beg more Westerlies to join the bubble and command them to dash around in whatever random pattern they want.

It seems to help—the next few explosions are nowhere near us. But it's definitely not awesome on my stomach.

"What is the anemometer sensing?" Arella asks. "I've never felt anything so cold and hollow."

"It's the suicide draft," Aston tells her. "I'm surprised you could detect it. Clearly the rumors of your talents have not been exaggerated."

"Of course they weren't."

I roll my eyes, glad when Solana asks, "What's a suicide draft?"

"Exactly what it sounds like," Aston says. "Think of it as Raiden's ultimate control. He doesn't allow his Stormers to be taken prisoner, but he doesn't trust that they'll all have—shall we say—*the dedication* to honor the requirement if they're captured. So he forms a suicide draft around their necks when they swear their fealty, and then all he has to do is give the command and . . ."

He mimes his neck being snapped.

"Does he really keep tabs on every single soldier?" I ask.

"He lets his ruined drafts do it for him. It's amazing how efficient the wind is when it *has* to obey. Meanwhile you seem to leave it all up to whatever whim a draft might feel."

"Uh, it's keeping us alive so far," I remind him, as yet another explosion misses us. "The wind knows what it's doing way more than I do. Why boss it around?"

Aston laughs. "That's either noble or incredibly naive."

"I see the tower!" Solana shouts. "Can you get us lower?"

I try several different commands, but the Westerlies won't go below the tops of the trees. "If you need me to go lower, we'll have to be on foot again."

"And the Stormers will ambush us in minutes," Aston warns. "Our only chance right now is in the air."

"Not if we split up," Arella says. "I'll go with Solana. She can search for the passage, and I can keep watch for any nearby Stormers. I doubt they'll be searching the ground if you two are buzzing around the sky, distracting them."

It's not a horrible plan, but . . . "What if you guys get caught?"

"Same thing you'll do if you're caught—fight," Arella says, patting her windslicer. "And if we find the tunnel, I'll send a bird to signal you."

I don't see any better options, so I ask the Westerlies to hold steady long enough for Solana and Arella to jump.

"Be careful," I call as Solana uses a Southerly to slow their fall.

"You do realize you just left your fiancée with your girlfriend's rather violent mother?" Aston asks as we get moving again, just in time to dodge another explosion.

"Solana can handle herself—and she's my *ex*-fiancée."

"It's adorable that you believe that. Though honestly, we should probably be more worried about your future mother-in-law. Our princess is quite a natural with the power of pain."

The words make my stomach squirm worse than the Westerlies' next evasive maneuver.

It's not a good time for this conversation, but I have to ask, "Is there seriously no way to heal after using that power?"

"So you *do* care," he says, and I *really* regret asking. "Hm . . . the look on your face tells me you won't like this answer. She's in early stages still, so it's possible she could reverse the effect. But it would take something . . . *dramatic.*"

"Like what?"

"You can't guess?"

"Little busy here controlling a dozen Westerlies!"

"You'd think that would help you figure it out. Think about it, Vane. What do you replace violence with?"

The word pops into my head and my heart drops, even though our wind bubble is holding steady.

You replace violence with *peace*.

"So you're saying . . ."

"Bonding with a Westerly should give her the balance she needs," Aston finishes. "If only she knew someone who was up to the task . . ."

His laughter makes me want to shove him out of the bubble.

"You don't even know if that's true," I argue. "You said *should*, not *would*."

"Ah, so you *can* use that brain of yours. Very good. This is all just a theory. A very well reasoned theory though, don't you think?"

It is, but . . .

No.

Uh-uh.

So not happening.

Solana was the one who decided to try Os's command—not me.

But she did it to help Audra, my conscience reminds me.

Aston smirks. "Suddenly being noble isn't quite so easy is it?"

No, it definitely isn't.

But I don't want to think about it anymore.

"This is taking forever," I say. "How much longer do you think we can hold out?"

"Not much. I'd wager they're readying the Shredder. It's basically like Raiden having a mile-long windslicer to slash at us from the safety of his fortress."

"Awesome."

I get my first glimpse of the Shredder in action when a dozen trees get sawed in half.

The next slice clips the top of our wind bubble, and we almost go *splat!* But I manage to regroup after a few seconds.

I ask the Westerlies to take us higher, but the winds resist my command and keep ducking back down toward the forest.

"More proof of the folly in trusting the wind," Aston says as an entire row of trees gets sliced and diced right beside us.

"We're still alive," I argue.

But it's not looking good.

We crash into something a few seconds later, and I'm sure it's all over.

"Would you stop screaming?" Aston shouts, and I realize my mouth is wide open and something that sounds like a dying hyena is blaring out of it.

"You hit a bird—see?" Aston points to the owl soaring beside us. "I guess that means the mythical tunnel is actually real."

We follow the owl into the forest—the swervy little bugger is *not* easy to keep up with—and touch down in front of an old water tower. There's no sign of Arella or Solana. Just a two-foot wide hole in the ground that drops down so deep, I can't see the bottom.

"Jump," Solana calls from the abyss below—which does *not* sound like something I want to do.

But . . . she's alive—and we definitely won't be if the Stormers find us—so one at a time, Aston and I drop into the darkness.

CHAPTER 14

AUDRA

Raiden doesn't believe me.

The doubt and fury practically drip off him as he paces back and forth in front of the door to our tower cell.

But he can't ignore me either—not when there's a chance I'm telling the truth about Gus.

So he lets us remain where we are.

He even calls down unbroken Northerlies to strengthen Gus.

They swirl around the cell, making me shiver—but I don't mind the cold.

Gus is almost breathing normally again, and his cheeks have more color. He's still far from recovered, but it gives me enough hope he might actually pull through this.

I just need him strong enough to follow me through the Shredder.

And enough time alone for us to slip away.

And wind.

I can feel the whisper of breezes in the cracks, but they haven't crept in yet.

They're biding their time.

Waiting on me.

I've always known the wind has a will of its own—but I never realized it could be so deliberate. It's as if all of Raiden's years of ruining drafts have taught them how to survive.

"I must say, this could be a record for the fastest change of heart I've ever seen," Raiden says slowly. "After such blatant defiance, you're suddenly eager to spill all your secrets."

"One secret," I remind him. "And it's technically not mine."

"We both know it's the only secret that matters." He steps closer to the bars and squats down to my eye level. "So what exactly brought on this *remarkable* change?"

I focus on Gus, wiping away the dried blood glued to his lips.

"I thought Gus would be strong enough to survive this," I whisper. "But I was wrong. And I can't imagine waking up every day knowing I could've saved him."

"You realize you'll be betraying your beloved by telling me any of this. In more ways than one."

He points to my hand, which is still cleaning Gus's lips.

I resist the urge to pull my fingers away.

Raiden stands to pace again, scratching the stubble on his chin. "So—assuming I believe you—what makes you think your friend will be willing to teach me his secret command? He and I have had several heart-to-hearts already, and this little fact never came up."

"I think I can convince him."

"I'm sure you do—it's another thing you and your mother have in common. You cling to your lies and keep right on pushing. But sooner or later they always come back to haunt you."

He moves toward the window, staring out at the night sky.

"Your mother never told you why she helped me capture you, did she?" he whispers.

"You were there," I remind him. "You heard her excuses."

"Yes, I suppose I did." He turns back to face me. "You didn't believe she had no choice?"

"My mother will sacrifice anyone or anything to benefit herself."

"She's a survivor," he agrees. "But that wasn't why she betrayed you."

He pauses, waiting for me to ask more questions—but I don't care about her reasons. No threat or trick or scheme of hers could ever justify the horrors she brought upon Gus.

I reach for his hand, glad to feel he has some grip.

"I know you're hoping to escape," Raiden says, stepping closer to the bars. "So let me give you a piece of advice. I have defenses you can't see—consequences you can't imagine. If you try to leave my fortress, your friend *will* die."

An earth-shaking boom saves me from having to respond.

Raiden rushes to the window. "Looks like your boyfriend is right on schedule," he says as another boom echoes.

Panic reaches inside me, grabbing hold of my heart and squeezing squeezing squeezing.

More explosions follow, some closer, some farther away.

"He's a better fighter than I anticipated," Raiden says.

"I trained him well."

Raiden laughs. "Yes, well no amount of training prepares anyone to face the Shredder."

My mouth is too dry to speak, my heart crumbling with every minute that passes. Every explosion.

But maybe this is the opportunity I've been waiting for.

"Sounds like your Stormers are struggling," I say. "Shouldn't you be rushing down there to lead?"

"I can lead them just fine from up here." He reaches through the barred window and catches a dull, yellow draft, closing his eyes and inhaling the wind with a slow, deep breath.

The wind sinks in, and he spits it back out, grumbling several commands before sending the sickly wind back out into the night.

I only understand one word.

Arella.

So my mother survived the Maelstrom.

That explains how Vane could be fighting so well, and how he found his way here.

I can't believe he was willing to trust her—though perhaps its wise he did.

Raiden looks . . . rattled by her presence.

His knuckles turn white as he squeezes the bars, waiting for another wind to report on the showdown.

Another explosion erupts, loud enough to make my ears ring.

But the silence that follows is much more terrifying.

Come on, Vane—keep fighting.

Another yellowed draft arrives, and this time Raiden smiles as he breathes it in.

"Apparently they found our special tunnel," he tells me. "I had it built in case some fool ever got it in their head to search for the Royal Passage."

I'm not entirely sure what he means, but I get the basic gist.

Vane and my mother just flew right into Raiden's trap.

CHAPTER 15

VANE

I t smells in this tunnel.

And it's too dark to see anything.

And I'm pretty sure I just brushed my hand against some sort of mutant-size rat.

But we're finally getting close to Audra.

At least, I think we are.

Right now we're just walking and walking and walking.

"How long is the Royal Passage?" I ask Solana, who's right behind me, followed by Arella, with Aston bringing up the rear.

We have to walk single file—don't ask me how *I* ended up the leader.

Solana doesn't reply. It doesn't even seem like she hears me.

"Is there a problem?" Aston asks her.

"I'm . . . not sure. The tunnel was wider in my father's memories. And the Southwell crest was carved into the wall."

"How can you see anything?" I ask.

"I can't—but that's another problem. The tunnel my father used had a bluish glow. I think it was some type of bioluminescence—and maybe the frost is messing with it, but . . . the walls were also made of stone."

I run my hand over the muddy sides, trying to feel if there's something solid underneath.

All I find is squishy stuff and creepy-crawlies.

"Well . . . maybe we're in a different part?" I say, shaking the yuck off my hand. "Or maybe your dad remembered it wrong?"

"Or," Aston says slowly, "the mythical tunnel was *too* mythical."

"That sounds like Raiden," Arella whispers.

"Am I supposed to know what that means?" I ask.

"Ask yourself this," Aston says. "What would Raiden do if he heard a legend of a secret tunnel?"

"How would I know?" I tell him. "I've never read the evil mur-derer's handbook."

"And there's no way he could've heard about the passage," Solana adds. "My family are the only ones who know."

"He's interrogated members of your family," Aston reminds her. "And Raiden would use that knowledge to his advantage. He'd make sure that anyone searching for the passage finds what they're looking for—only it wouldn't be what they're looking for."

I stop walking. "So . . . you're saying this tunnel is fake?"

"I'm saying it's a *trap*," Aston corrects. "This path probably leads to a dungeon, or some perfectly coordinated ambush. And I'm sure Raiden also has Stormers waiting at the entrance we used, in case we backtrack."

"But we found the entrance right where I remembered it being," Solana argues.

"Exactly my point," Aston tells her. "Raiden would stick to the legend as closely as possible."

"There were two sets of train tracks," Arella whispers. "They circled both sides of the tower. And the stone we moved was marked with the Southwell crest. The symbol was small, but it does seem too easy."

"Okay, so . . . what do we do?" I ask, fighting to stay calm.

Aston scratches at the walls. "I don't know about you—but I'll claw my way out of here if I have to."

"The ground is too frozen," Arella tells him. "And the Stormers will hear you escape."

"Then I'll destroy as many of them as I can until they crush the life out of me," Aston snarls. "There's no way I'm letting them take me again."

"Awesome as that plan sounds," I jump in, "there has to be a better way."

Aston snorts a laugh. "All right then—how do *you* propose we get out of this?"

He goes back to clawing at the wall, and I focus on my Westerly shield. It's only one little draft—but that was all Audra needed to start that haboob in Death Valley.

I don't have her way with the wind, but surely I can convince my own kin to help me.

"Please," I whisper to the draft in the Westerly tongue. "We need a way out of here. Can you use your force somehow?"

Great wording, man—what is this, Star Wars?

"Can you blast us a new exit from the tunnel?" I try again. "Or—um, what other way is there to get out from underground?"

"Oh yes, I can see why Raiden has killed so many for this power," Aston says when nothing happens. "I almost wish I could be there when he discovers its pointlessness."

"Come on!" I beg in Westerly. "Aren't you getting tired of everyone thinking you're worthless?"

That seems to get the wind's attention.

Its song shifts, flooding my head with new lyrics that definitely aren't what I'd been expecting.

I'd assumed the plan would involve a lot of running and hiding. But my Westerly wants something with a bit more *flare.*

"I don't suppose anyone has a lighter in their pocket," I mumble.

"By lighter you mean something to spark a fire?" Aston asks.

"Yeah. The wind wants us to head to the end of the tunnel and make something called a firewhirl."

"That's a *Westerly* plan?" Arella asks.

"Do you think I could make it up?" I ask.

"Definitely not," Aston says.

The manic edge to his voice seems to be fading as he adds, "It's not a terrible idea. But it depends on how large of a welcome party Raiden has waiting for us. One wind might not be enough."

"What about eleven winds?" Solana asks. "I have eight stored under my skin. And Vane and I can give up the Southerlies keeping us warm."

"None of that matters if we can't light a fire," I remind them.

"I have you covered there." Aston snarls a strange command and snaps his fingers.

Sparks flash through the darkness.

"How did you do that?" I ask.

"We control *air*," Aston says. "And what does fire feed on?"

He snaps again, and I realize he's clicking the bits of his exposed bone together to make enough friction.

It's beyond nasty, but all I care about is "So you think this will work?"

"It might," Aston says, a slow smile curling his lips. "Get us to the exit and have your drafts ready. I'll make sure the winds burn."

CHAPTER 16

AUDRA

The wind is stirring.

Rustling through the cracks all around us—each draft whispering the same words I feel deep in my core.

It's time.

Gus is as strong as he's going to get—still slipping in and out of consciousness, but able to move on his own. And Raiden is distracted by the near tangible silence beyond the fortress.

He stands with his back to me, the full force of his focus aimed at the window, where his sallow drafts trickle in with updates from his Stormers.

His replies are calm and hushed. The air around him radiates confidence.

But there's a rigidness to his posture. A tension seeping from his shoulders.

Clearly, his trap is taking too long.

Somehow Vane and my mother are eluding him.

Which means now is the time to change the game.

But what move am I supposed to make?

I'm still locked behind bars.

Still slowed by an injured companion.

Still under Raiden's watch, even if his eyes aren't on me.

The restless Easterlies whisper among the hidden depths in the walls, offering strength, courage, calm.

But if I'm going to do this, what I really need is a new plan.

We can't flee through the Shredder—not until I know whether Vane has been captured.

Vane.

Thinking his name makes my Westerly hum with an urgent sort of energy, flickering against my skin in strange, deliberate patterns, like it's trying to signal me—but I don't have the key to translate the message.

Gus coughs, and I'm relieved when no red leaks from his mouth. I help him sit up, and he leans his head against my shoulder, his fingers tracing the bloodstains on my back.

"I'm fine," I whisper. Whatever Raiden did was meant to mark me, not end me. "What about you?"

He gives me a weak smile. "Never been better."

"Sounds like someone is nearly ready for our important conversation," Raiden tells us. "As soon as I tie up a few loose ends . . ."

My Westerly presses tighter, repeating the same pattern as before.

I wait for Raiden to turn away and breathe into my breezy palm. "I can't understand you."

The wind stops for a moment, and I worry it's going to leave. But it picks up again, gathering around my face, whooshing so fast it makes my hair scatter.

Gus pulls me behind him, letting his broad shoulders hide me.

He presses his lips against my ear. "I think it's trying to trigger a breakthrough."

My eyes widen, and I can't decide if my heart is racing with excitement or fear.

The Westerly must sense my unease, because it grows softer.

Gentler.

"Trust the wind," Gus whispers.

I close my eyes and nod.

It's not easy to clear my head, but I let myself think of nothing but the soothing wind.

The rush of power.

The call of freedom.

And with my next breath, the Westerly slips into my mind.

My eyes water as it presses deep into my consciousness, whisking around my memories. I feel my essence stir, drawn toward the freedom of the sky. Even without understanding the words, the pull of the Westerly is irresistible, begging me to flee this grounded body and become pure motion and energy and strength.

If it weren't for the steady pressure of Gus's hand holding mine, I might surrender.

Instead, I focus on the mushy, garbled words, trying to shape them into something I can translate.

If only I weren't an Easterly.

I'm too cold.

Too unsteady.

I'm not worthy of the beautiful language the Westerly is trying to give me.

It belongs to someone sweet and soothing and stable.

Trust the wind.

I can't tell if Gus is whispering the words again, or if it's an echo from earlier. But the next sound I hear crashes against my essence like a wave on the shore, smoothing the battered places inside me and filling the cracks in my heart with a single, simple word.

Peace.

The thought is a hurricane, flooding my mind with wants and needs—so different from my last Westerly breakthrough, where every thought was tangled up with Vane. This time it's only me— just the wind and my consciousness, fusing our hopes and dreams into something new.

Something *powerful.*

My whole body trembles as the draft flees with my next breath, and I drift with an overwhelming sense of calm.

I've never felt so settled in my own skin. So *right* in who I am.

But my nerves spark when I hear Gus gasp with a startled breath.

I sit up and find him still—too still.

His pulse feels strong, though, and his skin is warm. His expression peaceful.

And that's when I realize . . .

Gus is about to have the fourth breakthrough.

My Westerly shield must've shifted to him.

I pull Gus close, tangle my arms around him—anything to help keep him grounded. His flesh is so weak, I can't be sure he'll hold on.

"You have to come back," I whisper. "Take the wind's strength and make it your own."

"So *this* is why you asked to be up here," Raiden says, reaching through the bars and grabbing my ankle.

He tries to drag me toward him, but I kick his hand away.

"You think you're safe from me over there?" he asks as I crawl out of his reach.

He calls for a guard, and the Stormer with the scars pounds up the stairs.

"She just had the fourth breakthrough," Raiden tells him, "and it looks like he's about to."

All eyes focus on Gus as he exhales a shuddering breath and rolls to his side, coughing and thrashing.

I hug him as tight as I can, too relieved to have him back to care that Raiden's shouting orders to the Stormer.

But as my Westerly shield blankets itself around me, I hear Raiden snap, "Take them back to the dungeon! Get them away from the wind."

Before the Stormer can act, a thunderous explosion shakes the tower.

Smoky red-orange light pours through the window—the unmistakable glow of a raging fire.

CHAPTER 17

VANE

Okay, so firewhirls are freaking awesome.

I can't believe they aren't the Gales' go-to weapon.

Mind you, they look pretty wimpy as I make them—just a tiny dust devil that I toss a few scattered sparks in.

But once I shout, "Engulf!" and the heat mixes with all the rushing oxygen? It turns into a hundred-foot spinning death spiral shooting red-hot flames in every direction—which might actually be why I haven't seen the Gales use them. I'm pretty sure I would've burned off all my appendages if I'd been in charge.

But Aston's a pro when it comes to violence.

He takes out half the Stormers with his very first blow. The rest put up a better fight—but he still wipes them out with three drafts to spare and uses the leftover winds to carry us to the top of a tree several miles away, so we can regroup.

"You're holding up rather well," he says, his eyes narrowing at me. "Especially considering we smell like roasted Stormer."

"Ugh—you didn't need to put it like *that*," Solana groans as she tangles a fresh Southerly around me to keep me warm.

I switch to mouth breathing to dodge the smell—but honestly, I'm doing okay.

"I wonder if it's because the firewhirls were the Westerly's idea," I mumble. "Maybe it knows what my limits are. Or maybe it knew how desperate our situation was. Or . . . I don't know, maybe I'm getting tougher."

"Definitely not the last one," Aston tells me. "But this is progress. From now on, you ask your little winds what they want you to do and obey. Maybe you'll actually get through this."

"Let's hope," I agree, calling down a fresh Westerly and tangling it into another shield. "So what now?"

"Now we play good news, bad news," Aston says. "The good news is, we survived Raiden's trap. I'm sure we've also succeeded in royally pissing him off. And the smoke and glare from the fires will make it much harder to track you."

"And the bad news?" Solana asks.

"Yeah, and what's with this 'you' stuff?" I add. "Don't you mean 'we'?"

Aston becomes very interested in his ruined hands. "The bad news is . . . my part in this little adventure has come to an end."

A million different reactions spin through my head—most of them involving another kick to the nuts.

But losing my temper isn't going to make him want to stick around.

"You said you'd help us rescue Audra and Gus," Solana reminds him.

"Actually, I said I'd help you come up with a plan. And I'll still do that."

"You're weaseling out on a technicality?" I snap.

His eyes flash, and I can tell he has one of his snide comebacks ready to go. But by the time he speaks, the words come out through a sigh.

"The truth is . . . I was force-fed a rather large dish of reality while we were stuck in that tunnel," he mumbles. "And I've had to admit that I can't risk letting Raiden capture me. Not because I'm afraid of what he'll do to me. Because I'm afraid of what *I'll* do. Raiden is as addictive as the power of pain. The more you're around him, the more you see the logic behind his decisions, until you can't remember why you ever resisted. I almost let him turn me into his shiny new tool last time, and if he gets ahold of me again, I'm not sure what I'll do. So you can hate me for abandoning you—but I promise, it's better that I leave you now than end up fighting against you."

It's the most humble, sincere thing Aston has said this whole journey—and I can't really fault him for it.

But I'd gotten very used to the idea of having him there to fight all the Stormers if we needed him. . . .

I take a deep breath. "Fine. We can do this without you."

"You can," Aston agrees. "And you can also do it without her."

He grabs Arella's arms, binding her in broken winds with the same motion.

"If you think—"

"Let me stop you from saying anything especially foolish," Aston interrupts me, "and remind you that she can't be trusted around Raiden either."

"Raiden holds no power over me," Arella argues.

"Oh really?" Aston asks. "So then you wanted to betray your daughter?"

When she doesn't respond, he adds, "If you truly want to save your girl, leave her rescue to people who might actually be able to help her."

"Don't pretend like you're doing this for Audra," Arella snaps. "You just want my pain."

Aston doesn't deny it. "But if that were all this was about, there are other much more exciting ways to force it out of you. So stop pouting and try doing what's best for your daughter for once in her life."

"You think *she* cares whether my daughter lives or dies?" Arella shouts, turning the full weight of her glare on Solana. "Do you think *she's* safe from Raiden's corruption? She's already succumbed to the power of pain!"

"To save your life," Solana snaps.

She turns to me to back her up, but I'm not sure I can.

I also notice she's twirling her link so fast it's probably rubbing the skin off her wrist.

"Maybe . . . you should go with them . . . ," I mumble. "It's getting pretty dangerous."

"You need me," Solana says. "You can't do this without me."

"She's right," Aston assures me.

I bite my lip.

"Why are you looking at me like that?" Solana asks.

Okay, I know I'm about to trigger the rage storm to end all rage storms. But she's still twisting her stupid link and I can't ignore it anymore.

"Why are you taking such a huge risk, Solana? Is this about us?" I whisper the last part, pointing to her gold cuff.

The silence is crushing.

Solana breaks it with laughter—cold, angry laughter. "Get over yourself, Vane. This fortress was my home. The man who killed my family is in there. And Gus needs my help. His mother died protecting me—I owe it to her to save her son. *That's* what I care about. So can we stop wasting time? We need to get back to the section of train tracks where I found the false tunnel. The real one has to be over there somewhere—and I already know which side of the tracks it *isn't* on. It shouldn't take me long to figure out where it *is*."

"You don't think Raiden's destroyed it?" Aston asks.

She shakes her head. "My winds keep telling me to have hope. And the entrance is protected by a password, so even if Raiden found it, he wouldn't be able to get in."

"But won't that area be crawling with Stormers?" I ask.

"Most likely," Aston says. "You'll need a distraction. A few well-placed firewhirls should buy you a few minutes—though there will likely be one Stormer who stays behind to keep watch."

"I'll take care of him," Solana and I say at the same time.

"Come on, Vane—be real," Solana tells me. "We both know the killing is going to fall on my shoulders. And that's fine. I've outlived three guardians. I know how to fight."

"Not as well as I do," Arella argues.

"But we've already established that you're coming with me," Aston tells her. "We both know what I'll do if you disobey me."

Arella pales at the words, and I can't help wondering what exactly Aston's holding over her. Before I can ask him, he adds another warning."

"If you face Raiden, remember that he's protected by his backlash."

"I still don't believe he's invincible," I argue. "Gus made him bleed in Death Valley."

"Did he now?" Aston asks. "I'm guessing it was just a scratch?"

He nods when I agree. "Then that's either a fluke, or another part of the trick. Raiden's a master of manipulation. Do *not* underestimate him. And if you decide to risk a shot, don't go for the heart or the head."

"Noted," Solana says. "Anything else we need to know?"

"Yes. The Royal Passage will only get you inside the fortress. From there, you'll have to navigate the labyrinth to find the dungeon."

"My father's memories included details on the different paths," she promises.

"Yes, but they don't include Raiden's new additions," Aston insists. "He's been a busy boy since he took over. The only way to know where you're heading is to watch for the pattern. Walls with smaller, rougher stones mean you're in the old, original pathways.

Those take you to the main courtyards and all the living quarters. Paths with precise, square-cut stones mean you're in Raiden's newer additions, heading to all the dungeons and towers. And any paths with metal slats are for the wind—be extra wary of those. I'm sure they were nice and safe when your family lived there. But the kind of tempests that fuel Raiden's fortress are not to be trifled with. And if I had to guess, I'd say your friends will be in the northern dungeon, so try there first."

"Actually, I was thinking we should swing by the turbine before we attempt the rescue," Solana corrects. "Might as well cripple his power source while we have a chance."

"Well, aren't you the clever girl," Aston says. "But surely you know a blow like that will dash all of Loverboy's hopes of sneaking in and out undetected."

"I think we're already past that," Solana says, and I hate her for being right.

Aston nods. "I'll do what I can from the outside. But I'll only be able to keep their attention for so long. And if they block you in, know that you can always escape through the Shredder. I carved a guide on one of the walls in the northern dungeon. The trick is to trust my instructions, not your eyes. Your eyes will only see the blades."

"Blades?" I repeat.

"Seventeen fans," Aston explains. "I nearly lost a leg at a couple of points—among other things. So only use it as a last resort. But it's good to have the option."

"How could you possibly find a path through seventeen fans?" I have to ask.

"Oh, believe me, Raiden made sure I was familiar with the slice of each of the Shredder's blades. I endured his sessions by isolating the different pains, imagining the angles and edges. And I'm here, aren't I? What better proof do you need that the guide works?"

I suppose he has a point.

"Anything else we need to know?" I ask.

"Yes, and you're not going to like it," Aston says. "Many of the paths can only be accessed by using a verbal command."

Solana guesses the problem before I do. "The power of pain."

"Can you handle that?" Aston asks.

She swallows twice before she nods. "A few commands won't destroy me."

She says it with confidence, but I notice she glances at Aston for confirmation.

Aston, meanwhile, is now focused on me. "If it does become a problem, there are ways you could help."

"What does he mean?" Solana asks.

I look anywhere except at her—which is a bad idea because I end up locking eyes with Arella.

The way she's glaring at me makes it clear she's guessed what Aston's referring to.

"Remember why you're doing this," she tells me. "And *who* you're doing this for."

I love how she can be worried about Audra's happiness one second, and selling her out to Raiden the next.

Besides, for all I know, Audra's thrilled to be free of her bond to me—but I'm trying really hard not to think about that.

Aston clears his throat. "Time to memorize some commands."

My stomach squirms every time he makes one of the scratchy, snarly sounds—and when Solana repeats them, it's a billion times worse.

"The passwords might have changed since I left Brezengarde," Aston warns her. "And if they don't work—don't panic. There *is* a way through the maze without the shortcuts. It's just infinitely harder."

"Great. Thanks for the pep talk!" I say.

"It's always better to be realistic," Aston argues. "Besides, you're resourceful, and not without your talents."

"Thanks," I mumble.

"I wasn't talking to you. *You* need to let *her* lead. And if you get in a bind, ask your Westerlies for guidance."

"So are we ready then?" Solana asks.

"Yes, I suppose it's time," Aston agrees. "The section of the tracks you need is that way."

All I see is darkness and trees.

"We'll leave first," Aston says. "Watch for the first signs of fire. I'll put on a good show, but they'll lose interest quickly, so I would work hard at finding that tunnel."

Arella grabs my hand. "Bring her home."

I get a crazy urge to hug her goodbye, which proves I can't trust my judgment at the moment.

"Brave faces on," Aston says. "And every time you start to panic, cling to that pendant." He points to Audra's blue cord around my neck. "She's waiting for you."

CHAPTER 18

AUDRA

All I smell is smoke.

We've been moved back to our lonely cells in the dungeon, so it's impossible to tell where it's coming from. But I can't imagine Raiden leaving us in an inferno—not now that we have his coveted prize.

I still can't believe we've had the fourth breakthrough.

Even thinking the words feels impossible.

But the lyrics of my Westerly shield fill my mind, and I can understand them perfectly.

It sings of change.

Of momentum.

Of new allies banding together.

If only Gus and I weren't locked away underground and could put our new power to use.

But Raiden cut us off from the sky.

I couldn't understand the commands he snarled before he left—they were all voiced in the language of pain. But the air is so still, even the dust motes don't stir. And my breath vanishes as soon as it leaves my mouth.

The stones rumble beneath me, echoes from the battle waging outside.

I press my palms against the floor, glad the explosions feel distant.

Hopefully that means that Vane and my mother are fighting their way to freedom.

"We need to get out of here," Gus whispers. "I think—"

"SILENCE!" the scarred Stormer shouts, clanging his wind spike against the bars of our cages.

The sharp ring of metal pierces my eardrums, and I send him my coldest glare. He's been assigned as our guard while Raiden leads his Stormers in the battle, and he's taking his role quite seriously.

"You should be helping us," I tell him. "The wind is on *our* side."

"And since when does the wind know what's right for our people?" he counters. "Since when does the wind *think*? It's a *force*."

"I used to believe the same thing," I tell him. "But the wind is changing. Maybe it's fighting against your cruel methods. Or maybe it was always this thoughtful and we were too arrogant to listen. Either way, it's showing us where our loyalties should be. We belong with the wind and the sky."

"Don't waste your breath on him," Gus tells me. "He took

plenty of turns with Raiden's whip during my interrogation."

"I spare no sympathy for those who face the consequences of their actions," the Stormer snaps. "You should've known what to expect the moment you dared to defy him."

"And you should know the risks of joining him," Gus shouts back. "Raiden's rule *will* fall, and when it does, he'll drag his armies down with him—and that's assuming he doesn't decide that you'd be much more useful as one of his Living Storms."

"Ah, but he's saving that privilege for his captives," the scarred Stormer says. "I'm sure that's what he's planning for you. Like father, like son."

Gus lunges for the bars, but the sudden motion is too much for his weakened body. He collapses to his knees, coughing and gasping.

My Westerly shield flits to his side, coiling around him.

"Do you see?" I ask the Stormer. "That Westerly is acting on its own."

"Rushing from one person to another hardly counts as a mighty uprising."

"It does in this case," Gus snarls.

He stands and shouts *"Meld"* in Westerly, and my jaw falls as he pries open his cell's bars. The metal bends as though it were made of feathers, and when the scarred Stormer lunges with his windslicer, Gus dodges easily, kicking out the Stormer's legs.

He dives on top of him, pinning the Stormer's shoulders with one hand, using the other to deliver blow after blow after blow.

Bones crack.

Blood splatters.

The Stormer's cries fade to delirious moans.

"That's enough!" I shout—but I have to repeat the call twice more before I'm able to pull Gus out of the frenzy.

"He's still conscious," Gus says, reaching for the fallen wind-slicer and pressing it against the Stormer's neck. "We can't risk that he'll raise the alarm."

"You can't kill him!"

Gus points to the hole in his shoulder. "He laughed as this happened."

I swallow, trying to understand how the same soldier who saved me from assault could be so cruel.

But it doesn't matter.

"You're under Westerly influence now," I whisper. "There's no telling how the violence will affect you."

Gus loosens his grip on the hilt, but keeps his blade pressed in place.

"Trust me on this, Gus. It's not worth it. You're going to need every ounce of strength to escape."

"Fine," he says, slowly lowering his blade.

He punches the Stormer one last time—a knockout blow that leaves him silent and still. "It's probably better to let Raiden deal with him anyway. I'm sure he'll have much more creative ways to punish him for letting us get away."

Each word drips with the purest, most potent kind of hate.

I don't blame him—but it's hard to watch Gus strip off the unconscious Stormer's uniform and drag his limp body to one of the empty cells.

He slams the barred door and crushes the lock so easily, it's like the metal melts at his touch.

"How are you doing that?" I whisper.

"My gift allows me to absorb strength from the wind and channel it into my muscles. That's why those Northerlies helped me recover as much as I have. And now that I can finally absorb Westerlies . . ." Gus pries open my cell as though it were paper.

"That's incredible."

"It's never been this strong before," he whispers. "I can't tell if it's a power of four thing, or because your Westerly was especially strong."

"Was?"

The word feels like a knife to my heart.

I know it's ridiculous, but . . . after all that little draft and I have been through . . .

"Don't worry." Gus closes his eyes and whispers "Release" under his breath.

His body shifts ever so slightly, as though his essence unraveled for a brief moment, and a soft rush whisks past my senses, singing its familiar melody.

"We need to get out of here," Gus says as my Westerly tightens into a shield around me. "But first, a little camouflage."

He shuffles to where he left the Stormer's clothes, and I notice he's limping again.

He tries to pull the jacket on, but his bandages snag on the fabric.

"Here," I say, scooting behind him and taking over.

It's a slower process than I want it to be, pulling the sleeves inch by inch. But Gus has lost too much blood—I can't tear open any of the scabs.

"I never thanked you for this," he says, touching one of the pieces of torn red fabric. "I don't even remember when you did it."

"You were pretty out of it." I pull his jacket the last little bit. "How are you doing—*really*?"

"It doesn't matter. I'll either get through this, or I won't."

"It does matter, Gus. We're in this together. I need to know what you're dealing with."

He swallows hard. "Let's just say I'm not planning on making it, okay? I'll help you as long as I can and—"

"We're both getting out of here."

"I don't think it's going to be up to you to decide."

He tries to button the jacket, but the fabric won't reach. He's far more muscular than the Stormer.

"Well . . . hopefully if anyone sees us, it will only be from behind," I say.

"Or maybe they'll think I got hurt in the battle," he says. "I guess my pants might give me away, though."

We both eye the Stormer's pants on the ground, and I feel myself blush. "If you need help . . ."

Gus shakes his head. "It'll take too long. Besides, I doubt they'll fit. You ready?" he asks, strapping the windslicer around his waist. "We should get moving."

He heads for the stairs, sucking in a pained breath as he climbs the first step.

I pull his arm over my shoulders and support him as we climb. "Maybe you should absorb my Westerly again. It seemed to make you stronger."

"You need it more than I do."

"Don't be absurd."

"I'm not. Come on, Audra—let's be real here. You've got people out there risking their lives to save you—"

"To save *us*," I correct.

"Eh—mostly to save you. We both know that."

I let out a sigh. "Vane is . . ."

I don't know how to finish the sentence.

Now that my Westerly instincts are back, I feel a bit more of a stirring at his name.

But not what it was.

"Breaking your bond messed with your head," Gus whispers. "But that doesn't mean you can't get it back. He came after you, Audra. You two need each other."

I shrug, not sure what to say.

The gesture tilts Gus off balance, and I have to scramble to keep him from falling.

"Sorry."

"Don't apologize. This is proving my point. If I slow you down too much, I want you to leave me."

"That's not happening." I stop and wait for him to look at me. "It's not, Gus. I mean it. And I need you to promise that you won't give up—no matter what."

Gus sighs, not looking at me as he mumbles, "I'll do my best."

It's not the most convincing delivery, but I have to take it.

"So where to?" he asks, as we get back to climbing the stairs.

With Vane and my mother still outside fighting, I can only think of one option.

"We need to find our way to the Shredder."

CHAPTER 19

VANE

I have no idea where we're going.

There are plenty of fires and explosions going on in the distance—but those are supposed to be leading the Stormers *away* from where we're headed.

Meanwhile we're flying through the dark, over trees and snow and shadows that all look exactly the same. Fortunately, Solana has no problem bossing me around, and it seems like she actually knows what she's doing.

Soon enough, I spot the outline of train tracks peeking out of the ice. A couple of minutes after that, the weathered water tower appears.

"I don't see any Stormers; do you?" I ask as we circle the curved tracks.

Solana unsheathes her windslicer. "No way it'll be that easy. Dip a little lower to drop me off, then hide somewhere in the trees."

"Uh, you're not going down there alone."

"I'm better alone—and it'll be easier if I don't have to worry about keeping you safe."

My Dude Instincts tell me I should feel insulted by that—and that I need to insist that *I* be the one to protect *her.*

"You're sure you can handle it?" I ask instead.

"I'll call for you if I need help."

She gives my hand a quick squeeze, and her warmth is still buzzing in my fingers as she jumps out of the wind bubble and lands in the snow with a somersault.

I fly to the top of the tallest tree and crouch on a sturdy branch, ready to swoop down at the first sign of serious trouble—and it comes fast. Solana's barely taken ten steps when two Stormers burst out of the highest snowdrift. Between their thick shoulders and burly arms, they add up to about four of her.

"I'm fine!" she shouts, which is apparently my cue to stay put.

I grip my dagger and lean down for a better view of the action, balancing on the balls of my feet. I agreed to let her handle this—but if she needs me, I'm ready.

"We'll get to you in a minute," the smaller Stormer shouts at me.

The other Stormer snarls a broken command, sending ruined winds tangling around Solana—but she sucks the drafts up and stores them under her skin.

"Looks like we'll need to do this the old-fashioned way," the bigger Stormer tells her, unsheathing two windslicers, one for each of his hands.

The other Stormer does the same, juggling the swords back and forth like a freaking circus performer.

Solana positions herself between them. It seems like the worst place to be—until she does this crazy spin-flip move and somehow manages to attack both Stormers at the same time.

Within a few seconds she's gotten them down to one windslicer each, and when the Stormers charge, she somersaults away, moving so fast she's just a blur of blond hair and scattering snow.

I knew Solana claimed she could fight—but *dang*. She does a spin-slash-backflip move this time, and both Stormers scream as she lands somewhere just out of their reach.

Red splatters the ice as the smaller Stormer clutches a deep calf wound and the bigger one holds his bleeding forearm. But their injuries don't slow them down as much as I'd like. They rush Solana again, keeping a wider space between them so she can't use the same move. She does at least dodge, but they strike back immediately—and then again.

I try not to think about how much time is racing past, but I can't help glancing at the sky, wondering how much longer we have before more Stormers swoop in.

Solana's cry drags me back to the battle, and when I see blood on her leg, I'm on the ground before I even realize I jumped.

"I was fine," Solana says as the bigger Stormer comes after me.

I'm pretty sure this guy could kill me just by stepping on me, and I beg my Westerly to come up with a plan—preferably one that doesn't involve using this dagger. I'm not sure how the violence will affect me, but mostly I really don't want to have to get that close.

That's the sucky thing about bringing a knife to a sword fight. The chances of me hitting him before he chops off my head definitely aren't good.

Retreat, the Westerly tells me, and I back off as much as I can.

Come on, I tell my shield. *You told me about firewhirls last time—what else have you got?*

The stubborn draft just keeps repeating for me to retreat. So I do—but I retreat toward Solana. I figure we might as well do this two on two instead of two battles waging at the same time.

"You okay?" I ask when I see how badly she's limping.

"It's only a scratch," she promises. But when she tries to do her spin move again, her leg crumples and she gets a pretty nasty face full of snow.

The big Stormer laughs. "Had enough?"

"Have *you?*" Solana tries to get up again, but her leg is too shaky. So she dives and swipes at his ankles instead.

He dodges, but she manages to clip the smaller Stormer near his Achilles tendon, and he lets out a yowl that's part dying cat, part humpback whale.

"I'm getting sick of this," he shouts, launching a dozen draining winds.

Solana absorbs most of them, but one manages to tie itself around my arms and pin them.

"Not as skilled as your little girl, I see," the big Stormer says, shoving me into the snow and adding a second bond around my legs.

I guess I should be glad the snow cushions my fall enough to spare my elbow, but it's freaking freezing. Plus I can't tell what's happening anymore.

"He's the only one we have to keep alive," one of the Stormers says. "Kill her."

"Come on, Westerlies," I beg as I hear metal clang and Solana yelp.

I manage to twist to my side and blink the ice out of my eyes—and find Solana down on her knees in a puddle of red, with one Stormer on each side of her.

"Enjoy your final breaths," the bigger Stormer says, raising his windslicer to deliver the deathblow.

My Westerly shield screams *SLIDE!* and I flop down like I'm a seal streaking across ice.

My shoulder knocks the bigger Stormer over, and he falls onto the needled edge of his own windslicer.

Darkness rims my vision during the squishy gagging sound that follows, but I'm much more traumatized by the sound of another bone-crunching windslicer swipe.

I turn toward the noise, terrified I'm going to find a headless Solana.

But hers is still attached.

The other Stormer . . . not so much.

"Hang on," she tells me, and I can't quite figure out why—until I taste bile on my tongue.

I'm not sure if I'm actually throwing up, or if I'm just about to. It's kinda like I'm having an out-of-body experience.

I watch blankly as Solana grabs one of the Stormer's black wind-slicers and shreds the winds binding me, then limps toward the water tower and counts her steps.

At some point she drops to her knees and starts digging in the snow. "In my memories this is about how far the entrance looked from the tower."

I fumble to her side and focus on helping her dig.

Don't think about the bodies. Don't think about the bodies.

"It has to be here," Solana murmurs.

I hope she's right, because I hear a rumbling that sounds a lot like approaching Stormers.

Okay, I tell my Westerly. *Got any ideas?*

The Westerly leaves me, twisting into a weak funnel and sweeping aside more snow.

"Wait," Solana says, pressing her ear to the ground. "I think it's sinking in somehow."

I trace the muck with my fingers until I feel the breeze slipping through a crack so thin, I doubt a hair would fit.

"Right there," I tell Solana, who's following my hands with hers. "Do you feel it?"

She nods. "But I don't see a latch or anything."

"Maybe the password is enough?"

"Let's hope."

She leans down and whispers through the crack.

I can't hear what she says—but it works.

A roar of wind knocks us back as it blasts open a hatch.

Solana drags me with her as she jumps, and my ankles definitely aren't happy about the landing. But I can see through the eerie blue light that Solana's family crest is painted on the stone walls.

We found the Royal Passage—and just in time.

Wind spikes explode above us as Solana shouts the command and seals us inside.

CHAPTER 20

AUDRA

We're going in circles.

Wasting energy.

Facing too many dead ends.

I knew the fortress was a maze, but I thought if we kept pushing forward, eventually we'd find our way through.

Instead we wind up back in the dungeon.

"Should we make him guide us?" I ask, motioning to where the scarred Stormer lies unconscious in his locked cell.

"He'd lead us straight to Raiden," Gus warns. "You can't trust your enemies—even when you force them."

"But how else do we find the way out of here?" I stretch the muscles in my neck—supporting Gus is taking its toll on my back.

Gus presses his ear to the wall, and I assume he's listening for sounds of battle.

When I copy him, I hear a low, constant hum.

"That's the Shredder," Gus says, backing away from the wall. He looks as pale and gray as his Stormer jacket.

"You okay?" I ask.

He closes his eyes, taking slow, shaky breaths. "I can still feel it, tearing around inside me, like the winds bored into my essence."

I reach for his hand.

"I'm fine," he promises.

But when he wipes his mouth, I see red.

"Is the sound making you worse?" I ask.

"It's probably the lack of wind. Or all this walking. And at least now we know how to find where we're going. If we keep following the sound, it'll lead us right to it."

The plan seems to be working, but the louder the hum grows, the paler Gus turns, if the sound alone makes him bleed, how will he stand among the Shredder's blades?

"Maybe there's another way out—"

"I'll be fine," he interrupts. "We're not changing the plan."

His words would be easier to accept if his teeth didn't have a reddish gleam.

I pull Gus's arm around me and try to move us faster, hoping he'll grow stronger if I can get him some fresh air.

The sound leads us through several more turns and then . . .

. . . we end up back in the dungeon.

The scarred Stormer laughs when he sees us. "Ready to give up?"

Gus kicks the bars so hard I fear he'll break his foot.

"We'll find a way through," I tell him before he can kick again. "I just need to think."

I try to remember every detail I noticed during my time in the tunnels, but nothing stands out.

And then I realize what we're missing.

"The power of pain," I whisper. "The Stormers always use broken commands to open hidden doorways."

"Indeed we do," the scarred Stormer says. "Which doesn't help you at all, does it?"

He rolls to face me, and I cringe when I get a better look at his mashed-up face.

"Please," I say. "If you help us, you can escape with us.

Gus pulls me away. "Forget him, Audra. He'll never betray Raiden."

"He's right," the Stormer agrees.

"Why?" I ask. "We both know what's going to happen when Raiden finds you like this. I'm offering you a chance to live."

"So long as I join the Gales and spill all of Raiden's secrets—and fight at their side as they destroy everything I've helped build? No thank you. I have no intention of becoming a traitor."

"So be a loner," I counter. "Get us out of here and disappear. It worked for Aston."

"Yes, well Aston had an advantage I don't have—though he paid for it with his skin." His hands move to his neck, rubbing his throat. "If Raiden senses that I've betrayed him, he'll trigger my suicide draft."

I'm not sure I know what that is—though the name speaks for itself.

I squint at his neck, but I can't see any trace of it.

"There's no way to remove it," he tells me. "In case that's what you're planning. I can't even feel it—if I hadn't been conscious when Raiden formed it, I wouldn't even know it's there. And if I try to tamper with it, Raiden will trigger the *slow* death. I've seen it in action once." He shudders.

I reach up to rub my neck and catch Gus doing the same.

I knew Raiden's methods were cruel, but I never imagined anything like this.

"And he makes all of the Stormers have them?" I ask.

"He doesn't *make* us. It's how we show our commitment—and the commitment is *mutual*. We swear to be loyal, and Raiden swears to teach us his ways."

"You honestly believe that teaching you to do his dirty work for him is the same as agreeing to sacrifice your life?" Gus asks.

"In exchange for the power we're given? You bet," the Stormer tells him. "And the suicide draft takes a toll on Raiden too. It drains so much of his strength he can only form one a day."

"Is power really all you care about?" I have to ask.

He shrugs—but I can tell by the tightness in his features that there's something more he's not saying.

"How did Raiden convince you to swear fealty?" I press.

"Why do you care?" he snaps back.

"Because I want to understand."

"No one ever understands."

I wait for him to say more, but he turns away.

"This is a waste of time," Gus says, heading for the stairs.

I've only followed him for a few steps when the Stormer says, "A groundling killed my father."

I turn back and find him wiping his eyes, and he has to clear his throat twice before he can add, "He caught my dad on his *property* after a storm and pointed a gun at him. I was hiding nearby. Saw the whole thing. He claimed my dad was a looter—like we gave a damn about his rusted junk. When my dad tried to calm him down, he shot him in the head. It didn't matter that my dad was the one who *saved* their filthy house from the storm. And the wind didn't knock the bullet aside fast enough."

"I'm sorry."

"Yeah. That's what everyone says. That, and 'I wish there were something I could do.'" Raiden was the first person who understood. And he *did* something. After I swore fealty? He brought me back to that house and we tore everything to shreds."

"Revenge isn't justice," Gus tells him.

"Then how do you explain the beating you gave me?" the Stormer argues.

"That was deserved," Gus says, taking my arm. "He's just stalling. Stalling until someone finds us."

"It's better than that," the Stormer says. "I'm also making sure we have time to capture your Westerly friend—if we haven't already."

An unearthly howl stops my reply, and the grating mix of rage and ruin crawls under my skin.

I've heard the sound before—and I hoped to never hear it again.

The cry of an unwilling victim being transformed into one of Raiden's Living Storms.

CHAPTER 21

VANE

Solana's bleeding a lot.

Like, a *lot* a lot.

She's even leaving a trail of red footprints on the stone floor.

I keep trying to get her to stop so we can bandage up her wound. But she claims we don't have time—and she's probably right.

Even if the password prevents any Stormers from getting into the passage, I'm sure they've guessed where we're heading. So my whole "stealthy heist" plan is trashed at this point. And I have a feeling the gut-wrenching wail that just shook the passage means Raiden's making a Living Storm Welcome Party for us.

I refuse to think about who it could be. The cord of Audra's guardian pendant is still blue, so I know she's safe. But Gus . . .

"How long is this passage?" I ask.

"Too long."

I can't tell if Solana's worried about Gus too—or if she's worried about how much she's having to lean on the wall for support.

Eventually she collapses, and I barely catch her in time.

"I'm fine," she mumbles.

"Yeah, it looks like it."

I ease her to the floor and unbutton my jacket.

"What are you doing?"

"Cutting bandages." I unsheathe my dagger and slice off the bottom of my undershirt. "Figured this was softer fabric."

Her wound looks pretty gnarly, so I cut a few more strips. Then I realize how stupid wearing a half shirt is and rip off the rest.

"That's a good look," Solana says, pointing to my bare-chest-plus-jacket combo.

I can't tell if she's teasing me or getting deliriously honest. Either way, I'm pretty sure I'm blushing.

"Warning," I say, taking a quick sniff of the sweaty fabric. "Apparently I stink."

"That's not exactly news. Besides, I'm sure I smell just as bad."

Actually, she smells like oranges or melon or—

I shake my head.

No time for playing guess-the-shampoo.

Solana tries to take the bandages from me, but I keep a tight grip. "It's my turn to help."

It seems like a totally normal thing to offer—until I have to pull her wounded leg into my lap. And it gets worse when I have to slide her dress up another inch to expose the whole gash. . . .

Okay—focus on the blood.

"Let me know if this hurts," I say as I dab at the wound with a piece of cloth.

She doesn't cry out, but she keeps sucking air through her teeth, and I don't blame her.

"This looks awful."

"Gee, thanks."

"I didn't mean your *leg*—not that I'm looking," I add quickly. "I just meant . . ."

My excuses trail off when she laughs.

"I'm giving you a hard time," she says, "so you'll stop looking so nervous. Honestly, I've never had a guy so afraid to touch me."

My cheeks feel way too hot.

Maybe they melt my brain, because I hear myself say, "So . . . you've been with other guys?"

"Are you seriously asking me that?"

"No—you're right. I'm sorry—I don't know why I said that."

Cue uncomfortable silence.

Actually, "uncomfortable" isn't a strong enough word. This is like if awkward and uncomfortable hooked up and had an ugly, miserable baby that won't stop screaming and pooping all over everything.

"For the record," Solana says, "I meant the Gales who treated my wounds over the years, and the guardians who trained me to fight. They had to get very hands-on at times, and they've never been this twitchy."

"Well, they have a lot more experience than I do—with fighting and stuff . . . not with, you know—not that Audra and I have . . . um . . . you know what? I'm going to stop talking now. Maybe forever."

"That's a good idea," she agrees.

I stare at the floor, wishing a sinkhole would open up and swallow me.

When it doesn't, I wrap her wound with the widest scrap of fabric.

"It needs to be tighter," she says.

"But that'll hurt."

"Yeah, well, sometimes pain's the only way."

It feels like there's a deeper meaning to her words, but I decide not to go there.

Instead I pull the bandage a little tighter—but apparently it's still not enough. She grabs my hands, forcing me to pull until her skin bulges.

A tiny gasp slips through her lips, but she moves her leg a few times. "Thanks. I guess I should've let you do that from the beginning."

"Wait—did you just admit I was right?"

"Don't let it go to your head. I'm sure it was a fluke."

I sigh. "Now you sound like Audra."

And with that, the moment hits an all-time low.

I stop wishing for a sinkhole and consider digging my own. I bet it wouldn't be hard to gouge the stone with my knife. . . .

"It's always going to be weird between us, isn't it?" Solana asks.

"I don't know. Maybe with time . . ."

"Yeah."

Neither of us sounds very hopeful.

I don't realize I'm playing with Audra's guardian pendant until Solana reaches out and touches the cord.

"I'm glad she's still alive," she whispers. "And I'm going to do everything I can to make sure she stays that way."

"Thanks," I mumble. "I wish we had a way to know how Gus is doing."

"Me too. Especially now that I heard that Living Storm. But I feel like I'd pick up his echo if he wasn't okay."

"Maybe."

I don't know much about the process—just that when sylphs die, they leave a small piece of themselves drifting with the wind to tell the world they've gone.

But we're so deep underground his echo might not be able to reach us.

"Think you're ready to walk again?" I ask.

"Only one way to find out."

She's still wobbly, but her limp is mostly gone.

I wrap her arm around my shoulder. "You'll save more energy this way."

"Thanks."

We walk in silence for several minutes, until the hall curves and she pulls away.

"I'm feeling better now," she promises.

And she does make it a few steps. Then she has to lean against the wall again.

"Is this a pride thing, or a girl thing?" I ask.

"What exactly is 'a *girl* thing'?"

"Oh come on. You know how girls are, pretending everything's okay when really they want to rip your face off."

"Assuming I agree with your broad generalization—which I don't by the way—I suppose you think guys are better?"

"Well, yeah. Kinda. At least when a guy is pissed at another guy, he tells him—or he punches him in the face."

Solana rolls her eyes. "Then how do you explain all the things you keep stopping yourself from saying?"

"Like what?"

"Never mind. Let's keep moving." She tries to walk again and nearly collapses.

I help her lean against the wall, but she scoots away from me. It's only a few inches, but it feels like miles.

"Maybe you're right," I say when I can't stand the silence anymore. "Maybe we're both holding things back, and if we just got it all out in the open, this would be easier."

Her eyes drop to her hands, and she twists her link.

I'm about to ask her why she does that when she stops to look at me.

"Fine, you want to know why I feel uncomfortable around you? It's because I can tell you blame me for what happened to Audra. And I know you hate that I use the power of pain. I also know you think you're going to have to bond with me to save me from that power—and you act like everything I do is some big scheme to seduce you."

Okay . . . whoa.

Holy Mountain of Honesty, Batman!

Maybe I should've left this alone. . . .

I don't even know where to start, except to mumble, "It's not like that."

"Then how is it?"

I stare at my compass bracelet, which seems to be spinning even faster.

"I wish I could've saved you both," I whisper. "And I wish you'd never had to use the power of pain. I get that neither of those things were your fault. It's just hard not to play the 'what if' game, you know?"

"Oh, I know," she says. "I play that game more than anyone."

She's staring at her family's crest carved into the wall, and I have a feeling I can guess what some of her what-ifs are.

"What about Aston's theory?" she asks, reminding me we still have a whole lot more awkwardness to get through before this is over.

I can't look at her as I ask, "He told you?"

"I figured it out. And for the record, I'm not convinced he's right. But even if he is, it doesn't change anything. I don't want to be bonded to someone who's only trying to *fix* me."

"But what if it's the only way to stop the power from ruining you?"

"Then I'll deal with it. It's not your problem."

We both know it kinda is.

"What about the last thing?" she whispers. "And don't make me say it again. It was embarrassing enough the first time."

Seriously—*where* is a sinkhole when I need one?

"I don't think you're *seducing* me," I tell my feet.

"But?" she prompts.

I can hear my brain screaming, *DON'T SAY IT.*

We've already come this far, though, so I blurt out, "You're really not still hoping I'll change my mind?"

"Please, Vane. How many times do I have to tell you—"

"Yeah, I know. You're not pining for me. But . . . if you're really over it, why are you still wearing your link?"

She stops spinning the cuff, almost like she didn't notice she's been doing it. "I'll get rid of it someday. I'm just not ready yet—and not because of you. Because of me. It just feels like, once I take it off—that's it. There goes my whole family's heritage."

Riiiiiiiiiiiiiight.

Because I'm stealing the throne.

"I don't *want* to be king," I tell her.

"You know that makes it worse, right? You're being handed my future and you don't even want it. All you want to do is run away."

"Yeah, because it's a *huge freaking responsibility*! And I have no idea how the hell I'm supposed to rule people."

"So you learn. And you try your best."

"It won't be good enough."

"I don't believe that. You could be a great king, if you decided you wanted to be. Your Westerly perspective is incredibly valuable."

"Tell that to Os—and the Gales—and anyone else who expects me to be this, like, ultimate warrior. That's the thing, Solana. Even if I do find a way to kill Raiden—that's it. Then I'm done with violence forever. And what happens the next time there's a threat to our world?"

"Then your Westerly instincts will teach you how to keep the peace."

I sigh.

That's asking an awful lot of the wind.

And not even the whole wind. Westerly is one language out of four—and let's not forget that it's a language that almost got totally wiped out.

Why is everyone so convinced it's the answer to everything?

Just because it's important doesn't mean it's the only thing we need. Otherwise, why are there three other languages?

I straighten up. "It should be four."

"Am I supposed to know what that means?" Solana asks.

I shake my head, taking a second to think it all through again before I tell her, "One ruler isn't enough. There are *four* winds."

"So . . . you're saying there should be *four* kings?"

"Or queens," I correct. "All that matters is that each language have a representative."

I'd still be stuck being King Westerly—but it wouldn't be *as* bad if it wasn't all on me.

And Solana could be the Southerly.

Then she wouldn't have to lose her family's heritage.

And it might be a way to calm Os down about Audra, too. She could represent the Easterlies—assuming she still wants to be with me, and we manage to survive today, and we kill Raiden, and and and . . .

"I think we're getting ahead of ourselves," Solana says, and I wonder if she's been thinking about the same things. "Let's get Gus and Audra back and *then* we can decide if we want to convince the Gales to reorganize our entire world."

When she puts it like that, the idea sounds impossible.

But . . . I still think I'm onto something.

For the first time since Audra told me about all of the Gales' crazy plans, I can actually think about my future without feeling like I'm hyperventilating.

It's made things less awkward with Solana, too. She has no problem leaning on me—though her leg does seem to be getting stronger.

We're moving at a pretty good pace when we turn a corner and find a dead end with an old metal ladder leading to another hatch in the ceiling.

The entrance into Raiden's fortress.

CHAPTER 22

AUDRA

try to focus on moving forward and solving the riddle of this labyrinth.

But every time I hear the Living Storm wail, I can't help thinking: *It could be Vane.*

It could also be my mother—which is more terrifying than heartbreaking.

Who could stand against a tempest of my mother's greed and rage?

"You okay?" Gus asks. "Are your wounds making you woozy?"

Actually, I'd forgotten all about the cuts on my back.

"Do you think Raiden would kill him?" I whisper. "Now that he knows we've had the fourth breakthrough—do you think that makes Vane expendable?"

"I guess it's possible," Gus says. "But I feel like Raiden would still want to bring him in alive. He'll want to make sure *one* of us gives him the power. Then he'll take us all out. So the better question is, can we get out of here before Vane gets himself captured? Because I *really* don't want to have to turn our escape into a rescue."

That makes two of us.

There has to be a trick to getting around this maze.

I concentrate on my shield, letting the Westerly language drift across my tongue.

"We need to reach the surface. Can you guide us?" I whisper.

My shield doesn't respond, but I continue repeating my request. Sometimes the wind needs to know how much you mean it.

A soft tug slows my feet as we near the top of a staircase, and I feel my shield pulling my shoulders to turn them.

I don't understand what it wants until I remember the day I was nearly assaulted. The scarred Stormer pulled me through a hidden door.

Could there be another path hidden here?

My Westerly seems to think so. It's singing of stronger air waiting on the other side. But when I search the wall, I see no handle— no seam. And I can't use the power of pain.

I wonder if the power of four could have some effect.

I stretch out my hands, trying to feel for the air the Westerly is singing about. The stone dulls my senses, but my shield switches to a lyric about trusting the unknown. So I close my eyes and whisper the words I've said more than any others. The call of my heritage.

"Come to me swiftly. Carry no trace. Lift me softly. Then flow and race."

The last syllable has barely left my lips when a gentle rush slips through an imperfection in the wall and coils around me like an embrace from an old friend—and in a way it is. The strong, healthy Easterly is every bit as brave and loyal as my shield.

"How did you do that?" Gus whispers.

"I think it was the wind. It seems to want to help."

I try calling a Northerly or a Southerly, but none respond. So there's no way to channel the power of four.

"Do you think east and west are enough?" I ask Gus when he's unable to summon any drafts either.

"It might be. Those winds belong to your natural heritage and your bonded heritage."

I open my mouth to remind him that I'm not bonded to Vane anymore, but even thinking the words triggers a jolt of pain deep in my chest.

That's new.

And yet, the sensation is also familiar. A slow, steady tugging, almost like . . .

I shake the thoughts away.

Now is not the time to be pondering my bond to Vane.

The Easterly and Westerly dance around each other, and I listen to their songs. The lyrics seem vague, singing of dual strength, dual force. But the final verse keeps championing the power to sever.

"Sever," I whisper, trying the Westerly tongue first.

Nothing happens, so I repeat the command in my native tongue.

I should've known from the beginning that Westerly was too

peaceful. Only a tricky Easterly would be willing to tear anything apart.

And it does.

The drafts stretch thin and slam into the rock. A narrow cloud of dust erupts from a seam I never would've been able to see on my own.

But the door remains shut.

"Now what?" I ask, listening to the drafts, but their song gives me no other clues.

"I wonder," Gus says, stepping forward and giving the rock a hard shove.

The door swings open with a scratchy crumble.

"I guess we need to do some of the work too," he says, coughing on the floating dust.

He's right.

It's going to take all of our efforts combined to make our way through this maze.

But if we work together, we have a chance.

CHAPTER 23

VANE

"Do you hear anything?"

I've already whispered the question at least twenty times. It's kind of a miracle Solana hasn't jumped down from the ladder and clobbered me.

But I still can't make myself believe her when she removes her ear from the ceiling and tells me, "No, Vane. I still hear nothing."

"Maybe the stones are too thick. Or the Stormers are being really quiet."

"Or they have no idea where the tunnel exits," Solana whispers. "Just like I'd hoped."

Hope.

I'm trying not to feel too much of that right now. It's safer to be realistic.

We're about to sneak into the enemy's lair—that's the kind of thing that requires fancy gadgets and superspy moves and *Mission Impossible* theme music.

But we don't have self-destructing messages to guide us—and I'm definitely not Tom Cruise. And we were too stupid to take the anemometer from Arella before she left, which would've at least warned us if there were Stormers around. So our odds of pulling this off are—

"Are you listening to me?" Solana asks, interrupting my thoughts.

"No. Sorry. What?"

"I said I think we're good. But I'll climb out first and give you the all clear."

"And if it's *not* clear?"

"Then I'll make it clear."

"But what if—"

"Vane," she interrupts, waiting for me to make eye contact. "This is what we're here for."

She's right.

This is it.

It's all-in time.

Either we pull this off, or . . .

It's probably better if I don't finish that sentence.

Not that I'm worried about *me*.

Okay, fine, I am a little.

A lot.

But I'm much more freaked out about seeing Gus and Audra.

All the things I've been trying not to think about—all the ways Raiden might have hurt them . . .

If it's actually happened, I'll have to see it—and I don't know how I'll handle it.

"Let's do this," Solana whispers, reaching for the hatch.

She gives me a smile that looks surprisingly confident, considering we're two wounded teenagers who haven't slept in several days, trespassing blindly into a warlord's mazelike fortress—and he knows we're here.

"Okay," she whispers, "if my dad's memories are right, this hatch should lead into a small storage room. But wherever we are, we'll need to make our way to the turbine. If we cross any Stormers, we'll need to dispatch them silently."

"And by dispatch you mean . . ."

"It's us or them, Vane. Try not to forget that. And remember that any of them could've done something to hurt Gus or Audra. They're the enemy. The only thing we have to make sure is that we don't leave a trail. I'm hoping the majority of the Stormers are still chasing after Aston and Arella, or trying to open the hatch we used to get here. But from this point on, no talking unless it's an emergency—or we know we're somewhere secure. Otherwise, communicate through gestures only."

She presses her palms against the ceiling and leans close to whisper the password.

I can't believe she's so calm and steady. It makes me extra glad she didn't leave when I tried to send her home.

Which reminds me . . .

"You don't have any winds stored inside you, right?" I whisper. "Remember what Aston said could happen."

"The only winds left are the ones that are already broken," she promises. "I've been saving them for this."

"You're planning to use the power of pain?"

"I'm planning to do whatever it takes to get the four of us out of here alive. Ready?"

No. But I nod anyway.

She takes three slow breaths. Then whispers to the hatch.

The door swings open, making only the tiniest of creaks—but it might as well be an air horn.

We both freeze and hold our breath.

Nothing happens.

Either we really are alone, or they're waiting for us to move deeper into their trap.

Solana glances at me before climbing another rung up the ladder and peeking out into the room.

Nobody chops off her head, so I take that as a good sign.

She climbs another step and slithers out into the darkness. I count the seconds after she's gone, realizing we should've come up with an emergency system—a special whistle, or at least a timeline so I know when to worry.

Thirty seconds crawl by.

Sixty.

Ninety.

By one twenty my twitchy legs move me to the ladder.

I climb a couple of steps at the two hundred mark.

Another at three fifty.

By that point I no longer have any idea how many actual

minutes have passed. But I'm up to the top of the ladder.

Solana told me to wait for her signal—but what if she needs me?

My brain is arguing in circles when Solana's face melts out of the shadows, and I barely manage to stop myself from scream-flailing.

She slides closer, pressing her lips against my ear. "It's totally empty. No one's been in here for years. It's still a storeroom, but not of what I was expecting."

"Is it dead bodies?" I whisper back. "That's the kind of thing you need to warn a guy about."

"It's not dead bodies. It's . . . you have to see for yourself."

That doesn't exactly sound like I should be excited to follow her into the dark. But I do anyway, and I find . . .

"A bunch of dusty trunks?"

"Open one," Solana tells me, "but be quiet about it."

I ease the nearest trunk open, relieved when it doesn't squeak.

"Toys?" I whisper, staring at the pinwheels and reed pipes and kites and windsocks all neatly arranged inside.

"*Raiden's* toys," Solana corrects. "Look at this."

I crawl to where she's opened a trunk filled with stuff I can only describe as "baby things." Rattles and tiny clothes in pale yellows and blues, and a couple of well-loved stuffed birds. Tucked among the blankets is one of those clay handprint things with the initials *R.N.* carved in loopy letters.

"N?" I ask.

"Must be his family name. He's a Northerly, but I only know him as Raiden."

Same here.

I never realized Raiden had a last name.

Or a childhood.

Or cute, tiny hands.

I know how stupid that sounds—obviously he wasn't born an evil dictator. But it's bizarre to see proof of the *before*.

Once upon a time, he was just a kid with chubby fingers, flying kites and hugging his stuffed birdies and living with his family.

"What happened to his parents?" I ask. "And does he have any brothers or sisters?"

"No idea."

"Shouldn't we know?"

We've all been so focused on stopping him that we haven't bothered getting to know him.

I wonder if that's a mistake.

Isn't that why "know your enemy" is a saying?

It makes me wish we had time to crack open every trunk and try to piece together his life story. Since we don't, I shove the clay handprint thing in my coat pocket—and while I'm at it, I grab an old mallard-shaped windsock from the other trunk. I hope Socky the Duck was his favorite.

Solana doesn't notice my thieving as she seals the hatch we came through and crawls toward the wall, where threads of light outline a heavy door.

"Any idea where that leads?" I ask.

She presses her ear against it. "Not really. But it sounds quiet out there. And it should be one of the old hallways. I doubt it'll take us to the turbine—but hopefully it'll have an air vent. If I'm not back in five minutes, come after me."

She draws her windslicer and tugs lightly on the door.

"Is it locked?" I ask when it doesn't budge.

She motions for me to duck into the shadows, then whispers the password that worked twice before.

Nothing happens.

"Let's hope Aston's commands work," she says.

The sound of her snarl makes me queasy, and even across the room I can see her eyes glinting with the rush of the *need*.

A soft click rewards her efforts, and the door slides open. She doesn't hesitate before slipping out, sending me back to waiting-and-counting mode.

I'm only at forty-seven seconds when I hear a grunt and a thud.

I scramble toward the door and crash into Solana, who's dragging something into the room. It takes my brain a couple of breaths to realize it's a body.

A Stormer with a yellow draft tangled around his face.

I can't tell if he's awake, but he's not putting up a fight.

"He was the only one," Solana whispers as she closes the door again so no one can hear us talking. "I couldn't tell if he was a guard or just passing by. Either way, this is good news."

"How?"

"Because we can take his uniform. He even looks like he's your size. I wish he'd been carrying an anemometer, but they must only carry those when they're out in battle. At least he has a windslicer."

She gets to work stripping him down, but I can't stop staring at his face.

He looks about my age—maybe a little older.

"Help me lift his legs," Solana whispers.

I obey—and then regret it when she pulls down his pants and the dude's going commando.

Solana laughs as I cringe. "What were you expecting?"

"Uh—how about some boxers? Even tighty-whities would've been better than nothing."

Solana looks at me like I'm speaking alien, which raises a super-weird question.

"Sylphs wear underwear, right?"

"Why would we? The less we have between our skin and the air, the better."

I have absolutely no idea how to respond to that—and I have to work very hard not to think about what's clearly not under Solana's tiny dress.

Then again, it does also cast a new, rather interesting light on all of my memories of Audra . . .

Solana kills the fantasies by tossing the pants at my head. "Get changed."

"Dude, his junk was floating around in these."

"Well, apparently yours won't be." She raises one eyebrow and my face gets hot. Especially when she adds, "You should consider it. Might make a difference. But either way, you're currently dressed like a Gale. And they know we're here."

I really really really really really hate her for being right.

I also hate how badly my cheeks are burning.

And I'm *definitely* not going freebird in these things.

"What about you?" I ask as I duck behind some trunks and struggle out of my coat.

"I'll change if we find another Stormer—or pass a supply closet. But now that you're in uniform we'll be okay. If we see anyone, we'll pretend I'm your prisoner."

"That's asking a lot of my acting skills."

"Hopefully it won't come up. How's it going back there? Need help?"

"Don't even think about it. You just worry about naked boy—and maybe cover his bits with Raiden's blankies." I emerge a minute later, fidgeting in the itchy fabric and wishing my new pants weren't so much tighter than my others The stuff from my pockets barely fits. "Should we tie him up so he can't walk out of here once he wakes up?"

"That won't be a problem."

Maybe it's the unnaturally calm way she says it. But it makes me take another look at the Stormer and realize the draft silencing him is covering his mouth *and* nose.

"Before you freak out," Solana says, holding out her hands like she's calming a rabid dog, "remember, he *chose* to serve Raiden. He deserves whatever happens to him."

"Not this." I grab my dagger and try to cut him free, but my swipe grazes right through the ruined draft.

By the time I realize I need to use his black windslicer, a cold, rattly sound echoes through his chest, and he goes a different kind of still.

"You didn't have to kill him!" I say—barely remembering to whisper.

"He would've killed us! And what if he'd escaped? What if he led them back to this room to wait for us? This is our exit. We have to keep it clear. This is why Aston said I should be the one in charge. He knew I'd be the only one who could make the tough choices."

"This wasn't a 'tough choice'—it was murder!"

"No, it was war—and keep your voice down or you're going to get us killed." She turns away from me, pulling at the hem of her dress, and I notice her hands are shaking.

When she looks back my way, there's a plea in her eyes, begging me to let this go.

But there's something else there too. That same junkie-glint as the last time she let the power of pain take over.

Even my Westerly shield agrees, switching its tune to a song about *traitors*.

"We need to get back on track," she whispers. "We're making too much noise and moving too slow. If we don't get Gus and Audra out of here now, we never will."

I know she's right.

And some part of me knows this isn't her fault. It's the disgusting power breaking her down bit by bit.

But I can't be a part of this.

"Here's how this is going to go," I say, heading for the door. "This is *my* mission, and we go by my rules from now on."

"You really think *you* can get us through this?"

"No, but I'm hoping the wind can. This isn't up for negotiation. We do it my way—or we split up. Your call."

Solana sighs. "We'll see how long this lasts."

I'm feeling pretty good about the whole taking-back-control thing, until we get to the door and I realize it's locked again.

"*I* can open it . . . ," Solana says.

Traitor, my Westerly whispers.

Got any bright ideas, then? I ask the wind.

I'm expecting it to sing some sort of vague melody about resisting temptation. Instead, it slips through the cracks and unlocks the latch.

Solana's eyes are as wide as mine as I pull the door open.

Maybe the fourth language can take down the power of pain after all.

CHAPTER 24

AUDRA

We're finally making progress.

    Slow progress.

    But progress.

Slipping through secret doors to new parts of the maze.

I have no idea where we are, but at least the halls have changed.

Rougher walls.

Uneven floors.

The path we walk even feels like an incline, heading for the surface.

I'd be celebrating if Gus's skin weren't turning as pale as a sun-bleached stone. His breaths also hold a gurgly rattle that makes my stomach knot.

I coiled the Easterly around him, but it seems to be making no difference. And Gus claims that if he absorbed it, he'd use the energy up even faster.

I keep calling for other drafts, but so far none have been around to answer. Even Raiden's ruined winds seem to be avoiding this hall—not that they would help us.

"So I just realized you never told me the whole plan," Gus whispers. "How exactly are we supposed to escape through the Shredder?"

"Aston's guide maps out a path through the fans."

Gus stops walking. "How many fans are there?"

"Seventeen."

It sounds so much worse out loud.

Seventeen leaps through spinning blades.

The slightest miscalculation—a split second of difference—and we're nothing more than a splatter of red.

Gus whistles. "Well, I guess it's a good thing I'm in such great shape then."

He smiles at his joke, but it still breaks my heart.

I remember Gus during the early days of my guardian training. He'd be doing sit-ups or push-ups or practicing fight moves long after the rest of us retired for the day. His focus was legendary, and it pushed me to try harder, be better.

And now . . .

"Relax. It's going to take a lot more than this to finish me off," he promises, getting us moving again. "I'm way more worried about the fact that we haven't run into any Stormers." "I've been thinking the same thing."

Not that I *mind* an easy journey—but I don't trust it either.

We're escaping the world's most impenetrable fortress. We should be constantly dodging guards.

"I can't imagine Raiden would only assign one Stormer to cover this area," Gus whispers.

Neither can I.

Even if Vane and my mother are distracting him, it's a sloppy, careless mistake—and Raiden doesn't make mistakes.

"Do you think we're heading for an ambush?" I ask, glancing over my shoulder.

"I think we're heading for *something*," Gus says.

He whispers to his Easterly, asking it to search the path ahead. The wind darts away, and Gus's knees buckle, dragging us both down.

"I wish you'd absorb my Westerly," I tell him as I pull him back to his feet. "It made you so much stronger."

"It did," Gus agrees. "But that draft has had more bright ideas than both of us combined. No way am I locking it up somewhere it can't help us if we need it."

The Easterly returns, reporting emptiness ahead.

"It can't be this easy," Gus says, reaching for the windslicer strapped to my waist.

As soon as he draws the sword, it slips from his weakened hand.

The *CLANG!* that follows sounds like a hurricane raging down the hall, announcing our presence to the entirety of the universe.

I retrieve the weapon and push Gus against the wall, standing in front of him to cover us.

A minute passes in silence.

Then another.

And another.

"I know I should be relieved," Gus whispers. "But *someone* should've heard that."

"Wait here. I'm going to sweep the area."

I crouch low as I move—checking the walls, the ceiling, the floor. Still, I don't notice the slightly raised stone until I step on it.

The second I hear the click I drop to my stomach, knocking the breath out of my chest as a wind spike blasts out of the wall and explodes.

Pebbles and dust cloud the air, making it impossible to see if I'm near any other triggers.

"DON'T MOVE!" I shout to Gus, forcing myself to remain still. "The floor is rigged."

"That blast was designed to maim, not kill," Gus says. "Someone's probably on their way to scoop up the injured."

I'm sure he's right. And I have no idea how to get us out of here. Gus is too weak to run—and who knows how many other traps we could set off?

Then again, the more traps we trigger, the worse they'll imagine our injuries . . .

"Maybe we should play with their expectations," I say as I spot another raised stone and tap the center with the edge of the wind-slicer.

Instead of the spike I'm prepared for, a mangled wind bursts out of the floor and tangles around me.

I've been caught in a crusher before, but this one is suffocating *and* sharp. Every time I try to twist free, it feels like the wind is peeling off my skin.

"Hang on!" Gus calls, careful of his steps as he rushes to help.

He slashes the vortex with the windslicer, but the black metal passes straight through.

One of my ribs cracks, and Gus grabs hold of the crusher with both fists.

Veins bulge in his arms, and his face contorts with agony as he lets out an unearthly scream and tears the crusher to shreds.

I collapse to my knees and he crumples beside me, both of us shaking and gasping for air. I recover first and drag us away from the rest of the trigger stones.

That's when I notice Gus has stopped breathing.

"He needs wind!" I beg my Westerly, and it coils around him. But it can't seem to sink under his skin without Gus giving the command.

I send the Easterly to find an exit, but I don't have time to wait.

Gus's lips are taking on a bluish tinge.

I faced this same dilemma with Vane—and I never did determine whether a bond would form if I pressed my mouth to his.

That did hold a much greater risk, since I already cared far too deeply for Vane.

Still, I care for Gus in other ways, and what if . . .

I don't have time for this debate. I prop his neck on my knee and open his mouth.

Maybe if I cover his lips with my fingers, the barrier will ensure there's no connection.

"It's going to be okay," I whisper as I lower my mouth to his and blow all the breath in my lungs.

Half of it breezes through the gaps around my fingers. The rest doesn't sink deep enough.

I pull my hand back and suck in another breath, checking the hall around me for signs of the Stormers.

I can't hear what the wind is doing—can't tell if any guards are drawing close.

I lean down again and breathe straight against his mouth.

Our lips barely touch—but I can feel how cold they are.

I lean back for a new breath and repeat the process again.

And again.

By the fifth time, I notice his mouth turning warm.

"Come on, Gus," I whisper. "You're so close."

Three more breaths and my lips turn tingly.

The next time, Gus gasps on his own.

I scoot back, letting him cough and wheeze. That's when I realize I can hear footsteps charging closer.

I search for the Easterly and find it slashing at the ceiling.

I send the Westerly to help and order them to *Sever* as I drag Gus toward the exit I hope the winds are making.

Silt rains down, stinging my eyes as the drafts cut the seams around a square hatch.

I drop into a deep crouch, begging my Westerly to fuel my jump as I burst off the ground. The stone is heavier than I expected, and my wrists scream in protest, but I manage to knock the hatch aside and make an opening.

I land next to Gus and throw him over my shoulder, wondering if I can leap high enough with his added weight.

My Westerly has a better solution, coiling around us both and repeating the command it wants me to use.

"Elevate."

The wind pulls taut and drags us like a rope. It's not a comfortable process, but it's worth it when we launch through the hatch. I've barely pulled my legs inside when the Stormers burst into the room, and I shove the hatch closed and collapse on top of it.

"Is there a way to seal the door?" I ask the winds.

Neither have any suggestions.

And Gus is barely conscious.

And I left the windslicer down below.

I scan our new tunnel, searching for actual options.

The thin metal slats lining the ceiling could possibly serve as a weapon—but when I try to pry one off, the metal is welded too tight.

The best I can manage is to coil the Easterly and Westerly into a weak sort of wind spike. The point feels dull—wind spikes need the strength of the Northerlies. But it's better than nothing.

I drag Gus behind me, glad to see he's still breathing. If only his eyes weren't closed and his wounds weren't seeping through his bandages.

I'm wishing for wind—and maybe the sky hears me—because the metal slats tilt and cool air rushes in.

For two seconds I let hope swell in my heart. Then I realize the Stormers haven't tried to follow me. And when I pull on the hatch, I find it sealed shut.

I press my ear to the floor and hear the voice of the Stormer who ripped my dress.

"Flood the tunnel with flurries. She's useless in the cold."

The metal slats tilt farther, and the wind picks up speed, tearing at my face and hair.

I unravel the wind spike and blanket us each in a shield before I pull Gus close and try to find something to grab on to.

The walls are perfectly smooth—the tunnel too wide to use my feet for leverage. And the wind keeps rushing rushing rushing.

I hold firm as long as I can, but the gusts are relentless. Eventually, the river of air drags us away.

CHAPTER 25

VANE

I'm *rocking* this leader thing.

Okay, fine, maybe I've had a ton of help from the wind.

But the point is, I'm totally kicking butt!

We're moving fast. We've avoided dozens of Stormers—a couple were close calls, but we still got out of there without being seen. And my Westerly isn't having any problems finding the hidden doors we need.

So take that, power of pain and all your dark, evil, creepiness.

You just got stomped by a Westerly!

I'm planning the endless ways I'll be bragging about this to Os when we pass through the next door and my mind blanks out.

"Is this . . . Raiden's bedroom?" I whisper.

"I think it must be." Solana traces her hand across the wall, which is painted with a perfect sky in a hundred shades of blue. Birds of every color soar from one side of the room to the other, and windswept trees disappear into the floor.

"He kept my grandmother's murals," she whispers. "I've always wanted to see them."

I don't blame her.

I'm not even into art, and I can tell they're amazing.

The whole room is crazy beautiful. Everything is clean and white and pristine. The marble floor is polished, and the wall of windows gives us a view of the whole range of snow-capped mountains. Even in the dark—with the fires and smoke—it takes my breath away.

"I'm guessing this is all your family's stuff?" I ask, pointing to the huge canopied bed covered in more pillows than one of my mom's decorating magazines. The posts are carved to look like trees, and hundreds of wind chimes dangle from the ornate branches. The center chimes hang lower than the others, and they're strung with a few clumps of colorful feathers and something that kinda looks like a miniature silver flute.

"No, this is all new," Solana whispers. "Only the paintings are familiar."

I study the room again, noting silver mirrors and vases full of reeds cut to different heights.

Who knew Raiden was so . . . decorate-y?

The better question is: Why are we here?

I told my Westerly to take us to the turbine, since sabotaging the crap out of this place is even more crucial now that they know we're here. Maybe that'll keep everyone distracted while we head for the dungeon, and if not, it'll hopefully cripple them when they attack us.

I search the air for my shield and feel it calling me from what I'm guessing is Raiden's closet. I'm on my way there when I turn back and snatch the chimes hanging from the center of the bed.

I'm not sure why I want them—and I kinda regret the decision when the rest of the chimes start tinkling like crazy. But it's too late now. Plus, it makes me realize something.

We're standing in the bedroom of the guy who's basically declared himself King of the Wind, and . . . the air is perfectly still.

It almost feels stale.

I don't know what that means—but it has to mean *something*.

Solana shakes her head at me as I shove the wind chimes in my pocket—which is pretty full now between the chimes and Socky the Duck and the handprint thing.

"You'd better hope there were no Stormers around to hear that," she whispers.

"Yeah, I know. I should've picked something quieter. But imagine Raiden's face when he plops down in bed and realizes we were here, messing with his stuff."

"See, and I'd rather find a way to ensure he never rests again," Solana mumbles.

Okay. Yeah. I guess that's a better plan.

I head for the closet, which turns out to be more like a master bathroom. There's a huge tub in one corner, and a dressing table covered in colorful bottles that look like cologne. I peek into the walk-in closet as we pass it, and it's floor to ceiling clothes.

"Where does he get all of this stuff?" I ask.

"I'm sure most of it is spoils of war. Why?"

"I don't know. It's just weird. This place is so normal—if normal people wore this much white fur and feathers."

"What did you think his living quarters would be like?" Solana asks.

"I honestly had no idea."

I always picture Raiden in a war room with a map of the world spread out on the table and giant knives stabbed into the countries he's taking over.

Plus I've never seen a sylph *house*. That serial-killer place Arella lives in hardly counts. And Audra squatted in a burned-down shack on my parents' property. The Gales sleep in holes in the ground so the Stormers can't find them. Even my few childhood memories are all filled with the deserted human houses we crashed in during our days on the run.

"I guess it's easy to forget there's a person behind all of this," Solana whispers, and somehow the idea makes it all worse.

The more I learn about Raiden, the more I can't figure him out.

Does he stand in his closet asking himself which outfit would look the coolest for a long day of murdering children and then soak in a giant bubble bath afterward?

"I think your wind's over there," Solana says, and I follow her to a small cubby room with nothing but a toilet.

Side note—I guess it really is true: *Everyone* poops.

I kick down the seat and stand on the lid, feeling the section of the ceiling where the Westerly is circling. "Pretty sure there's a door here."

"Let's hope it leads to a wind tunnel."

I know I should be rooting for the same thing, but Aston made it sound like the wind tunnels are a whole other nightmare.

I give the command to open the hatch anyway.

"Need a boost?" I ask Solana, kneeling and cupping my hands.

She steps over them, hops up onto the toilet tank and stretches high enough to grab hold of the edge of the doorway, then pulls herself up like a pro.

"You coming?" she asks. "This isn't the kind of place I want to linger."

I can't climb with my bad elbow, so I have to convince my Westerly to pull me—and it doesn't go smoothly. When I finally flop into the tunnel, I totally get why Solana's desperate to keep moving.

The air feels hot and sour, like we're standing in Raiden's armpit—and it smells just as disgusting.

The sticky drafts pull at me, chanting, *Go! Move! Faster!*

We start out at a walk, but it quickly turns to a run—then a flat-out sprint.

And still I want to go faster.

Faster!

FASTER!

My focus narrows to the next breath, the next step, the next burst of speed—which is probably why I don't notice the giant, spinning fan until I'm seconds from charging through it.

"Whoa," Solana says as I grab her arm and screech us both to a stop. "How did you see that?"

"My Westerly got my attention." And I'm pretty sure its current song about watching where you walk is the wind's way of calling me an idiot.

The song shifts again as I concentrate on the fan, repeating a single word in a very specific rhythm.

"How much do you trust me?" I ask Solana.

"Why—is it telling you to jump?"

"It is. And I'm pretty sure if we do it at the same time, we'll end up as Windwalker smoothies. So since you can't hear the Westerly telling you when to go . . ."

"You're going to have to push me," Solana finishes.

She blinks hard several times. Then steps in front of me. "I guess we should get it over with."

Her hair blasts my face until she gathers all the blond waves at the base of her neck.

I seriously can't believe we're going to do this.

We can't even see what's on the other side. For all we know, it's another fan—or an army of Stormers.

Now! my Westerly tells me.

Now!

Now!

"In case this doesn't go well," Solana whispers, "I just wanted to say . . . you were right about his power. I can feel the need corrupting me. But I don't know how to stop it."

Aston's solution flits through my mind, and I squeeze the

thought away. "The less you use it, the safer you'll be."

She nods. "That's why I'm letting you push me into a fan instead of using a command to stop the blades."

"There's a command to stop the blades?"

"That's what the need is telling me. It senses what I want and comes up with a way to make it happen."

Crap—now *I'm* tempted.

One more time isn't going to make *that* big of a difference for her, right?

Except . . . the power sounds even creepier when I really think about it.

How can the need *know* what she wants—and what if she wants something bad?

My Westerly has gotten us this far. It's safer to keep trusting it—even if nothing about this decision actually feels safe.

"You ready?" I ask.

Solana nods, but her shoulders are shaking.

Now! my Westerly orders.

Now!

NOW!

On the next repetition I close my eyes and shove Solana as hard as I can.

I'm fully expecting a sound like something squishy dropping into a blender. Instead there's an excruciating silence before Solana calls out, "I'm okay! It's not as bad as I thought. But there's a pretty steep drop on the other side, so you'll need to use the Southerly I gave you to stop your fall."

I nod—which is stupid because it's not like she can see me. Then I scoot closer to the fan and try to get a handle on the rhythm again.

Now.

Now.

Now—crap, I should've gone but I wasn't ready!

Now!

Now—Audra's waiting, come on, dude—NOW!

I leap through the blades, preparing to be smoothiefied. But all I feel is a buzz of rushing air. The drop hits me then, and it takes me several seconds to remember the right command, so I land a little harder than I want to—but I'm alive!

We've ended up on the ground floor of a tower, its round walls stretching at least five stories. And there are about a zillion fans covering the wall, alternating with round vents in a checkerboard pattern.

Streams of hot and cold air blast through the fans and vents and collide against a giant motor in the center, making all the cogs and springs spin like we're inside some sort of giant steampunk clock tower.

The stones tremble beneath our feet, pulsing with the energy generated by the turbine.

"Okay," I tell Solana. "Time to break this thing."

CHAPTER 26

AUDRA

can't stop the spinning.

I can't even slow us down.

Now I understand how a tumbleweed feels, caught in a sandstorm.

But this isn't the desert.

We're tangled in an indoor squall—blasting maximum velocity through a frosted funnel.

At least the wind seems to be reviving Gus's strength. I wish I could say the same for myself. Instead, the cold sinks deep, smothering my consciousness in mental snow. The shivers shake away my reason, and when I beg my Westerly for guidance, it offers no solution.

Gus's Easterly remains silent as well, and I sink deeper into the haze of cold. Sheer stubborn will helps me fight my way back, and I stretch out my senses, stunned when I feel a faint itch on the edge of my left thumb.

A brave Northerly reaches for me from somewhere high above.

I whisper its call, and the draft seeps through the cracks and coils around both of us.

Before I can celebrate, I catch the lyrics of its disjointed melody.

The Northerly sings only two words, repeating them with a thundering authority.

Not a suggestion.

A command.

Let go.

My Westerly joins the song.

So does the Easterly.

And when I chance a look at Gus, he's mouthing, *Trust the wind.*

I tighten my grip, not sure I can risk his life again. He's far too weak to brave these torrents on his own.

But we'd never have gotten this far if the wind wasn't on our side. . . .

It takes five steadying breaths before I pull my fingers slowly from Gus's and let the drafts rip us apart, slamming us into opposite walls. Pain screams through my back as the cuts Raiden gave me tear open.

But as the shock fades, I realize: *We're no longer moving.*

Somehow, on our own, we're able to stand against the relentless winds.

Leave it to Raiden to turn his fortress into a game of everyone for themselves.

"I'm pretty sure my insides have frozen," Gus says, dropping to his knees and clutching his stomach.

"Mine too." I press my ear against the stones, trying to get a read on our location. "The drafts are drowning out the Shredder. But if we walk against the wind, it should lead us back to where we entered."

"The Stormers will be waiting for us there," Gus reminds me.

"I'm sure they will. But it sounded like there's only one way in or out of this place."

"That doesn't make sense. This wind has to go somewhere."

My Westerly seems to agree, ending every verse of its song with *Charge forward!*

But when we try to get moving, Gus's legs collapse beneath him.

"You need to rest," I say, resisting the urge to help. If I draw close, it would only send us airborne again.

"I'm fine," Gus promises.

"I don't think you realize how close you came to dying. I barely brought you back."

"Yeah . . . about that." His eyes lower to my lips, and my heart jumps into my throat.

He remembers. . . .

"I'm really sorry," I mumble.

"For saving my life?"

"For triggering that trap in the first place, thinking I was being clever."

I could leave the apology there—pretend there's no awkwardness hanging over us. But Gus is still focused on my mouth, and I know my face must be ten different shades of red.

"I'm also sorry for the way I saved you," I whisper. "I know it was very . . . personal."

"It was," Gus says, a small smile curving his lips. "Don't worry, I didn't feel any connection, in case you're worried."

"Neither did I."

"Yeah, I figured." His smile fades. "What you did though . . . that was *way* above and beyond anything anyone has ever done for me. So I just wanted to say . . . thanks."

My cheeks burn hotter, and all I can think to say is "Anytime."

"Yeah, I don't think Vane will want me taking you up on that."

I focus on my hands.

For all I know, Vane and I will never—not that Gus and I would *ever* . . .

"You're overcomplicating it. You know that, right?" Gus asks. "You and Vane chose each other once—why wouldn't you choose each other again?"

"I don't know. Things change."

"They clearly haven't for Vane. Mr. Lazypants flew across the country, scaled a mountain, and took on an army of warriors—for you."

"And you."

Gus rolls his eyes. "He loves you, Audra. And I know you love him, too. Otherwise you wouldn't have been able to resist the power of these."

He puckers his lips.

I want to laugh, but the gesture draws too much attention to his wounds, and I find myself wondering how much his handsome face will forever be ruined by scars.

Gus leans across the hall, closing some of the space between us. "Whatever you're thinking about that's causing that wrinkle between your brows? Stop it. And promise me you won't give up on what you have with Vane just because you're afraid."

"I'm not afraid."

But I am.

Loving Vane was the bravest thing I've ever done, and I barely survived it the first time. It's terrifying to imagine making that journey again.

And yet, I can feel pieces of myself stirring—like my essence is shifting, making room for something.

Or someone.

"Come on," Gus says. "The sooner we get out of here, the sooner we can find him."

I let Gus take the lead so I can keep a better eye on his wobbly movements.

"Is it getting colder?" he asks, his breath clouding the air.

"They're trying to freeze us out."

The winds are also getting stronger, speeding our feet, erasing our caution. I'm moving at such a blur that I don't notice the metal grate ahead until the sharp, angled slats glint in my eyes, and I barely manage to grab Gus and pull him backward in time.

The contact sends us into another tailspin and Gus shoves me away, sending us both crashing hard to the floor.

"Thanks," I mumble, rubbing my bandaged side.

"Yeah, you too," he says. "Good eye. I don't know how I missed that."

"Might be the cold getting to us. But I think these winds are toxic."

"Then let's get away from them, shall we?" He inches toward the grate. "I wonder if Raiden has a welcome party waiting for us."

He peeks through the slats and gasps.

"That bad?"

He shakes his head. "You . . . have to see this."

I'm imagining every possible worst-case scenario as I shuffle toward the grate. Still, I'm definitely not prepared to see two figures standing in the room far below, watching the spinning gears of a giant turbine.

One is a blond girl in a tiny dress.

The other is a boy I'd recognize anywhere, even wearing a Stormer uniform.

Vane and Solana.

CHAPTER 27

VANE

What was that?" Solana asks, grabbing my arm—and totally screwing up my throw.

My windslicer sails in a wobbly arc and lands nowhere near where I was aiming.

Even better: It settles between the teeth of one of the giant cogs, and when the gears spin together . . .

CRUNCH!

"What the hell?" I timed that throw perfectly, and now I've lost my weapon, *and* the freaking turbine is still spinning.

Solana turns a slow circle, studying the fans and vents. "I saw something," she tells me, reaching for her windslicer. It's all mangled from banging it against the gears in our other failed attempt to sabotage this stupid thing—who knew a turbine could be so indestructible?

I ask my Westerly for a report, but I can't separate its song from the roar of the wind and the gears. And the constantly swirling air throws off my senses, with all the waves of hot and cold and swishes of sour and bitter.

And then . . . I see a flash of light.

I can't tell which vent it came from, but I'm guessing it's some sort of signal for a bunch of Stormers to attack from every direction. They probably followed our trail through the maze—or maybe this turbine is sending our trace through the fortress.

Solana pulls me behind her. "I'll get us out of this, but I need you to let me fight my way."

"You're not using the power of pain—"

"We don't have time to argue." She snarls a garbled command and two yellowed drafts seep out of her skin and coil around her hands like sickly gloves.

"How is that supposed to help?" I ask.

"The need will tell me."

Her voice sounds flat and far away and her eyes look glazed, like she's turned into a zombie—which definitely isn't selling me on the power of pain.

Then again, it's probably a good thing we have it. The light just flashed again, and this time I saw where it came from. One of the vents way up high looks like its bending, and I swear I saw a quick glimpse of something gray.

"They're coming," Solana says, still in that faraway voice. "Stay back and let me fight."

"You can't take them all by yourself."

"I only feel two. It will be easy."

I'd be a lot more excited about this plan if she didn't sound like a possessed kid in a horror movie.

But two Stormers is good.

We've already done that and won before—surely we can pull it off again.

"We have to keep this quick," Solana says. "The air here is too turbulent. As soon as they land I'll use the need to end them. Cover eyes so you don't have to see."

I want to tell her I can handle it, but I'm not sure if I can. I'm getting flashbacks to the bloody carnage after our last battle, and the dead Stormer we left in the storage room, and—

Don't think about it.

My legs shake as I watch the last of the vents' metal slats get ripped apart by a seriously scary-looking Stormer.

He's too high up to see details, but I can tell he's bloody.

He shouts something I can't understand, and he and another Stormer dive for us.

Solana starts murmuring a creepy command, and I beg my Westerly to come up with something useful. But as the Stormers drop closer, I notice the bloody one's a guy with long blond hair. And the other—

"Solana, STOP!"

I shake her out of her frenzy right as she releases the drafts and they spiral away from her hands, *barely* missing the two figures as they land.

"Why would you . . ."

Solana's question trails off when she takes a closer look at the "Stormers."

Meanwhile five million emotions have taken up the epic battle of What Should I Feel Right Now? as I ask, "Audra?"

CHAPTER 28

AUDRA

Vane won't look at me.

He did when he first said my name. But then his eyes moved to Gus, and they haven't strayed.

I can't fault him—even *I* haven't gotten used to Gus's altered appearance.

But every fiber of my being is screaming, *Why won't he look at me?*

That first quick glance—those brief seconds he gave.

It wasn't enough.

The craving is both new and familiar. Hot and cold. Terrifying and exhilarating.

I want him to see me. Talk to me. Reach for me.

But I also want to run away.

I'm not ready for this—any of it.

Vane clears his throat, his eyes still focused on Gus. "Gus, I . . ." His voice breaks.

"It's okay," Gus tells him, limping closer.

"No it's not." Vane wipes his eyes with shaking hands. "You . . . I can't . . ."

"I know," Gus tells him. "But I'll heal. Don't worry about it, all right?"

"I can't believe *you're* comforting *me*." Vane shakes his head hard, tearing his hands through his hair. "I'm sorry—I don't know how to do this."

He smears away more tears as he finally turns my way, meeting my eyes for barely a second before shifting his full attention to my nose.

His eaglelike focus helps me understand what he's really avoiding.

"I'm fine," I promise. "Just a few cuts and bruises."

"Her Westerly's been protecting her," Gus adds.

Vane's whole expression shifts to something heartbreakingly tender. "You still have your shield?"

"She does," Gus says when I forget that I'm supposed to answer. "The winds have done some amazing things—but we'll get to that later. Do you know where the Stormers are?"

Vane shakes his head. "We've barely run into any. What about you guys?"

"We saw a few, but not as many as we should have," Gus says, "so I'm pretty sure they're setting up an ambush somewhere."

"Sounds about right," Vane grumbles.

"How did you guys get out of your cell?" Solana asks.

"Kinda a long story," Gus says. "Right now, we should keep moving."

"We should," Vane agrees.

"But first we need to stop the turbine," Solana reminds him.

She explains their sabotage plan, and it's actually a smart play. I hate myself for not thinking of it—and I hate myself even more for glaring at her tiny dress and shiny hair.

She's risked her life to help us—that should be my only focus. But I can't stand the way she keeps using the word "we" as she describes how she and Vane snuck into the fortress through a secret tunnel.

A bitter, unreasonable anger clouds my thoughts, devouring several seconds before I remember something actually important. "Wasn't my mother with you? I heard Raiden say her name."

The worry in my voice surprises me—as does the flood of relief when Vane says she's still alive.

"Aston was worried they'd end up betraying us if they had to face Raiden," he explains. "So they created a distraction to help us sneak in, and now they're probably on their way back to his cave."

"Aston helped you?" I ask.

Gus chooses the smarter question. "How do you know they're not betraying us right now?"

"I don't," Vane admits. "But . . . sometimes you have to trust people."

The brief look he and Solana share turns my insides to needles.

I try to listen as they hash out ideas for how to sabotage the turbine, but it's hard to focus when I'm standing this close to Vane.

Every twitch, every blink, every stolen glance he gives me. I can't help studying them, searching for answers—and I don't even know the questions.

The words won't take shape in my mind. Only the feelings.

So many feelings.

Too many feelings.

"We're not doing it your way!" Vane snaps, dragging me back to attention.

"What's her way?" Gus asks.

"It's . . . also a long story," Vane says. "Add it to the list of things we need to talk about if we get out of here."

"Oh, we're getting out of here," Gus says. "Lend me that Westerly of yours—and any other winds you have—and I'll tear this thing apart."

"Westerly?" Vane and Solana ask.

Gus nods.

Vane's lips twitch with questions, but he manages to shake them off. He sends Gus his Westerly along with a Southerly, and I watch his eyes widen as Gus absorbs them and heads for the turbine.

Even with the extra burst of strength, the pull of the motor nearly sucks Gus in. Solana darts to his side—annoyingly sure-footed among the flurries—and grabs him by the waist, keeping him grounded.

"Do you need help?" Vane calls.

"Nah, we got this," Gus tells him. "You guys have other things you need to take care of."

Vane tenses at the words, and goes back to not looking at me.

What does that mean?

Seconds pass, each one making it harder to breathe.

Eventually Vane mutters something I can't catch before he finally strides toward me.

Three steps and he's at my side, his words bursting out in a frenzied breath. "I'm so sorry, Audra. Will you ever be able to forgive me?"

It's not the question I was expecting—and I hate that he's noticed my jacket, his eyes locked on the bloodstains crusting my shoulders and back.

I need to tell him this wasn't his fault. Convince him I'm okay. Thank him for risking everything to come get me.

But the words won't push past the lump in my throat.

How did I get this broken?

I didn't think I was this broken.

"It's okay," Vane says, and the softness of his voice feels like clean, sweet air. "You don't have to say anything."

He starts to turn away, and a swell of panic brings back my voice.

"Vane, I . . ."

That's all I have.

But it seems to be enough.

He reaches for my face, brushing away a tear I didn't realize was there.

His soft fingers vanish just as quickly—his hands dropping firmly to his side—but the heat of his touch lingers under my skin.

Tiny sparks left from better days.

I close my eyes and soak them in.

"I know this isn't the time or the place," he says, his face close enough for me to feel his breath on my cheeks. "But there's one thing I have to say."

He stops there, and I realize he's waiting for me to look at him.

When I do, his beautiful eyes burn with the most desperate sort of longing—no attempt to deny it or disguise it.

"I'll do whatever it takes to prove that I still deserve you," he tells me. "But only if that's what you want. And I don't need you to decide now. I just . . . needed you to know."

Our eyes hold one second longer.

Then he turns and walks away.

CHAPTER 29

VANE

I want to race back to Audra, wrap my arms around her, and screw this whole slow-and-steady plan I came up with.

But the sadness I saw in her eyes keeps me moving away.

It reminds me too much of the first time we got together, and I know what it means. She needs to heal again before she'll be ready for anything more—and not just emotionally this time.

I'm sure that bloodstained jacket is hiding something way worse than she's letting on. Especially when I look at Gus.

I watch him and Solana scale the mechanisms of the turbine, and all I can think is . . . *How is he still alive?*

I'm glad he is—but his injuries?

There. Are. No. Words.

He catches me staring and gives me an exaggerated wink, like that will somehow make me forget his swollen face and shredded chest.

Audra comes up beside me—close enough that I can feel her heat through the air. I take a breath and remind myself: *slow and steady*.

"How bad is he?" I ask. "Tell me the truth."

I wasn't sure if she would, but she gives me the full horror story. By the end I have to bend over to get some blood to my head so I don't pass out.

"Are you okay?" she asks.

Once again, I can't believe that *I'm* the one being comforted.

I suck in a huge gulp of air, trying to drag myself together. "I'm just worried about you. Having to see all of that . . ."

"It was nothing compared to what Gus had to face."

Maybe—and *thank God*, even if I know it's crazy selfish to think that.

But still.

"You don't have to downplay what you've gone through, Audra. It had to be awful."

She swallows hard and looks away. "It was."

They're two teeny words—but they crush every part of me.

I reach up to wipe away her fresh tears. "I wish I knew how to help."

"You *are* helping. You're here."

"I am—not that you really needed me. I should've known you'd find a way to escape."

"It wasn't me," she says. "It was Gus. I don't know how I would've gotten through this without him."

I . . . don't know what to say.

I'm glad Gus was there for her—well, not *glad*, given that Gus is basically a walking wound right now because of it.

But I'm glad she wasn't alone.

It's just . . .

"I wish I could've been there."

If this were a movie, that would be her cue to give some big sappy speech about how I *was* there—always on her mind—and how the very thought of seeing me was what kept her going.

But this is Audra, so she tells me, "I'm glad you weren't."

She does take my hand, though, and sparks tingle everywhere our skin touches.

Even without our bond.

Even in this horrible place.

Even with all the complications piling up between us.

She's everything.

My less noble side starts screaming, *SCREW THE SLOW-AND-STEADY PLAN!*

Even my noble side tries to convince me that bonding again might help her heal.

I lean a little closer—and I swear she leans closer to me. Her eyes are even focused on my mouth, making it pretty dang tempting.

But a thundering *CRUNCH* sends us both jumping back.

I turn toward the turbine, where Gus has peeled back a huge piece of metal, revealing a cluster of smaller gears spinning way faster than the others.

"If they didn't know we were here before, they do now," Audra warns us.

"Who cares?" Solana asks. "We're shutting them down. Look!"

She pries one of the gears off with her windslicer—then another and another—each gear causing a chain reaction through the turbine.

Sprockets screech. Cogs clank. Springs snap. And everything slooooooooooooooooooows, until the hum of the fans fades away, and the floor stops vibrating.

The final nails in the turbine's coffin are the vents lining the walls around us, which clamp shut one by one.

I should be celebrating the victory, but my chest feels too heavy. I can't speak—can't breathe—and from the way everyone else is clutching their throat, I'm guessing they're having the same problem.

My vision dims and I grab on to Audra, using the last of my strength to drag her toward anything that could be an exit.

We only make it a few steps before the world fades to black.

CHAPTER 30

AUDRA

I wake up in chains.

Cold, heavy metal pulling against my wrists, ankles, and waist.

Jagged stone at my back.

Blackness all around.

The pit is so deep, it's only a shadow stretching into oblivion. I thought nothing could be worse than my damp cell in Raiden's dungeon. But this is beyond reason.

I try to piece together how I ended up here—something to do with a tower.

And a turbine.

And . . .

"Vane?" I whisper, hoping he won't reply.

Please don't let him be here—don't let Raiden have that much control.

"Audra?" Vane asks groggily, shattering the last of my hope.

I try to turn toward the sound, but there's a chain weighing down my forehead, restricting even the smallest motion.

"Are we all here?" Solana asks from somewhere farther away.

"I think so."

Gus's voice carries a heaviness that wasn't there earlier. I don't know if that means he was injured during our capture, or if his previous wounds are flaring up. The air here certainly can't be helping. It's disgustingly stagnant.

We must be deep under the earth.

"Welcome to my oubliette," Raiden calls from somewhere high above us. "Clearly I should've kept you here all along, but I believed in the competency of my guards. That problem has now been corrected."

Metal rattles, and a chained body is lowered in front of us—all I can see through the dim light is black skin and thin white scars.

I gasp.

"Yes," Raiden says. "No doubt you recognize the fool who let you get away. Rest assured, that mistake will *not* be occurring again."

The scarred Stormer thrashes, his words reduced to grunts and groans.

"Let me show you why you should be grateful for those chains holding you to the stones," Raiden says.

The scarred Stormer's eyes lock with mine as his bonds unravel, sending him plummeting into the darkness.

His groans fade as he falls—but the crash I'm expecting doesn't come.

Instead, Raiden snarls some sort of command, and the groans choke off with a crunch.

"His years of loyal service bought him a much quicker death than any of you will experience should you try to escape," Raiden tells us, and I wonder if that means he triggered the Stormer's suicide draft. "Do not fool yourself into believing that your pitiful gifts will aid you. There's no wind here. No power for you to draw on. Even I couldn't stop myself from plummeting, and if you fall . . ."

A stretch of silence follows, until it's broken by the sickening thud of a body spattering against the floor.

The sound of gore doesn't bother me as much as the fact that I never learned the scarred Stormer's name.

He was misguided—even cruel at times.

But he had his complicated reasons.

He also came to my aid once.

And now he's dead, because Gus and I tried to escape.

"Please," Vane says, his voice more angry than desperate. "I'm the one you want. Let the others go."

Raiden's laughter is darker than his pit. "You're the least interesting at this point. But I'll deal with that when I've finished cleaning up your mess. So I'd advise you to let the reality of your situation settle in. Your deaths are inevitable, but you still have the chance to spare yourselves countless hours of agony."

Metal clangs as my chains tangle so tight, it feels like my neck might snap.

"Fight against your bonds, and my guards have orders to drop you. And those who might consider themselves *valuable* should know that they'll cost the lives of others."

Seconds blur into minutes, then Vane whispers, "Is he gone?"

His chains clatter, and he coughs and hacks as though the guards tightened his bonds to punish him.

So we can't talk—can't move. And Raiden's not lying about the air. There's nothing here to aid us. My Westerly shield remains, but the turbine must've swallowed our other winds. And no drafts are brave enough to sink this deep into the earth.

That would explain why the Stormers didn't follow us after we entered the wind tunnel. They knew we'd either lose consciousness from the flurries, or trap ourselves another way.

My shield's song begs me to remember that the harshest storms eventually pass. But I find no comfort in the words.

How can any of us stand against such reckless cruelty?

Tears stream down my cheeks, and I surrender to the self-pity. After all the fighting and struggle and sacrifice—to end up here.

It's such a disgusting waste.

I lose track of time. I lose feeling in my body. I've let myself slip so far away, I barely hear Solana whisper, "I'm getting us out of here."

The guards rattle her chains to punish her, but it doesn't stop the unsettling stirring.

The oubliette hums with a crackly sort of energy that rises from the darkness, filling the stagnant air with a willful purpose.

The swells grow stronger. Sharper. Tearing at my chains and clawing at my limbs.

All my instincts scream for me to resist the unnatural pull. But my Westerly's song has changed. It sings of necessary sacrifice, and begs me to trust the danger.

So I release my hold as the air tangles into a cyclone of wicked wind. My chains bruise and batter until they eventually tear free—but instead of a deathly fall, I rise with the ruined drafts.

I crash into something nearby, not realizing it's a person until their arms tangle around me, and I hold tight as we launch up with the strength of a hundred winds.

Jagged rays of light split the darkness, and we explode through shards of stone and bits of cold.

Whiteness swallows everything as I crash back to my feet, fighting to keep my balance in the mound of ice.

The storm fades and the cold takes over and I recognize the courtyard—and the hum of Raiden's Shredder.

"This way," I shout, struggling toward the sound.

The arms around my waist move with me, but someone else grabs my wrist and tries to drag me the opposite way.

"The tunnel we need is back through the fortress," a deep voice says, and my brain takes a second to recognize that it's Vane.

Gus replies before I do, and I realize he's the one I'm holding on to.

"If we go back into that fortress, we'll never get out," he says. "There's a way through the Shredder. Audra has the guide."

"Aston left instructions for how he escaped," I say, clinging to Gus for warmth to keep my head clear. "It's our best chance."

"I think they're right," Solana says, wobbling through the snowdrifts.

Her eyes look glazed, her limbs unsteady.

Whatever she did to launch us out of the oubliette was not without a price.

"Aston told us the same thing," she tells Vane as he drops my hand to steady Solana.

"He also said it's super risky," Vane reminds her.

"No riskier than where we just were," I say.

Vane turns to look at me, and I can't read his expression.

"Okay," he decides. "Take us to the Shredder."

CHAPTER 31

VANE

Never mind—I vote for a new plan," I say as I stare at the spinning blades.

I know it's a dumb thing to say, but . . .

I don't see how we're supposed to survive this.

Seventeen fans, spinning so fast they look like a solid wall of metal.

"What about the trick you just used?" I ask Solana.

I'm guessing she blasted us out of the oubliette with the power of pain—and staring down this many fans, I'm okay with that. Especially since she didn't seem to be as affected by the power. She's weak and wobbly, but her eyes don't have that creepy glint.

Solana shakes her head. "I used up everything to get us out of there. And I can't sense the command I felt when you and I faced that other fan. I'm either too empty, or these blades are too strong."

"We're losing time," Gus says, pointing to the grate behind us.

Through the gaps in the metal slats I can see a group of Stormers searching the courtyard. Soon enough, one of them is going to notice that the hinges to the grate are stripped from Gus prying it open.

"They can't turn this thing on, can they?" I ask.

"It's already on," Audra says. "All Raiden does is narrow the beam of wind and aim it at his targets."

She shudders at the memory, and Gus turns a greenish color.

I feel a different kind of green when she takes his hand.

It only lasts a second. Then she's bending to pull up her pant leg and promising, "Aston's guide will get us through."

Gus crouches beside her, and as his hand brushes the red scratches on her calf, I gotta admit, I kinda want to deck him—even after I realize the scratches are the guide.

I know it's the stupidest thing I could possibly be thinking about right now, but Gus and Audra seem . . . different.

The way they clung to each other as Solana blasted us out of the oubliette.

The way he keeps leaning on her.

And let's not forget that GUS CAN ABSORB WESTERLIES!

I can't tell if he's had the full breakthrough, or just picked up a new talent. Either way, there's a story there—and I'm starting to think I'm not going to like it.

I get that they've been through a ton of crap together, and that it had to bring them closer. But *how* close—and how will I survive it if they've gotten *too* close?

I shake the doubt away, realizing I have bigger things to survive first.

"So what do these marks mean?" I ask, squatting beside them—but giving Audra as much space as I can.

Audra points to the deepest scratches. "I'm assuming these marks are the path we'll need to take. They seem to indicate the specific point we should aim for."

I guess that sorta makes sense, and it fits with how Aston created the guide, but when I check the first mark—around the two o'clock position—"Uh, I still don't see how we don't die."

"Aston warned us it would be like that, remember?" Solana jumps in. "He told us to trust the guide, not our eyes."

"Right, but . . ." I grab Socky the Duck out of my pocket and fling him through the marked place on the blades.

We all get blasted with facefuls of shredded lint.

"I'll go first," Gus says, wiping the Socky carnage out of his eyes.

"You're too weak," Audra argues.

I have to agree with her on that one. Gus looks worse than when I first saw him. His skin is as gray as his Stormer jacket, and all of his bandages—side note: Are those made from Audra's *dress*?—seem to be leaking red.

"That's *why* I'm going first," Gus says. "I'm the expendable one—"

Audra reaches for his hands. "No, you're not."

The look that passes between them definitely doesn't help my downward-spiraling rage-jealousy.

Even Solana seems to notice, because she places a hand on my shoulder—and not in a possessive way. More like a "there, there" head pat.

Great.

"I'll go first," Audra says.

"Uh-uh," I jump in.

"Yeah, you're the one with the guide," Solana reminds her. "If something happens to you, we won't know the path to follow."

Okay, that's definitely not the reason I was going with—though I hate to admit that it's actually a valid point.

"If anyone's expendable here, it's me," I tell them. "Raiden said as much back in the oubliette. Plus, I'm the one with the least injuries, so I should be the first up."

I'd be lying if I said I wasn't hoping they'd talk me out of it—or at least *try*. But of course this has to be the one time they decide to agree with me.

I turn to Audra as I move into fan-jumping position, ready to tell her I love her in case I turn into Vane-splatter. But the words vanish when I realize there's a chance she might not say it back.

"Okay," I say, pretending my eyes are watering because of the fan. "Here goes nothing."

"Be careful," she begs, and that gives me a little boost as I raise my hands above my head like I'm about to dive into a pool, and launch myself into the fan.

The air vibrates all around me, and my ears throb from the hum, but there's no pain—until I face-plant onto the cold metal floor.

"I'M ALIVE!" I shout, checking all the key body parts to

make sure everything's where it should be. "And there's not a lot of space over here, so be careful with your landing."

I'm still scrambling to my feet when Audra leaps through, tucking her legs as she lands. I'm so happy she's okay that I can't help it—I throw my arms around her.

She hugs me back, and I think maybe—*maybe*—she and I are going to be okay. Assuming we survive the next *sixteen* fans.

I let go of her as Solana lands beside us, and a few seconds later Gus follows, hitting the ground even harder than I did.

"It's the Shredder," Audra explains as Gus struggles back to his feet. "Some of its winds are still in his essence."

Gus coughs up blood, and I want to punch myself for my earlier jealousy.

"We need to move faster," I say, checking the guide, which shows the eight o'clock position on the next fan.

Audra insists on going first, and we fall into a pattern for the next seven jumps. You'd think it would get easier—but every leap is just as terrifying. All it takes is one mistake and we're splattery pulp.

Gus has to go and prove it on the tenth fan by clipping his left arm on the blades.

He doesn't chop it off—though it sure sounds like it as it happens. And he loses enough skin that when I try to help him I almost throw up.

"I'm slowing you down," Gus says as Audra rips off part of her pant leg to bind the wound. "Just leave me and I'll catch up later—"

"No way," we all interrupt.

But Gus is super wobbly. No way he can jump high enough to make it through.

"What if we throw him?" Solana asks, and I assume she's kidding.

Scarily enough, Audra's game, which is how I end up holding Gus's feet as Solana and Audra each hold his shoulders and we shove him through the blades of the next fan.

"That worked," Gus calls—though he didn't land well. But a bruised shoulder is way better than anymore missing Gus-bits.

We do the next fan the same way, and I'm starting to feel pretty good about it, until a Stormer screams, "THEY'RE IN THE SHREDDER!"

The walls around us slide to the left, nearly knocking us into the blades.

"Oh goody—this thing can move!" I grumble as we struggle to get into our Gus-tossing positions. "Because this wasn't impossible enough already."

"All Raiden wants is a shot at learning Westerly," Gus says. "So let him have me. I'll keep them distracted long enough for the rest of you to get away."

So he *has* had the breakthrough.

I'm digesting that revelation when I realize Gus is still talking.

"I'll protect your language," he tells me. "Raiden will never learn *anything*."

I have no doubt about that.

But I'm not ready to give up yet.

"Come on," I say, hoisting him over my shoulder in a fireman's carry. "We'll make this quick."

Audra shows me the position, and I rally all of my strength and jump through the fan.

The blades clip my shoulder, leaving a pretty gnarly gash—but I keep going.

Three down.

Then two.

Only one.

I'm running on pure adrenaline at this point, and feeling pretty delirious.

But I can do this.

One. More. Leap.

Audra jumps through to make sure the outside is clear and Solana goes next, promising she'll have a wind ready to catch us.

"Hey," Gus says as I catch my breath before the final jump. "Thanks for not giving up on me."

"Never," I promise. "We're getting you out of here. And then we'll figure out how to get you better."

"Maybe," he says.

But he sounds like he finally believes he has a chance of surviving this.

And he does.

We all do.

Raiden doesn't get to win this time.

I take one more second to gather my strength and leap through the final set of blades.

I clip the side of my right leg—but it feels like just a scratch. And there's a steep drop on the other side, so thank goodness for Solana's quick-catching Southerly.

Audra takes Gus from me, and I try to believe she's giving me a chance to rest. I'll stress about how tight she holds him later.

Right now I just want to celebrate that we all survived the freaking Shredder.

But of course nothing is ever that easy.

We're only free a few seconds before a Stormer shouts, "THERE THEY ARE!" and the fortress gates open to unleash the army.

CHAPTER 32

AUDRA

We'll never outrun them.

Not in our condition.

Not with healthy winds too few and far between as the Stormers close in.

But I refuse to accept only this brief glimpse of freedom.

If we can't flee, I'll fight as hard as I have to.

I beg my Westerly shield for wisdom, and search the air for other brave drafts. Amazingly, I find a Westerly, an Easterly, a Northerly, and a Southerly.

I'm about to weave them into a wind spike when all four drafts change their songs, singing of teamwork and embracing our heritage—and each draft is stretching in a different direction.

The Southerly pulls toward Solana. The Northerly toward Gus.

The Westerly toward Vane. And the Easterly wants to stay with me.

I hadn't considered that combined, our heritages represent all four languages. But the winds seem to have decided to put that into action.

"My wind is giving me a command," Vane says.

"So is mine," Solana agrees.

"I think we're all supposed to say the word at the same time," Gus adds, his voice already stronger now that he's surrounded by fresher air.

"But we should wait for the best opportunity," I whisper, even if my instincts are already twitchy.

The Stormers move closer.

Closer.

"Now!" I shout.

Together, the four of us switch to our native tongues and give our winds the same command.

Swelter!

The winds weave into a cyclone, but spin the opposite direction, and the rushing downdraft feels like a foehn. The heated, snow-melting winds usually form on the leeward side of a mountain. But the power of four seems to be able to harness the same force and amplify it.

The foehn creates a wave of melted ice as Raiden's unnatural winter seeps away in the rush of dry heat. The water crashes into the Stormers, washing them down the mountain and causing enough chaos for us to flee.

A pipeline would be a huge help, but I can't feel enough untainted drafts to build one. And honestly, I'm not sure if Gus could handle the blast. As it is, I'm dragging him through the sky, begging my Westerly shield to carry us faster.

Vane and Solana catch up, and we head for the forest. I'm hoping the trees will hide us until we have a chance to form an actual plan.

"There's too many of them," Vane shouts, pointing to the trail of reinforcements chasing us down.

I shudder when I see two Living Storms among the ranks, and I can't help worrying it's proof that Aston and my mother never got away.

"Solana, can't you do anything?" Vane asks.

"The need isn't giving me any commands!" she shouts back.

I'm not sure what that means, but a funnel of fire erupts behind us, turning the world to flashes of blinding color and deafening howls and squeals.

"Was that you?" Vane asks Solana.

"No, it was me."

The familiar voice doesn't seem real until two figures dart out of the shadows.

One wears a ripped hooded cloak. The other has long dark hair.

My emotions turn to thunder as I gape at Aston and my mother.

"I thought you left," Vane shouts.

"So did I," Aston says as he snaps his fingers and sends another firewhirl spinning to life.

The burning spiral cuts a wall of flame through the tress, and when a Living Storm tries to push through, its funnels ignite.

"That should hold them off for a bit." His smile fades when he notices Gus. "I see Raiden's tricks haven't changed. I can carry him. You both look . . . weakened."

"How do we know you're really on our side?" Gus asks.

"The fact that I launched the fire at *them* seems like a pretty big clue," Aston tells him. "And because I could be safely back in my cave, but I was convinced to linger in case you got yourselves into this kind of mess. And . . . because I know your pain."

He holds up his punctured hand.

"If you want to stick with the pretty girl, I don't blame you," Aston adds. "But only do it if you're both strong enough."

"I can handle it," I promise, readjusting Gus for a better hold.

"We should control our speed," my mother says, keeping her eyes anywhere but on me. "Too much force might tear apart his injuries."

"That's what happens when you send someone off to be tortured," I snap.

She still doesn't look my way, but her whole body goes rigid as she mumbles something I can't hear over the squealing.

"What's that noise?" Vane asks, making me realize the sound is more than the pressure in my head. "Is that the Stormer's gadget?"

My mother nods and holds up a silver spinning anemometer. "It sprang to life when you led the army this way. That's how we knew to be ready."

"The Stormers use them to keep track of each other," Vane explains to me. "So when it goes off, we know they're close."

"How many Westerlies can you gather?" Aston asks Vane.

"I feel three," he says.

"There's a fourth one if you stretch your consciousness closer toward the mountain," I tell him.

That earns me far more attention than we have time for, so I head off their questions with a quick "Yes, Gus and I had the fourth breakthrough. Once we get somewhere safe I'll explain how it happened."

There's something sad about Vane's posture as he nods, and I wonder if he's bothered we share his language.

But I don't have time to consider such trivialities. I'm helping Vane gather the Westerlies when the sky goes still and the winds holding us waver and fade.

We barely manage to stay airborne as Raiden shouts, "You'll never leave this mountain!"

His voice is everywhere and nowhere. A ghost of shadow and flame.

"Surrender now," he snarls, "or experience a new realm of pain."

"I think we'll go with option C!" Vane shouts back.

Only two Westerlies manage to break through whatever wall Raiden has created, and it doesn't feel like enough. But Vane weaves them around us anyway.

"You'll regret leaving," Raiden warns us. "You have no grasp of the price you'll pay."

"Grasp *this*!" Vane shouts, ordering the Westerlies to rise.

Aston launches another firewhirl as the winds blast us away— the forest blurring with sparks and smoke as we streak through the sky.

I'd feel more triumphant if Gus weren't coughing and sputtering.

"We need to slow down!" I shout. "The speed is tearing him apart."

"If we do, they'll be on us in seconds," Vane argues, pointing to the anemometer, which is still squeaking, warning us there are Stormers on our tail.

"Maybe not," Aston says, testing the air with his fingers. "I don't feel any Stormers nearby."

"But I still feel the chill," my mother whispers.

Gus coughs again and Aston's eyes widen and he shouts a dozen curses as he grabs my mother's needled blade and swipes it toward Gus's throat.

"What are you doing?" I scream.

"Trying to save him."

He slashes Gus's neck before I can pull away.

The blow barely grazes Gus's skin, and there's so much shouting and squealing and flailing, I can't figure out what anyone is saying, until my brain catches two words:

Suicide draft.

"NO!" I scream. "GET RID OF IT!"

Aston slashes again.

But the windslicer does nothing.

Neither do any of the commands Aston and Solana shout.

And Gus keeps choking harder and harder, right up until the moment his neck snaps and his body goes limp and cold.

CHAPTER 33

VANE

G us is . . .
    I can't.

CHAPTER 34

AUDRA

failed.

CHAPTER 35

VANE

don't understand.

How can Gus be—

A sharp sting across my cheek knocks me back to reality.

"Finally," Aston says, and I realize he slapped me—and that I've lost control of the winds.

"I need you to set us down," he tells me. "Can you handle that?"

I try.

It's a bumpy landing, but the snow softens it—mostly.

I sink into the cold, letting the numbness take over. It helps me face the question I don't want to ask.

Was there something we could've done?

I try to search for warnings we might've missed, but nothing stands out—except Raiden's last threat about the price we'd pay if we escaped.

"Where's Audra?" I ask, flailing to sit up.

"She's fine," Aston promises. "You all are. The anemometer's been silent, ever since . . ."

He doesn't finish the sentence. But his eyes dart to where Audra sits half buried in the snow, clinging to Gus's body.

Gus's *body*.

My stomach heaves, and I have to crawl away and puke into some bushes.

I keep gagging long after I run out of bile. And even when that stops, I can't seem to get up.

"Come on," Solana says, her voice thick with tears as she grabs my good arm and tries to pull me to my feet. "The storm's getting worse."

I hadn't noticed the wind, but she's right. It's tearing branches off the trees. And the thunder sounds like a war zone.

"You need to get inside," Arella tells us.

"Inside?"

I thought we were in the middle of a forest. But I turn to where she's pointing and see we're actually in the middle of . . . I'm not sure.

There's a huge red-and-white building with pointed roofs and narrow windows. It almost looks like a castle, but I'm guessing it's probably a hotel.

"You have to get away from the wind," Arella says. "I'm sending Raiden a false trail, but he won't believe it if he picks up the real one."

She must be using the same trick she used after she killed my parents to make him believe we were all dead. Sylphs lose a piece of ourselves when someone we love dies, and Arella knows how to change the loss and make it carry a message. The concept makes zero sense, but if it buys us some time, I'm not going to stop her.

We need to clean our wounds and rest for a second. But we've only gone a few steps before I hear Audra let out a sharp cry.

I'm picturing snapped necks and suicide drafts as I tear through the snow to her side.

It's almost as heartbreaking to find the real problem is Aston trying to pull her away from Gus.

"I'll take care of him," he promises.

She tightens her hold, kicking and sobbing and flailing.

Until she notices me.

The pain in her eyes nearly knocks me over, and I try to think of something to say.

All I can do is stretch out my arms and offer her a place to hide.

Slowly—very slowly—she lets go of Gus and stumbles over to me, burying her face in my shoulder.

I hold her as tight as I can, just like I did after the storm that shattered our families.

A different kind of bond formed between us that day.

But right now . . . I can't feel it.

I can't feel anything except a rage so thick it fills me with the darkest, coldest kind of hate.

A crunch of branches makes us jump, and we both turn to watch Aston carrying Gus into the trees.

I don't know what he's going to do with him, but I'm glad I won't have to see it.

"He's gone," Audra whispers. "How can he be gone?"

"I don't know."

But I know everything's changed.

My instincts have fallen silent.

I'm finally ready to do what has to be done.

I'm going to end this the only way it will ever really be over.

I'm going to find a way to kill Raiden.

CHAPTER 36

AUDRA

should've paid closer attention.

Should've seen something that could've saved Gus.

Instead, I hovered helplessly by and let Raiden snuff the life out of him.

After all the sacrifices Gus made.

All the suffering he endured.

I failed him.

And then . . . I breathed in his gift.

I didn't want to.

But Gus chose me.

His final message said, *To make sure you keep fighting.*

So I inhaled the power and let it settle into my essence, just like the day I breathed in my father's gift.

A tiny piece of him to cling to.

But it will never be enough.

And I will never be worthy.

Aston returns from the forest with empty arms and an empty stare, and I can't bring myself to ask what he did with the body.

"I know you're not going to believe this," he says, turning his face to the stormy sky. "But there was nothing you could've done to change this. Your friend was lost the second Raiden tied that draft around his neck. I would know. That's how Raiden broke me."

He pulls back his cloak and points to the holes lining his shoulder.

"I made it through twenty-nine days of torture. But on the thirtieth, Raiden threatened to bind me with a suicide draft. I knew that meant I'd never be able to leave. So I gave in to the power of pain to save my neck—literally."

Vane pulls me closer when I shiver.

"Why didn't Gus tell us?" Vane asks.

"He probably didn't know. Raiden bound Gus to break *you*." Aston's eyes focus on me. "I'm sure he expected there would be some sort of escape or rescue, and he wanted to ensure you'd regret it."

"I do," I whisper.

But there are questions that go with that—questions I can't seem to hide from.

Would I have stayed if I'd known?

Would I have remained in that dungeon?

Sent Vane and Solana away and stayed at Raiden's mercy?

I know what the answers *should* be, but . . . I don't know.

"It's okay," Vane says, brushing tears off my cheeks. "I'm here."

He is.

And I don't deserve him.

I don't deserve anything.

"I see the war you're fighting," Aston tells me. "Don't let Raiden win. Take your freedom and use it to resist him."

"I'm going to do more than resist him," Vane says.

"Hm. I believe you," Aston says. "Though you realize that comes with challenges."

"I don't care—there has to be a way to do it."

I know what they're discussing.

I know it's my cue to be strong and join them. That's what Gus is counting on. He wants me to keep fighting.

But I can't help whispering, "Raiden always wins."

"Not always," a new voice says, and my blood boils when I realize it's my mother.

"How would you know?" I shout. "Do you think you beat him just because you refused to be his queen?"

"Wait—what?" Vane asks as my mother blanches.

By the time she answers, her voice is as smooth as ever, and I want to claw her eyes out. "I wondered if he'd tell you."

"Is that why you're here?" I ask. "To figure out how many of your secrets I uncovered?"

"No. I came to help my daughter."

"Help me? YOU LET RAIDEN TAKE ME!"

I tear away from Vane, grabbing my mother by her shoulders. "Do you have any idea what I've been through? What he did to me?"

Vane's strangled choke makes me regret the words, but it's too late to take them back.

"Stay away from me," I tell my mother. "I've had enough of your help."

I only mean to shove her away.

But I'm not used to my new strength.

My mother flies backward, crashing into one of the trees with a crunch that sounds like breaking bone.

I don't check to see how badly she's hurt.

I don't wonder about the red that splatters the snow.

I let Vane wrap his arms around me and lead me away, telling myself I'm finally free of her.

CHAPTER 37

VANE

have no idea how badly Arella's injured—but I can't deal with it right now.

We have to get out of the wind—and Audra and I both need to get away from the blood.

So I leave Aston to clean up, and lead Audra over to the hotel.

Solana's waiting for us outside the main doors.

I . . . sorta forgot about her.

I feel even crappier when I see her eyes are puffy from crying.

Gus's death is a huge blow for her, too—he's the whole reason she agreed to help me.

I offer her my free arm as an apology, and after a second, she takes it, leaning against my shoulder as the three of us make our way into the lobby.

The place is *huge*—arched ceilings and dangling chandeliers. Music plays softly in the background, and it smells like flowers and money. But what throws me is the mass of people. Hundreds of them, crowding around the scattered furniture.

And of course chaos erupts when they notice the three bleeding teenagers.

They all shout on top of one another and hustle us to one of the couches.

A guy in a stuffy blazer drops to his knees beside us and starts asking ten thousand questions. I thought he might be a doctor, but he sounds more like the hotel's manager.

He seems to think we're hikers who got caught in the storm.

I don't bother correcting him. It's not like I can tell him we escaped from a sylph fortress and have an army of wind warriors trying to kill us.

"I'd call for an ambulance," he says, "but we're snowed in. Have been for days."

That explains why there's such a huge crowd in the lobby. I bet everyone's freaking out, wondering when they'll get home.

"That's fine," I tell him, since it's not like we can take human medicine anyway. "We just need a first aid kit."

"And maybe some clean clothes, if you have them," Solana adds.

His eyes narrow at my leg, and I notice it's dripping blood on their fancy rug.

"Sorry," I mumble, covering the puddle with my shoe. "It looks worse than it is."

"I hope so." He turns to a girl wearing a shiny vest and a bow tie, who looks like she couldn't possibly hate her job any more. "Can you help them to the bathrooms? I'll meet you there with the first aid kit, and anything else I can find."

She nods, but stares at us like she's just been asked to defuse a bomb. "Can you guys walk or . . . ?"

I nod, and help Solana and Audra to their feet. "Just show us which way."

The crowd parts as she tells us to follow her, and our footsteps sound too loud on the marble floor.

I notice a bunch of kids hiding their faces as we pass, and they look even more terrified when I try to smile at them.

Vest Girl heads for the ladies' room, and doesn't stop me when I go in with them. I set Audra on the chair—since when do bathrooms have chairs?—and she stares blankly into space.

"The paper towels are over there," Vest Girl says, pointing to the counter. "And soap is by the sinks. And, um . . . yeah."

"You don't have to stay," I tell her, when she stands there shuffling her feet. "I'm sure this isn't going to be pretty."

I hike up my pant leg and show her the oozing cut from the Shredder. The one on my shoulder is worse. I can feel it dripping down my back.

"Ouch," she whispers. "Did you get attacked by a moose?"

"A moose?"

"Moose can be mean," she explains.

There's a joke there somewhere. But I don't have the energy to make it.

She leaves us then, and I hobble over to a sink, catching my first glimpse of myself in the mirror. Between the mud and the blood and the red-rimmed eyes, I definitely get why the kids were hiding from zombie-Vane.

Solana looks almost as bad as she limps up beside me. She's covered in scratches and bruises, and her leg wound has started bleeding again.

"Here," I say, soaking a paper towel and handing it to her.

She takes it and crouches down, using it to clean the cut on my leg.

Shame burns my cheeks. "I didn't mean for you to take care of *me*."

"It's my turn. Sorry," she adds when I hiss through my teeth.

"It's fine. It just stings."

"It does."

Her eyes turn glassy.

I pull at my sleeves, realizing I'm still wearing a Stormer uniform. I want to tear it into mangled shreds. But I should probably make sure they can find me something else to wear first.

"Are you okay?" I mumble. "Do you need to talk about . . . anything?"

Yes, I know I sound lame.

"Maybe later," she says. "You should be helping Audra."

My eyes stray to the chair, where Audra hasn't moved.

"Do you think she's in shock?" I whisper.

"I don't see how she couldn't be. What happened with Arella? I heard screaming,"

"Honestly? I have no idea. Arella might be okay, but . . ."

Solana closes her eyes. "I don't hear an echo."

"Would you really be able to hear it? We're inside—and the storm is super loud out there."

"I can still hear whispers of Gus's."

She wraps her arms around herself, and I try to hear what she's hearing, but my senses are too dull.

Or maybe I'm too numb.

"So you don't think Arella's dead?" I whisper.

"I feel like we'd know if she was. She has such a powerful presence. The sky will shift when she joins it."

I can't decide if that's good news or bad news.

"How exactly did Audra hurt her?" Solana asks.

"She flung her like she weighed nothing more than paper. It was crazy."

Solana covers her mouth. "I wonder if that means Gus gave her his gift. I thought I heard something transfer as he died, but it was hard to tell."

I guess that makes sense, given what I know about Gus's ability. And I know it shouldn't bother me—at least not for the *reason* it bothers me. But my hands still curl up so tight, my nails cut into my palms.

"Want me to find Aston and see if he has any news on Arella?" Solana asks. "He won't be able to come inside without drawing too much attention."

Yeah, I can't even imagine what would happen if he walked in here with all his holes.

"It can wait," I tell her. "We should stay out of the wind as long as we can."

Our eyes both drift back to Audra.

"Go," Solana tells me. "She needs you,"

She needs *someone*.

But I'm not sure if it's me anymore.

"Seriously, Vane," Solana says, "don't overthink it."

I try to breathe the words in, but they feel too raw and scratchy in my chest.

"How bad do you think her wounds are under that jacket?" I whisper.

Solana bites her lip. "I don't know. After Gus . . ."

My stomach sloshes with a fresh wave of bile as Solana soaks a stack of paper towels and hands them to me. "If you need any help, just ask."

I give myself three deep breaths. Then I make my way over to the chair.

"Hey," I say, crouching in front of Audra.

She doesn't blink.

I don't know what I'm supposed to do here. Shake her? Wait for smelling salts?

I settle for taking her hands, surprised at how much heat sparks at her touch.

"There you are," I whisper when her eyes slowly clear.

She turns to scan the room.

"We're in a hotel," I tell her. "They're letting us use their bathroom, and they're hopefully getting us new clothes and bandages. Do you need water or something? I know you don't like to drink or eat, but—"

Audra shakes her head. "My mother?"

It's such a relief to hear her voice, I have to resist the urge to throw my arms around her.

I brush the hair out of her eyes, instead. "I don't know. But Solana doesn't feel an echo."

She looks just as torn by the news as I feel.

I'm trying to think of something brilliant and healing to say. Best I can come up with is: "Can I check your wounds?"

"I'll be gentle, I promise," I add when she flinches.

"It's not that. I . . . don't want you to see."

Oh.

My face burns as I remember what I've learned about sylphs and underwear. I'm guessing that applies to bras and stuff too . . .

"I can turn away while you take off your jacket," I tell her. "And then you can use it to cover your, um . . . you know."

"I didn't mean *that*," she says, and I'm pretty sure she's blushing.

My smile dies really quick when she says, "I don't want you to see what he did to me."

Fury lumps up in my throat, and it's not easy to choke it down. It's even harder to find the words to explain what I'm feeling.

"I hate him for hurting you, Audra. And I hate seeing you in pain. But . . . that's it, okay? It's not going to change anything. I'll still . . ."

I stop myself from saying I'll still love her.

I can't tell if it'll make things worse or better.

She swallows several times, then nods and starts unbuttoning her jacket.

"I'm going to turn away until you tell me it's safe."

I look toward the sink and find Solana watching us. She's spinning the link on her wrist, but when we make eye contact, she goes back to cleaning the wound on her leg.

Audra takes her deepest breath yet as she tells me she's ready.

I still need a few more seconds.

"Is it that bad?" she asks when I suck in a breath.

"No, it's nothing like . . ." Probably better not to mention Gus.

There are only five cuts, and they're not as deep as I'd feared.

But . . . they're very *specific*.

"I know the cuts are a mark," Audra says. "You don't have to be afraid to tell me. What did he carve?"

I sigh and dab the three cuts on her right shoulder. "Right here, he carved a *W*. I'm guessing he wanted to mark you as a Westerly."

She nods. "I suppose that's fitting." Her fingers tease the breeze still sliding over her skin. "It was my shield that triggered my breakthrough, if you're wondering," she whispers. "I didn't even know what was happening at first. I thought I needed you there. But apparently not."

I'm guessing she doesn't mean the words to feel like a windslicer jab to my gut, but . . . they have that effect anyway.

"What else?" she asks, and it takes me a second to realize she's gone back to wondering about her cuts.

I move to her left shoulder and dab the long, curved gash. "He carved his storm cloud over here. I'm guessing that was to brand you as *his*."

Her hands curl into fists.

Mine are doing the same thing, wringing the red-stained water out of the paper towel I'm holding.

"And the last one?" she asks.

My fingers move to her lower back. "This one's just a jagged line. But it's the deepest. I think he wanted to hurt you."

"Probably," she mumbles. "But I still got off easy."

"This isn't *easy.*" My hands are shaking so hard, I nearly drop the paper towels.

I don't want to ask my next question, but it has to be done. "Did he . . . I mean . . . are there any other wounds I should check? Or . . . did he . . ."

Nope. I can't say it.

"There's nothing else," she says, focusing on the floor.

I turn away, so she won't see the tears I'm blinking back. And that's when I notice we're not alone.

The blazer guy stands in the doorway holding two plastic first aid kits and a stack of clothing in his shaky hands.

His eyes are focused on the cuts on Audra's back. "What happened to you guys?" he whispers. "Is it something we need to be prepared for?"

I'm guessing he's imagining, like, serial killers or something.

If only it were that easy.

I could tell him the whole complicated truth. But I don't have the time or the energy to make him believe me.

Plus, his question made me realize something way more important.

There are hundreds of people trapped in this hotel—and we're putting all of them in danger just by being here.

"We'll leave as soon as we're done cleaning up," I tell him as Solana takes the supplies. "And once we're gone, you need to bar the doors. Don't let *anyone* go outside."

"Why? What's out there?"

"Just stay out of the wind. And when the storm clears in a few hours, get everyone out of here."

"There's no way it'll clear up that soon," he argues.

But he's wrong.

It will.

I'm going to lure Raiden away from this mountain.

And then, I'm going to end this.

CHAPTER 38

AUDRA

The groundling's clothes feel strange against my skin.

Everything feels strange.

Especially when I check my reflection.

I look . . . normal.

A bit banged up, and definitely exhausted.

But still me, even in the tight groundling clothes.

If only I could *feel* like me.

I try to braid my hair, but lifting my arms pulls at the wounds on my back.

"Need help?" Solana offers.

I shake my head.

It's not important.

I'm not really a guardian anymore.

I'm not sure what I am.

"Is it okay if I come in?" Vane calls through the door, and I feel my lips curl with half a smile.

He left us alone to get dressed in privacy, without our even asking.

"Yep, we're all covered," Solana says, fussing with the sleeves of her pale green coat.

Between that and the pants, it's the most clothing I've ever seen her wear. And it makes my eyes linger on her face, which has such soft, sweet features it's hard not to—

My thought drops away when Vane shuffles into the room.

He's changed into dark pants and a shirt that doesn't really count as a shirt at the moment, since he's only managed to pull on a portion of one sleeve. The rest of the blue fabric is tangled and bunched between his neck and the thick bandage on his elbow, leaving his chest and stomach exposed and . . .

Wow.

"Can I get a little help here?" he asks.

I'm wondering how many sit-ups he's been doing when Solana says, "I think I'll let Audra handle this one."

She smiles as she says it, but I hear the tight edge to her voice.

It makes me glance at Vane, wondering if he's wishing she'd volunteered. It's a crazy doubt, I know—but I can't help feeling it.

Redness colors Vane's cheeks, and he shrugs his free arm. But it's the intensity of his eyes that makes my heart leap into my throat.

He's focused only on me—his stare like a rope, pulling me closer.

"Getting dressed with a bum elbow is harder than it should be," he says as I try to ease the tight fabric over his bandage. "Plus, I'm not sure if this shirt is really my size."

It's probably not.

Were his shoulders always this broad?

I have to lean closer to untangle a twist in his sleeve, and end up brushing my hand against his stomach.

Again. *Wow.*

I'm positive I'm blushing. And the air has turned tingly, making my head fuzzy.

I give his shirt a final tug to cover him, and the fabric suctions against his muscles like a second skin.

"Thanks," Vane whispers, leaning so close his breath skips across my cheek.

His hair is damp and his face scrubbed clean, bringing back a hint of the boyishness I remember. But his features still look more angled and shadowed than they were.

These last few days have aged him.

My eyes wander back to his tight shirt without my telling them to, and I notice a necklace that must've been hidden by the bunched up fabric.

"You have a guardian pendant now?" I ask, sliding my finger across the blue cord.

"Actually, it's yours," he whispers. "Do you want it back?"

I shake my head.

I like knowing he has it. Somehow it makes the space between us feel smaller.

"Aston gave it to me," he explains, "so I'd have a way to see you were still alive. I don't know what I would've done . . ."

His voice catches then, and he clears his throat, his eyes glistening with tears.

My hand slides to where he's clutching the silver feather pendant, and I wrap my fingers around his.

"I'm sorry I worried you," I tell him.

"Are you seriously apologizing for Raiden capturing you? If anything, I . . ." He shakes his head and steps back, putting a gap between us. "Are you *really* okay?"

"I'm fine."

I scratch at my sleeves, needing to keep my hands busy.

"Is your shirt itchy?" he asks.

I run my hands over the smooth purple fabric. "Actually, it's too soft."

My guardian uniform was coarse and heavy. Comfort makes me uncomfortable.

"Well, I feel like Captain America in this thing," he says, pulling his shirt, trying to stretch it out. "Though I guess I wouldn't mind if it turned me into a supersoldier."

"You're doing fine on your own," Solana promises. "Plus, you have awesome backup."

She smiles, but Vane's lips stay straight and serious, and his eyes shift to the floor. "Actually I've been thinking about that—"

"Uh-uh," Solana interrupts. "I'm seeing this through to the end."

"So am I," I tell him.

"Just hear me out," Vane argues. "Aston can fly you to his cave and keep you safe—"

"I don't want to be safe," Solana tells him. "And I don't need to be taken care of. You've seen me fight. You know I can handle myself. And whether you like it or not, you're going to need my power."

"What power?" I ask, realizing there's an even better question. "How did you get us out of the oubliette?"

Vane and Solana share a look.

"Maybe we shouldn't think about that right now," Vane says.

"No, she might as well know." Solana leans against the wall, trying to look confident. But her hands are twitching. "Just promise me you'll hear me out before you judge me, okay?"

She waits for me to agree, then adds, "I . . . know how to use the power of pain."

I fall back a step.

I can't decide what bothers me more: That I never noticed? Or that they didn't tell me.

"You knew?" I ask Vane. "How could you let her—"

"He hasn't *let me* do anything," Solana says. "It was my choice—and it saved all of our lives."

"At what cost?" I demand.

"I haven't ruined any winds, if that's what you're asking. All I've done is store drafts that have already been damaged, and draw them out when I need them."

"That won't stop the power from taking over," I tell her.

"Yeah, I've been warned—a *lot*." She shares another look with Vane, and I feel my stomach turn.

"You're okay with this?" I ask him.

"Of course not."

I'm calming a little. Until he says, "But . . ."

He sighs when he sees the look on my face. "Sometimes there isn't a perfect solution—and I know what you're thinking—"

"I don't think you do."

Westerlies are supposed to value peace above everything else.

Does he really trust Solana more than his own heritage?

"You didn't let me finish explaining," Solana reminds us. "I had a revelation when we were trapped in the oubliette—and it changed everything. I realized the power of pain feeds off my needs—and that's an incredibly selfish process. So I thought, maybe that's why it's so destructive. It's there to serve my every whim, of course that would be addictive. And I wondered what would happen if I focused on the needs of others instead. So I told myself that I didn't care about me. I just wanted to get you guys out of there. I didn't care if I had to be left behind, or sacrifice myself to save you, and I repeated it over and over until it felt true. When it was, the need came up with a command that blasted us out of there. And the power didn't have as strong of an effect on me."

"I guess that explains why you were able to stop us from falling even though Raiden said he wouldn't be able to do it," Vane mumbles. "I'm pretty sure he hasn't thought about anyone besides himself in . . . ever."

I suppose it does make sense.

"But I still think it's dangerous to keep using the power," I tell her.

"I know," she says. "I'll stop as soon as I can. But we all know it's going to take *everything* we have to beat Raiden."

"No, it's going to take everything *I* have," Vane corrects. "*I'm* the last Westerly. I'm the one this is all about."

"It may have started with the Westerlies," Solana argues, "but then Raiden stole Brezengarde from my family. I'm just as involved as you are. And Raiden has the power of pain—and his backlash. You can't expect to handle all of that by yourself."

"I don't," he says. "I have it all planned out. I'm going to lure him somewhere far away from people, so I can make sure no one else gets hurt. And then I'm going to bring in the Gales. They've learned the power of pain, so they can keep the Stormers busy—"

"Wait," I interrupt. "The Gales are using the power of pain?"

Now I truly do feel sick.

"Os started training them when we left," Vane says. "I tried to stop him. But . . ."

There's the "but" again. And this time it destroys the whole Gale Force.

"They made their choice," Vane tells me. "So I might as well not let the power go to waste."

"You don't sound like a Westerly," I tell him.

His smile looks painful. "Maybe not. But I've still got a little bit of Easterly left in me. I've held on to as much as I could."

His hand moves to his heart as if he's reaching for the strands of our bond.

I thought they'd all been severed, but I can almost feel them tangling around me, connecting us together.

"I can use the emergency call to bring the Gales to me," he says. "And with their help, I can end this. And you guys can go somewhere safe. I'll make sure I tell the Gales what Solana learned—"

"I'll tell them myself," Solana interrupts. "This is my fight too, Vane. You're not going to change my mind."

He opens his mouth and lets out a heavy sigh before he focuses on me.

"I'm going," I tell him.

He moves closer, his eyes as desperate as his voice. "Please, Audra. I need to know you're safe. If anything happens . . ."

"I'll be fine. I know how to handle myself in a fight."

"Not against Raiden. He has this backlash thing that rebounds any attacks. Plus Aston thinks what happened to Gus was because Raiden knew there was a chance you'd escape. That means he planned for this to happen—who knows what other horrifying things he'll do? And if I lose you again . . ." His voice cracks, and he squeezes my guardian pendant. "Please, if I ever meant anything to you, please do this for me."

I'm so lost in the impossible choices it takes me a second to catch his deeper worry.

"Of course you meant something to me," I whisper. "Why would you even say that?"

He shakes his head. "I'm not saying this to try to pressure you."

"And I'm not saying it because I feel pressured."

Hope clears the sadness clouding his expression, but he blinks it away.

"I just need to know that Raiden will never touch you again," he tells me.

"Then let me help you kill him," I say, glad my words hold steady.

My Westerly instincts seem to be silenced by my hunger for justice and revenge. I wonder if Vane is feeling the same.

"But what if . . . ," Vane starts, until I reach up and cover his lips with my finger.

I meant only to silence him, but the spark of heat nearly knocks me over.

It's such a simple thing, touching him like this.

I don't know why I've built it up in my head to be so complicated.

I stare into his eyes, and it feels like falling into a memory and glimpsing the future all at the same time.

"We've done all of this together," I whisper. "Even when we were kids, it's always been you and me, standing strong against the storm. And that's how we have to end it."

My other hand moves to his cheek, pulling him even closer, until there's nothing separating us but the last of our hesitation.

I never thought I'd be ready for this moment again.

But it's like Gus said.

We chose each other once.

I just have to show Vane that I still believe.

My eyes focus on his mouth, and Vane sucks in a shaky breath.

He wants this.

So do I.

And yet, as I lean that last little bit, Vane turns his face aside and pulls away.

CHAPTER 39

VANE

Audra was going to kiss me.

WHY DIDN'T I LET HER KISS ME?

Why did I listen to that tiny, niggling voice in the back of my head?

The rest of my brain was whooping and hollering and shooting off confetti cannons—but that stupid freaking voice had to go and ask, *How can she actually be ready for this?*

Gus died like an hour ago.

And she still doesn't know how badly she hurt her mom.

And she's been a hostage for days.

And all of that just doesn't seem like the right time for her to be making a major life decision.

So I turned my freaking head away, and now she's looking at me with so much shock and betrayal I'm tempted to cling to her ankles so she can't leave until I've had a chance to explain.

Instead, I open my big, stupid mouth and say, "Sorry, it's just . . . Solana's over there. . . ."

And with that, Audra walks away.

The door slams behind her, and I sink to my knees.

"Well," Solana says as I punch the floor—and then curse at myself for punching the floor. "*That* was unexpected."

I bury my face in my throbbing hands.

I wanted to do it right this time.

Not just right—*better.*

I mean . . . the first time we bonded was in the middle of a freaking battlefield, with a dead Stormer, like, *right there.* And our next big, important kiss was in Death Valley, right after Gus killed his father's Living Storm and there were Stormers attacking us.

Is it so bad that I didn't want the third time to happen in a bloodstained girls' bathroom with Solana standing by watching?

Especially since I don't see how Audra could really be ready to make that kind of commitment. I just want to make sure I don't end up on her list of regrets.

"For what it's worth," Solana says, "I think you did the right thing."

"Do me a favor and tell Audra that, will you? Actually—don't, she'll probably read something *really* bad into that."

In fact, the longer I stay in here alone with Solana, the worse I'm making all of this look.

"Why does love have to be so complicated?" I ask.

I mean seriously, none of those sappy movies my mom loves to watch have betrothals and suicide drafts and broken bonds in them. Can't I just be the guy who stands outside her window holding a boom box or something?

"Well, I don't exactly have a lot of experience in this area," Solana says, "but I *know* you guys will work this out. She'll be thanking you in a few days."

A few *days*?

Why does that sound like *forever*?

Solana offers me a hand up so I'll stop being a Vane-lump on the floor. I'm about to take it when I realize how not cool it is to make her deal with *my* love drama.

"We should go," I say, getting up on my own.

Audra's waiting for us on the other side of the door with her coat buttoned up to her neck and her eyes glued firmly to her brown hiking shoes. I'm pretty sure she's been crying—proof that doing the right thing sucks for everybody.

But there's nothing I can do about it right now, except lead the way back to the entrance.

The lobby seems twice as full as it was before, including several moms holding tiny babies.

"We have to get Raiden away from here," I mumble.

"Where are we going to lead him?" Solana asks.

She emphasizes the word "we," and I know there's no point arguing—though I can't help hoping all the fresh awkwardness might convince Audra to go with Aston.

"I'm still figuring out the best place to go," I admit.

It would take too much energy to head all the way back to the desert—and my hometown has suffered enough, anyway.

The closer we get to the Gales, though, the faster they'll be able to meet us, so we need to focus on places that are in the middle.

"It should be Nebraska," Audra says without looking at me. "The winds are strong there. And there's plenty of empty land. And . . . that's where it all began—for us, at least."

Actually, that's kind of . . . poetic.

Let's crush Raiden the same place he tried to crush us.

"We'll need to take a pipeline," I tell her. "That way we have a little time to prepare."

"Prepare for what?" Blazer Guy asks, coming up beside me.

"Nothing you need to concern yourself with," Solana promises.

He looks pissed at her answer, and the last thing we need is a big scene, so I tell him, "It's going to happen far away from here. Just don't forget what I said about getting everyone out when the storm clears. And keep them away from the windows for the next bit too."

"Why?" he asks.

"Let's just say there's a chance the storm will get a lot stronger once we head out there."

I can tell he thinks I'm a million miles beyond crazy, and in some ways he's kind of right.

"Thanks for the help," I tell him.

"And the clothes," Solana adds.

"You can thank the other guests for those. Everyone searched their suitcases for spare things. Keep that in mind when you do . . . whatever it is you're going to do out there. You owe these people."

"We do," I say, and he must believe me, because he leaves us there and calls for everyone to get back when we open the door.

The cold crashes into us like a tidal wave, the winds trying to knock us over as we sink into the thigh-deep snow. We have to hold hands and trudge together to make any progress, and Audra makes a point of clinging to Solana instead of me.

Aston emerges from the trees after we've distanced ourselves from the building. "Judging by the tension radiating from the three of you," he calls over the storm, "I'm guessing there's a rather interesting story to tell."

"How is my mother?" Audra asks.

"Ah, so you *are* concerned about her. Then perhaps it's happy news that she's very much alive and resting just over there." He points to a clump of trees on the far side of the hotel. "She's a bit unhappy about the branch I had to remove from her shoulder, but I keep telling her holes are the new rage. She's also in a delicious amount of pain. I think I absorbed two fixes already."

"Fixes?" Audra asks.

"That's how she's repaying me for helping. Didn't Loverboy tell you? What *have* you two been talking about?"

"Gus," I jump in, glad when Aston's cocky smile fades. "We've also been coming up with a plan to take down Raiden."

"Having any luck with that one?" Aston asks.

"It's still a work in progress," I admit. "But we know we're taking a pipeline to Nebraska and luring him there so he can't hurt any more humans."

"And I presume you know how to aim your pipeline to make

sure you don't blast us to the other side of the planet?" Aston asks as I gather enough winds to weave one with the power of four.

"Not really," I admit. "But I'm going to trust the wind. I'll tell it where we need to go, and hopefully it'll take me there. And wait— did you say 'us'?"

I thought this was the part where Aston tells me it's a horrible, stupid plan and he'll be zipping back to his cave.

Instead he says, "I'll go check on Arella. Let me know when we're ready to leave."

"We?" Solana asks, clearly as surprised as I am.

"Of course. I can't trust you three not to screw this up—and if you do, Raiden will be far too powerful for my liking. And Arella needs some time for a heart-to-heart with her daughter."

"Uh-uh," I say. "You can come, but she stays away. I don't trust her, and Audra—"

"No, it's fine," Audra interrupts. "We're going to need her."

"Her gift isn't worth it," I argue.

"Maybe not, but she'll be valuable in other ways."

"Like what?" I ask. "Betraying us? Making sure we're captured?"

"Well now, entertaining as this lovers' spat is, I'd better go gather your mother," Aston tells us. "I wonder how her injury will fare through the pipeline. Here's hoping it's excruciating."

He trudges off to get Arella, and I start building the pipeline, whispering a plea to the Westerly for it to get us to Nebraska in one piece.

The wind's song doesn't change, so I have no idea if it's going to help. Still, I give the final command and spin the drafts into the sky-high funnel we need.

"Oh good, our transport looks even more unstable than I imagined," Aston says, hobbling over, carrying Arella like a baby.

Her shoulder is tied in a shred of his cloak, and her skin has about as much color as the flurries of snow. But her eyes are open and her breaths look steady, so it's better than I was expecting.

Until Arella draws her windslicer.

"Oh, relax," she says as I grab the nearest winds and weave them into a wind spike. "I only wanted to give this to my daughter. I thought she might be glad to have a weapon. And she's rendered my sword arm quite useless."

Audra hesitates a moment before she takes the windslicer.

She slashes it a few times, and doesn't put it away.

I decide to keep my wind spike as well. It can't hurt to have a solid weapon handy.

Arella points to the pipeline. "I'm sure Raiden can see that—if he hasn't picked up your traces already."

"That's kind of the point," I say. "Can you make sure he knows where we're going?"

Arella nods. "As soon as we arrive, I'll send him a very special invitation."

"I'm sure you will," Audra mutters, slashing her windslicer again. "That's what you do best."

I want to reach for her hand, but that would probably be a bad idea—especially now that she's armed.

"I'll go first," I tell everyone. "And if any of you decide you'd rather not be part of this, I won't blame you. This is *my* fight—"

"It's *our* fight," Solana corrects. "Raiden killed my family."

"And my husband," Arella adds.

"And took about twenty pounds of my flesh," Aston reminds me.

"And Westerly is my language too," Audra adds—*finally* meeting my eyes. "The winds chose to protect me. I'll do the same for them."

I guess there's nothing else to say.

Silently, though, I beg the sky to keep them safe.

Please don't let this be another mistake.

I repeat the plea twice more.

Then I step into the pipeline and let the winds blast me away.

CHAPTER 40

AUDRA

The last time I stood among these rolling hills, my father died.

I can feel him in every rustle in the air.

In the stirring leaves in the scattered trees.

And yet he's never felt so far away.

I turn my face to the sky and search for my favorite Easterly. Somehow it always made me feel like he was still watching over me.

I haven't called for the draft since it convinced me to break my bond—and not because I regret the decision.

It's just hard to crave the thing that brought me such pain.

And yet . . . I still crave Vane.

Thinking his name makes my insides wither.

Arrogant as it may sound, I never considered he might reject me.

He turned his head away, like the very idea of kissing me was disgusting.

Some small, rational part of me remembers the regret and worry I saw in his eyes as he did it, and knows there were likely factors behind the decision that I'm not considering.

But the crushed, wounded parts can't stop watching him with Solana.

They pace across the field, her at his side, hanging on his every word. I'm sure they're discussing strategy, but . . .

She's still wearing their link.

And they've been traveling together.

And she's so soft and beguiling.

And the only word I caught of his mumbled excuse was *Solana*.

And . . .

I'm being a fool. Even if my worries are founded, this is the absolute last thing I should be thinking about before a battle.

I close my eyes, trying to imagine my former walls rising up inside me, sealing off any emotions.

I need to be cold.

Still.

Numb.

"I can feel the Gales approaching," my mother says beside me, making my insides tangle. "They should land in a few minutes."

That's faster than I was expecting.

I triggered the emergency call less than an hour ago.

They must be speeding their flight with the power of pain.

My mouth tastes sour at the thought.

"What about Raiden?" I ask.

"He knows how to hide from my senses. But I can feel enough turbulence to tell he's on his way. I can't guess his precise trajectory, but I suspect we have a bit longer. He'll wait for us to take our places and he has the air prepared. *Then* he'll reveal himself."

"Thank you for the report."

I assume she wanders away. But after several seconds she tells me, "You should be preparing with the others."

"I *am* preparing."

"No, you're mooning over a boy."

My grip tightens on my windslicer, but I keep my eyes closed, refusing to let her bait me.

She's like a mosquito—if you can't swat her, the only option is to let her sate her taste for blood and flit away.

"In case you're worried," she whispers, "I'm not angry at you for hurting me."

"I wasn't worried."

I hear her sigh. "So this is how it is now? We can't even talk to each other?"

"When have we ever talked?"

All I remember are the years she let me carry the blame for my father's death—years I sweated under the desert sun, living in a crumbling shack because I wasn't welcome in her home.

She lets out a second sigh. "I never realized being a mother would be this difficult."

"Yes, it must be awful for you having to think about someone besides yourself. And now you sit there, expecting sympathy—"

"I don't expect sympathy," she interrupts. "All I hope for is understanding. I know I haven't been a perfect mother—"

I have to laugh at that.

"—but that doesn't mean some part of me doesn't wish that I had been," she finishes. "I did try at times, though I'm well aware of my failings. Is it so wrong to admit I wasn't prepared?"

"Yes," Vane says, and every nerve in my body tingles to life.

I can tell he's standing over me, but when I force myself to look up, all I can see is a blinding halo of blond waves, standing close by his shadow.

"I'm not trying to defend myself," my mother says. "I'm trying to apologize."

"Well, you suck at it," Vane tells her.

I feel my lips smile. But it fades when I force myself to turn to my mother. Spots of brown freckle her face, and I realize they're dried blood.

I try to feel guilty—but all I feel is tired.

"Nothing you say will ever change the fact that Gus is dead because of the trap you set for us." I dust the grass off my legs and stand to walk away.

"How about an explanation then?" my mother calls after me.

I can't imagine any explanation could possibly make me understand.

But I stop walking.

"Make it quick," Vane tells her. "We've got armies coming in from every direction. And I'm not sure if any of them are actually on our side. The Gales weren't exactly happy with us when we left."

My mother nods and stretches her uninjured arm, letting the breeze send goose bumps over her skin. Long seconds pass before she whispers. "I was trying to protect your father—or whatever little is left of him. Raiden's Stormer crushed his form and stole his final breaths. But his songs live on. Surely you've noticed. They visit you far more than they've ever come to see me."

A cold chill washes over me. "The Easterly?"

My mother nods, turning her eyes to the sky, where a flock of birds sails among the clouds. "I don't know how to explain it. But I can feel that it's him—some tiny glimmer of his former essence. And Raiden threatened to destroy it. With one snarled command he could turn the last whisper of your father into one of his mindless slaves. I couldn't bear to even imagine it. So I agreed to call you over. I knew you were strong and could fight him. And I half expected to be ignored. Hoped for it, honestly."

Vane shifts his weight, probably remembering that he was the one who convinced me to go.

But Gus was behind the idea as well.

"What do you expect me to say to that?" I ask. "That all is suddenly forgiven?"

"No," my mother says. "But I hope you can at least learn from it. Raiden is the master of impossible choices. And before this is over, I have no doubt that you'll be forced to make one. That's always his strategy, so that even his losses can be called victories."

I think of what happened with Gus and the cost of my escape.

It wasn't truly a conscious choice that time, but I still paid the price for it.

It's always more than a battle with Raiden.

It's a game of wits.

"So what are his weaknesses?" I ask her. "You?"

Her smile is sad. "Even my vanity won't allow me to believe he still cares for me."

"But he did once, right?" Vane presses. "That's what Audra meant about you being his queen?"

"Yes. Though I hardly knew he had such grand aspirations. When Raiden and I were together, he was simply a charming guardian rising through the ranks of the Gales, and I was the notorious beauty flirting my way through life, trying to decide my best option. There was something magnetic about him, and for a brief time I thought . . . maybe?"

"So why'd you reject him?" Solana asks. "Did you realize he had a darker side?"

"I'd love to claim such wisdom and foresight. But my motives were much more selfish."

Vane snorts. "Big surprise there."

"What does that mean?" I ask her.

"It means . . . I realized that Raiden needed me as much as I needed him. He was broken in ways—and don't ask me for specifics. He never spoke about it, and I wasn't interested in asking. I wanted someone to shelter *me*. Someone to help me shoulder my burdens. Not someone I had to fix. So I stayed with him until I found a better offer, and left him for your father. I knew I'd chosen the better husband, but I didn't realize the mess I'd avoided until a few years later."

I can't decide how to feel about her story, except to drown in the irony that my mother's fickle selfishness led her down the safer path.

"And you really have no idea what issues he was dealing with?" Vane asks. "Not even any guesses?"

My mother studies her hands. "Like I said, I wasn't interested in knowing—though I did suspect it had something to do with his family. He told me his parents were both dead, and he never seemed sad about it—except one time, when he lost his whistlepipe and panicked—"

"Whistlepipe?" Vane interrupts.

"It's a child's instrument. Raiden always wore it from a chain around his neck. I assumed his parents gave it to him—"

"Do you mean this?" Vane asks, reaching into his back pocket and pulling out a small, silver instrument strung among several feathered hair ornaments.

My mother's eyes widen. "Where did you get that?"

"It was hanging above Raiden's bed in Brezengarde. I took it mostly to piss him off, so he'd know I was in his room, messing with his stuff. But you're saying it's important?"

"Incredibly so. He never told me why, though. The most he ever said was, *It helps him to remember.* And like I told you, I wasn't the type to ask questions."

Vane's lips twist into a cold smile. "I guess I know what to do with it now. I'll crush it right in front of him."

"I wonder if Os knows more about its significance," I say, mostly to myself. "He and Raiden were close during their time in the Gales."

"Well, you'll be able to ask him"—my mother closes her eyes—"right about . . . now."

The word has barely left her lips when dozens of Gales drop out of the sky, forming a circle around us, their windslicers raised for attack.

CHAPTER 41

VANE

M y army doesn't look happy to see me.

I guess I can't totally blame them, given the fact that I kinda ran off and abandoned everybody.

Still, you'd think they'd give me at least *some* credit for getting Audra back and making it out of Raiden's fortress alive.

At least there are more guardians than I was expecting. It looks like maybe fifty—and they're all strong and healthy and loaded up with weapons.

It'd just be better if those weapons weren't . . . y'know . . . pointed at my head.

"Thanks for coming," I say, giving them my best no-need-to-stab-me smile.

Os ignores it and decides to kick off the convo with the worst possible question. "Where's Gus?"

I clear my throat. "He . . . um . . ."

God—I can't seem to say it.

These are Gus's friends. They trained with him and fought with him and knew him way longer than I did.

Os guesses the meaning of my silence and raises his eyes to the sky.

When the rest of the Gales copy him, I figure they're giving Gus a moment of silence. Then I realize they're actually listening for his echo.

I do the same, surprised when it works. I've never heard one before—and it's not how I've pictured it. I always thought it would be the last remnants of the person's voice, saying their final goodbye. But it's more like . . . their entire essence tangled up in a song.

"How did he die?" Os whispers, wiping his eyes.

I can barely choke out "Suicide draft."

The term gets a mixed reaction, with only some of the Gales seeming familiar with the concept. Os explains it to the rest, and one of the Gales I don't know steps forward.

"Does that mean you almost got him out?" he asks.

I notice he's about my age, so he was probably friends with Gus.

"We did get him out," I say. "And we'd almost broken free of the Stormers chasing us. And then . . ."

Poor guy looks like I just kicked him in the chest.

"What about you?" Os asks Audra. "You seem *unharmed*."

I'd better be imagining his annoyed tone, because I will seriously blast him off the face of this planet.

"Only minor injuries," Audra says, reaching back to rub her right shoulder. "Raiden mostly tried to use Gus to break me."

"Did it work?" Os asks.

"Of course not," she snaps. "Though Gus deserves most of the credit. He endured more than any of us will ever know."

I notice she doesn't mention that they had the Westerly breakthrough.

That's probably better—especially when Os points to me and says, "And I'm assuming you two have already rebonded?"

Yeeeeeeeeeeaaaaaaaaaaeah . . . what am I supposed to say to that?

We came close, but I was worried she wasn't ready—and also that she had maybe developed some feelings for Gus—so I stopped it, and now she's probably disgusted with me?

Even saying "not yet" feels too presumptuous.

So I kinda want to hug Aston when he calls from outside the circle of guardians. "Since when are the Gales so interested in teenage romance?"

The guardians spin around and create a gap in their ranks to let Aston saunter through.

"Is it really you?" Os whispers.

"In the flesh," Aston agrees. "Well . . . mostly." He lowers his hood and knocks everyone back a step. "If you think this is bad, you do *not* want me to take off this cloak."

He waves his arms back and forth, making air whistle through the holes in his hands.

All the Gales squirm and wince.

"Now you see why I stayed away," Aston tells them. "That, and . . ." His focus drops to his ruined fingers. "I let Raiden find my breaking point."

"You did," Os says after several seconds of silence. "Though I'm not sure any of us can claim the same wouldn't happen to us. And yet here you are. Reappearing after so many years—so many battles where your knowledge and experience could've aided us—and you've chosen to stand with *him*."

"You mean our *king*?" Aston asks when Os points at me. "Isn't that the side we're all on? Or did I miss something during my time in the dungeon? Don't tell me that just because he turned out to have a mind of his own—and occasionally decides to use it—"

"Hey!" I say.

"—that you've decided to undo a decade of planning," Aston continues, ignoring me.

"That plan was a relic," Os says. "From a time when we put far too much faith in the power of four."

"Oh, I wouldn't be so quick to write off the power of four," Aston tells him. "It may work differently than how we were expecting—and at first I thought he was being lazy—"

"Again—hey!" I interrupt.

"—but I've realized that's how the power functions," Aston finishes. "It's about trusting the wind, relinquishing your control and handing it over to the sky. That's the Westerlies' influence, I suspect. They like to make up their own mind, not be told what to do. So should we really be surprised their people are just as stubborn? You're only mad because he won't go along with your little betrothal plan. But surely you've realized by now they never would've worked out anyway."

"Dude!" I say at the same time Solana says, "Hey!"—though I'm not sure why I'm arguing.

"Oh, you know it's true," Aston tells us. "You've been traveling together less than a week, and you've been at each other's throats most of the time."

Yeah, but half of our fights were because of the betrothal hanging over us.

Then again, why am I defending this?

"The matter of his marriage is only one of many points that we do not see eye-to-eye on," Os reminds us.

"Yes. I can see that." Aston steps closer, leaning in to stare into Os's eyes. "That is quite a craving you're bearing. It's like looking at my own reflection—though with a bit less blue on the lips."

"I have it under control," Os says, backing away and blinking. "*We* have it under control."

"That's the lie we tell ourselves," Aston says. He studies the nearest guardian and shakes his head. "You've all been training hard, I see."

"We have," Os agrees. "We're trying to *protect our people*."

"And who will protect them from you," Aston asks, "when the need offers you anything you desire, so long as you surrender to the craving? What happens when you're so empty and ruined that you'll do anything for the rush of pain to pull you back together?"

"If that's the price we have to pay to finish this, so be it!" Os snaps back. "Even you know we don't stand a chance on our own—and they know it too, otherwise they wouldn't have sent that."

He points to the emergency signal in the center of the field—a thin, white funnel of speeding winds stretching to the highest point of the sky.

"I'd even wager that's why they involved you in the first place," Os adds, glaring at me. "Someone to do their dirty work."

Aston shrugs. "That doesn't mean it was wise to corrupt the entire force with a power you don't understand. And every time you use it, you're dragged further under."

"Maybe not," Solana mumbles, then shrinks slightly when all eyes focus on her. "I think . . . I found a safer way to channel the power."

"Have you now?" Os asks. "Does that mean you've used the commands I taught you?"

"She did," I answer for her. "And it really messed her up."

"I'm fine," Solana starts, then stops herself. "It's been hard. And part of me wishes I'd never used it. But it's a little better now that I figured out the trick. If I focus on the needs of *others*, instead of what I'm craving, the power doesn't take over the same way. The hard part is letting go of the selfish thoughts and making sure I truly mean the sacrifice."

"But you still have to ruin the wind, don't you?" Arella asks.

"Not if I use winds that are already broken," Solana tells her. "Raiden has shattered thousands of drafts—and I'm sure he'll destroy hundreds more today. We can use those to fight against him. Give them back their meaning. Otherwise what will their fate be? To drift aimlessly with no value or purpose ever again? They may be damaged—but they're not useless. So long as we make sure we're working in harmony with their needs, I don't see why it would be cruel to let them help us, whatever way they can."

I hadn't thought of it like that before.

I kept thinking of it like shielding ourselves behind dead bodies. Taking advantage of the violence of others in order to survive.

But the winds aren't *dead*.

If she's found a way to give them purpose—why not?

I feel even better when I see Audra nodding, like she agrees with Solana's reasoning.

"So is this your plan, then?" Os asks me. "Put us on the front lines of your battle while tying our hands and limiting our power?"

"Thinking of others doesn't tie your hands," Solana insists. "And it definitely doesn't limit your power. It made us stronger than even Raiden claimed to be."

"And you can organize yourselves however you want," I add. "You're the experts on battle strategy. All I need is for you guys to keep the Stormers busy, so I can find Raiden and end this."

"*You're* going to end this?" Os asks. "You realize what that means?"

"Yeah, I'm going to kill Raiden," I tell him.

Hopefully slowly and painfully.

It's kind of amazing how little the idea shakes me. All I have to do is keep my mind focused on Gus.

"I'll be helping," Solana jumps in.

"As will I," Audra adds.

"*Only* if I need it," I correct.

"Oh, you'll need it," Os says. "Or is selflessness supposed to be the magical cure for your aversion to violence?"

"No, the magical cure is rage," I tell him. "Raiden murdered Gus right in front of me. He tortured the girl I love. So yeah, I have absolutely zero doubt that the first chance I get, I'll be ready to end him."

I'm pretty proud of how confident I sound in my little speech. Until I realize I slipped the *L* word in there too.

The coward in me wants to put my head down—look anywhere but Audra's face.

But the needy, desperate boy has to know what she thinks.

I steal a glance, and . . . she's not looking at me.

But she's blinking a lot.

Are those tears?

If they are—are they good tears?

Something hits my side, and I realize Solana elbowed me.

"Os asked you a question," she says under her breath.

Right. I'm supposed to be focusing on battles and things.

"One more time?" I ask, losing what little credibility I might've gained.

Os sighs. "I asked if you have a preference on how we organize the ranks."

"I do," Aston jumps in, and once again I want to hug him. He knows everything about Raiden's battle tactics and gets to work bossing everyone around, sending the guardians to different positions, and telling them how to prep for battle.

Arella wanders off to "get a better reading on the air." And Solana takes off her jacket to absorb as many winds as she can. Even Audra's keeping busy, testing her strength and range of motion with her windslicer.

And I'm . . . standing here uselessly—which is pretty much par for the course, but it feels like I could do better.

I still have the pain pills I grabbed from my house, so I divide them up among the Gales, telling them to crush them and throw the powder in the Stormers' faces if they lose their weapons during the battle.

I'm debating whether I should make them wind spikes, too, since I know Os will probably shatter the drafts in them. I decide to put it off when I remember a question I meant to ask.

"Do either of you guys know anything about this?" I ask Aston and Os, showing them the whistlepipe.

Their jaws fall open.

"I'm guessing that's a yes?"

"That belonged to Raiden's sister," Aston whispers.

"Raiden has a sister?"

"*Had,*" Os corrects. "She returned to the sky when he was nine. He never told me the whole story. Something to do with groundlings. Add it to the list of reasons he despises them."

Okay, now we're getting somewhere.

Dead sister. Humans responsible. And Raiden probably felt super powerless when it happened.

I'm not a shrink or anything, but that sounds like a pretty good reason why someone might head down the I-want-to-kill-everyone-and-have-absolute-power path.

I'm trying to figure out if my hands are strong enough to crush the pipe right in front of him, or if I'll have to drop it and stomp it with my boot when I hear Aston worrying about our number of guardians.

"You don't think fifty will be enough?" I ask.

"Sixty-three," Aston corrects. "And no, I don't. Raiden will bring at least a hundred."

"How many Stormers does he actually have?" I ask.

"Not as many as you'd think. He has trust issues, if you can't tell by the suicide drafts. He usually keeps his force between one hundred twenty and one hundred fifty, recruiting and replacing as needed."

Wow—that's definitely not as many as I'd been imagining.

"I'm sure he'll also bring Living Storms," Os adds, squishing the tiny bit of hope I'd been building. "Depending on how many innocents he can find and transform."

My mind flashes to the people in the hotel, and I really really really hope he needs sylphs in order to make his creepy warriors. But I can't help imagining hundreds of Living Storms tearing toward us.

"And this is really everyone?" I ask Os. "There aren't any other Gales we can call for aid?"

Os shakes his head. "Raiden has decimated our forces over the last few years. And we were always a small uprising. All we have are those you see, those too badly injured to fight, and a handful of reserves I left behind to cover things should the worst happen."

"Is it still the same contingency plan?" Aston asks him.

"Essentially. We have a system of tunnels where anyone loyal can flee, and the guardians on reserve will make sure anyone who needs them can find them. Everyone will be safe underground, so long as they stay out of the wind until they're strong enough to rise up again."

"That . . . could be a very long time," I mumble.

The reality of what we're facing hits me then—like *really* hits me.

This isn't just about risking our lives, or settling our score with Raiden.

It's about our whole world crumbling.

"Fear is your greatest enemy in battle," Aston says. "Don't surrender to it. Take it one fight at a time, one enemy at a time, and hope you're still standing when the storm settles."

That's definitely not as comforting as he seems to think it is.

"Besides," Aston adds. "You'll have the strongest defense during the fight."

"You really think the power of four is that strong?"

"I was talking about *me*. I'll be providing your cover so you can get to Raiden. And trust me, I am very motivated to make sure you get there."

Something about his tone—or maybe it's the intensity in his eyes—makes me feel a little choked up when I tell him, "Thanks."

It also makes me hand over my wind spike.

"In case you need it," I mumble.

"It's worthless against Raiden unless you break the Northerly inside it," Os warns.

"Perhaps," Aston whispers, tracing his fingers along the blue edges. "But I hate to disturb such purity."

I weave myself a new wind spike and scan the field. It doesn't have much to it. Mostly rolling hills and a few scattered trees. "Where do you think I should look for Raiden?"

Aston points to a weird pointed rock in the distance—or maybe it's a mountain. It's hard to tell. It kinda looks like a hill that's giving the sky the finger.

"Raiden always watches from a distance," he tells me. "He'll only swoop closer if the flanks are failing—or to celebrate his victory. So my guess is, he'll be somewhere over there. It's the highest point in the area, and it's a difficult approach from the ground. I can also feel groundlings not far from there, and I'm sure he knows we'll try to spare them."

"Wait—there are humans nearby?" I ask, craning my neck and seeing nothing but empty plains. "Why?"

"I think that rock is famous," Solana tells me. "I know I've seen pictures of it before."

Great. So we're back to putting people's lives in danger—and it's too late to change location.

"Shouldn't we claim the high ground for ourselves, then?" Os asks. "Minimize the risk of casualties?"

"Not if we want to win. Raiden's overconfidence will be our greatest asset. The more he thinks everything's going his way, the more likely he is to make a mistake. Let him have what he wants. Let him think he has all the advantages. By the time he realizes there are other forces at play, it will hopefully be too late."

I hate gambling with people's lives that way. But . . . I know Aston's right. "So what's the smartest way to approach?" I ask, vowing to fight ten times harder to keep people safe.

"We'll have to see how the battle plays out," Aston says. "And you'll have to keep an ear to your winds, asking them for help getting around his backlash—and *don't* try for the kill until they give you an answer. Assuming there *is* an answer."

"There has to be one," I mumble. "Otherwise why have any Stormers at all? Why go after the power of four if he's invincible?"

"I used to tell myself the same thing, when I was plotting my escape. Never did get the answer. But don't look so glum, Loverboy. Your winds haven't failed you yet."

Yeah, I guess not. "But what if—"

The rest of my question is swallowed by the wave of heavy, gray clouds that pours in from the north, blacking out the sun.

In the same breath the sky goes eerily still.

Lightning flashes across the sky as hundreds of Stormers emerge from the thunderheads.

With a loud, ground-shaking rumble, the battle begins.

CHAPTER 42

AUDRA

Stay close to Vane.

It's my only plan for this battle.

No matter what happens, I won't be separated from him again.

Not because he said he loved me—though I'd be lying if I said that didn't help.

Because this is how it was meant to be.

I've been his guardian.

His girlfriend.

And now I'm not sure what I am.

But I need him.

And I'm the only other person here who speaks Westerly.

Stormers pour into the field like gray rain, gathering in the center with their backs to one another. A beast with too many heads and no heart to guide it.

I don't understand why they hold their attack, but I decide to be grateful for the extra time.

I find Vane crouched in the long grass, his eyes trained on the strange rock formation in the distance.

"Is that where you think Raiden's hiding?" I ask.

He jumps and clutches his chest. "Gah—are you trying to scare me to death?"

"No—but maybe now you'll realize you should be paying closer attention! I could've been a Stormer. You need to—why are you smiling?"

"Sorry," he says, trying to bend his twitching lips into a frown. "It's just nice to have you lecture me again. I've missed it."

My throat turns thick. "I've missed it too."

A hundred other words bubble up, but I swallow them back. Instead, I offer him my hand to help him to his feet.

His sparks prickle my fingers, and I'm tempted to not let go—but Aston comes charging toward us. "Save the touchy-feely stuff for when we've survived this. Right now we need to get out of the circle of death."

He points to the distance, where dozens of Living Storms are untangling themselves from the sky, stacking into an impenetrable barrier all around us.

So that's Raiden's strategy.

Crush us from without and within.

Leave nothing in the center but dust.

"This is more Stormers than I was expecting," Aston says. "Raiden's not holding any reserves. Apparently he's determined to end this today too. Os is on his way to make us a path out of here so we can track Raiden down."

He points to a figure in black charging across the eastern plain, heading for one of the smaller Living Storms. "He's going to make it chase him," Aston explains. "To create a gap for us to slip through. After that, we'll be on our own."

"I'm coming with you," Solana says, landing beside us.

She's rolled up her sleeves and knotted her shirt to reveal her midriff, despite the flakes of ice peppering her hair.

"Were you windwalking in this?" I ask, checking the sky.

Lightning crackles in threads of gleaming white and electric pink, painting the storm with erratic, unpredictable patterns. Ice and snow swirl among the flashes, their violent flurries building toward a roar.

Even *I* would never brave such a sky—and I have my father's gift to guide me.

"I needed to absorb some of the ruined drafts," Solana says, untying her shirt and covering herself with the wrinkled fabric. "But I only caught a couple. The Stormers are doing a good job of cutting us off from the wind."

"What are the Gales going to do if they can't call the wind?" Vane asks.

"The same thing we are," Aston says. "Fight with anything we have and try not to die."

I search the air for any brave drafts, and catch the weak pull of a distant Westerly.

It takes a bit of convincing to call it to my side, and I notice Vane watching me the whole time. His smile looks almost proud, but it fades when he catches the wind's song.

"It's singing about traitors," he mumbles. "Lets hope it's not talking about the Gales."

I listen to each lyric carefully, trying to piece the full meaning together.

We're trying to protect you, I tell the wind. *We're on your side. But we need your help.*

I beg the wind to whisk away and gather its friends.

Not just Westerlies, I add. *We need the full strength of the sky.*

It's time for the wind to rise up and prove that it's far stronger than any of us have ever been.

I can't tell if the Westerly understands me, but the draft vanishes toward the horizon.

"Maybe I should send my shield, too," I mumble. "It gathered the drafts we needed in Death Valley."

"Uh-uh," Vane says. "I want that wind as close to you as it's willing to stay. I'm pretty sure it's the only reason you're still alive."

I'm certain of it—and that's the truth I'm hoping Raiden's missing.

If a single wind can save a life—or take it—what will happen when the winds unite?

"Time to go," Aston says, dragging Vane toward the Storm.

The uneven ground fights to topple my legs as I sprint after them, with Solana right behind me.

We aim for the narrow gap Os has carved into the wall of

Storms, but halfway there Solana jerks me to the side.

A wind spike explodes where I'd been standing, showering us in dirt and grass and petals.

"Where are they coming from?" I ask as another volley swallows Aston and Vane in a cloud of debris.

"We're fine," Vane shouts, coughing and hacking. "But getting the hell out of here would be a really good idea."

We try to run in a crouch, the position every bit as fumbling as it is painful.

The wounds on my back stretch, and I feel the *W* tear open as I twist to avoid a wind spike aimed at my head.

The next blast sends us tumbling across the field, and Solana cries out.

"I'm fine," she promises, but I notice she's limping hard.

"They're out of range over here," Aston calls, waving his arms as we barely dodge another round of explosions.

I draw a burst of strength from my Westerly shield and let it fuel my arms as I lift Solana and half carry her over to safety.

"You guys okay?" Vane asks, taking her from me.

"You can put me down," she tells him. "My ankle's sprained, but I don't think it's broken."

She winces as he sets her in the long, scratchy grass, but when she tests her ankle, it holds.

"They're closing ranks," Aston says, pointing to the gap Os made, which is narrowing as the other Storms move to cover it. "We're going to have to move *fast*."

"I can handle it," Solana tells me when I go to carry her again.

She leads the way, and we charge forward, pushing our tired, aching limbs as hard as they can go.

But it's not fast enough.

The pull of the Storms is too strong, and they drag us toward their merciless funnels.

"Lock arms," Vane shouts. "The heavier we are, the harder we are to pull."

Solana grabs him first, and I cling to her, my feet lifting off the ground as the Storm tears closer.

"Pull harder," Solana shouts, and our group surges forward, step by agonizing step until my feet drop back to the ground and I regain traction.

"Toss me your wind spike," Aston shouts, and Vane untangles his arm to throw it.

Aston lets go to catch it, and without his weight, we're sucked back toward the Storm.

"Hang on," Aston says, clinging to a tree with one hand and aiming the wind spike with the other.

The weapon is sickly with pain now, and he hurls it straight through the Storm's chest.

Sallow steam leaks from the unraveling funnel, and the Storm unleashes a bellowing howl.

"That's our cue," Aston shouts, grabbing Vane's arm.

"Not without this," Vane says, commanding the wind spike to "come."

I wasn't sure if it would obey, but it snaps to his hand as Aston drags him away.

The air tries to pull Solana and me back, but we synchronize our steps and push through, collapsing as we cross the boundary of the circle.

"Over here," Aston orders, and we crawl to where they've taken shelter behind a cluster of boulders.

None of the Storms break rank to follow us.

"Just like I thought," Aston says. "Raiden ordered them to focus on the battle. We can rest here for a second before we move on."

Vane crawls closer to me, taking my arms and searching for blood.

"I'm okay," I promise. "Nothing major."

He looks safe as well. A few cuts and scrapes on his face, but nothing deep enough to scar.

"How's your ankle?" I ask Solana.

She circles her foot a few times. "I won't slow you down."

"I'm not worried," I tell her. I'm fairly certain I owe her my life. "How did you hear that first wind spike? I never would've seen it if you hadn't grabbed me."

She curls her arms around herself. "My senses are stronger now that I'm carrying ruined drafts."

I try not to shudder, but the thought of being filled with tainted winds . . .

"Yeah, I know it's creepy," she mumbles.

"I don't think creepy's the right word," I tell her. "More like . . . uncomfortable."

"So you aren't disgusted by the power of pain anymore?" Aston asks.

I'm stunned to realize I'm not. "The way she's using it doesn't seem to bother the sky. Why should I feel any different?"

"Yes, but you realize she wouldn't be able to use it her way if others weren't abusing the power?" Aston reminds me.

"So she's managed to make the most of a difficult situation," Vane says, but his voice sounds distracted.

I follow his gaze and see him staring at a grayish building stationed near the base of the pointed rock.

"I count twelve cars in the parking lot," he mumbles. "So I'm guessing that means there's about fifty people in there."

"I think you're overestimating," Aston tells him. "The structure feels mostly empty to me."

"Mostly empty isn't the same as *empty*," Vane reminds him.

"It's not," Aston agrees. "Welcome to a moment when you'll have to settle for 'good enough.' Shades of gray. Necessary evils. Much like what we're letting happen over there."

He points to the battle we've just escaped, and from our higher vantage point things look far bleaker. The Gales are fighting the Stormers with windslicers, so there must still not be any useable winds. And for every Stormer fighting, there are two more watching from the sidelines, ready to swoop in as reinforcements if the others fall or tire.

"Where's my mother?" I ask, realizing I haven't seen her.

"She said she'd find higher ground and send reports on what's happening. I doubt she'll be much help, since you already made her mostly useless with that dramatic shoulder injury."

"Higher ground," I repeat, checking the field again. "We're at the highest point right now, aren't we? Other than the rock face where Raiden's waiting? And she's not here, is she?"

"Oh, wonderful," Vane grumbles. "What deal do you think she's striking with Raiden this time? Handing all four of us over—maybe with whipped cream and a cherry on top?"

"I can't imagine she'd be that foolish," Aston says.

I roll my eyes. "Clearly you don't know my mother."

"Actually, she and I are closer than you'd think. Every time I absorb her pain I understand her better—but that's not what I meant about her being foolish. She's very aware that I've made the same threat as Raiden. I know what draft she's protecting. And I know the command to destroy it."

"You wouldn't," I whisper as everything inside me coats with frost.

"Oh, I think you know me well enough to know that I very much would. I'm like a thunderhead that way. I can look soft and fluffy. But get too close and I will blast the heart right out of you."

"No one's blasting the heart out of anyone," Vane tells him, "unless it's Raiden. Or Arella—if she really is off cutting another deal. And if you do anything that hurts Audra—or her father's songs—I'll show you just how violent a Westerly's capable of being."

"Good," Aston says. "Keep that darkness close. You're going to need it when we get to Raiden."

"Speaking of which," Solana jumps in, "shouldn't we get working on that? The Storms are closing in on the Gales."

"I was hoping your little Westerly might return with a few reinforcements before we press on," Aston tells me.

I've been counting on the same thing. But no matter how far I stretch my senses, I can't feel any winds.

"I have five drafts tucked away," Solana offers. "Three Southerlies, a Northerly, and an Easterly—plus the two ruined winds I caught."

"And I used four in that wind spike," Vane adds. "And I have a Westerly shield."

"Still not enough for what I was thinking," Aston says. "We'll just have to improvise."

"What if we . . ." Solana's voice trails off, and she closes her eyes. "I think I know a command that will blur our forms as we move—I just have to think it through to make sure it's useable."

She reaches for my hands and stares into my eyes.

It takes me a second to realize she's testing her motives.

I suppose protecting the girl who stole your betrothed is about as unselfish an act as possible.

"Okay," she whispers, her hands starting to shake. "I don't think it'll stretch very wide, so we're going to have to huddle together."

She takes a deep breath before hissing a string of garbled words.

"Fascinating," Aston breathes as a gray draft crawls out of her skin and forms a loose funnel around us. "I never would've thought to make that request."

"What did she say?" I ask.

"It's best not to explain to someone who doesn't use the power," he says. "We wouldn't want to awaken the hunger."

The air whips faster and faster, turning to a blur.

"Are you okay?" Vane asks, steadying Solana as she wobbles.

"It's just a little draining," she says. "How's the craving in my eyes?"

He leans closer, and she seems to hold her breath. "Wow, I only see the tiniest glint."

"As do I," Aston agrees. "I must admit, I'm rather disappointed. I've been hoping you were wrong about this selflessness thing, since it doesn't sound like a whole lot of fun. I guess I should count myself lucky that I'm too far gone for it to matter. You ready to move?"

Solana nods, and we creep out of the rocks, trying our best not to kick one another's heels as we move.

"How is this hiding us?" Vane asks.

"It's similar to how we disguise our forms when we fly," Solana tells him. "I convinced the draft to combine our traces, so it'll feel like there's only one of us. And it's weak and muffled, so Raiden might not even notice it. But if he does, he'll think it's a lone Gale. He definitely won't be prepared for the four of us."

We move in silence after that, making the slow climb up the rock formation.

I stretch out my senses, trying to home in on Raiden's exact location. But either we're too far away, or Raiden's too good at hiding.

"By the way," Solana whispers, turning to look at Aston. "I don't believe that anyone can ever be too far gone."

"Even Raiden?" Vane interrupts.

"He's different," she says. "He's the one who started messing with the power. And even if he could change his ways, he's done too much to be redeemed."

"As have I," Aston tells her. "I know you still see me as that eager-to-help Gale—but I can't even remember being him. And the things I've done since then would give you nightmares."

"But you're here now," Solana whispers. "I saw how terrified you were in that tunnel outside Brezengarde. And still, you came back—and now you're marching up to face Raiden, knowing our chances aren't good."

"So really, we should be questioning my sanity," he says with a forced smile. Several seconds later he adds, "I just . . . want this all to be over."

I can't tell what he means, but the sadness in his tone turns my heart heavy.

He clears his throat. "We should pause in that crevice ahead. It's making me twitchy that I can't get a reading on Raiden. I know he's good—but he's not this good."

We ease into the crack—which is much cozier than it looked from the outside—and I end up pressed rather tightly against Vane.

"Sorry," he whispers, trying to find somewhere to put his arms.

"It's okay," I tell him, pulling his hands to rest on my hips. "I don't mind."

A teasing glint sparks to life in his eyes, but it's gone just as fast, and he turns his face away, eyes on the ground.

I want to grab his chin and force him to look at me—talk to me. Explain his complicated mixed signals.

But time is never on our side.

"Is anyone getting anything?" Aston whispers. "Though I should probably limit the question to Solana since you lovebirds clearly have your minds *other* places."

His raised eyebrows fuel my blush, and I close my eyes and listen to the sky. "Everything feels empty."

"That's what I'm sensing too," Solana agrees.

"Everything *is* empty," a new voice says, and my brain screams, *NOT AGAIN!*

We all look up to find my mother standing over our crevice with one of her loyal crows perched on her shoulder.

"You can't sense Raiden," she says, "because he's not here."

CHAPTER 43

VANE

"What do you mean Raiden's not here?" I ask as I scramble out of the crack we've been hiding in—trying not to bruise Audra in the process.

"I thought the statement was self-explanatory." Arella reaches up to stroke her ugly crow, and I wish it would bite her. "Raiden's not here—and I don't just mean on this rock. Apparently he's skipping this whole battle."

"How do we know this isn't another one of your tricks?" Audra asks, jumping out of the crack and pointing her windslicer at her mother's heart.

Arella rolls her eyes. "Your senses are giving you the same message, aren't they? It seems Raiden elected to let his army handle the matter for him."

"That doesn't sound like him," Aston says as he hefts himself out of the crevice and helps Solana climb out with her weak ankle. "Maybe for a quick snatch-and-grab mission. But he sent his entire force."

"That was my thought as well," Arella says. "And why I've circled every inch of the battlefield. I even called on a bird to be my eyes when the sky grew too treacherous."

The crow caws, making me jump.

Freaking birds.

"Do you think he's waiting for something before he arrives?" Solana asks. "Trying to catch us off guard?"

"Or maybe he knew he'd lose this time, so he's cowering at Brezengarde," I say, trying to think positive.

"I suppose both are possible," Aston says, "though the latter seems unlikely—especially since the Gales aren't exactly triumphing out there."

He's right.

The sound of the fight keeps echoing this way, and . . . it doesn't sound good.

I kick the ground so hard it showers us in bits of rock and dirt. "Sorry."

It's just . . .

Raiden not being here ruins our whole plan—which is probably the *real* reason he's playing hooky. And if he's holed up in Brezengarde, I . . . *can't* go back there.

I know we escaped once. But I can feel it deep in my gut. We'll never beat Raiden on his home turf.

309

And God—does this mean all those people are still snowed in at that hotel?

I kick the ground again, and Audra places her hand on my shoulder to calm me.

"So what do we do?" I ask.

"Maybe we should circle back and fight with the Gales," Audra says. "They could definitely use some backup."

We all turn to study the battle. The Gales are outnumbered five to one—and soon it'll be six or seven to one, judging by all the red stains on the ground.

"Why are there still so many Stormers hanging in the mush-pot?" I ask.

"I'm assuming you mean the cluster of soldiers waiting in the center," Aston says. "And I'd wager they're the ones who've been charged responsible for our capture. If Raiden was going to skip a battle, he'd make sure his best warriors save their strength to scoop up his spoils and bring them back to where he's waiting. I doubt he cares about learning Westerly anymore, but I'm sure he wants you to die knowing he stole the one thing you gave your life to protect."

"Then we can't go down there, right?" Solana asks.

"So we just stand here and watch them all die?" Audra argues.

"Besides, won't the rested Stormers just come after us anyway?" I ask.

Either way—Raiden wins.

It all feels so pointless.

I keep trying to take control—keep trying to tell myself I can beat this.

But Raiden's like the kid in my fourth-grade class who liked to catch Japanese beetles, tie string around their bodies, and hold on to one end.

The dumb bugs would fly around in circles, and sometimes he'd let the string go slack. Let the beetles think they were finally going to fly free—and then *SMACK!* They were splatters of green goo on his baseball bat.

I'm tired of being a dumb bug—and I really really really don't want any of us to end up green goo.

Raiden thinks he can beat me without even showing up.

Well . . . *screw that.*

We're the good guys, dammit!

We're supposed to pull it together and have that "group shot" moment. Like in the comic book movies when all the heroes gather up and the score gets louder and the camera does one of those fancy 360-shot things and everyone's like, "RAWR—GO TEAM AWESOME!" And then they dive back in, kicking butt and taking names until the bad dudes explode or get blasted into another dimension or something.

That.

We need that.

But how do we pull that off in reality? Especially a funky reality where we can control the wind, but the bad guys can too?

Except . . . they don't have the power of four—and that's what this whole mess is about, isn't it?

"Solana, didn't you say you had a Northerly, an Easterly, and some Southerlies stored away?" I ask.

She nods. "Why? What are you thinking?"

"I'm thinking . . . are you a Northerly?" I ask Aston.

"I am, actually," he says. "But if this is a power-of-four thing, haven't we established that your tricks falter against the power of pain?"

"Have we really?" I ask. "Or have we established that the two powers are *different*? Because we pulled off something pretty awesome when we were trying to get away from Brezengarde. I kinda forgot about it, since what happened to Gus totally killed the victory. But before that, we used the power of four—and it worked."

"It did," Audra chimes in. "There were four of us then, too. And we each used our native wind and gave the command in our native tongue. Our drafts told us what to say, and somehow we made a foehn, and it melted the snow and took out most of the Stormers, before reinforcements arrived. If we ask the wind for help again, maybe it'll come up with something even better."

Aston sighs. "It would be a lot easier to get behind this plan if we hadn't been so horribly abandoned by that Westerly you called over."

Yeah, that really does suck.

I don't get why that wind didn't want to help.

"But just because one draft lets us down," I say, "doesn't mean they all will."

"I think it's our best chance," Solana adds. "At least we'll be coming at them with something they won't be prepared for."

She releases three of her drafts, sending the Easterly to Audra, the Northerly to Aston, and keeping the Southerly for herself.

I untangle my Westerly shield, begging it to swirl with the others and not drift away.

"What about me?" Arella asks.

"We don't need you."

I might be imagining the joy in Audra's voice, but I'm pretty sure she's wanted to say those words to her mother for ten years.

"So what am I supposed to do?" Aston asks.

"Right now, it's all about listening." Audra holds out her hands, and Solana and I each take one.

Aston sighs as he reaches out and completes the circle—and I'll admit the whole process does feel a little "Kumbayah." But as I beg the winds for help and focus on their lyrics, I can hear their songs slowly synchronizing.

The whirlwind picks up speed, whipping into a frenzy as a single word rings out over all the others.

"Everyone else is hearing 'simoom,' right?" I ask. "That's an actual thing?"

"It is," Audra tells me.

"And I doubt they'll be prepared for that," Aston murmurs.

"Why, what's a simoom?" I ask.

Audra tightens her hold on my hand. "It means 'poison wind.'"

CHAPTER 44

AUDRA

I've never seen a simoom before.

They're rare in this part of the world.

And Windwalkers tend not to use them.

Partially because they can be erratic and untamable. But mostly because they're terrifying.

To let the earth choke out all the air . . .

My shudder makes me realize what I'm forgetting.

"I need you to warn the Gales," I tell my mother, hating that we have to rely on her after all. "Tell them to hold their breath and cover their hands and faces—without tipping off the Stormers."

I wish I could order a retreat, but that could ruin everything. And I doubt the Gales would be able to get past the Living Storms anyway.

"I'll use the birds," my mother tells me, marking the feathers on her crow's wing. She whispers directions for it to follow and sends it soaring into the stormy sky.

"Okay, what the heck is this thing we're about to make?" Vane asks as my mother calls more birds to warn the other Gales.

There aren't many willing to brave this weather, but a handful of sparrows responds as I tell Vane, "It's a heat-driven dust storm."

"How is that different than a haboob?" he asks. "Besides the way less awesome name, of course."

He winks and I can't help smiling.

Now is definitely *not* the time for another round of his infamous boob jokes.

But I love that he always manages to ease the tension.

"Haboobs are formed by sudden downdrafts. Simooms are cyclonic," I explain. "And they carry heat along with the dust, and sweep through an area so fast they choke everything in their path and scorch it."

"I've heard stories of whole pastures of dead animals after a Simoom passes," Solana adds. "And men with blistered skin."

"That definitely doesn't sound like anything I want to be signed up for," Vane says. "Are we sure the Gales can survive it?"

"We're not sure of anything," I hate to admit. "Except that our winds are telling us the command, and they haven't failed us yet."

"If it helps," Aston adds, "the Gales are as good as dead in this battle anyway. At least this gives them a chance."

No. That doesn't help.

But I can hear Gus's voice whispering through my memories.

Trust the wind.

Keep fighting.

"So how do we actually do this?" Vane asks. "Do we stay up here and watch, or ..."

I wish.

"I think we'll have to follow through on foot, don't you?" I ask Aston.

He nods. "I doubt the simoom will have much affect on the Living Storms. They don't breathe or have skin to burn."

"Wait a second," Vane says. "Are you telling me that once we use up half of our winds to make this simoom thing, we're still going to have to fight"—he turns to the battle and counts—"*thirty-six* Storms?"

"You're the one who thought we should listen to the wind," Aston tells him. "If you don't like their plan, take it up with them."

Vane checks the drafts' songs again, and I find myself doing the same. They're still focused on the simoom, and they've added another lyric about hoping in the unknown.

"Well then," Vane says. "Anyone got any plans for fighting the Living Storms? Last time it didn't go very awesome."

He rubs his injured elbow, and I try not to remember how many Gales died in that battle—or the fact that we were only facing twenty-nine Storms at the time.

"I have a few ideas," Aston murmurs. "But most of them require wind, so we'll have to hope the simoom wipes out whatever the Stormers are doing to keep the sky empty. And another involves breaking the rest of the drafts in this wind spike. Or breaking the ones I'm capable of shattering, at least."

"Why would that matter?" Vane asks.

"Simple math," Aston tells him. "If shattering one draft boosts its strength, breaking the others should triple the effect."

Vane doesn't look thrilled with his reasoning.

But he nods.

"Try to focus on the Gales you're hoping to save—not on saving yourself," Solana advises, before Aston can give the command. "Keep saying it over and over in your mind and make yourself believe it. Then say whatever words the need tells you."

Aston sighs. "You're really killing all the fun of this."

"It's not supposed to be fun," I snap. "Those winds are being sacrificed to save us—at least give them some small choice in the matter."

Aston sighs again, but closes his eyes and lets several seconds slip by before he hisses a string of commands.

The wind spike crackles and shifts to a shade of yellow so bright it practically glows.

I can feel the power radiating from it, sick and scratchy but so intense it gives me hope. Until Vane tries to command it to "come" and the spike refuses to respond.

"Maybe it needs you to say the command in the power of pain?" Vane suggests.

Aston and Solana both try, to no avail.

"At least that makes it harder to steal," Aston says, slashing it a few times.

"It also means you'll probably only get one shot," Vane reminds him.

"Then I'll make it count," Aston says, slashing the spike several times. "And hopefully build more when I have access to wind."

Vane turns to the battlefield, probably taking another count of the Storms. "I'm not sure I want to know the answer to this," he says quietly, "but . . . do we know who these Storms are—or were—or whatever the right phrase is?"

"I'd wager they're the Stormers who failed to capture us on the mountain," Aston tells him. "And the ones who allowed you to escape from Brezengarde. Raiden wouldn't let such failure go unpunished."

I know I shouldn't feel sympathy for the Stormer who tore my dress and tried to assault me. Or Nalani, who was happy to let Gus die in that cell.

But it's all such an incredible waste.

So many lives stolen.

So much pain and ruin.

And for what?

For one sylph's greed for ultimate power—a sylph who couldn't even bother showing up to fight his own battle.

Please, I beg the winds, *give us the strength to end this.*

"Os got the warning," my mother announces, stroking her newly returned crow. "And the other birds are finishing up their rounds."

"I guess that means it's time to do this, right?" Vane asks, tightening his grip on my hand. "You sure you're up for it?"

"I have to be. We need an Easterly."

He leans closer, whispering only for me to hear. "But I need *you* more. We could use your mother—"

I shake my head. "I don't trust her. Besides, I'm staying with *you*."

"Will you two please remember that there are people with eyes here, having to watch this sugary mushiness?" Aston interrupts.

Vane shoots him a glare—but Aston's right.

Still, I feel myself twining my fingers tighter with Vane's. "Okay, we'll give the command on three. And then—depending on what happens—we'll charge into battle. Ready?"

I wait for each of them to nod.

Vane agrees first.

Then Solana.

"Oh, why not?" Aston tells me.

"One," I count. "Two."

I steal an extra breath before I call, "Three!"

In perfect harmony, we all shout, *"Scorch!"* in our native languages.

The winds double their span, blasting the four of us backward. We skid across the ground as the winds swirl so fast they tear off chunks of rock and pulverize them.

The battle goes quiet as the Stormers halt to stare.

"Is that how this is supposed to work?" Vane asks as the funnel stretches higher and higher. "I thought it was going to, y'know, *move.*"

"It's heating up," Aston says. "Ever rub a stick between your palms and watch the friction spark?"

The air does seem to be getting hotter.

And hotter.

And hotter.

"Maybe we should back up," Vane says.

But there isn't far to go. The hill slopes down on one side, and butts us up against the spire of rock on the other.

"EVERYONE COVER YOUR MOUTHS!" Aston shouts, and I bury my face in my hands as the storm blasts into a cyclone and swirls toward the battlefield.

The simoom stretches wider with every second, gouging the earth as it moves, smashing it into silt and fanning it through the sky until the air is so thick I can barely see my hands. The grit burns my eyes and throat, and I wish we'd been smart enough to tear strips of fabric from our jackets and make face masks.

Someone grabs my hand and I scream—then choke on the dust.

"It's okay," Vane shouts, pulling me to my feet.

We stumble toward the others, all of us coughing so hard it nearly knocks us over.

"This storm will burn out in a few minutes," Aston rasps. "So we should start making our way down. We'll want to hit them when they're scrambling to regroup."

The air feels too heavy to move—or that might be my head. Between the searing heat and the shallow breaths and the scratchy eyes, it's hard to concentrate. Still, we manage to lock arms and form a chain, and Aston takes the lead, sending us charging down the rock face as fast as our shaky legs will carry us.

Maybe the winds fuel our sprint.

Maybe I'm just dreading the fight ahead.

But it feels like only seconds before we reach the battle.

The smell is indescribable.

Filth and waste and roasted flesh all mix with the dry scent of parched earth. I'm gagging with every breath, and then choking on the dust.

Everywhere I look, gray figures writhe on the ground, some still, others wailing and clutching their faces with blistered hands. I notice a few Gales collapsed among them and try to convince myself they'd already fallen in the battle. It helps to see so many guardians still standing.

They move as weak and wobbly as we do, but they're ready for a fight, weapons raised as they fan the dust away from their eyes.

The Living Storms have broken their ranks and scattered—their roars mixed with the hiss of the unraveling simoom—but through the haze of grit I can see them tearing our way.

"We'd better head over there," Vane shouts, pointing to where two Storms are closing in on an injured Gale.

"We'll never get there in time," Astons says, letting go of me to aim his wind spike. "I'd rather hoped to hang on to this longer, but . . ."

He lets the spike fly.

His aim is flawless—hitting one of the Storms through the shoulder before exploding the other's head in a burst of yellow steam.

"Two down," Vane calls. "Thirty-four to go. And that was our only weapon. Just, y'know, in case anyone's keeping track of these things."

"Actually," Aston says, squinting through the murk. "I think the spike survived. I'm going after it."

He takes off toward the carnage, and we start to follow, until a roar to the east stops us cold.

I turn and find Os and another Gale battling five Storms between them.

"They need our help!" Solana shouts.

"Okay, but *how*?" Vane asks. "I'm still not feeling any winds down here, are you? And there's also *that*." He points to three Storms tearing toward us from the other direction.

"We need a distraction," Solana says, closing her eyes as she snarls a scratchy command.

A ruined draft and a Southerly seep from her skin and coil around her.

"This looks like a terrible plan!" Vane shouts as the drafts launch her toward the Storms. "What are you going to do up there without any weapons?"

"No idea!" she calls over her shoulder. "But I begged the winds for something to make them lose interest in you guys, and I guess this is the answer."

She waves her arms and hollers insults until the Storms turn to chase her, and she flies toward where Os is fighting.

"You realize she's basically bringing them three more enemies to fight, right?" Vane asks. "I'm not sure the wind thought this one all the way through."

I'm not certain either.

But we don't have time to worry about it.

Four more Storms shift paths and head our way.

We race the opposite direction, but they gain with every step. Aston tries to fight his way back to us, but he's tackling three of his own. And all the other Gales are fighting battles. Which leaves me with one final, desperate idea.

I'm certain Vane is going to hate it, so I turn my face away from him as I focus on my Westerly shield.

We need help, I tell the loyal wind. *I need you to do what you did in Death Valley. If we don't get more winds, everyone is going to die.*

My shield tightens its hold, not wanting to abandon me.

Please, I beg. *We need wind more than anything.*

The draft sings of impossible choices as it untangles itself.

"Thank you," I whisper in Westerly. "And hurry!"

"Please tell me you didn't just do what I think you did," Vane says.

"It's our only option."

"No, there's still this." He asks his shield to wrap around me, and the wind blankets my skin. I try to send the shield back, but Vane covers my mouth with his dusty palm. "Please, just let me do this. It's the only way I'll be able to concentrate."

I want to argue—or pull him even closer—but the four Storms chasing us have drawn so near that I can feel their pull dragging us toward their funnels.

My feet float off the ground, and Vane jumps on top of me, rolling us away as soon as we crash. I lose track of which way is up. Everything is tumbling tumbling tumbling—until we crash into a pile of bodies.

A couple of them are still alive, clawing and flailing with their blistered hands.

"Yeah, no thanks," Vane says, kicking a Stormer away and grabbing another's black windslicer.

I do the same, and we both point them at the injured Stormers.

"What do we do?" Vane asks. "Kill them so they can't come after us—and maybe put them out of their misery? Or leave them and not get our hands bloody?"

"I can't tell," I admit. "My instincts are all over the place."

"Mine too."

Another second passes before he grabs my arms and pulls me east. "I feel like if killing's the right choice, we'll *know*."

I squeeze his hand harder, taking a second to marvel at how steady he's become. Despite the horrors raging around us, he makes me feel safe, even when two more Storms angle their paths to head us off.

We screech to a halt, and I feel the draw of two other Storms behind us.

"They're boxing us in," Vane shouts as we try to pivot east, only to spot another Storm blocking our way.

"DON'T MOVE!" Aston calls from somewhere to the west.

"EASIER SAID THAN DONE!" Vane shouts back.

We both grapple for a hold to keep us tethered to the ground.

I'm about to lose my grip when yellow flashes through the nearest Storm, and the mangled funnels explode into bellowing mist.

"GRAB THE SPIKE AND TAKE OUT THE OTHER!" Aston orders.

I pull a muscle in my shoulder as I stretch to reach for the spike, but it's worth the pain when I close my hand around it.

I only have time to check my aim once before I let the weapon fly.

The explosion buries us in rock and rubble, and Vane drags me out of the debris and gets us moving again.

"Where are the other Storms?" he asks, trying to see through the fog of sand.

I tighten my grip on his hand. "I can't tell, but they sound close."

"GET DOWN!" Aston shouts. "INCOMING ON YOUR LEFT!"

I dive to the dirt, covering my head.

Five seconds pass.

Then ten.

"ANY TIME NOW!" Vane calls, lifting his head to scan the field.

The wind spike blows past him, striking the rocky ground in a shower of dust.

"DID YOU SERIOUSLY JUST MISS?" Vane asks.

"I TOLD YOU TO GET DOWN!" Aston shouts. "YOU'RE LUCKY I DIDN'T HIT YOUR GIANT SQUARE HEAD!"

"I have a square head?" Vane asks.

I have to laugh, even surrounded by so much misery.

I'm still smiling as I fight my way to the wind spike and let it fly toward the Storm's main funnel.

It hits dead on the mark, and Aston launches it back through the final Storm near us, dissolving it into a puff of sickly smoke.

"How many have we taken out?" Vane asks as we grab the spike and run.

"My best count says we're down to twenty-four," Aston says as he falls into step beside us. "But it might be twenty-five—which is better than I'd expected, honestly. I don't see how we're going to hold out. This wind spike is getting weaker with every toss. I'm betting it has about three good hits left before it unravels. Also, I'm getting rather tired. This body isn't exactly built for running."

"Can't you draw strength from all this pain?" Vane asks.

"Not without wind. And even then . . . this is a far darker kind of suffering."

My stomach turns as I survey the battlefield, and the rot and ruin heaped everywhere.

This is the great legacy Raiden has brought to our world.

But I can't worry about the dead.

Our guardians are still outnumbered three to one, and without weapons, their fights have been relegated to running and dodging. And Solana's veering erratically through the sky with at least a dozen Storms chasing after her.

"If only we had some wind," I whisper when I note three more Storms bearing down on our position.

I swear the sky hears me, because in the same breath Vane murmurs, "I don't believe it."

I turn to follow his gaze and see he's stretched out his hands to the west. When I open my senses I can feel the pull of my Westerly— and it didn't return alone.

My shield streaks toward me, swirling around my face as hundreds of drafts flood in from every direction.

"You're hearing this, right?" Vane asks as he listens to the winds' chanting song.

I can only nod, my eyes welling with tears at the beauty of so much unbridled power.

I doubt the winds need us to give the command. The song seems more of a warning for us to be prepared.

Still, as the drafts coil themselves around us—Easterlies, Westerlies, Southerlies, Northerlies—and Vane and I lock eyes, we both raise our voices and shout, "Rise!"

CHAPTER 45

VANE

I have no idea how to describe anything that just happened.

I'm not even sure if it *did* happen.

Maybe a Living Storm ate me, and my mind made the whole thing up while my body was being digested.

All I know is, one second the battle was falling apart and I was thinking that Audra and I should spend our last few minutes making out. And the next second the winds were swarming in out of nowhere, telling us to "*Rise!*"

And then . . .

I don't even know.

The wind became a beast with a million invisible heads and arms and teeth, like some sort of hydra-kraken woven straight from the air. And it used all of that weirdness to devour everything it touched—including us. But we weren't destroyed. We were just sort of . . . sucked up.

Audra. And me. And Aston. And Solana. And Os. And any other Gales that were still breathing—even Arella.

We were all pulled into . . . was it a cocoon?

I guess I could also call it a *womb*—but that sounds way too gross.

So we were in this freaky cocoon-thing, floating around with all these warm breezes that were singing about salvaging our heritage. Meanwhile we could still see the battle going on all around us—kinda like watching a movie but somehow knowing you're not just watching?

And then . . . everything went quiet, and we were set down gently in the crushed grass, and we all just stared at each other like, *WHAT THE HELL HAPPENED???*

So yeah.

I don't know.

But I guess it doesn't matter.

WE'RE ALIVE!!!

And, WE WON!

Os celebrates by ordering everyone to gather up the bodies, proving that he seriously knows how to kill the buzz.

I offer to help. But yeah . . .

The gore is *way* too much.

Especially when I realize that most of the Stormers have their necks snapped.

"Suicide drafts," Aston breathes. "He terminated his whole army."

"Why would he do that?" Solana whispers. "Would he truly give up that easily?"

No one has any real answers, though they debate a bunch of different theories.

I try to pay attention, but I can't stop thinking about all the dead dudes watching me. Audra has the same *I'm gonna hurl* look in her eyes that I'm sure is in mine, so I take her arm and lead her to the fringes, to a soft spot of grass peppered with wildflowers. When we keep our backs to the battlefield, it's almost like we're sitting in a park somewhere, watching the sunset. You know, if we *really* pretend.

"Do you think it hurt?" Audra whispers. "When the drafts ..."

I picture Gus's face the moment his draft triggered.

One second he was Gus.

The next he was blank.

"No, I don't think they feel anything. It happens too fast."

Minutes tick by, and I count the cars in the visitor center parking lot, glad to see they're still in the same neat rows, untouched by the storm.

"What if the people over there saw the battle?" I ask.

"They probably went underground to a storm shelter," Audra says. "And if they didn't, I'm sure they'll come up with some sort of rational explanation. Groundlings are good at making excuses for the impossible. Even you did it when you thought you were one of them."

"Not always," I tell her. "I never let myself make excuses for believing in you."

Her eyes turn soft at that, and half a smile curls her lips.

I scoot a little closer, deciding to press my luck. Our legs touch, and the rush of heat gives me a burst of courage. "I knew it was crazy to believe that the girl I dreamed about every night was really out there somewhere. I just wanted you to be real so bad that I didn't care."

That earns me the rest of the smile, and I reach for her hand, surprised to feel the soft rush of her Westerly shield draped around her skin.

"The draft didn't want to leave," she says as I brush the breeze with my thumb. "Is it weird that I hope it never does?"

"Hey, you and that wind have been through a lot. Maybe more than you and I have."

"Not quite." She traces my palm with her fingertips—such a simple gesture, but seriously: *sparks and shivers*. "You told me once that I was the one constant thing in your life," she whispers. "But you've been the constant in mine, too. I know you probably don't remember—and I'm so sorry about that—"

"It's okay," I tell her.

And actually, it is.

I still need to sort out my past—and I will.

But right now I care way more about our future.

I reach for her other hand, and her heat rockets up my arm so fast it settles into my heart.

Does she have any idea what she does to me?

Our eyes meet and my breath catches.

Maybe she does.

"So," she says, licking her lips and leaning a little closer. Close enough that my brain screams, *THIS IS IT!!!*

I decide I'm not stopping it.

I don't care that we're only a few feet away from death and destruction.

Maybe battlefield kissing will be our "thing."

I'm trying to remember the last time I brushed my teeth—and hoping I'm not blasting her with BO—when she takes a deep breath and asks, "What are we going to do about Raiden?"

That's what she was thinking about?

Why doesn't the universe just punch me in the nuts???

Especially since . . . I'd kinda forgotten about him.

His army's gone—mostly. Doesn't that mean it's over?

I wish it could be that simple. But Audra's right.

Raiden's still out there, and as long as he is, he can start this mess all over again.

But what the hell are we supposed to do now? He's locked away in his fortress, still protected by his backlash.

I lean back on the grass and stare up at the darkening sky, feeling like an insignificant ant.

It'd be awesome if we could just beg Audra's shield to get its windy friends back together and blast over to Brezengarde to finish the job. But . . . I don't think the wind works that way.

If it did, wouldn't it have crushed Raiden a long time ago?

I think . . .

The wind definitely has a personality—but it's also still a force.

If we really need it, maybe it'll pull through for us.

Otherwise we're on our own.

This feels like one of those times when it's up to us to figure it out—and I know I *can* do it.

I can kill Raiden.

I owe it to Gus, and my parents, and all the Westerlies who died protecting my language.

This is *my* fight.

It's time for me to end it.

It's just the *how* part that's especially tricky.

We're down to him and me now, so . . . am I supposed to, like, smack him with a white glove and challenge him to a duel?

Better question: How do I beat him?

"Please," I whisper, my words automatically switching to Westerly. *"Help me figure out how to end this."*

Audra lies back beside me and together we listen to the melodies drifting through the air. At first it all sounds the same—just songs about the turbulent day fading into a calmer night. But slowly the lyrics shift, and one in particular catches my attention:

> *Born of the sky*
> *Resting on the earth*
> *So much lost. Even more to gain*
> *Seek your ally*
> *Discover their worth*
> *Triumph through peace and pain*

Audra told me one time that sylphs are caught between two worlds, since we have ties to both the wind and the ground. So I'm guessing that first part is basically the wind agreeing that yep, this fight's up to me.

But who is my "ally"?

And more importantly—*why does the process have to involve pain?*

Can't I triumph through peace and something else? How about fluffy bunnies?

Actually, now that I'm thinking about it, "attack of the bunnies" sounds super terrifying. I'm imagining a pack of red-eyed, fanged, killer rabbits when Audra mumbles something.

"What did you say?" I ask, shaking my head to de-bunny my brain.

"All my instincts tell me that if we try to invade Brezengarde, we'll never get out."

I agree—though I'm not loving how casually she slipped the word "we" in there.

Then again, maybe she's the "ally"?

Except I already know her "worth."

"There has to be a way to lure him away from his fortress," she says. "Something he can't resist."

"Like the language he's been trying to steal for the last couple of decades?" I ask. "Or a chance to recapture the prisoners who embarrassed the crap out of him by escaping? We offered him both, and instead of showing up, he sent his whole freaking army—and then he offed them. It's like the guy has finally snapped. And, uh, if he was scary when he was just an evil dude trying to take over the world, imagine what he's going to be like now that he's gone nuts? He's probably turning Brezengarde into a maze of deathtraps, and he'll just stay in there, blasting stuff with his Shredder before taking long bubble baths."

"Bubble baths?" Audra asks.

"You should've seen his bathroom."

Audra sits up. "That's right! Do you still have the whistlepipe you stole from his bedroom?"

I only make it through half a nod before she's on her feet, mumbling about finding her mother as she runs through the battlefield.

The Gales have the bodies mostly cleaned up, and now they seem to be preparing the wounded for transport.

"Where do you think they're going to take them?" I ask Audra.

"There's a base not that far from here. They set it up after your parents were killed, so they could keep an eye on you during your adoption process."

Well, that's . . . weird—but I guess all that matters is that they have supplies to treat the injured.

If everyone pulls through, we might have about twenty-five guardians left—still a ton of losses, but not as brutal of a ratio as the last battle. And hey, it's more than Raiden has, which still feels so wrong. I wish I could figure out why he killed everyone.

We finally find Arella at the highest point in the field, perched in the center of the hill with her arms stretched toward the sky.

"What are you doing?" Audra asks her.

Arella jumps, and then rubs her injured shoulder. "I'm trying to find your father's songs. I haven't seen his Easterly since the day I left the Maelstrom, and I'm starting to fear Raiden has taken control of it."

The words stop Audra cold.

"If he has, we'll get the wind back," I promise her. "I'm ending Raiden as soon as I can get close to him."

She nods, blinking hard before taking a deep breath and focusing on her mother. "I think I know how to convince Raiden to leave Brezengarde," she tells Arella. "But I'm going to need you to send him a message."

Arella smiles. "I thought you didn't trust me."

"I don't." Audra's jaw is so tight, it looks ready to snap. "But I need you to send a bird marked with the code you and Raiden used to use."

"Why would you want to waste time with that?" Os asks, coming up behind us. "Sending the wind is much faster."

"Yes, but sending the wind won't shake him up," Audra tells him. "I saw how tense he was around my mother's ravens."

"He still has them?" Arella whispers.

Audra dips her head. "He only has one now. He snapped the male's neck after I wouldn't give him what he wanted."

Tears drip down Arella's cheeks, and she murmurs something none of us catch. Then she slips her fingers between her lips and makes a high-pitched whistle.

I'm expecting her ugly crow to sweep in, but a huge brownish-gold eagle soars above us instead. It circles three times and dives to Arella's wrist. Its talons look painful as they dig into her skin.

"What message am I marking?" she asks, pulling out the eagle's wing.

"Tell Raiden we have his sister's whistlepipe," Audra says. "And that if he doesn't meet us here by sunrise we'll destroy it."

It's a solid plan—though it's hard to believe Raiden would care more about a flute than the power of four.

"Tell him to come alone," Audra adds. "And unarmed. And give him this as proof."

She asks me for the whistlepipe and snaps off one of the feathery things dangling with it.

"I'm assuming these were his sister's hair clips," she says as Arella makes the eagle clasp the feathered piece with its talons. "But even if I'm wrong, he'll recognize it from the chimes."

"Do you really think he'll come?" Os asks. "Raiden doesn't respond to demands."

"He will if we make it irresistible." Audra glances at me as she adds, "Tell him he'll be meeting only with Vane and myself. The last Westerly, and the Easterly who escaped him—and before anyone argues, remember, he has to believe he can defeat us."

"And if he overpowers you," Os argues, "he'd have everything he's wanted. I wouldn't be surprised if the whole reason he skipped this battle was to push us into taking such a risk. He wants us to believe him weak so he can prove himself strong."

"It doesn't matter," Aston says, marching up to join the debate, with Solana right behind him. "If you want to make the puppy come, you have to offer it a treat."

"Except the puppy is actually a wolf, ready to devour everything," Os argues.

"Which is why we'll be ready for him," Audra says. "Vane and I both channel the power of four."

"And that won't be enough," Os says. "You need the power of pain as well."

They argue back and forth, and I know I should probably chime in—not that Audra can't handle herself.

But Os's points got me thinking about the lyrics to the winds' song.

I check it a few more times, making sure I really have the right translation, because if I do . . . this is gonna be ugly.

The song seems to get louder as I listen, like the wind is cheering me on, encouraging me to make a big mess out of everything—which does seem to be the thing I'm best at.

Eventually I clear my throat and tell Arella, "Don't send that bird yet. I need you to change the message."

Cold sweat drips down my back, and I can't look at Audra as I mumble, "We need to change Audra's name to Solana."

CHAPTER 46

AUDRA

W hy her?"

It takes me a second to realize the petty question came from me. But now that I've asked, I need to hear the answer.

I turn to Vane, feeling very small as I add, "Do you truly trust her more than you trust me?"

"Of course not!" Vane reaches for my hands, but stops himself halfway. "Listen to the wind—tell me that line about peace and pain doesn't mean what I think it means."

I listen to the lyrics.

Then check them again.

And again.

"I feel the need to point out that I too know the power of

pain," Aston says, his smile making it clear how much he's enjoying our awkwardness. "As does our captain here. And any of the Gales."

"Yeah, but the song's not about them," Vane says. "Look at the other lyrics. We all know I haven't always appreciated Solana, because of the way you guys tried to force us together. I bet that's what it means about discovering my ally's worth. Plus, she's the one who got us out of Raiden's oubliette. She's also the one who learned the better way to harness the power of pain—though all of this is assuming you're willing," he tells Solana.

"Oh, I'm in," she says. "I've been preparing for this my whole life."

A fresh wave of envy ripples through me.

Especially when Vane adds, "I think this is how it should be. Solana and I are the only ones here who've had absolutely no choice about being involved in any of this. I'm here because I'm a Westerly, and Solana's here because she's part of the royal line. Both of us lost our families, and have had our entire lives controlled because of Raiden. This is our chance to take back our futures."

It's a very honest, well-reasoned, impassioned speech. But it doesn't ease the queasiness in my stomach.

"If that's what you want," I say before I walk away.

Behind me, I hear Vane tell my mother to change the message. A second later the eagle takes off, soaring through the dusky sky in a bubble of Easterlies to fuel its speed.

With that many winds, I wouldn't be surprised if it reaches Brezengarde within the hour.

I suppose that means I should be leaving too.

But I have nowhere to go.

No home.

No family.

No—

"Hey!" Vane calls, running to catch up with me. "Can we talk about this?"

When I keep walking, he jumps in front of me.

"Please, Audra. I know how this looks."

"It doesn't look like anything. You're right, that *is* what the wind wants."

"Riiiiiiiiight," he says. "So then . . . why are you saying that through gritted teeth?"

I relax my jaw. "Just because I agree with it, doesn't mean I have to like it."

I try to weave around him, but he manages to block me.

"If you think I'm letting you leave like this, you're crazy," he says. "I'll be super annoying if I have to—we both know I'm good at it. Wait, is that a smile?"

I hadn't realized my lips had twisted.

"Please," he says as my face falls back to a frown. "Tell me what's wrong."

I shake my head. "It doesn't matter."

"It does to me." He sighs when I stay silent. "This isn't you. You're not like this."

"Like *what*?"

"Like . . ." He tears his hands through his hair, clearly realizing this is a make-or-break answer. "You're confident. And smart. And beauti-ful. And you have to know that I trust you more than anyone. You're the only girl who has ever—seriously *ever*—mattered to me. I loved you even when I thought you were imaginary. Even when you were throwing bugs at my head and dragging me out of bed at five a.m. for training. I waited for you when you left me with only three words and a dusty jacket—and when you broke our bond, I kept holding on anyway. I've never had even the slightest doubt that you're the one I want—and I don't give a crap if anyone disagrees. So please don't let this stupid, unimportant detail make you question any of that."

It's another really great speech.

My heart begs me to believe it.

But . . .

I take a deep, slow breath.

"Then why did you turn away?" I whisper. "When I tried to . . ."

I can't say it.

He reaches for my chin, tilting my face to look at him.

"That wasn't what I *wanted* to do. But I was trying to do the right thing. You'd been a prisoner for days. And Gus had just died. And . . . I wanted to make sure . . ." He looks away. "I didn't want to be something you regretted a few hours or days or months later. I owed you a chance to really figure out what you wanted."

"You're sure you didn't also want some time to figure out what *you* want?" I have to ask.

The only thing I've ever had to offer Vane is my protection. And now the sky has rejected me as his guardian, and handed my job over to the same girl the Gales chose for him.

Vane takes a step closer. "I know what I want, Audra. It's you. *Only* you."

"He's not lying," another voice says behind me.

I cringe.

"Sorry to interrupt," Solana says as she joins us. "But I figured, since this is kind of about me, I should probably be a part of it—a quick part," she adds, holding out her hands to calm Vane. "There's really only one thing I want to say. Well, I suppose it's several things, but it all relates to the same theme."

"I thought this was going to be quick," Vane grumbles.

"It is," Solana says, scooting closer to me. She waits for me to look at her before she says, "The thing is . . . I want what you have."

Vane groans. "Somebody please kill me now."

"Oh, relax," Solana tells him. "I didn't mean it like *that*."

She bites her lip, and a bit of her confidence slips as she tells me, "I know you think I've been making some sort of sneaky play for him all this time—and I guess I'd be lying if I said there weren't moments when I was—"

"I knew it," Vane mutters.

"You're *not* helping yourself," she warns him. "But yeah, I'll admit, part of me wanted to know if I could change his mind—and I figured I had a right to try, since he was betrothed to me first. So I wore my favorite dresses. I tried to give him a chance to get to know me. And none of it mattered—which is what I mean about wanting what you have. I want someone who looks at me the way I see him look at you. And while I'm at it, I want someone who treats other girls the way he treated me: always polite—well, *mostly*—but also always *so* careful to stop himself from crossing even the tiniest of lines. It was frustrating when I was trying to get his attention. But in a weird, backward way, it showed me what I'm missing. So before I face this final battle, maybe it's time we settle things."

She turns back to Vane, giving him a sad smile as she holds out her wrist and unclasps the wide golden band of their link.

Someone gasps and I realize Os has moved close enough to eavesdrop.

"Not a word over there," Solana tells him as she grabs Vane's hand and drops the link onto his palm. "I'm not going to bond myself to a guy who's hopelessly in love with someone else."

"So you're ready to walk away from your heritage?" Os asks her. "Ready to hand the crown over to *her*?"

"Assuming, of course, that Audra is still even interested in our king," Aston says as he sidles up to join us.

Vane sighs. "Thanks, dude. And you know what? Let's talk about that for a second. I was going to wait until everything with Raiden was actually settled. But assuming we survive"—his voice cracks on the last word—"I don't want to come back to a mess of drama. If we beat Raiden today, you have to consider my plan."

"And what exactly is that?" Os asks.

Vane focuses on Solana before he tells Os, "We follow the same model as the wind. Four languages. Four rulers. None of this one-king-to-rule-them-all crap. Humans have been trying that for centuries and it's never gone well—and it hasn't exactly been awesome for you guys either. But you saw how well the power of four worked when it had each of us channeling our own language. Why would it be any different when it comes to ruling our people?"

"Because four leaders would do nothing but dispute and dissent," Os argues.

"Or maybe they'd balance each other," Vane snaps back. "We could keep each other in check. Make sure a power trip like Raiden's never happens again. Come on, you have to admit the idea makes sense."

Silence follows.

Even the sky seems to be holding its breath.

I can't decide if I should be impressed that Vane put so much thought into this, or sad that I'm hearing his plan the same time as everyone else.

"I suppose it depends on the four," Aston says after a moment. "Vane would obviously be the Westerly."

"Yeah, I can't seem to dodge that one," Vane agrees. "And Solana should be the Southerly."

"And I suppose you want *her* to be the Easterly?" Os snaps, pointing at me.

"Audra's fought harder for our cause than almost anybody," Solana says before I can form a reply. "I'd be honored to serve alongside her."

"As would I," Vane adds. "Assuming that's what she wants to do."

"Well, isn't this working out conveniently," Os mutters. "So who did you have in mind for the Northerly?"

"That one's harder," Vane admits. "It should've been Gus. But since he's gone . . . what about Aston? He made an awesome fourth today. And he survived Raiden's fortress longer than anyone."

"And cracked under the pressure," Os reminds us.

"I'd like to see you do better," Solana snaps. "Besides, what better way to make sure the Northerlies never stray down Raiden's path again than to have their leader be someone who's tasted his power and found the strength to escape it?"

"Careful, you're going to make me blush," Aston says. "Plus, I'm betting our captain was planning to nominate himself."

Os denies it, of course. But I can see the shift in his expression. That quick glint of power, mixed with hunger.

Which is exactly why it should never be him.

"We're not taking *nominations*," Os says. "I'm not even sure why we're discussing this."

"Because I'm about to pick a fight with Raiden, and I need something to tell me I'm not going to regret it," Vane says. "I'm not asking for a final decision. I'm not saying there can't be more discussion. I just want you to agree that you'll at least consider it. If you're willing to let me risk my life for you, you should be willing to let me have some choice in my future if I survive. At least give the idea a fair try."

Os rubs the edges of his scar. "Fine. The suggestion will be presented—assuming you survive your fight."

"We will," Solana says, and I envy her confidence—and so many other things—as she tells Vane, "We have the sky on our side—though we should be discussing *some* strategies."

"And *we* should be leaving," Aston jumps in. "If Raiden finds us here when he arrives, he won't bother stopping."

Everyone shifts into action, gathering up the last of the wounded and preparing to carry them away.

Vane grabs my hand as I join them. "Just give me five minutes, okay?"

He leads me to a quiet spot under a leaning tree. I stare at the crooked trunk, wondering if it stood straight and tall before the battle, and if it will ever sort itself out and grow straight again.

"So," Vane says, "are we okay?"

I try to nod. But the air between us still feels murky.

"I thought it was going to come down to us," I whisper. "I thought we were going to take down Raiden together."

"So did I. But I have to admit, part of me is relieved that you'll be safe."

"And what am I supposed to do? Go back to my mother's house? Watch the sky? Worry each breeze will carry your echo?"

"You're not going back to my house?"

"I . . . don't know."

"Oh."

The hurt laced into that single syllable feels like salt pressing into my wounds.

"What are you thinking?" I have to ask when he shifts his face to the slowly rising stars.

"I'm thinking . . . I can't hear Gus's echo anymore. Can you?"

I stretch out my senses. "No. He's gone."

"I'm so sorry." He smudges the tears off my cheeks. "Listen—I'm just going to ask this quick, so we can get it over with, okay?"

He takes a shaky breath.

"When you and Gus were in Brezengarde, did you . . ."

"Did we what?" I press.

He clears his throat. "Did something *change* between you guys?"

The words weave through my head, tying up unanswered questions.

So all this time, he thought . . . ?

"It's okay," Vane whispers. "Gus was a good guy. And he was there to help you when I wasn't. He even gave you his gift. I just . . . need to know."

It's my turn to step closer, take his hands, wait for him to look at me.

"We had to lean on each other," I tell him. "But it wasn't *that* kind of closeness. I even gave him mouth to mouth and nothing changed between us."

"Wait—what was that last part?"

I smile at the shock stretched across his face, but it fades as I remember my time with Gus in that horrible hallway.

"He stopped breathing at one point, and it was the only way to bring him back. I wasn't sure what would happen. But nothing did. *Nothing* changed the entire time we were together. If anything, he mostly tried to convince me that you and I were going to be okay."

"You didn't think we would be?"

I sigh. "I didn't know what to think. Breaking our bond was very . . . confusing. It didn't take my memories of you. But it stripped away all the feelings."

He closes his eyes, and when he opens them again, they're glassy.

"Okay," he says. "I understand."

"No. You don't." I reach up to cradle his cheek with my hand. "The feelings started coming back as soon as I saw you. Why else do you think I . . . ?"

A few tears spill out of his eyes, trickling over my fingers.

"I'm so sorry," I whisper. "Please don't be sad."

"I'm not," he promises. "Not if there's any chance you can love me again. All I need is a chance."

"You have more than a chance, Vane."

I pull his face closer.

Then closer still.

Our breath mingles, so warm and sweet in the cooling air.

"Are you sure this is what you want?" he whispers.

"Yes." The rightness of the word feels like the song of a steady Easterly, grounding me in who I am.

"Is it what *you* want?" I ask.

"Are you kidding? But I feel like I should wait to make it more special this time—or at least until we're somewhere a bunch of people didn't just die. Maybe even take you on a real date first—have we ever actually done that? I guess that day at In-N-Out sorta counts."

"Of course it counts." I smile at the memory.

That was the day Vane showed me how to live for myself—how to take what I needed and not feel any remorse. And since I'm starting to feel like I might actually lose my mind if he holds back any longer, I decide to take the decision away from him.

"I love you," I whisper, bringing my other hand to his face. "That's all that matters."

I wait long enough for him to say, "I love you, too."

Then I pull his lips to mine and kiss him like it's the first, last, and only time.

CHAPTER 47

VANE

O kay, I thought I knew what it felt like to kiss Audra.

I thought I'd replayed all the details so many times over the last few weeks that I was ready for the soft silkiness of her lips and the sugary taste of her mouth and the dizzying rush of heat as a new bond unites us.

But either that old cliché about absence making the heart grow fonder really is true—or she's been holding out on me.

Because seriously: *damn.*

She nearly pulls me over.

We both stumble a few steps before her back finds the crooked tree, and she deepens the kiss and pulls me against her. Every doubt and worry I've ever felt seems to crumble at her touch, and it's overwhelming how much strength and courage and devotion she shares with me as we connect.

I hope whatever she takes from my essence gives her the peace and happiness she deserves. I'd do anything to blot out whatever darkness her days with Raiden might've left behind.

She breaks away for a breath, and I kiss along her jaw, then up and down her neck, until I find a spot right below her ear that makes her tremble every time I press my lips there.

Her hands trail down my arms and make their way to my waist, slipping under my shirt and tracing across the lower part of my stomach. The sensation makes me shiver, and I'm tempted to do the same to her, but I'm afraid I might brush across more injuries. So I keep one hand on the side of her face and the other buried in the long, wild strands of her hair.

It's such a gift to feel her this way—free of all the burdens she's always forced herself to carry. Surrendering everything.

As I kiss my way back to her mouth, I promise her I'll do anything in my power to keep her this happy and strong and brave.

I have absolutely no idea how many times Aston clears his throat before we notice, but when we finally pull apart we have *quite* the audience.

Solana's redder than I've ever seen her, and Os looks like he's ready to punch a few puppies. Aston's smirk is equal parts *I told you so* and *Get a room*. And then there's Arella who looks—

You know what?

I *really* don't want to think about the look on my girlfriend's mother's face after she's caught us making out. Especially since that mother is a psychopath—or is it a sociopath?

"Well now," Aston says, "clearly we've settled the who-will-be-bonding-with-whom question—and just in time, since our boy could probably use a little Easterly influence for this showdown with Raiden. Might take the edge off the whole violence aversion."

I actually hadn't thought about that, but he's right.

Score another point for *all the kissing*!

"I don't know," I say. "Maybe we should make sure the bond is really in place, just to be safe."

Audra makes a sound that could probably be described as a giggle, and I'm on my way to steal one more kiss when Aston clears his throat again.

"You really *do* need to pay attention—unless you don't care about what happens to mommy dearest. Turns out Os here is planning on bringing her back to the Maelstrom, and I thought you might not be happy about that."

"She's a murderer," Os argues. "And a traitor. And a danger to everyone. And she has to be contained."

He's not wrong.

But the Maelstrom is a death sentence.

I take Audra's hand, hating to see the color draining from her face—especially since she'd had such a sexy flush a few seconds ago.

"Is the Maelstrom really the only option?" I ask.

"It's not," Aston says. "That's where we come in. I've managed to convince the Gales to let the four of us try our hand at deciding. Consider it a test for how this process might work should they decide to make us rulers. So let's not mess this up. I'm starting to think I'd rather like to live in a castle—though I'll want my own. No way am I living with the kissing couple."

"Me either," Solana agrees.

Yeah, right there with them—and while we're at it, I'm never setting foot in Brezengarde again, so if Solana wants it, she can have it.

Though wait—*does this mean Audra and I are moving in together?!* How will I explain *that* to my parents?

"Focus," Aston says, snapping his holey fingers in my face. "This is the part where we're supposed to come up with brilliant alternatives."

"I make no guarantee that we'll hold to your decision," Os jumps in. "But it will be interesting to know your thoughts. The Maelstrom was my last resort after I exhausted every other avenue, so I can't imagine you'll come up with much."

"What about banishment?" Solana asks.

"Do you really think she'll stay away?" Os counters. "And what even constitutes proper banishment? Our people are scattered throughout the planet."

"Then what about full-time guards?" I ask.

"I tried that already," Os says. "She slipped away within hours."

"I came back," Arella reminds him.

"No—we hunted you down."

"I *let* you find me," she corrects. "Believe me, if I wanted to disappear, I could. I know I've made mistakes, but I'm trying to be better. All I'm asking is for you to trust me."

Audra snorts, and I tangle our fingers tighter as I lean in to ask her, "What do *you* want to do?"

"I don't know," she whispers. "I don't think I can choose."

"Wonderful," Os says. "So our four potential leaders can't even render a single decision."

"I'll give you a decision," Aston says. "Make Arella my responsibility. I know how to control her. And this is an arrangement she already agreed to."

She did—I was there.

But now . . . I don't know.

"Allowing you to torture her three times a day doesn't sound much better than sending her back to the Maelstrom," I have to admit.

"She wouldn't be dead," Aston argues, "so that's a pretty big improvement. She'd also have my charming company. But for the record, I have no intention of feasting on her pain. I've actually decided to go on a bit of a diet as far as that's concerned. Solana's new methods seem to be slowing my cravings."

"Are you okay with this?" I whisper to Audra. "It's better than the Maelstrom, right?"

She has her face turned to the wind, blinking back tears as she listens to their songs.

Os sighs. "We don't have time for this."

"You don't have time to consult the wind?" Solana asks.

"Is that what she's doing?" Os snaps back. "Or is she stalling?"

"It started as stalling," Audra admits. "But the wind does have an alternative suggestion."

I concentrate on the winds' song and notice its singing about a lost bird. It doesn't mean anything to me, but it has a different effect on Audra.

She sounds equal parts weary and nervous as she whispers, "The wind wants her to be my responsibility."

CHAPTER 48

AUDRA

should've known the wind would side with my mother—though I suppose I should be grateful it didn't tell me to forgive her.

Only to help.

And to attempt to understand her.

I hear the words of the Easterly's song in my father's voice—deep and rich and resonant. And I can imagine him standing in front of me, his eyes glinting with too much love and joy to ever match the wind's melancholy tone:

> *A lost bird with tired wings*
> *Never rests and never sings*
> *Begs the sky for a place to land*
> *Never finds a friendly hand*

Passing time fades hope into a darker shade of gray
Wayward winds drag calm and reason much too far away

Hearts go cold
Paths get crossed
Strength fades to bitter doubt
Sometimes the end only begins when someone reaches out

My father was the first to offer my mother shelter—the first to steady her against the turbulence of her power.

But it wasn't enough.

How am I supposed to be more than he was?

"What do you mean she'll be your responsibility?" Os asks, giving me a chance to take the words back.

It's one of those rare split paths, where I can choose the easy and safe. Put myself ahead. Take what I want.

Or not.

I know which path my mother would choose.

And I never want to be her.

So I choke down my bitter anger and tell Os, "I meant that I'll be the one to monitor her. The place she's been hiding these last ten years is sufficiently isolated and safe. I'll make sure she stays there, finishing her days in peace and never harming another life again."

"Wait—what?" Vane says, as Os asks me, "How?"

"I'm still piecing it all together," I tell them both.

I can't stay with her in that stuffy house—my sanity will unravel.

But how else can I keep a vigilant enough watch?

Vane takes my hands, his eyes searching my face. "I'll support whatever you decide—and I'll help any way I can," he promises. "But do you really want to be your mother's babysitter?"

"*Want* isn't the right word," I whisper. "But . . . she's my mother."

And there it is—the truth I've been running from for longer than I can remember.

Unstable and cruel as my mother can be, we share the same blood.

And . . . she's had her moments, however rare and far between.

She flew to Raiden's fortress to aid in my rescue. She also convinced Aston to remain after he'd chosen to flee.

Also—probably most tellingly—she didn't fight back when I attacked her after Gus died.

She's not the same crazed woman who attacked me after I learned her role in my father's death. I thought I saw my *real* mother that day. But maybe I only saw another part.

A dangerous, deadly side that must be restrained and monitored.

But not her entire essence, either.

And with that admission, I feel the truth settle—like that lost, lonely bird, finally finding a place to rest.

Sometimes the end only begins when someone reaches out.

"So this is your vote, then?" Os asks.

I focus on my mother as I nod.

Her expression is unreadable—but I'd expect nothing less.

Vane tightens his hold on my hands as he says, "Then it's mine, too."

"The matter can always be revisited if the arrangement doesn't work," Solana adds. "So for now, that's my vote as well."

"Well, I suppose that means I should add my vote," Aston says. "And hey, look at that! The four of us found a way to agree. Bet you thought we wouldn't be able to do that, didn't you, Ossy?"

Os shakes his head, more in frustration than disagreement before he launches into further reminders that our decision-making powers haven't actually been granted.

Those still lie up in the air, like so many other things.

Too many other things.

The most important things.

"How am I supposed to leave you here?" I whisper to Vane as everyone shifts back into motion. "How can I fly away when any moment now, Raiden could arrive. And if . . ."

"Hey, maybe this will be good," Vane says, pulling me closer. "We'll prove we're not one of those like . . . needy, codependent couples."

He tries to smile, but I notice he hasn't let go of my hands.

It should be *me* fighting with him—or me fighting *for* him.

But the wind is telling me to go.

I focus on the feathery soft clouds—clouds that promise calm and quiet ease—and beg the sky to lend Vane its full power and protection.

I'll do anything the wind asks, if it rises up this one last time.

I'm still finishing my plea when I notice a tangle of movement on the northern horizon.

"What is that?" Vane asks, pointing to the same blurry spot.

The dark smudge is too small to be Raiden, and yet I still hear the scrape of drawn windslicers.

My mother covers her mouth. "No! The poor thing . . ."

Her words choke into a sob.

I don't understand her grief until she calls the swirling winds to her side, and a tangle of long, golden-brown feathers flutters to our feet.

"Is that . . . ?" Vane asks.

"Yes," Aston tells him. "It looks like our eagle messenger met a rather unpleasant end."

My mother drops to her knees, tracing her long fingers over the plucked carnage.

Another innocent life stolen.

Another sacrifice without reason.

Let this be the end.

"It's a message," my mother whispers, drying her eyes with the back of her hand. She counts the notches in the feathers, and I try to do the same, but Raiden used the code only *she* can translate.

"He says that if you and Solana are brave enough to face him, you need to leave all your weapons and let his wind carry you to where it began."

"What does that mean?" Vane asks.

"It means he's asking for a change of location," Os tells him.

"Yeah, I got that," Vane says. "But *where*?"

"He doesn't specify," my mother says, checking the feathers again. "But based on what I feel in his wind, I'd guess you'll be traveling several hundred miles south."

"Oklahoma," Os whispers. "That's where it has to be. He spent most of his childhood there."

"And judging by his message," Aston adds, "I'd wager it's also where his sister died."

The words settle in, each one a cold, jagged stone.

"So . . . we have to go, right?" Vane asks. "The wind is still giving me the same advice."

"You do realize it sounds like Raiden doesn't expect to survive this little meeting, don't you?" Aston asks. "In which case, it's unlikely he's still hoping to collect your power."

The same worries thunder through my mind, mixed with the sound of Raiden's laughter.

"But isn't that a good thing?" Vane asks. "It means even *he* knows he can't win."

"Never underestimate the desperation of a trapped animal," Os reminds him.

"Sinking ship mentality," Aston agrees. "If he has to go, he'll take the precious ones with him."

"Then wouldn't he ask for Audra to come too?" Vane asks.

"He knows you'll never bring her near him," Os says. "The fact that you excluded her from the original plan made that clear."

"Or he has other plans for her," Aston warns.

"You can speculate all day," my mother tells them. "And never be any closer to the answer. Raiden's a Northern squall. You can't predict him. You can only battle the storm."

"But they're not battling the storm," Os argues. "They're letting it lead them blindly to the slaughter."

"I think I've lost track of the metaphor," Vane mumbles.

His hand shakes as he pulls it away from mine and holds up the whistlepipe. "But we should be safe as long as I still have this. He clearly wants it back. So I'll shield it with Westerlies so he can't tell if I'm carrying it, and use that to stall him while we wait for the wind to tell us how to end him."

I can see dozens of flaws with that plan.

Hundreds.

Thousands.

But I also see no other option.

"We should probably get going," Solana says, sounding far more enthusiastic than I can ever imagine feeling. "Every second we delay gives him more time to prepare."

"And what about *your* preparations?" Os asks. "You haven't discussed a single strategy. You haven't gathered any weapons. All you've done is end your betrothal and waste time on vulgar public displays of affection."

"Best decision ever," Vane says, grinning at me. "And come on, Os. We all know we're not going to take Raiden out with a windslicer or a wind spike—in fact, if we tried that, we'd just get destroyed by his creepy backlash thing. So screw planning—that's Raiden's trick. And it's all an illusion. Time and again we've proven that no matter how hard he tries, he can't control the wind. All we have to do is keep trusting the sky."

"Keep in mind that the wind doesn't actually care whether you live or die," Aston warns him. "It's very clever. But that doesn't mean it has compassion."

I despise the words for being true.

And I despise the helplessness that pours over me as Solana

gathers the fallen feathers and calls for Raiden's wind.

Tears blur my eyes as Vane pulls me closer, turning us away from the crowd so it's just him and me.

"This isn't goodbye," he tells me. "It's 'see you soon.' Really soon. As fast as I can be there. And I need you to be careful in the meantime, okay?"

"*I'm* not the one we need to be worrying about," I remind him.

"Hopefully not—but we both know I'm going to worry anyway. So promise me you'll keep your guard up."

"I always do."

He grins and whispers, "I love you."

"I love you too," I breathe. "So you have to come back to me."

"Like you could ever keep me away."

"I worry you're not taking this as seriously as you should be," I whisper. "Raiden just killed hundreds of people. He's up to something—"

"I know," Vane interrupts. "Believe me, I'm very aware of how freaking scary what I'm about to do is. But I'm going to win, Audra. You know why? Because I have too much to live for."

He leans and kisses me then, his lips tender and soft and sweet. It fills me with warm flutters—but it's not the desperate rush I crave.

I know what he's trying to show me.

He's saving the rest for later.

Still, I take a little more for myself now, dragging him closer, parting his lips, breathing in his breath as he gasps to keep up with me.

This isn't goodbye.

But it's a reminder of how much I need him.

Someone clears their throat, and I finally let Vane break away.

His eyes look as wild as his tousled hair, and it's such a beautiful thing.

"Where can I find you when this is over?" he asks, brushing a hand across my cheek.

"Your house," I decide, earning one of his glorious smiles.

"*That* will be the best homecoming ever."

He steals one last kiss, leaving a sweet taste in my mouth before he steps away and joins Solana.

His eyes never leave mine as Solana tangles Raiden's wind around them, sealing them inside the bubble without another word.

There's nothing more to say.

One way or another, this ends tonight.

All I can do is hope and wait.

CHAPTER 49

VANE

So far I haven't thrown up.

Or peed my pants.

Which is pretty awesome, considering this ruined wind is flying us way faster and bumpier than any wind should be allowed to move.

"You okay?" I ask Solana as we hit an especially hurl-worthy patch of turbulence.

She nods, and I realize she's been awfully quiet since we left.

I guess we've both been quiet—though I've let out a bunch of yelps and squeals during some of the scarier dives. But I wonder if it's still a little awkward for her, since, y'know, she did just have to watch me rebond with Audra. . . .

Actually, no, she's probably trying to prepare for the upcoming battle, and I seriously need to get over myself.

I close my eyes and try to copy Solana's focus, but it's hard to concentrate around the steady tugging in my chest.

I'd forgotten how strong the pull of a healthy bond feels, like part of me is tethered to Audra, stretching thinner with each mile I put between us.

There's a steady pain that comes with it, but it's strangely comforting. It tells me she's safe. And that she's slowly drawing me back to her.

"By the way," I say, hoping this is an okay thing to tell Solana. "Thank you for giving back your link."

"Yeah, well . . . I figured you two might never get together otherwise. Honestly, for two stubborn, willful people, you both can be super insecure and wishy-washy."

I have to laugh at that, glad things finally feel more normal between us.

She even adds, "You guys really are good together."

I should probably stick with "thanks." But for some reason I add, "You'll find the same thing someday."

God—why not just tell her *Someday your prince will come?*

I'm all set to apologize, but Solana laughs it off.

"Let's worry about my love life after we survive tonight, okay?"

Riiiiiiiiiiiiiiiiiiiiiiight.

The whole, flying into Raiden's Trap of Inevitable Doom thing.

"Any idea what we're in for?" I ask.

"I thought your new motto was 'screw planning.'"

"Hey, just because I don't want to try to out-control a control freak doesn't mean I don't think we should brace ourselves."

"Well, in that case, I think it's going to start slow. I think Raiden has something he wants to say to us before he does anything violent."

"He *is* a bragger. . . ."

"Right, but I think it'll be more than that. He went to a lot of effort to bring us somewhere personal to him. I'm assuming that means he's going to tell us *why* we're there. What I can't figure out is, why us? And why now? If he's really planning to kill us afterward, what's the point?"

It's a good question, actually.

Villains in movies tend to "monologue" a lot—but that's usually just the screenwriter stalling things so the hero has enough time to make their dramatic escape.

Raiden's way too smart for that.

Then again, it'd be awesome if he does it. Especially since our whole plan is: *Stay alive long enough for the wind to tell us how to end him.*

"Are you going to be okay?" Solana whispers, breaking my train of thought. "I mean . . . there's no way this isn't going to be violent. . . ."

"I'm ready to do whatever I have to do in order to finish this."

I wish my mouth weren't so dry as I say the words.

I try to focus on Gus—stay angry—remind myself of all the evil things Raiden has done. But really, it all comes down to one thing:

"I'm trusting the wind. I know we keep saying that, but it's all I have. Either my heritage will save me—or . . . it'll break me. Either way, it'll be up to the sky."

A long silence follows, until Solana asks, "It feels like we're flying lower, doesn't it?"

"I think so. But it's hard to tell when I can't see the ground."

There's a moon out there somewhere, but it must be blocked out
by clouds. And I can hear thunder rolling in the distance.

It was a dark and stormy night . . .

I can't remember what book that comes from—but I really hope
it doesn't end with *and then they all died.*

"Do you think—"

My question morphs into a yowl as our draft drops so fast and
hard that I feel the need to shout, "You don't think he's going to splatter us like bugs, do you?"

"He can try," Solana says. "I have enough winds stored up to
catch us."

That *would* make me feel better except . . . "Isn't holding on to any
winds around Raiden kinda like holding a bunch of grenades around
Magneto?"

"I have no idea what that means!"

I'm ready to explain the entire X-Men universe to her, but our
plummet gains even more speed, and I decide to spend the next few
minutes screaming my throat raw instead.

Right before we go *KABLAM*, the wind screeches to a halt, leaving us hovering over some long, scratchy grass.

"Are you okay?" I ask Solana.

"Yeah. But ugh—what is that smell?"

"I think it's 'cow.' Might be 'horse' though. All I know is, it's
some sort of animal poop." Which seems . . . strangely appropriate.

"I'm going to set us down," Solana warns, then hisses a command that makes us drop into the knee-high grass.

"You're quite talented with my power," Raiden says from somewhere in the darkness.

The wind stirs to life around us, singing in mangled, ruined words.

"Seriously?" I ask. "You're going with the ghostly-voice trick? Is that supposed to scare us?"

"How about this?" Raiden asks.

A dozen bolts of blue lightning blast across the sky, illuminating a figure in a white billowing cloak standing about twenty feet away.

I'll admit it.

I scream.

But I mean—the dude just controlled *lightning*.

One well-aimed bolt and I'm a Vane-sizzle.

The glow of the lightning flickers away, leaving me squinting to catch the glint of his eyes.

Minutes crawl by.

Okay, it's probably only seconds, but it seriously feels like *forever*.

So much for Solana's theory about Raiden inviting us here to tell us the Woeful Tale of His Life.

I check my Westerly shield's song, hoping it's already solved the how-do-we-end-him conundrum. But so far all it's telling me is: *stall*.

"So," I say, clearing my throat. "Nice place you chose here. Was it the poop smell that sold you, or the prickly burrs?"

"Is this how you feign bravery?" Raiden asks. "Worthless jokes and pathetic complaints?"

I shrug. "It works pretty well. What about you? Fancy wind tricks are great and all, but don't they ever get boring? Is that why you've been so desperate to learn my language? Looking for some inspiration? If so, this is one of my favorites."

I call a Westerly to my side and tell it to mess up Raiden's hair.

It doesn't do a whole lot, but it does make Raiden flinch—and seeing that flinch feels *good*.

"What's wrong?" I ask him. "Afraid the peaceful tones are contagious?"

"Careful," Solana whispers.

I know she's right.

I should stop poking the bear—at least until I've found the way to kill him. But now that Raiden's this close, all I can hear is the sickening sound of Gus's neck snapping.

Plus, not showing up for our last battle was a pretty freaking cowardly move. Makes me wonder if Raiden's really as scary as we think.

Have we ever actually seen him fight?

What if he's like one of those magicians who use a bunch of illusions to convince you that they're cool enough to make a car disappear and really they're just a guy standing in front of a mirror?

"Saw your army today," I tell him. "Can't say I was impressed."

"Neither was I," Raiden agrees. "I'd forgotten how few of them truly deserved to wield the power of the sky. I kept a handful of the worthy with me, and the rest? Well, I'm sure you saw how they ended up. Really, I should be thanking you. You gave me the perfect opportunity to clean house while taking out your guardians in the process."

"Yeah, well too bad a bunch of guardians survived," I snap. "And now you have no army to fight them."

"I don't need an army. I'll take care of your Gales personally—you have my word on that. But first, I need to tie up a few loose ends."

The edge to his words makes it clear: He's definitely here to kill us.

I don't think he cares about the fourth language anymore.

I doubt he even cares about the stupid whistlepipe.

He brought us here so he could end us.

Any time now, I tell my shield. *Stalling isn't going to work much longer.*

The only answer it gives me is: *patience.*

Yeah, easy for it to say when it's not about to get lightning-fried. But I grit my teeth and ask, "So . . . what's up with all the white clothes? I got a peek at your closet and, dude—you know there are other colors, right?"

"And we're back to the pointless ramblings and insults. It's really your only move, isn't it?" Raiden asks. "I guess that's what happens when your winds won't stand up and fight for you."

"Uh, my winds have taken you down plenty of times, thanks."

AND NOW WOULD BE A GOOD TIME TO DO IT AGAIN— ARE YOU LISTENING, WESTERLIES???

"What about you?" he says to Solana. "You're awfully quiet over there. I'll admit, I was surprised he chose to bring you. But I suppose he was afraid I might carve more scars into his beloved."

My hands curl into fists, and I start to weave a wind spike.

Even if I can't stab his kill spots—I can make him bleed.

Solana absorbs my drafts, her eyes pleading with me to not escalate things before the wind is ready.

Raiden smiles like a Cheshire cat and takes a step closer to her. "Ah yes, you're a windcatcher. A family trait, I believe—not that it did them any good. Your father had been so smug about his escape, I had to make sure I took my time with him. And the rest of your relatives—tell me, how did it feel to walk the halls of Brezengarde? Did you know I slaughtered your grandparents in the very room you stood in? I bet if you'd looked hard enough you could've seen the stains on the floor."

I reach for Solana's hand, hating to feel her shaking.

"It was almost pathetic how desperately they pleaded for their lives," Raiden continues. "I expected so much more dignity from the royal family. They even told me about their precious secret passage. They kept the password protected, but I learned enough to set a trap."

"A trap we got out of super easily," I remind him.

"Yes," Raiden agrees. "As I said. You showed me the folly of relying on an army. But that mistake has been corrected. And now you get to face me. We'll see how your foolish tricks stand up against my power."

Lightning crackles all around us.

I glance at Solana, hoping she's got a plan, but her eyes are closed and she's focused on the wind.

"It must be lonely," she says quietly. "Your winds so clearly despise you. Their shattered songs are filled with loathing. Is that why you keep your bedroom still? Does their hatred haunt you?"

"Careful," Raiden warns, as thunder rolls across the plain. "I could end you with one word."

"I don't believe you," she says.

FYI: It's a bad idea to call Raiden's bluff.

He growls a command, and Solana claws at her stomach, screaming and thrashing until I'm pretty sure he's shattering the winds inside her.

"Stop it!" I shout, pulling the whistlepipe out of my pocket. "Or do you want me to smash this into tinsel?"

Raiden stops, and I'm relieved for about half a second.

Then he laughs. "So you *do* have it with you. That makes this much easier."

Well . . . crap.

Come on, Westerlies—think!

And maybe start gathering some other winds, since I'm sure Raiden's next attack is coming—and it's gonna be a big one.

"You know this wasn't the only thing I stole from you, right?" I say, fighting to buy time as I check on Solana, glad to see her breathing is steadying.

"I haven't missed anything else," Raiden says. "So it can't be too important."

"You're sure?" I fumble in my pocket.

Socky the Duck is long gone, but I still have the handprint thing—and it's a good thing I do.

Raiden stumbles back a step when I hold it out to show him.

"Does that mean this is special?" I ask. "So, like . . . you wouldn't want me to do this?"

I pinch the edge and tear off a crumble of the plaster.

"STOP!" Raiden yells, as lightning flashes and thunder blares and the winds switch to hurricane mode.

"I take it that means you want your chubby handprint back."

"That's not my hand," Raiden snaps.

It's not?

"It's your sister's, isn't it?" Solana asks, proving she's smarter than I am.

She leans on me, and I'm assuming she needs the support. But the strength in her grip makes me wonder if she's planning something.

Man, I hope so.

My Westerly is giving me nothing but a constant chant of *Stall! Stall! Stall!*

"Rena," Raiden whispers, glancing at the sky.

"How did she die?" Solana asks.

Thunder shakes the ground.

"Why is that always the first question?" Raiden asks. "She *lived* for five years—but no one ever wants to hear about that. All they want to know about is the end."

"I want to know about her life," Solana promises. "Tell me about her—isn't that why you brought us here?"

Raiden's laugh is darker than the next crack of thunder. "I came here for *me*. You were just my excuse—and a reason to send a message. Do you know, I haven't been to this field in forty-seven years?"

"The day she died, right?" Solana asks.

"The day she was abandoned by the sky, and ruined by a disgusting groundling."

He moves into the darkness, and Solana and I debate a second before we follow, keeping a safe distance from the tree he stops to lean against.

"Rena was fascinated by the groundling's flying machines," he whispers. "I never understood the appeal. But I was a good brother, so I'd sneak her away and we'd stand right here, where we could see them circle over this field, puttering and humming and spewing smoke. I brought her at least once a week, and it was always the same. But she didn't tell me she'd had her breakthrough. If I'd known, I would've held her hand. I would've made sure she stayed beside me. I never would've let her fly so close."

Solana covers her mouth, and I kinda feel like doing the same.

Everything I'm imagining involves some wicked sharp propellers.

"She might've lived," Raiden whispers. "She'd only lost a leg. But the shock made her fall. And when I ordered the wind to catch her, the draft disobeyed."

Okay, *now* we're getting somewhere.

It even makes me feel a little sorry for Raiden—not enough to excuse anything he's done. But still.

Watching your little sister die like that . . . ?

I trace my fingers over the chubby handprint in the clay, feeling like a jerk for what I'm about to do. But the winds still haven't given us a plan, and I can feel our time running out.

"Surrender yourself," I tell him. "End this peacefully. Or I'll smash this into powder."

Solana grabs my arm as the storm shakes the ground again.

"You know," Raiden says, "I'm almost tempted to agree. I'd

love to watch you live with what you've let happen tonight."

"What does that mean?" I demand.

He laughs.

"There goes her thumb!" I shout, snapping off another piece of the plaster. "Tell me what you mean or I'll destroy the rest."

The winds roar with Raiden's rage, and Solana clings to me, mumbling something about the sky being too charged for us to fly.

"You honestly can't guess?" Raiden asks. "You haven't wondered why I brought you here? Who I might be trying to keep you away from? Who else I might have wanted to reach with my message?"

"Oh God," I say, and Solana has to hold me steady. *"What have you done to Audra?"*

The rest of the handprint crumbles to grit when he only smiles. I fling it at his head and grab the whistlepipe, squeezing it in my fist. "If you touch her again—"

"I'm not doing anything," Raiden interrupts. "That's on my associate. She and I made another deal."

"Your associate?"

No.

It's not possible.

How could Arella . . .

The metal squeals as I crunch it, echoing the sounds in my brain.

"You're going to regret that," Raiden tells me.

"We'll get her back," Solana promises. "Whatever happened, it's not too late."

But it is.

That's why Raiden wasted so much time taunting us and telling stories. The monologuing was a stall for *us*. To stop me from saving her.

The only way to help Audra now is to end this for real.

I reach for her guardian pendant to calm my panic.

The cord is still blue—and my chest still aches with the pull of our bond.

There's still time.

And there's still wind.

Four drafts within my reach—one from each direction.

I weave them into a wind spike and beg for the full weight of their power.

"Well, then," Raiden says, weaving three winds into a sickly gray spike of his own. "Shall we begin?"

CHAPTER 50

AUDRA

The sky is quiet in the desert.

Almost too still.

Just a slice of moon surrounded by dust and stars.

It makes me uneasy, though I'm sure that's mostly the pull of my bond. The constant reminder that Vane is much too far away.

"Aren't you coming inside?" my mother asks for what must be the fifth time.

"I told you, I will."

I lasted five minutes after we arrived.

Five minutes of staring at the still, silent chimes my father gave her, once again locked away from the wind.

Then I needed air.

I move to the shadow of her lonely oak tree, the only place in this sad stretch of land that feels welcoming.

I made my guardian oath here.

Sacrifice before compromise.

I thought I was done with that life.

And yet, here I am—voluntarily my mother's keeper.

I don't regret the decision. But I dread it all the same.

Her birds have already begun to gather—fierce crows and twitching sparrows and leering vultures. They line the roof, the branches, the rocks and weeds. Their eyes follow my every move, their stares both wary and unwelcoming.

They always choose my mother over me.

I've assumed it was some testimony to her superiority.

But I wonder if it's a simple matter of authority.

I march back inside, pluck my father's chimes from above her empty table, and carry them out to the porch, stringing them from the same hook I used the last time I freed them.

My mother shouts for me to stop, but already their soft tinkling has made the air less lonely.

"I'm going to move them back as soon as you're gone," she tells me.

"No, you're not. You risked my life—and cost Gus his—all to protect whatever remains of Dad's songs. And yet you lock his chimes away and refuse to let them sing?"

"I'm protecting them!"

"No, you're ruining them. I know how it feels to be a prisoner. I know how it drains the heart slowly out of you. I won't let you dull Dad's legacy the same way."

The words knock her back a step, and I watch the emotions flicker in her eyes. Flashes of guilt and sorrow and remorse—but there are too many darker notes for me to care.

"Fine," she says, her focus on the stars. "We'll try it your way—for now."

"If it helps you to tell yourself that, go ahead. But this is permanent. You have to follow my rules."

"My, we're taking our role as potential queen quite seriously, aren't we?" she asks.

"You think I care about a title? I care about my vow. I swore to keep you under control. I swore to protect our people from your influence. And I will. You don't leave this house without me—ever. I don't care if it's a raging inferno. Suck the air away to squelch the fire and stand in the ashes. And no sending messages to anyone except me."

"So is that what you're going to do with your life now?" my mother asks. "Constant vigil monitoring me? I don't think Vane would be too happy with that arrangement."

He wouldn't—though if I asked him to, he'd do it.

But I'm not alone in this. I have the sky—and my gifts.

"The wind will tell me if you disobey," I warn her. "As will my birds."

I turn toward our feathered onlookers, glad to see I already have their focus.

"You answer to *me* now," I tell them. "And your task is to watch *her*."

I stretch out my hand, and a brave sparrow flits to my finger.

He nuzzles his beak against my thumb as I stroke the bold stripes along his head and tell him to report to me twice a day. I can feel his loyalty swell with my touch, and I know he'll keep a steady eye.

I order the rest of the birds to be his backup.

The wind will tell me if they fail.

"If you prove you can't be trusted, I'll let Aston find another solution," I warn my mother. "And if he can't find one, I'll send you to Os, and we both know his answer."

"Well," my mother says, smoothing the fabric of her silky blue gown as I send my new sparrow friend back to his oak branch. "I see you have it all figured out."

She's trying so hard to be the elegant creature she's always been. But she's too frail and scarred to pull it off.

Too weak and wounded to ever intimidate me again.

My mother sighs. "Why does it always have to be like this? Can't we . . ." She shakes her head, scattering whatever else she'd been planning to say. "Why don't you come inside? I can help you clean your wounds."

"I should get going."

I promised Vane I'd be waiting for him—and after all the waiting he's done for me, that's one promise I intend to keep.

His bond tightens its hold on my heart, the crushing pain proof that he's still breathing.

Still fighting.

Please let him win.

My eyes will be glued to the sky. Listening. Hoping.

"We can't leave things like this, Audra," my mother says. "Just come inside for a few minutes."

"Why are you so insistent on that?"

She stares at the singing chimes, and her hand darts to her wrist. "Maybe . . . I'm not ready to be alone," she whispers.

I watch her fingers twitching across her bare skin, itching to polish the gold cuff that should be there. And I have to ask. "What happened to your link?"

"Os took it. Before he sent me to the Maelstrom. He said I dishonored my bond with my choices."

"You did."

"I know." The wind seems to shift, and she turns her face to the breeze, her expression peaceful even as her fingers gouge red trails across her skin. "I've lived with my mistakes every day for ten years. Sometimes I'm not sure how I'll bear it any longer."

"That's your fault."

"It is. But you could fix it."

"If you're asking me to forgive you—"

"I'm not asking anything. I'm simply telling you what your father told me. When Vane pulled me out of the Maelstrom, I was mostly gone—and I had no plans to fight my way back. But your father's songs found me and called me toward him. He filled my heart with new lyrics. Reminded me that while he gave you his gift, he gave me *you*. And he said I could live without him—but never without you."

I close my eyes, hating that I have to hear the message in her voice instead of his.

"Is that why . . . ?" I whisper.

"Yes. It's why I helped Vane rescue you. I had to see if your father was right."

The next logical question burns on my tongue, begging me to ask it.

But I can't.

I don't want to care about her answer.

So I turn to the wind, searching once again for my father's Easterly.

"You won't find him," my mother tells me.

I hate her for being right.

Why can't he be there?

Why can't he—

I suck in a breath. "I feel him."

My mother grabs my arm, her whole body shaking.

"He's coming from the north," I whisper. "I'm calling him over."

"Go inside," she tells me, dragging me toward the door.

I lock my knees. "Why? What are you doing?"

"I'm bringing you inside. For once, can't you simply listen to me?"

"Not until you tell me why."

My mother laughs, clawing harder at her skin. "Stubborn right to the end."

She reaches down her dress and pulls a golden-brown eagle feather from what's left of her cleavage.

"Yes," she says as my eyes widen with recognition. "Raiden sent me a special message. He told me to bring you somewhere and keep you occupied so his Stormers could collect you."

"And you agreed," I finish, though it goes without saying.

"I didn't have to. He was sending them either way. And if I resist, he'll destroy your father's wind. So go inside, Audra. Don't make me force you."

I have to laugh at that. "You think I'm going to surrender that easily? You can't beat me anymore. I have the power of four! I have Gus's gift!"

"GO INSIDE NOW!" she screams, launching a whipping wind that drags me through her front door and slams it behind me.

I tear at the handle, but somehow the wind holds it closed.

She can't contain me that easily.

I grab one of the chairs from the table and smash it through the nearest window, kicking away the jagged shards of glass so I can crawl through.

My feet have barely touched the ground when two Stormers land in the yard.

"Let's make this quick," the tallest one says—though they're both enormous.

Raiden sent his best.

"GO INSIDE!" my mother screams as I gather any nearby winds.

The Stormers have tried to clear the sky, but they can't chase away my Westerlies.

"They're not taking me again!" I shout.

"Please, Audra," my mother begs. "I don't want you to see this."

"See what?" the smaller Stormer asks.

It all happens too fast then.

Wood crackles as my mother whips her arms, tearing huge branches off my favorite oak and slamming the jagged ends through the Stormers' chests.

No one has ever survived her trademark trick.

No one can match my mother's speed.

But . . . she wasn't fast enough.

With his final breath the largest Stormer snarls a broken command.

I scream and drop to my knees as the wind he'd been carrying writhes in pain and unravels. Slowly the draft's essence crumbles away, until there's nothing left but a sickly yellow whirl.

It used to be an Easterly.

It used to be everything.

"I didn't want you to see," my mother whispers.

I realize her arms are around me, and that we're both shaking too hard to move.

It's impossible to think surrounded by so much destruction.

Shattered branches.

Shattered bodies.

Shattered wind.

"I'm so sorry, Audra—there was no way to save you both, and I wasn't going to make the wrong choice again."

She chose me.

"Please come inside," she whispers. "The violence . . . remember, you speak Westerly."

Somehow I make my legs carry me into the house. Or maybe it's my mother carrying me. My mind is too stuck on the fact that *she chose me.*

And my father . . .

"He's really gone," I whisper.

That last tiny piece.

I hadn't realized how much it meant until . . .

"He's not gone," my mother tells me. "That's what I finally see. He lives in you—everything powerful and incredible about him lives in *you*. I'm sorry it took me so long to realize it. And I'm sorry I let the madness ruin us."

"Are we ruined?" I whisper.

It feels like it.

But I don't want to give Raiden that power.

My mother has played the villain—but Raiden's always been the true enemy. He set our world on this path and left everything scattered and broken.

I won't let him break me.

I won't let him take anything else.

So I hold tight to my mother—let her wipe my tears and check me for wounds. And when she's done, I do the same for her.

"I can hear your Westerly singing," she tells me, tracing her fingers through the breeze against my skin. "What is it saying?"

I close my eyes and listen to a song about a steady tree, braving every storm because of its strong hold.

My mother has always been my tempest.

But maybe she can also be my roots.

I sing the lyrics for her—but stick to a loose translation to avoid risking any breakthrough.

"Thank you," she whispers. "I'll try to remember that so I can hold steady until the next time you come to check on me. In the meantime, go. Get ready for Vane."

I check my bond, not sure if I should be relieved or terrified that the pull feels just as far away as before. Clearly there was more to Raiden's plan than any of us anticipated.

But I'm too far away to get there in time.

And . . . he doesn't need my help.

He has the wind—and Solana. He has his training.

"What about you?" I ask my mother. "Do you need help with . . ."

She shakes her head. "I can handle the cleanup. I've done it before."

She helps me stand and move my shaky legs to the door, and I find my strength with every step.

I know there's probably something I should say—some grand speech that could cement these new connections.

But words are failing me at the moment.

So I borrow some from Vane, clinging to the hope that they'll soon be true for him and me as well.

"It's not goodbye. It's see you soon."

CHAPTER 51

VANE

'm just going to say it—I'm *really* sick of wind battles.

Like, I can't even begin to explain how over them I am.

Crushing cyclones.

Exploding wind spikes.

Getting constantly sucked up and tossed around.

I don't have time for this crap.

I need to get back to Audra.

She's strong enough to take down Arella—and she promised she'd be on her guard. But it still kills me that I'm stuck playing Who Has the Scariest Wind Trick? when I could be on my way to help.

And I know Audra gave me a big speech one time about how human weapons have nothing on the might of a hurricane. But, dude, what I wouldn't give for a tank to hunker down in and keep on blasting.

But no.

All I get is a steady supply of Westerlies, which still haven't come up with any freaking ideas for how to end this madness.

And Raiden's wind tricks just keep right on coming.

"Is that really all you've got?" I shout from our hiding spot behind a few trees as Raiden launches another volley of wind spikes and Solana uses some special command to deflect them away.

I mean, I'm glad we're able to hold our own—but seriously, what's the deal? I'm seeing a lot more *average wind fighter* and a lot less *legendary warrior*.

Unless he's tiring us out, and saving the good stuff for the end....

Yeah.

It turns out it's the last one.

"You *had* to push," Solana snaps as Raiden forms a massive tornado and somehow tangles it with a ton of flashing purple lightning.

I don't understand the physics of that—but the zapnado is headed our way, and fun bonus: Its suction is pretty much on the level of a supermassive black hole. So it definitely has that *NO WAY WILL WE SURVIVE THIS* feel I've been expecting from Raiden.

I scramble to get us airborne, but that only buys us a few seconds before the zapnado's pull drags us toward its sizzling funnel.

"What was that?" Solana shouts as some sort of animal gets sucked past us and crispified by the lightning.

"Pretty sure that was a bison. Or maybe a buffalo? Is there a difference?"

"Never mind, just get us out of here!"

"I'm trying!"

My Westerlies fight as hard as they can, but I feel the electricity getting stronger, rippling across my skin, making my hair stand on end.

"Okay, new plan." I have to look away from Solana, because even with the gravity of our situation, I want to make fun of her giant static hair explosion. "How many winds do you have left?"

"I only have broken ones."

Another bison whizzes past us, and we barely miss its flailing hooves. "Can you weave them into a wind spike?"

"I can try." She murmurs a few different commands and ends up with some sort of yellowish curved thing.

"That looks more like a wind boomerang—what did you ask for?"

"I asked for something that would give us a fighting chance."

"Well . . . let's see if it works!"

I aim for the funnel's base, hoping that might knock it over or something.

It *does* make a dent—but not enough to stop the zapnado.

"Incoming!" Solana shouts as the wind boomerang proves I nicknamed it correctly. It blasts back our way, exploding our wind bubble before I can catch it.

I can't find any winds to slow our fall, so we're stuck with the tuck-and-roll method. It's equal parts painful and disgusting when I end up with a face full of manure.

"For the record, I just bruised every inch of my body."

Solana has no sympathy, screaming "GET UP!" and hauling me to my feet.

We stumble away just in time to avoid a lightning blast that definitely would've turned us to ash.

Solana launches the boomerang back at the zapnado, nailing it right in the center.

Lightning and sparks explode everywhere, like it sucked up a big box of fireworks. And when the lights dim, the funnel finally unravels.

Raiden celebrates our victory by creating three more zapnadoes.

"I am seriously done with this guy," I grumble, glad to find enough Westerlies to get us airborne again.

We have to kill him.

The certainty of it feels like ice in my veins—every bit as unsettling as it is awakening. All my senses come to life, and I stretch them farther than I've ever reached.

I can feel dozens more Westerlies—maybe hundreds—waiting on the fringes. Almost like they're watching me.

Only a handful answer my call—which is both annoying and confusing—but with their help, I'm able to fly a lot higher this time. High enough to avoid the storm's suction—but all we can do is circle above the battle, and the thunderheads around us keep flashing with more lightning.

Please, I beg. *Tell me what I have to do. If we don't kill him soon, he's going to win.*

The winds stir a little faster, and their songs shift to something new.

But their brilliant new lyric tells me: *A shield is more dangerous than a sword.*

"Are your winds giving you any ideas?" I ask Solana. "Because mine are giving me philosophies. Or is it a platitude? Whatever—it's useless. I think this fight might be beyond them, but I'm hoping that still fits with the winds' plan. I'm here to keep us safe while you figure out the killing."

"Gee, no pressure or anything," Solana mumbles. "And I'm not having much luck. I've tried thinking about avenging Gus and my family. I've tried thinking about saving the rest of the Gales. I've even tried thinking about all the groundlings who've died in all the crazy weather Raiden's always causing. But every time I try to think about getting around his backlash, it gives me nothing."

"Okay, this is going to sound awful—and I swear I'm only asking because it's what you said worked for the oubliette—but . . . have you made it clear that you're okay if you don't make it out of this? Just to take any selfishness out of the equation?"

"Of course. I've made it very clear that I'm not concerned with my safety—only yours. But it still hasn't given me anything."

My idea trigger goes off, but I try to shut it up.

I really really really don't want *that* to be the right answer.

But its way more exhausting for us to dodge storms than it is for Raiden to make them. We barely take out the three zapnadoes—only to have him form three more—and when one gets way too close to frying us, I take a deep breath and force myself to ask, "What if *I'm* throwing off the need? What if the way you keep trying to protect me is too selfish? I mean, I appreciate that you are, but . . . when you compare saving my life to *saving our entire world from Raiden*, I . . . kinda don't stack up."

"So . . . you want me to focus the need without trying to keep you alive?"

"Well, feel free to make it clear that's not our *first* choice, but . . . yeah."

I try to tell myself it's not as devastating as it feels. After all, if we don't come up with a plan, we're both dead anyway.

But all I can think about is my promise to Audra that I *would* come home to her.

I can still feel the pull of our bond—even through all this chaos.

She's drawing me toward her.

How can I abandon her?

"A new command is starting to form," Solana whispers, which does *not* feel like good news. "I think . . . if you can fly us close enough to Raiden, I might know what I'm supposed to do to take him out. But I'm not feeling a way to avoid the backlash."

"So basically, you know how to kill him—but it'll kill us, too?"

"I think so . . . it's hard to tell. I never know exactly how it's going to work until I try it."

I take another ten seconds to admit we're officially out of options, and a few more after that to let go of a couple of tears.

"We don't have to do it, Vane. If we keep fighting, we might find another way. I'll try again, telling the need to keep you safe."

I have to laugh at that, though it's not funny at all. "That's ridiculous. Why is it okay for you to die, and not me?"

"Because I'm using Raiden's tainted power, and you're using the language of peace." The thickness in her voice tells me she's crying too.

"Neither of us deserves this, Solana. Just like our families didn't deserve what happened to them. It's like Aston said. War is about hard choices. This is ours. If you don't want to do it, teach me the command."

"But what about Audra?"

I choke back a new wave of tears—and resist the urge to shout at the sky: *THIS ISN'T FAIR—YOU OWE ME!*

It's *not* fair—but it doesn't matter. All that really matters is one thing.

Please let Audra be okay, I beg the wind. *Let her survive whatever she's facing. And don't let losing me make her unhappy. I mean, she can cry a few tears—but then I want her to move on. She's grieved enough in her life. Please let her get over me.*

I'm so focused on my plea that I don't notice that we're circling lower, like my Westerlies have gotten behind this brutal suicide mission.

At least the storms have calmed, and the last of the zapnadoes have unraveled.

"Are you ready for this?" Solana whispers, clutching a new wind boomerang thing.

"Let's just get it over with quick this time," I whisper. "As soon as the need tells you what to do—do it, okay?"

She reaches for my hand, and I squeeze hers back, glad I get to face this with a friend.

"Here goes nothing," I tell her, ordering the winds to set us down in front of Raiden.

He chose his spot well—a ridge so narrow we can only keep a couple of feet between him and us. A guarantee that we'll be within range of his backlash.

"So this is how it ends," Raiden says. "The last stand of the last Westerly. Any final words?"

I'm about to tell him no when I notice my winds have added a new lyric.

They're still singing about a shield being more dangerous than a sword, but there's a new line that comes right before it.

Trust your enemy.

"You have two choices," Raiden tells us. "Teach me a word of Westerly and I'll kill you both quickly. Refuse, and you'll get to watch your little friend experience a multitude of indescribable agonies."

He grabs Solana by her hair, wrenching her neck as he drags her closer.

Trust your enemy, my Westerlies sing. *Trust your enemy. Trust your enemy.*

TRUST YOUR ENEMY.

"You want to know a word of Westerly?" I ask Raiden, hoping I'm guessing the wind's meaning. "Fine. I'll teach you a word. Just don't hurt her."

Solana's eyes get almost as huge as Raiden's.

"Just like that?" he asks. "After all of this"—he sweeps his arms toward the battle-scarred field—"you're ready to betray your heritage before I place a single blow?"

"I saw what you did to Gus," I mumble. "Solana doesn't deserve that."

Maybe I'm a better actor than I think. Or maybe Raiden's just power hungry and doesn't stop to ask the questions he should probably ask.

He doesn't even argue when I demand he let Solana go. He releases his hold, and I pull her close enough to whisper, "Watch for my signal."

"I'll teach you their strongest command," I tell him. "The one that's saved me the most. If that doesn't trigger your breakthrough, nothing will."

Raiden's in full power-junkie mode, his mouth practically salivating as I ask the Westerlies to whisk around him.

A shield is more dangerous than a sword.

"I'm going to teach you how to form a shield," I say. "It only takes one word."

Solana and I share a look, and I hope she's ready, because she's going to have to time it perfectly.

"Listen to the way I say it first," I say, glad my instincts aren't making me hurl yet. They've done that every other time I've tried to teach anyone, so this really must be what the winds want.

I whisper the word, highlighting each of the sighing, swishy sounds.

"Repeat it one more time," Raiden tells me.

I notice Solana tightening her grip on her boomerang, and nod.

This is it.

Please let this be the end of him.

"Ready to try it?" I ask.

Raiden's too focused on the pronunciation to notice Solana whispering her own command and turning her boomerang from yellow to red.

He nails each syllable of the Westerly command perfectly, and right as the final sound rolls off his tongue, Solana flings the weapon, nailing him dead in the chest.

We both drop to the ground as the force of the backlash ricochets, and I suck in a breath, wishing my last taste of air wasn't so dusty.

I will always love you, Audra.

I repeat the words, hoping they brand themselves to my echo.

Let her find it. Let her know how sorry I am to leave her alone.

But as the explosion rings in my ears, I don't feel any pain. And after another second I have to brave a look.

I don't know how to describe the sound I make—it's a mix of a thousand different emotions.

Solana makes a similar noise as she sits up beside me.

In the split second after her boomerang passed through Raiden's backlash, the Westerly shield draped around his body, sealing in the explosion and leaving him to bear the full force of the blow—which triggers the backlash again. And again. And again.

Justice, the Westerlies tell me, the word easing my nausea at the gore.

Raiden's the one who sealed his doom, forcing himself to face the pain of his own evil power.

It's a slow death.

A painful one.

And then, he's gone.

I leave him in his shell a few minutes longer, just to be certain the explosions are over.

And when I finally release the Westerly shield, his body crumbles to dust.

Rejected by the sky. Left to rot on the earth.

CHAPTER 52

AUDRA

It's done.

I can feel it in the air.

A newfound peace I don't know how to describe.

The winds aren't calm—but I've never felt such joyous ease.

The air feels lighter, softer. Like Raiden's existence had been a physical burden, dragging down the sky and burying it in gloom.

And Vane . . .

Our bond feels stronger than ever. Almost electric with the rush of his urgent journey.

He's coming home.

He's safe.

And he's mine.

The Gales are frenzied with preparations—already a unanimous vote has passed, approving Vane's plan for a ruling power of four.

Coronations and celebrations are being planned, even as the surviving guardians head to Brezengarde to wipe out any remaining Stormers.

There are stories that need to be told, life-changing decisions that must be made.

But I've asked them all to wait.

I want one day.

One day with Vane, when we're not Easterlies or Westerlies or guardians or groundlings or kings and queens.

One day when I can give him a small sliver of the normal I know he craves.

His parents returned not long ago, thanks to a lucky fluke of timing. I'd been resting in his room when I was woken by the twittering sound of his phone ringing. It took me several tries to figure out how to answer—and I'm sure the conversation on my end was lacking—but I managed to convince them it was safe to come home.

They rushed here straightaway.

I'd expected our reunion to feel stilted.

Complicated.

Two worlds struggling to find a common place.

I'd had speeches prepared—most of them apologies.

But they weren't needed.

The second they walked through the door, they wrapped me in their arms and thanked me. There were questions of course. But mostly laughter and tears.

They keep telling me I'm part of the family—which I guess I am.

Sort of.

Bonding is a complicated thing.

There's still one more step to seal our commitment—but we'll get to that when we're ready.

In the meantime his mom flutters around me, trying to stay busy.

They'd stocked up on bandages and other supplies preparing for this moment, and she insists on helping me dress my wounds.

I can see the fury in her eyes when she finds the marks Raiden left. And she cries all over again when I tell her about Gus.

"Vane should be fine," I add, because I know she must be worrying. "When I left him, he only had minor injuries. And if he'd suffered anything more serious, I think I'd be able to tell."

Still, I know she'll feel better when she can see him herself.

As will I.

Soon.

I can feel he's closer, but still not quite close enough.

I ask if I can borrow one of Vane's shirts, since my other clothes were ruined, and his mom blushes and tells me she bought me a dress.

"I don't know if this is a weird gift—and it's not as fancy as the other one I saw you wearing—but as soon as I saw it, I thought of you."

The pale blue fabric is the softest, smoothest thing I've ever felt. And it's printed with tiny soaring birds.

"It's perfect."

She leaves me to change, and I stare at myself for far longer than I probably should, trying to recognize the girl staring back at me.

She carries more scars than my other self.

And yet, she carries fewer shadows.

She looks . . . happy.

His mother's eyes get misty when I emerge from the bathroom, and even his father looks moved.

"You're welcome to wait for him in his room," he tells me, earning himself an elbow from Vane's mother and starting a hushed debate about sleeping arrangements.

Yet another complicated thing we'll have to figure out.

But right now, I have other plans.

"Actually, I was wondering if you could do me one more favor," I tell his mom.

Of course she immediately agrees.

She smiles even wider when I tell her what I'm thinking.

"Leave it to me."

CHAPTER 53

VANE

The sun is just starting to rise as I crest the San Gorgonio Mountains and fly the familiar path through the pass.

The windmills of the wind farm spin slow and steady, their signal lights winking at me as I follow the line of the freeway into my valley.

I'd been dreading seeing all the damage again, but honestly?

Things don't look nearly as bad as I remember. Either the cleanup crews have been busy, or I've seen too much other destruction.

I hope it's the first option.

It took me longer to get home than I planned, but I had to make sure Solana had somewhere to go. I'd offered to let her stay with me, but she chose to go back to Aston's cave. She wanted to be around someone else who understood the power of pain. I'm hoping that doesn't mean the battle took a big toll.

Her eyes weren't glinting with any sort of craving, but I'm not sure if that's because we're both too exhausted.

Coming home felt like the longest journey *ever*.

We could've blasted here with pipelines—trusted our lives to the wind one final time. But we both chose the safe path, to fly and clear our heads.

I'm doing okay with all the violence.

Definitely no remorse over killing Raiden.

It's just a lot to process.

We kinda changed our entire world—in a good way, of course.

But still.

Change.

And responsibility.

And all kinds of other things I'm so not ready for.

All I really want to do is collapse on the couch and binge watch TV—unless Audra's around, then . . . *all the making out!*

The thought gives me a final burst of energy, and within minutes I'm back at my parents' house.

I didn't expect them to be home yet, but there's their car, parked in the driveway. I'm equal parts excited and exhausted.

I'm wondering if it'd make me a jerk if I snuck in through my bedroom window and did the whole big dramatic reunion thing once I'd gotten a little sleep.

But then I think about everything I've put them through these last few weeks—all the times I made them run for cover, and the mysterious injuries I showed up with, not to mention the whole *Guess what? Your son isn't human!* weirdness.

They deserve to know I'm okay.

My parents seem strangely unsurprised when I walk through the door—though of course there's still plenty of hugging and crying. They ask questions I don't know how to answer yet. So I tell them the only thing that really matters.

"It's over."

They hug me a whole lot tighter and promise they're here for whatever I need.

"So wait—how did you guys know to come back?" I ask.

My mom smiles. "Audra answered your phone."

"So you've seen her?" I ask. "She's okay?"

"She's more than okay," my dad says.

"She has a surprise planned for you," my mom adds. "But, uh . . . I think you might want to shower first."

"Yeah," my dad chimes in. "You smell like crap—literally."

He smiles at his corny joke, and I think about all the facefuls of manure I got during the battle and head toward the bathroom. "Good call."

It takes me longer than I meant to shower, but it's not easy with my injured elbow and all the other wounds I have to clean and bandage.

Plus I keep trying to guess what Audra's surprise is, and it's very . . . *distracting.*

My favorite Batman shirt feels tight across the shoulders. All this fighting really has made me stronger. Even without food—

Food.

God, I had no idea I was so starving.

I'm hoping my mom's making me about ten of her famous torpedo burritos, but when I head out of the bathroom, she's sitting with my dad on the couch, both of them giving me those horrifying *our baby looks so grown up* smiles.

"So . . . where's Audra?"

"She's waiting for you on the roof," my mom says.

The *roof*?

That kills almost all of my favorite theories.

It's already starting to get warm, and the air is turning still. But I find a Westerly and coil it around me.

As I do, I notice the compass on my bracelet has stopped spinning.

In fact, it seems like it's pointing straight to the rooftop.

The wind floats me off the ground, carrying me to where Audra's waiting, perched on the red tiles, her face turned away from me, focused on the sky.

She's wearing a dress.

Not a skimpy dress like I've enjoyed before.

But I like this one even better.

She looks so . . . normal.

So real.

And when she turns my way and smiles . . . *wow*.

I mean, seriously.

I don't know what I did to deserve this beautiful, incredible girl. But I'm never letting her get away.

I try to think of something deep and poetic to say. But the best I can come up with is: "I'm so glad you're safe."

"I'm glad you're safe too," she tells me. "I was starting to think you were never going to get here."

"I know. Sorry, I—"

She holds up her hand. "You don't have to explain. In fact, I think we should make a deal not to talk about anything stressful—unless you need to. I told the Gales we're taking today to relax."

I laugh. "Are you sure you know how to do that?"

She pats the roof tile next to her, offering me a seat. "I figured you could teach me."

I make my way over to her side—and by the way: Walking on roofs is *way* harder than it looks. I nearly trip twice—but I get there.

When I do, I notice a red-and-white bag peeking out of a thermal lunch case, resting near her hip.

"Okay, am I hallucinating, or do you have In-N-Out?"

"Not hallucinating," she says, opening the bag and filling the air with the smell of cheeseburgers and French fries.

My stomach growls so loud, we both have to laugh.

"I had your mom get it for me. I remembered what you said about how we haven't really had many dates. So I thought I'd give it a try. I know we're just up on a roof—and the food is mostly cold because I didn't realize you'd be back so late—"

"It's perfect," I tell her.

And it is.

I sit next to her and she hands me my cheeseburger and it's seriously the best moment ever. I get a little choked up by it, actually.

I watch her dive into her own burger without any hesitation or worries about sacrifice—see that look of *oh my God this is amazing* cross her face—and I have to kiss her.

I lean in and—

Gavin lets out a huge screech.

I nearly flail right off the roof, and fling a few French fries at him. "Dude—do that again and we're having roast hawk for dinner!"

He screeches and hops over to the fries, gobbling them up as he watches me. I guess I should be glad he's still alive—and that he has good taste in snacks—but it's easier to like him when his beady eyes aren't glaring.

Audra whistles something, and he flaps his wings and takes off toward the date grove.

"I told him to leave us alone," she tells me.

"Alone is good," I whisper, reaching up to wipe a spot of ketchup off her face.

I'm trying to decide if I should kiss her, or let her finish her burger. She makes the decision for me, grabbing my face and pulling me to her.

As soon as our lips meet, it's like breathing clear air. Or when the sun finally breaks through on a cold, stormy day.

The leftover darkness haunting me from the battle fades with each press of her lips, and I kiss her back, hoping I can erase anything her mother did.

When we finally pull away, the sun's much higher in the sky, and the sweltering heat is starting to settle in.

"Do you want to go inside?" she asks, waving a fly out of her eyes.

"Maybe in a minute. Right now, I just want to enjoy this."

She scoots closer to me, resting her head on my shoulder, and we both stare at the bright puffy clouds and listen to the wind.

It sings about new beginnings, and that's exactly what this is.

The first day of our every day.

With nothing but clear skies ahead.

ACKNOWLEDGMENTS

Every book takes its own unique journey from inspiration to publication, and this one was my greatest adventure by far. So I want to start by thanking my readers for their love and support—and especially their patience—as I fumbled through all the craziness to bring this story into the world.

An infinite amount of thanks goes to my fabulous agent, Laura Rennert, for her ability to play the roles of adviser, champion, and shoulder to panic on. The amazing people at Andrea Brown Literary also deserve an abundance of thank-yous, as does Taryn Fagerness and all my wonderful foreign publishers.

To my editor, Liesa Abrams Mignogna, thank you for believing in Vane and Audra and giving me the chance to write the ending their story deserved. My deepest gratitude also goes to Mara Anastas, Mary Marotta, Katherine Devendorf, Sarah McCabe, Carolyn Swerdloff, Jennifer Romanello, Faye Bi, Lucille Rettino, Jodie Hockensmith, Michelle Leo, Anthony Parisi, Betsy Bloom, Matt Pantoliano, Amy Bartram, Mike Rosamilia, Tom Daly, Sara Berko, Julie Doebler, and the entire sales team at Simon & Schuster for the time, care, and creativity they each pour into my books. And thank you, Regina Flath, for giving me three covers I absolutely adore, and Shane Rebenschied for creating the most gorgeous art-work ever.

Thank you, Kari Olson, for enduring hours and *hours* of brain-storming (Vane would also like me to thank you for constantly advo-cating All the Kissing!) And thank you, C. J. Redwine, for braving the deadline trenches with me. I'm not sure I would've made it through without our check-in chats. Thank you, Victoria Morris, for being an awesome cheerleader (and an absurdly fast reader). And Sara McClung and Sarah Wylie—no matter how far I drop off the radar, I'm so thankful to know you're both always there when I need you.

Thank you, lovely writer friends, for letting me lean on you (and hanging with me at events), especially Erin Bowman, Zac Brewer, MG Buerhlen, Lisa Cannon, Christa Desir, Debra Driza, Nikki Katz, Lisa Mantchev, Lisa McMann, Ellen Oh, Andrea Ortega, Cindy Pon, James Riley, Amy Tintera, Kasie West, Natalie Whipple, and Suzanne Young. And thank you to the brilliant teach-ers, librarians, bloggers, and booksellers who help readers discover my books, especially Mel Barnes, Alyson Beecher, Katie Bartow, Jo Gray, Maryelizabeth Hart, Jillian Heise, Faith Hochhalter, Heather Laird, Katie Laird, Kim Laird, Barbara Mena, Brandi Stewart, Kristin Trevino, Andrea Vuleta, and *so* many others. (If I've forgot-ten you, you officially have my permission to yell at me!)

To my parents, thank you for never letting me give up or doubt myself, and for not judging me (too much) when I find it far too easy to think like my villains.

To my long-suffering husband, Miles, thank you for help-ing me turn my office into the perfect writing space, and for not complaining when I still set up camp in your man cave during the endless deadline days.

Finally, I have to thank Vane and Audra. Yes, I'm aware that you're fictional (really, Mom—I am!) but in some ways you feel very real. You were there when I needed to fall back in love with writing, and again when I needed a boost of hope and faith. And even though I'm done telling your story, you'll still be with me. I'll think of you every time I look at the sky or feel the wind on my face. But I'm done tormenting you now—I promise! Go forth and enjoy your happy ending!

CHECK OUT ANOTHER THRILLING ADVENTURE FROM SHANNON MESSENGER!

Read on for a look at the first book in the *New York Times* bestselling Keeper of the Lost Cities series.

Blurry, fractured memories swam through Sophie's mind, but she couldn't piece them together. She tried opening her eyes and found only darkness. Something rough pressed against her wrists and ankles, refusing to let her move.

A wave of cold rushed through her as the horrifying realization dawned.

She was a hostage.

A cloth across her lips stifled her cry for help, and a sedative's sweet aroma stung her nose when she inhaled, making her head spin.

Were they going to kill her?

Would the Black Swan really destroy their own creation? What was the point of Project Moonlark, then? What was the point of the Everblaze?

The drug lulled her toward a dreamless oblivion, but she fought back—clinging to the one memory that could shine a tiny spot of light in the thick, inky haze. A pair of beautiful aquamarine eyes.

Fitz's eyes. Her first friend in her new life. Her first friend ever.

Maybe if she hadn't noticed him that day in the museum, none of this would have happened.

No. She knew it'd been too late even then. The white fires were already burning—curving toward her city and filling the sky with sticky, sweet smoke.

The spark before the blaze.

"Miss Foster!" Mr. Sweeney's nasal voice cut through Sophie's blaring music as he yanked her earbuds out by the cords. "Have you decided that you're too smart to pay attention to this information?"

Sophie forced her eyes open. She tried not to wince as the bright fluorescents reflected off the vivid blue walls of the museum, amplifying the throbbing headache she was hiding.

"No, Mr. Sweeney," she mumbled, shrinking under the glares of her now staring classmates.

She pulled her shoulder-length blond hair around her face, wishing she could hide behind it. This was exactly the kind of attention she went out of her way to avoid. Why she wore dull colors and lurked in the back, blocked by the other kids who were at least a foot taller than her. It was the only way to survive as a twelve-year-old high school senior.

"Then perhaps you can explain why you were listening to your iPod instead of following along?" Mr. Sweeney held up her earbuds like they were evidence in a crime. Though to him, they probably were. He'd dragged Sophie's class to the Natural History Museum in Balboa Park, assuming his students would be excited about the all-day field trip. He didn't seem to realize that unless the giant dinosaur replicas came to life and started eating people, no one cared.

Sophie tugged out a loose eyelash—a nervous habit—and stared at her feet. There was no way to make Mr. Sweeney understand why she needed the music to cancel the noise. He couldn't even *hear* the noise.

Chatter from dozens of tourists echoed off the fossil-lined walls and splashed around the cavernous room. But their mental voices were the real problem.

Scattered, disconnected pieces of thoughts broadcast straight into Sophie's brain—like being in a room with hundreds of TVs blaring different shows at the same time. They sliced into her consciousness, leaving sharp pains in their wake.

She was a freak.

It'd been her secret—her burden—since she fell and hit her head when she was five years old. She'd tried blocking the noise. Tried ignoring it. Nothing helped. And she could never tell anyone. They wouldn't understand.

"Since you've decided you're above this lecture, why don't you give it?" Mr. Sweeney asked. He pointed to the enormous orange dinosaur with a duckbill in the center of the room. "Explain to the class how the Lambeosaurus differs from the other dinosaurs we've studied."

Sophie repressed a sigh as her mind flashed to an image of the information card in front of the display. She'd glanced at it when they entered the museum, and her photographic memory recorded every detail. As she recited the facts, Mr. Sweeney's face twisted into a scowl, and she could hear her classmates' thoughts grow increasingly sour. They weren't exactly fans of their resident child prodigy. They called her Curvebuster.

She finished her answer, and Mr. Sweeney grumbled something that sounded like "know-it-all" as he stalked off to the exhibit in the next room over. Sophie didn't follow. The thin walls separating the two rooms didn't block the noise, but they muffled it. She grabbed what little relief she could.

"Nice job, superfreak," Garwin Chang—a boy wearing a T-shirt that said BACK OFF! I'M GONNA FART—sneered as he shoved past her to join their classmates. "Maybe they'll write another article about you. 'Child Prodigy Teaches Class About the Lame-o-saurus.'"

Garwin was still bitter Yale had offered her a full scholarship. His rejection letter had arrived a few weeks before.

Not that Sophie was allowed to go.

Her parents said it was too much attention, too much pressure, and she was too young. End of discussion.

So she'd be attending the much closer, much smaller San Diego City College next year—a fact some annoying reporter found newsworthy enough to post in the local paper the day before—CHILD PRODIGY CHOOSES CITY COLLEGE OVER IVY LEAGUE—complete with her senior photo. Her parents freaked when they found it. "Freaked" wasn't even a strong enough word. More than half their rules were to help Sophie "avoid unnecessary attention." Front-page articles were pretty much their worst nightmare. They'd even called the newspaper to complain.

The editor seemed as unhappy as they were. The story was run in place of an article on the arsonist terrorizing the city—and they were still trying to figure out how the mistake had happened. Bizarre fires with white-hot flames and smoke that smelled like burnt sugar took priority over everything. Especially a story about an unimportant little girl most people went out of their way to ignore.

Or, they used to.

Across the museum, Sophie caught sight of a tall, dark-haired boy reading yesterday's newspaper with the embarrassing black-and-white photo of her on the front. Then he looked up and stared straight at her.

She'd never seen eyes that particular shade of blue before—teal, like the smooth pieces of sea glass she'd found on the beach—and they were so bright they glittered. Something flickered across his expression when he caught her gaze. Disappointment?

Before she could decide what to make of it, he shrugged off the display he'd been leaning against and closed the distance between them.

The smile he flashed belonged on a movie screen, and Sophie's heart did a weird fluttery thing.

"Is this you?" he asked, pointing to the picture.

Sophie nodded, feeling tongue-tied. He was probably fifteen, and by far the cutest boy she'd ever seen. So why was he talking to her?

"I thought so." He squinted at the picture, then back at her. "I didn't realize your eyes were brown."

"Uh . . . yeah," she said, not sure what to say. "Why?"

He shrugged. "No reason."

Something felt off about the conversation, but she couldn't figure out what it was. And she couldn't place his accent. Kind of British, but different somehow. Crisper? Which bothered her—but she didn't know why.

"Are you in this class?" she asked, wishing she could suck the words back as soon as they left her mouth. Of course he wasn't in her class. She'd never seen him before. She wasn't used to talking to boys—especially cute boys—and it made her brain a little mushy.

His perfect smile returned as he told her, "No." Then he pointed to the hulking greenish figure they were standing in front of. An Albertosaurus, in all its giant, lizardesque glory. "Tell me something. Do you *really* think that's what they looked like? It's a little absurd, isn't it?"

"Not really," Sophie said, trying to see what he saw. It looked like a small T. rex: big mouth, sharp teeth, ridiculously short arms. Seemed fine to her. "Why? What do you think they looked like?"

He laughed. "Never mind. I'll let you get back to your class. It was nice to meet you, Sophie."

He turned to leave just as two classes of kindergartners barreled into the fossil exhibit. The crushing wave of screaming voices was enough to knock Sophie back a step. But their mental voices were a whole other realm of pain.

Kids' thoughts were stinging, high-pitched needles—and so many at once was like an angry porcupine attacking her brain. Sophie closed her eyes as her hands darted to her head, rubbing her temples to ease the stabbings in her skull. Then she remembered she wasn't alone.

She glanced around to see if anyone noticed her reaction and locked eyes with the boy. His hands were at his forehead, and his face wore the same pained expression she imagined she'd had only a few seconds before.

"Did you just . . . hear that?" he asked, his voice hushed.

She felt the blood drain from her face.

He couldn't mean . . .

It had to be the screaming kids. They created plenty of racket on their own. Shrieks and squeals and giggles, plus sixty or so individual voices chattering away.

Voices.

She gasped and took another step back as her brain solved her earlier problem.

She could hear the thoughts of everyone in the room. But she couldn't hear the boy's distinct, accented voice unless he was speaking.

His mind was totally and completely silent.

She didn't know that was possible.

"Who are you?" she whispered.

His eyes widened. "You did—didn't you?" He moved closer, leaning in to whisper. "Are you a Telepath?"

She flinched. The word made her skin itch.

And her reaction gave her away.

"You are! I can't believe it," he whispered.

Sophie backed toward the exit. She wasn't about to reveal her secret to a total stranger.

"It's okay," he said, holding out his hands as he moved closer, like she was some sort of wild animal he was trying to calm. "You don't have to be afraid. I'm one too."

Sophie froze.

"My name's Fitz," he added, stepping closer still.

Fitz? What kind of a name was Fitz?

She studied his face, searching for some sign that this was all part of a joke.

"I'm not joking," he said, like he knew exactly what she was thinking.

Maybe he did.

She wobbled on her feet.

She'd spent the past seven years wishing she could find someone else like her—someone who could do what she could. Now that she'd found him, she felt like the world had tilted sideways.

He grabbed her arms to steady her. "It's okay, Sophie. I'm here to help you. We've been looking for you for twelve years."

Twelve years? And what did he mean by "we"?

Better question: What did he want with her?

The walls closed in and the room started to spin.

Air.

She needed air.

She jerked away and bolted through the door, stumbling as her shaky legs found their rhythm.

She sucked in giant breaths as she ran down the stairs in front of the museum. The smoke from the fires burned her lungs and white bits of ash flew in her face, but she ignored them. She wanted as much space between her and the strange boy as possible.

"Sophie, come back!" Fitz shouted behind her.

She picked up her pace as she raced through the courtyard at the base of the steps, past the wide fountain and over the grassy knolls to the sidewalk. No one got in her way—everyone was inside because of the poor air quality. But she could still hear his footsteps gaining on her.

"Wait," Fitz called. "You don't have to be afraid."

She ignored him, pouring all her energy into her sprint and fighting the urge to glance over her shoulder to see how far back he was. She made it halfway through a crosswalk before the sound of screeching tires reminded her she hadn't looked both ways.

Her head turned and she locked eyes with a terrified driver struggling to stop his car before it plowed right over her.

She was going to die.

About the Author

SHANNON MESSENGER grew up among the sandstorms and giant bugs of the desert and was not sad at all when her family finally escaped the heat. She's studied art, screenwriting, and television production, but realized her real passion is writing for kids and teens. The Sky Fall trilogy is her first young adult series. She is also the author of the bestselling Keeper of the Lost Cities middle-grade series. She lives in Southern California with her wonderful husband and far too many cats and believes In-N-Out cheeseburgers are the perfect food. Find her online at shannonmessenger.com.

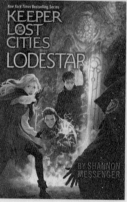

WITHDRAWN

DISCOVER NEW YA READS

READ BOOKS FOR FREE

WIN NEW & UPCOMING RELEASES

RIVETED

YA FICTION IS OUR ADDICTION

JOIN THE COMMUNITY

DISCUSS WITH THE COMMUNITY

WRITE FOR THE COMMUNITY

CONNECT WITH US ON RIVETEDLIT.COM

AND @RIVETEDLIT